BLACK FALL

THE JESSICA BLACKWOOD NOVELS

Black Fall

Name of the Devil

Angel Killer

BLACK

A JESSICA BLACKWOOD NOVEL

FALL

ANDREW MAYNE

HARPER

NEW YORK · LONDON · TORONTO · SYDNEY

BLACK FALL. Copyright © 2017 by AndrewMayne.com LLC. All rights reserved. Printed in the United States of America. No part of this book may be used or reproduced in any manner whatsoever without written permission except in the case of brief quotations embodied in critical articles and reviews. For information, address HarperCollins Publishers, 195 Broadway, New York, NY 10007.

HarperCollins books may be purchased for educational, business, or sales promotional use. For information, please e-mail the Special Markets Department at SPsales@harpercollins.com.

FIRST EDITION

Designed by Jamie Lynn Kerner

Library of Congress Cataloging-in-Publication Data has been applied for.

ISBN 978-0-06-249198-5 (pbk.)

17 18 19 20 21   LSC   10 9 8 7 6 5 4 3 2 1

Dedicated to "Princess Irene," Irene Larsen

CIVILIZED SCIENCES

Occurrences in this domain are beyond the reach of exact prediction because of the variety of factors in operation, not because of
any lack of order in nature.

ALBERT EINSTEIN,
Out of My Later Years

It has been concluded that compulsory population-control laws
could be sustained under the existing legal framework if the population crisis became sufficiently severe to endanger society.

CIVILIZED SCIENCES FOUNDATION,
CSF Congressional Report 1975

BLACK FALL

CHAPTER ONE

ENRAPTURED

WHEN SHE SAW the telephone pole with the yellow plastic base again, Olivia Fletcher slammed on the brakes of her mail truck, bringing it to a skidding halt. She checked the postal computer GPS on the dashboard one more time. It still insisted this was the intersection.

But that was impossible. There was supposed to be a gas station and mini-mart at the corner. She remembered the old man who sat behind the counter and the two mutts that would slobber on her ankles when she'd stop by to get her bottle of Diet Shasta. The lot was now just dirt, scattered with rocks. It was hard to even call it a lot. The land blended into the rest of the landscape.

As she stared out at the empty plot, perplexed, a dust-filled breeze blew into the cab, forcing her to roll up the window.

This had been her route two years ago. She was positive she'd passed the station only a couple of weeks back on her way to Runyon. Charlie, the carrier who normally had this route, hadn't mentioned anything about the station or the old man going away.

There was no PROPERTY FOR SALE sign or anything else indicating it had been torn down. Of course, Charlie also hadn't said anything about skipping town a few days back, leaving her to take over.

Deciding the postal computer GPS was lying, Olivia pulled out her phone to check Google Maps. There was barely one bar of signal. All things considered, she thought herself lucky to get even that much in the Colorado high desert.

The map slowly loaded on her phone. In league with the postal computer, it insisted this was the right turnoff.

"Well, heck," Olivia muttered, then turned the truck down the dirt road toward Moffat. Maybe somebody there could tell her what happened to the station.

The last time she'd driven through Moffat, it had been a collection of paint-stripped houses and a trailer park where people had kept to themselves. They all seemed a little churchy to her. They weren't Mormon fundamentalists or anything as far as she knew, just folks who liked to be left alone.

Based on the landscape and the shape of the ridge she was driving toward, Olivia was certain this was the road to Moffat after all—except there was no farmhouse and run-down shack like she remembered. It was just open plain on either side, with patches of weeds and stunted trees half-petrified from the dry air.

She reached the top of the ridge that overlooked Moffat. But there was no town to see. Even the road, covered in dirt and gravel, was only partially visible. It was the only sign people had ever been here, and barely at that. It reminded her of one of those atomic bomb test sites out in Nevada—*after* the bomb had gone off.

She drove the truck to the exact spot her postal computer GPS said was the center of Moffat, and put it in park. She found herself in the center of nothing.

"Hell," she grumbled, shaking her head. Bracing against the grit-filled wind, Olivia slid open her door and stepped onto the road. She shielded her eyes with a tanned hand and looked for some trace of the town. If this was Moffat, there should have been a row of houses to her left, a garage and a Laundromat to her right, and a small grocery store next to the farm services building straight ahead.

Olivia remembered the name of the woman who worked the grocery store counter. Eunice. She had an orange tabby cat that sat on the counter like a pudgy king, demanding to be petted by everyone who entered. But there was no store. No Eunice. No pudgy cat.

Olivia pulled strands of hair from her eyes and wiped away the dust that kept coming. The trailer park where Eunice lived should have been at the end of the street. Now it seemed the trailer park only existed in Olivia's memory. She glanced back at the bundle of mail in her truck, which she was supposed to leave at the PO box in the store. That wasn't going to happen.

What was she supposed to do?

There was no way around it: she felt foolish. But she'd already spent two hours going up and down the road that led to the Moffat turnoff.

Suppressing an expletive, she dialed her son-in-law, a deputy sheriff in Cooper. He'd be able to straighten this out. The two got along well, and often talked several times a day.

"What's up, Olivia?" he casually asked.

"Eric, this is gonna sound stupid, hon. I don't want you thinking your mother-in-law has lost it."

"You kill somebody?" he joked.

"Not exactly."

His tone suddenly got serious. "What's going on?"

"I . . . lost a town."

A long pause. "Moffat?" There was no trace of surprise in his voice.

Olivia froze. "Yeah, how'd you know?"

"I got a man with a produce truck in front of me asking the same thing. Hold on. I'm getting something over the radio."

Olivia kicked the toe of her shoe into the dirt while she waited for him to finish. There was something metal under the dust. Curious, she knelt down for a closer look.

"Well, that's odd," Eric said, returning to their call. "The telephone exchange says all the numbers appear disconnected. I haven't heard of any recent tornado reports. I better call the sheriff. Any idea how many people live out there?"

"Fifty-eight," she replied, without missing a beat.

"You know that off the top of your head?"

Olivia swept her hand across the metal sign at her feet. It said:

WELCOME TO MOFFAT, POPULATION 58.

She read it aloud over her phone, then said, "Eric . . . I think the town is flat-out gone."

"Gone? No people?"

"Gone, as in not here. No people. No town." Olivia stood up and felt cold.

Gone. The word echoed in her head as she tried to imagine the town as it once was: the buildings—*the people*.

The sun was setting and the shadows were growing longer. She noticed bits of charred, broken boards poking out of the dirt. A cracked cinder block stuck out of the ground like a giant chipped tooth.

She was taken back to the stories in high school history class about ancient cities buried under the dirt. One day, the people just covered everything and left. Nobody knew why.

She climbed back into the truck and locked the door as the wind grew stronger.

Either something took these people and their town, or they went willingly, erasing every trace of their existence.

She wasn't sure which scenario scared her more.

CHAPTER TWO

DEATH'S DOOR

Dᴿᴇꜱꜱᴇᴅ ɪɴ ᴀɴ Akris pantsuit, with platinum-blond hair, high cheekbones, and a slim nose—both crafted by a high-end Beverly Hills plastic surgeon—Diane McGillis looks more like a model-turned-K Street-lobbyist than a serial killer as she turns the key to the door of the townhouse that houses her office, located a few blocks from the White House.

It's 9:47 am, which means she's just finished her Pilates class and stopped by a juice bar on her way to work for her kale cleanser shake. My unkempt hair pulled back in a tie, I'm in jeans and an unwashed sweater, sipping a three-hour-old Starbucks latte and wishing I had time to make it to the gym, much less do a load of laundry or even shower.

I glance at the half-empty cups and fast-food containers scattered around the monitors and cameras set up in our rented loft across the street from McGillis's office. I guess I should clean those up. I guess I should be doing a lot of things.

Right now, what I'm really wishing for is a break in the McGillis case. She's not your typical serial killer, and her victims and their families—hell, most of the FBI—don't see her for what she is.

I'd had to call in a few favors to even get this investigation going. One of the conditions of the surveillance operation was that I would work the crap shifts so others in the detail could spend normal hours with their families.

"Has she done the egg trick?" my grandfather asks over speakerphone.

I'm watching McGillis while my grandfather rummages through old files in the basement of his ramshackle mansion in Los Angeles. I'd forgotten he was even on the line. "The egg bag? She's not doing kiddie shows, Grandpa."

The "egg bag" is pretty much what it sounds like: an egg, made of wood, and a small velvet bag. The egg goes in the bag, and it vanishes. The magician will turn the bag inside out to prove the egg isn't there. It's actually more impressive than it sounds in the right hands. Grandfather, one of the last magic greats, could have an audience rolling in the aisles while he made a hapless volunteer search in vain for the egg. This was a far cry from McGillis's performance. Her volunteers tended to die.

He sighs, exasperated. "No. No. The gypsy egg thing."

"What's that?"

"It's supposed to be a purifying ritual. The medium tells the client to bring a fresh chicken egg to a session. They rub the egg all over the client's body, then ask the client to crack it open. Inside there's blood, hair, other putrid things. The client is duped because they brought the egg."

I adjust a tripod to get a better view through a gap in the loft's curtains. "And the medium switches it for a prepared one when they're not looking?" I reply.

"Yes. You can hide the seal with superglue. Sometimes they do the switch right behind their back, or they use an accomplice. Does this witch have a helper?"

"Yeah," I reply, leaning in to look through the telescope aimed at McGillis's window. I can see she's talking to her assistant, Leo Martine. He's rail thin, in his late twenties, and nearly as well dressed as McGillis. "I'm looking at him. Mousy kind of guy. Went to Vassar. We're not sure if he's in on it."

"He *has* to be," Grandfather replies. "He's the one doing all the dirty work for her. Have any of the victims come forward yet?"

"No. We're trying to build a list of clients by watching who comes in and out of the place. Maybe one of them will help us out."

"You can always send me," Grandfather offers.

"I may have to take you up on that."

If I didn't know any better, I'd say his offer sounds genuinely sincere. Of course, I have to keep in mind he's a professional faker who has spent countless hours staring into a mirror perfecting his skills as a liar. However, over the last year, I have to admit that things have improved between us. Either he's become less of a bastard, or I've become a little more of one and can give it right back to him.

We've always had an awkward relationship, to put it mildly. I left home as soon as I could, mainly to get out of his shadow. Technically, I left Mexico City. It was on the night I almost drowned while performing an escape he'd engineered on international television. I wasn't really sure if he'd have been upset with that outcome, as long as it got him enough publicity.

My dad, bless his heart, was always more of an older brother to me than a father. He was young when I was born, and still very much my grandfather's son. My mother didn't stick around long enough to make an impression on me. I used to imagine that I took after her, projecting whatever qualities I wanted on my made-up version of her. I blamed Grandfather for her absence.

Despite his present helpfulness, when I was growing up he was an overbearing bastard who would cut my father and uncle down right in front of me. Nothing was ever good enough for him. Now I realize he was projecting his own insecurities on everyone around him. Not that this makes his behavior right. But as I got older, I saw what real evil was. Grandfather growled a lot and said mean things, but when it came down to it, he's always been there when I've needed him. Learning to ask for his help has been the hardest part.

Diane McGillis, on the other hand, is one of the evilest sociopaths I've ever encountered. She's set herself up in Washington, DC, as a spiritualist, but besides reading fortunes for bored politicians' wives and neurotic lobbyists, she also masquerades as a holistic healer offering medical advice and prescribing unproven, if not flat-out fake, remedies.

But this isn't the truly sinister part of her enterprise, or the reason I hate her with a passion. Her specialty is victimizing people in the late stages of cancer. McGillis performs crystal healing ceremonies, dispenses special teas, and offers a grab bag full of other claptrap options tailored to each victim's belief system— none of which come cheap. She befriends them, earns their trust, gets them to make her a life insurance beneficiary via some bogus spiritual charitable organization she controls, and then manipulates them into stopping chemotherapy or any other form of conventional treatment that might really save their lives. She gives them false comfort with a soothing quilt of lies—a contrast to the cold, hard reality of cancer specialists and hospitals. When her bullshit fails to help them and they pass away, she collects on the insurance policies. She empties their bank accounts on the way to the grave and then hits the jackpot when they die. They think she's a friend, even to the point of getting her victims to alienate their families and loved ones. A skilled manipulator, she knows all the right triggers to press.

She's led at least four people to their deaths so far. Who knows how many others she conned before showing up in the capital eighteen months ago. The twenty thousand dollars she pays for rent every month has to come from somewhere. It's sick. She picks on people at their most vulnerable. The hardest part is explaining to the victims' families that the person their loved one trusted, who provided so much comfort during the final stages of their loved one's life, was actually hastening their deaths for personal gain.

McGillis's mistake was the choice of her most recent victim, the wife of a sitting senator. He was bitter about the money she'd been paying to McGillis while his wife was alive, and even angrier when he found out after her death that McGillis was a beneficiary. McGillis probably just saw this wealthy woman as an ideal target. But had she done her research, she would have learned that Senator Foster is a member of the Senate Committee on Appropriations, and in charge of appropriating funding for the US Department of Justice.

It's sad that this is what it took for McGillis to appear on our radar. But that's the way things work in this city.

"Has she done any psychic surgery?" Grandfather asks.

Popular in the Philippines and South America, psychic surgery involves a so-called healer pretending to make "magical" incisions in someone's body to remove tumors without cutting the skin. Actually, they're using sleight of hand techniques to produce bloody chicken guts. It sounds ridiculous, but thousands of people seek this out, believing it's a viable alternative to the cost and pain of actual surgery or a terminal diagnosis. Even famous, otherwise intelligent people like Peter Sellers and Andy Kaufman fall for the scam out of desperation.

Back when I went to the University of Miami, I once used the principle of psychic surgery to remove a card from a guy's stom-

ach during a college psychology class presentation. I'll never forget his high-pitched scream when he looked down and saw all the
blood. I'd thought he was kind of cute. Not after that.

"Not that I know of," I reply. "She mainly lights candles and
waves crystals around."

"You seeing anybody special?" Grandfather asks out of nowhere.

I ignore the question. We're in a good place right now, but I'm
not at the point where I'm ready to talk to him about the men in
my life, or the lack thereof. "We might send one of our agents in.

There's a woman in narcotics with a treatable lymphoma.
She's recovering, but still looks underweight."

"Your father is up for the Academy of Magical Arts lecturer
of the year," he says, trying again to take the conversation into
personal territory.

"Do you know anything about candle magic?" I reply. I'm
still thinking about my grandfather's psychic surgery question,
remembering the relighting candles and the ones with colored
flames I played with in my room as a little girl. They looked almost like a living thing, not a blatant magic trick. McGillis's cli-
entele are largely too sophisticated for psychic surgery and gypsy
stunts, but might be persuaded by something like that.

"You can scry with a candle."

"Scry? Like see into the future?"

"Yes, or just see images. Stare at a candle long enough and
you'll hallucinate. There was a yogi out here who was running an
ashram in the basement of a producer at Paramount. He used to
get people high on mushrooms and then have them stare into the
flame."

"Interesting." I hadn't thought about a drug angle.

"You should think about coming to the awards show for your
father. He's got a new girlfriend, by the way."

"That's great," I say, without any additional comment. I really want to avoid another conversation about my own personal life. My mind is racing on to something else. "Ever hear about a healer using a hallucinogen in a tea?" McGillis could be adding a little extra kick, like ayahuasca, to her herbal teabags. We might be able to get a felony drug charge this way. That would be something at least.

"You kidding? Out here in LA? I can't imagine what they haven't tried."

There's a knock at the loft's front door. I ignore it. Even though our cover story is that I'm a software consultant renting a room from two other freelancers, our policy for this stakeout is to not answer the door if we can avoid it.

McGillis and Martine move out of view. If she is using some kind of drug in her therapy sessions, her assistant would probably be the one procuring it. If we can catch him red-handed, we might be able to turn him against her. A few years ago, I never would have thought about prosecuting a case like this that way. My boss, Dr. Ailes, says I'm learning to think laterally.

Another knock. I check the monitor for the hallway camera, which is aimed at the door. A young woman in a blouse and jacket, holding a small bundle in her arms, is standing there. Underneath her red hair and dark, almost black, lipstick, she looks distressed.

I rap my fingertips across the table, debating if I should answer the door. McGillis isn't visible at the moment, but I don't want to step away. I decide to keep ignoring the woman, hoping she'll give up.

She knocks again. "Damn it!" I grumble.

"Something wrong?" Grandfather asks.

"I'll call you later." I hang up and grab my University of Miami hat and nerd-girl glasses.

The woman knocks a fourth time. "Hold on," I call out,

tucking my sidearm into the waistband of my jeans under my sweater.

I unlatch the door, pretending to wipe sleep from my eyes, and the woman gives me a small smile.

She adjusts the weight of the bundle in her arms. She seems to be holding a baby. "Hello, neighbor, I was wondering if I could talk to you for a moment?"

I don't recall seeing her around. She could be someone's guest. "I'm sorry. I'm a little busy," I reply, forcing a smile, trying not to be too terse.

She's pale. Her red hair is pulled tightly into a bun, and plainly visible around her neck is a chain necklace made of red links. I try to get a glimpse of the baby's face, but she's holding it tightly to her chest. "I just have a question," she says.

The cop in me decides to take the upper hand by responding to a question with a question. "Boy or girl?" I ask.

Without looking down, she replies, "Girl." Her tone is almost lyrical, her words spilling out like a well-rehearsed song. "Have you noticed how turbulent things have been lately in the world?"

Oh great, a religious freak. "Not really," I reply, trying to shut her off. Grandfather would have said he was a ghost and told her to go away.

"Well, I'm here to tell you about your personal salvation." She absentmindedly raises an arm, letting the baby almost slip.

I saved the Pope, I think to myself. *What more do I need to do to get salvation?* This conversation got real nutty, real quick. "I'm sorry, but I don't have time to talk about Jesus right now." I'm about to shut the door, but I keep staring at the bundle. Her baby is quiet. I haven't seen her stir once. Even swaddled, she seems so small.

"I'm not here to talk about Jesus." The woman's eyes bore into me.

Then who, Cthulhu? "No?"

The woman reaches into the blankets and I catch my first glimpse of the baby's face. She's blue. She's so unnaturally blue I don't see the woman pull something shiny from the folds of the blanket.

"I'm here for your soul, Jessica," she snarls, raising a knife into the air.

Instinct kicks in. I grab for the infant and kick the woman hard in the stomach. As she falls backward against the hallway wall, the child begins to slide from her arms.

My left arm reaches out and catches her. My right hand goes for my gun.

The woman looks up at me, rage in her eyes.

"Drop the knife!" I shout, pointing my pistol at her chest.

She gets to her feet and glares at me, trying to figure out what to do next. I'm trying to keep the baby from slipping out of my grasp, and while I can't disarm the woman without dropping the child, I could shoot her.

"It's coming, Jessica!" she screams, and then she runs away down the hallway.

There's no time to worry about how she knows my name. I want to give chase, but I have this child in my arms. I glance down. Glassy eyes stare up at me. Red veins feather her bluish skin.

This baby isn't breathing.

CHAPTER THREE

HUMMINGBIRD

You DON'T STOP to think at a time like this. You act.

Everything is a blur. I lay the child down and make sure her airway is open. Two of my fingers rapidly press on her chest thirty times. When I first started volunteering at the children's hospital, teaching the kids magic to take my mind off my own stress, I took an infant and child CPR class. Being around so many vulnerable children, I felt it was my responsibility, even though we'd learned the adult basics in the FBI. But compared to the rigid practice dolls, under my fingertips this baby feels like a hummingbird. Her skin is soft, but cold. Her bones are fragile, as if they're made of thin porcelain. I breathe into her tiny mouth, afraid I'll somehow break her. Her small chest rises. I breathe into her again.

Thirty taps, breathe, breathe.

Again, I force my fingers down on her chest. Another thirty taps, breathe, breathe.

The children's hospital was where I met Elsie, a young girl brutally scarred after her abusive mother threw a pot of boiling

water at her. Now, after a hard year of plastic surgery, and because
of her resilience, the scars have faded and she's like every other
tween. Her Instagram feed is filled with smiling selfies and photos of her crushes. Her terrible past is more and more just a bad
memory.

I don't even know this baby's name.

I don't know if she's going to be okay.

Thirty taps, breathe, breathe.

She's still cold.

She's still not breathing.

Please breathe, little thing. Please. *Please!*

Someone grabs my shoulder. I look up as two paramedics
push me aside to treat the infant. I don't remember calling them,
but my phone is on the ground next to the child. The 911 operator
is on speakerphone. Instinct. You drill something into your head
until you don't think about it. That's the point of training.

I follow them into the ambulance, my hand cradling the
child's head as the paramedic continues CPR.

Thirty taps, breathe, breathe.

His hands push forcefully into her chest and I want to shout at
him to be gentle, but he knows what he's doing.

I just caress her head and whisper that she's going to be okay.
I tell her she's safe.

Even as I say it, I know it's a lie. Nobody is safe in this world.

As an only child in a dysfunctional family of traveling magicians, I was always taking in small animals and trying to save
them. I think I was trying to re-create my own little nuclear family
unit with whatever balls of fur or feathers I could find. I hid mangy
cats, retired show rabbits. When I was nine, I even rescued one of
my grandfather's doves after it was hurt in a performance. He'd

produce a dozen of them from a glowing Chinese lantern, and then they'd fly out over the audience to applause. But this time, perhaps confused by the bright lights and unfamiliar stage, one of the doves struck a pipe and fell to the ground offstage near my feet.

Its wing badly crumpled, the dove looked up at me with fearful eyes. I carefully picked it up and rushed it to the dressing room where, among my books and suitcase, I made a nest out of crumpled newspapers. Father wanted to put it out of its misery, but I cried, throwing myself in front of the wounded bird. He relented, knowing he was no match for the force of my will, and let me try to nurse it back to health. I named it Hummingbird. An odd name for a dove, but I was an odd child.

I took Hummingbird with us from town to town, feeding her sunflower seeds by hand, coaxing her to walk. But her wing was too badly broken to set right and she could never fly again, so she spent most of her time sitting in my newspaper nest, staring out the window. It was a sad life, but I refused to let her go. Grandfather and my dad gave up trying to persuade me to let them take care of her. I knew Grandfather's promise to take her to the vet really meant shoving her into a garbage can on his way to the bar.

"She'll learn," was my grandfather's last comment on the matter after a half hour of arguing with me. A stern and impatient man, he liked to believe everyone who disagreed with him was due karmic retribution from the universe.

Back home in California, I fashioned a cage for Hummingbird out of a discarded rabbit hutch. I put her on the crooked back porch of Grandfather's grand but ramshackle mansion. I wanted her to be happy, and I figured she'd be happier outside in the Los Angeles sunshine.

But when I woke up the next day and went to refill Hummingbird's water dish, I found the cage smashed on the ground and the chicken wire ripped open, blood and pearly gray-white feathers stuck to the torn mesh.

One of the coyotes that prowled the grounds at night got to her.

I'd saved her, but for what? To die a horrible death? In my childish desire to help, I'd prolonged her suffering only to leave her to a worse fate. What kind of person does that?

I LEAN AGAINST the wall of the corridor outside the operating room. A nurse tries to get me to wait in the reception area. I flash her my badge—and a glare that tells her no one is moving me.

Two orderlies rush past pushing a large machine into the operating room. It looks like a ventilator. A doctor, a compact man in his fifties, strips off his white coat as he enters the prep room to throw on scrubs, then stops and shoots me an accusing glance over his shoulder. "You the mother?"

"I found her," I reply weakly, still too numb to say anything else. All my energy is in the operating room with that child.

He waves me off and disappears through the door.

"Agent Blackwood?" someone says.

I turn to my left and see a gray-mustached man in a police captain's uniform. He must be the senior officer at the hospital. "Yes?"

"We've got your description out now."

I don't remember calling in a description of the woman. But I don't remember a lot of what had just happened. All I could think about was trying to get the child to breathe. Getting air into her lungs was my only thought.

"She was kidnapped from here a few hours ago." He points down the hall. "They pulled her right out of an incubator."

Good lord! Who could even consider such a thing? I just nod my head and stare back through the glass window of the operating room door as men and women in blue scrubs race back and forth.

"If you don't mind, we can wait in the lobby. She's in the right hands now."

"Is she?" I lock eyes with him. "Where were you when she was pulled from the incubator? Was she in the right hands then?" My anger is barely contained.

"That's not—"

His words are cut short by a low rumble. The floor underneath our feet trembles. He looks at me in surprise, as if I have an answer. The lights flicker, then go dark. I feel the pit of my stomach sink. Something horrible is happening. Again.

Shouts echo from inside the operating room. I push past the captain and through the doors. The medical team is trying to keep the equipment from sliding around. A florescent light fixture snaps free and dangles from its electrical cords. I lunge forward and brace my body over the small shape in the middle of the operating table.

The world shakes again. Something breaks, slamming into my spine. A doctor yells as a rack crashes down. Nurses try to keep the carts from spilling surgical instruments to the ground. Someone brushes debris off my back. The emergency lights flicker on.

"We're good now," says a middle-aged doctor in blue scrubs with bushy eyebrows beneath his skull cap. He gently grasps my shoulder after the rumbling stops. "We need to work. There's still fluid in her lungs."

"Is she . . . ?" I rise slightly, to make sure I'm not crushing her.

"She's going to be fine, but we need to keep going," he tells me firmly.

In the faint glow of the emergency light, I can see the child looking up at me. Her tiny hand is wrapped around one of my fingers, squeezing it. Holding on. Not letting go.

I glance around at the doctors and nurses in their blue scrubs and masks, then down at my hoodie and jeans. The butt of my pistol is poking out from my side. I feel so out of place, so unclean.

"You did everything right," the doctor continues. "Any longer . . ."

I pull away from the baby, even though her hand still firmly clings to my finger. The nurses quickly get the operating room back together as orderlies rush in to clean up the chaos.

Her tiny eyes are still staring at me. She's alive.

A nurse, clearly frustrated by my presence, touches my elbow. "Let's go into the hallway."

I don't know if she can even see me. But she knows someone is there. I caress her head with my free hand. "I'm so sorry," I whisper. "I'm so sorry."

I lift my finger away. Her hand reaches out as I tear myself away from the table, letting the doctors and nurses surround her.

I STEP BACK outside to the hallway and wait. The lights come to life as the regular power kicks in. Hospital staff run back and forth making sure everyone is okay.

Someone turns the volume up on a television at the nurse's station. Images of the damage appear, buildings with fractured windows, a collapsed parking garage, with more reports flooding in. A newscaster says a train may have been derailed.

I'm still trying to wrap my head around the last hour. I don't know how to process any of it. I've been so numb since I saw the flash of the knife. Nothing is real.

The doors to the operating room burst open, revealing two orderlies pushing the cart that carries the baby. The doctor who pulled me aside earlier strips off his gloves and gives me a thumbs-up. Then he follows the others down the corridor.

Over the PA a woman asks all visitors to clear the hospital

so they can make room for incoming victims. The floor trembles again and my knees buckle. Aftershock. Fortunately it's a mild one.

The stairs are a madhouse, but I make it outside. Broken panes of glass stand out on the hospital's exterior like spiderwebs. Wailing ambulances converge from every direction.

My phone rings. It's my father.

"Jessica? Are you alright?"

I catch a glimpse of a frightened face in an ambulance window.

It's my own.

"I'm fine, Dad. I'm fine. Everything is fine."

CHAPTER FOUR

REVELATIONS

My boss, Dr. Jeffery Ailes, gives me a long look before asking if I'm okay. His eyes are more tired than they were when we first met two years ago, and the gray at his temples seems more severe. It stands out against his dark skin, and instead of making him look older it makes him simply look *old*. Stress ages men differently than it does women. It's the way they carry themselves.

Over the last year, he's been dealing with his wife's ailing health. He's a compartmentalizer who would never let what's going on at home blow over into work—at least, he would never take it out on anyone else. But it's becoming apparent that the compartment for his personal life is weighing heavily on him.

Weary or not, his eyes still look right into you, and he has the calm, deliberate manner of someone who thinks deeply about what he says and never says anything just to fill the air. He and my grandfather, for better or worse, are probably the two most influential men in my life. The contrast couldn't be greater. Whereas Grandfather would look at you in a way that suggests you're being assessed and not measuring up, Ailes sees potential. He sees what you can be. As a special appointment to the FBI, leading our island office of misfit toys and assigning us cases that don't fit into the usual categories, finding untapped potential is what he does.

Before coming to the FBI in an advisory capacity, Ailes ran a black box hedge fund. It was the kind of firm that uses supercomputers and secret software to tell them how to invest and game the market. It made him a rich man—wealthy enough to play golf with CEOs and the president. The truest example of a public servant, he gave up a lucrative career to put his mathematical prowess to work for his country. He could be on the golf course right now with other rich and powerful men, or running for political office, but instead he's in a nearly abandoned building on the outskirts of the FBI campus at Quantico, where they used to store carpet fibers and tire tread patterns, working with a team of just three people and trying to slowly modernize the bureau from the inside out while helping us tackle the impossible cases, the ones the rest of the FBI isn't even sure exist.

"I'm just rattled," I say, instantly regretting the poor choice of words as images of the earthquake damage play out on a monitor at the back of our open office.

I'd had to catch a ride in a squad car back to the stakeout location to grab my work car. The city is in pandemonium. It took flashing my blue light just to make it three blocks. Traffic signals are out all over. Commuter rails and the Metro are shut down because of safety concerns. Transit officials have to inspect hundreds of miles of track and tunnels before they can let people back on the trains. For a city that depends on them, this is the apocalypse.

As I left DC for Quantico, people were walking around dazed, staring at their phones, some getting service and some not, all trying to figure out how they were going to get home. And we still have to find the people who could be trapped. The radio in my car said there was a report of a Metro car buried in the longest stretch of tunnel. The thought of being buried alive gives me shudders. I've been there. Not fun.

It's frustrating to be sitting here in an office miles away while rescue workers are out there doing something. But my orders were unambiguous. I was to return to my unit at Quantico and await assignment.

My two other coworkers, Gerald and Jennifer, are hunched over a computer with their headphones on working on something. Other than a nod when I arrived, we haven't communicated. Although they're not much younger than me, the differences between us feel apparent as I watch them conferring like students planning the latest edition of the school newspaper.

Solidly built, like a volleyball captain, Jennifer always wears an expression even more serious than mine; she apparently hadn't been coached from a young age how to force a smile. The secret is to do it with your eyes. If they didn't know she was armed, she's the kind of woman men would condescendingly tell to smile. When faced with others' stupidity, her withering glances barely contain how much more intelligent she knows she is. Neither of us has much capacity for small talk, and any conversation we share over box chicken salad lunches tends to be case related. But to say that we get along professionally makes our relationship sound colder than it is. A better way to say it is that we get along *efficiently*.

Gerald—lanky and usually smiling—seems like Jennifer's opposite, but intellectually he's her soul mate. With his unkempt brown locks constantly falling into his eyes, he looks less like a G-man and more like some wunderkind working on a startup in his parents' basement.

Both of them could have gone to work in the private sector for greater pay, but they chose the FBI and answered Dr. Ailes's call to service. I've since learned that Ailes's reputation in academic circles is quite significant—and one of the reasons both Gerald and Jennifer decided to take this path.

Watching the three of them geek out over some new code-breaking algorithm or a puzzle Gerald has brought back from a conference is like watching a family of geniuses. I'm welcome, to be sure, but I'm clearly the raven-haired stepchild.

Everyone is focused on the earthquake. Everyone, except me. As I wait for Ailes to sort through e-mail and bureau bulletins, I find myself staring down at my finger, the one the child had grasped.

"She said my name," I say out loud.

Ailes glances up at me from his laptop and thinks for a moment. "The woman who kidnapped the infant?" He reaches over and pulls a sheet of paper from a printer behind him. It looks like a transcript. "Did she recognize you?"

"I had my hat and glasses on. It's not the best disguise, but nobody has ever stopped me before. She knew it was me."

He gives this some consideration. "Do you think McGillis had anything to do with it?"

My first impulse would have been yes, but I'd been thinking it over since I left the hospital. "She's not that dumb. If she suspects we're building a case, I'm sure she doesn't want even more federal attention. She's too calculated. The woman could have followed me to the stakeout." I have an unlisted address, but that doesn't mean much these days.

My line of work puts me in contact with people who tend to take things very personally. DEA agents going after drug lords have to deal with the same situation. They're often rotated out of the field to avoid personal reprisals. Unfortunately, for me a change of address or even a career move wouldn't make a difference at this point. I tell myself I'm safer staying in the FBI doing what I do, because on the outside I'd be just another civilian victim. However, I don't know if my enemies follow the same logic.

"I'll stay on the Metropolitan Police Department," Ailes replies. "I'll make sure they coordinate with us on the woman. Chances are she's just some random crazy that saw you in a coffee shop one day and got fixated on you."

He's trying to downplay it, but this is what bothers me—the idea that it could just be some crazy rando. My most high profile case—the one that placed me in the national spotlight—has attracted legions of nut-job followers. When you take down a man who calls himself the Warlock, a man some people think is a god because of his ability to disguise magic tricks as evil miracles, you tend to get attention from disturbed minds. The FBI receives threats addressed to me on a daily basis. Equally disturbing are the pleas from people asking for my supernatural intervention to rid them of demons and other imagined dark forces.

It'd be one thing if the dangerous ones only came after me. Agents who take down mobsters and other vindictive crooks have to deal with this for the rest of their lives, sometimes even have to enter protective custody. But the potential harm to innocent people is what scares me the most. Ever since a bomb nearly took out my apartment complex, simply because I saw something I didn't realize I wasn't meant to see, I have to take everything into careful consideration. My current apartment is in a gated complex, where a number of people who work for CIA and NSA front companies live. It's a good thing I don't have expensive tastes, because rent is ridiculous. This is after Ailes secretly had another agent offer to sublet a place he owned at a ridiculously cheap rate. I'd called him out on it when I noticed the company that held the lease was named after Bernhard Riemann, a nineteenth-century German mathematician. He wasn't trying to be clever. He'd just underestimated how diligent I would be.

"I'm pulling you off the McGillis case temporarily," Ailes says.

I snap out of my daze. "What? You can't!" I fought hard for this case. It's the first major case I've initiated. Going after criminals like her is why I joined the FBI. It's what I'm good at.

"Knoll says he can take it over. He just finished a couple of his cases."

"But . . ." I try to find the words for my counterargument, but they all sound petulant. Knoll is a good man. We've worked together in the past and it's never about ego for him. It's about putting the bad guys away. I'd be mad at him for offering to take this one behind my back, but I'm sure Ailes called him once he heard what happened at the stakeout.

"It'll be in capable hands. We'll lean on Martine, see if we can get him to turn. Knoll will be good on that."

Knoll is by the book, not at all imaginative, but he's also very thorough. If I have to turn it over to someone, it might as well be him. But I'm not ready to give it up. "Why? Because of this?" I point to the 911 transcript Ailes had taken from the printer. As a magician, I'm good at reading upside down.

Ailes drops it to the desk. "No, no. Something urgent just came up."

"More urgent than McGillis?"

He gestures to Gerald and Jennifer. "I got something I think we're going to need you to clear up."

"What?"

"Right now it's a computer forensics issue. My gut tells me it's going to turn into something else." Ailes waves Gerald over to us.

Gerald slides around the table in a swivel chair and places his open laptop in front of me. A video is queued up. He hits Play, and an older man with a thin goatee sitting at a desk in front of a bookcase begins speaking. He has an eloquent British accent and speaks like a professor explaining time travel or something in a movie.

"Based upon my calculations, the mid-Atlantic region will experience a magnitude six or higher earthquake within a six-day window of August tenth, twenty seventeen."

That's today. I glance at Ailes, looking for an explanation; he nods back to the screen.

The man continues, "These calculations are approximate, based upon the formula, but the outcomes are unequivocal. I have other calculations I shall be releasing. My hope is that you will understand that these events are inescapable. All we can do is prepare ourselves for Black Fall." The video ends.

"Okay. Black Fall?" I ask.

"We're still figuring it out," says Ailes. "What are your first impressions of the video?"

Although his delivery is dry, my honest impression is that this video is creepy. But I know I can be tricked just as easily as anyone else when I'm out of my element. "When did it come out?"

"A little over an hour ago," replies Gerald.

I check my watch. "The earthquake was almost three hours ago." I point to the screen. "Anybody could put that together in no time. To *predict* something, you have to identify it before it happens." I say the last part a little more smugly than I'd intended. But these people are geniuses. They should have figured this part out.

Jennifer and Gerald exchange looks across the desks. Something has gone right over my head. Suddenly I'm feeling less confident about my assessment.

"What?" I ask.

"That's Peter Devon," Ailes explains.

I shrug. "Okay. So Peter Devon has a YouTube account."

He realizes that I have no idea who Peter Devon is. "The

mathematician and physicist? Won a Nobel Prize for his work in quantum mechanics."

"So?" I reply. "Smart guys make up stuff all the time."

Jennifer speaks up. "This smart guy has been dead for eight years."

CHAPTER FIVE

THE ALGORITHM

Being dead does put an interesting wrinkle in things," I reply, now understanding why everyone was surprised at my lack of surprise.

Ailes points his pen at the man on the screen. "Peter Devon was a specialist in chaotic systems. Back in the real world, I based a lot of my work on his early research."

I scroll back the video and move through it frame by frame. "Not a simulation?" We've encountered uncanny computer simulations of people in the past. It's crazy how something that was theoretical just a few months ago is now a smartphone app. Technology moves so quickly, making it even more difficult to tell the real from the unreal.

Gerald shakes his head. His haircut seems a little better than usual. It looks like the new girlfriend is working out. "No evidence so far. After we nearly got spoofed in the Warlock case, we've gotten pretty good at spotting fakes. You'd have to build your own 3-D engine and create original algorithms to get past us now."

"But it's possible?" I ask, trying to figure out the angle.

"The video was uploaded seven minutes after the quake," says Jennifer from across the table. "It's four minutes long. I don't even think Pixar could do all that in three minutes."

Okay. This is getting interesting. "How'd we find out about it?"

"It was uploaded to a YouTube account and e-mails were sent out to every news station and to YouTubers."

"They spammed it into going viral?" I ask.

"Basically," replies Gerald.

"Someone went through a lot of trouble to make sure the world knew about this fast." People can call me a cynic, but the little girl who used to sneak down to her grandfather's dusty basement library to swipe volumes of *the Tarbell Course in Magic* for reading under the covers is inclined to suspect trickery. "How hard is it to predict earthquakes?" I ask Ailes.

"Hard. We miss the vast majority of them. And nobody has been able to call one anywhere near this far in advance. Basically, you know one might hit give or take within a few decades. Beyond that, your next indication is seconds before the tremors start."

"So it's bogus," I decide. If Ailes is telling me you can't predict an earthquake, then I'm inclined to believe him. I just don't know how he did it. But my instincts tell me it can't be real.

"Bogus?" Jennifer replies sharply. "A dead man just called this. Nobody alive saw this earthquake happening." When something does not compute for her and she feels challenged, she sometimes reacts more forcefully than she intends to. But I'm sure the same can be said for me.

I try to explain my reasoning. "The video came out after the earthquake. Not before. Assuming you guys are right, and it wasn't made after the quake using some kind of computer software, then that leads to one conclusion: it was made before and someone was waiting to release it. Which raises the question, why?"

Gerald and Jennifer exchange confused looks. Ailes just observes. He takes a certain amount of enjoyment in watching his work children banter over things. Gerald and Jennifer tend to focus on the physics. I'm the one who starts with the human problem. What are we assuming? What are we overlooking?

"Are you saying the earthquake was some kind of trick?" asks Jennifer.

I roll my eyes. Then a thought comes to mind.

"Fracking didn't cause this," says Gerald, incorrectly anticipating my question.

"No, that's not where I was going. Anyway, you guys are supposed to be the super geniuses here." But even brilliant minds learn best from experience. I look around the table. "Hold on. Is there a large pad of paper around?"

"In the conference room," says Gerald.

"One second." I go retrieve the pad. When I return, they're all hunched over the computer as Gerald taps through the video, examining frames. "Who wants to write?" I ask from across the table.

"I will," offers Gerald.

I hand him the pad and a fat black marker. "Point to something around us."

Gerald thinks for a moment and points to the computer sitting in front of him.

"Okay, write it down on the pad."

He spells out "computer" in his precise script.

"Great. You volunteered and that was a free choice?" I ask.

Gerald nods.

"Turn to the last page of the pad."

Gerald flips to it and grins. He shows Jennifer and Ailes what I'd written: *Gerald will write "computer" on this pad.*

"Of course he was going to choose the computer." Jennifer

shrugs. She hates to be fooled by my tricks, and she'll stew for days if I get her good. I'll toy with her, like use a trick deck of cards and then leave a normal one in my desk across from her, knowing she'll steal a peek in there when she doesn't think anyone is looking. It'd be fun to catch her with her hand in the cookie jar, but it's even more rewarding for me to watch out of the corner of my eye as the high school Intel science fair winner tries to figure out how the hell I fooled her. It's the little things in life that give me joy.

"Was he going to choose it?" I ask. "How did I know *you* weren't going to volunteer?"

Ailes has a smile on his face. He loves watching me stump the geniuses. It keeps them humble. "Okay, Blackwood. Care to tell us muggles how you did it?"

I'd bet anything he's already figured it out and is just too classy to say anything.

"Hold on," Jennifer interjects. She's not ready to give this up. "It's a probability thing. Hmm, based on proximity of objects to Gerald?"

"Not quite," I reply.

She turns to Gerald, looking for some backup. "Did you think about writing down anything else?"

"I was thinking about the chair or the table." He's more amused by this than Jennifer is. "The only rational explanation is that Jessica is a wizard. The sooner you accept that, the easier it will be."

"Never," Jennifer growls. She's suspicious of us all. I once taught Gerald a trick that burned her for weeks.

"Look inside the cap of the marker," I tell Gerald.

His eyes light up when he pulls it off and sees the Post-it note I'd shoved inside there. He reads it aloud. "Gerald will choose the chair."

"What if he said desk?" she asks.

"If he'd chosen the desk I would have sent him back into the conference room. I wrote 'Gerald will choose the desk' on the whiteboard."

Gerald gives me an approving grin. "Okay, but how did you know I'd volunteer?"

"I didn't. I asked for someone to write. I didn't say what they were going to do. If Jennifer had offered to write, I would have still asked you to choose an object. Because I wrote 'Gerald' in all the predictions, you assumed that I predicted he would be chosen. But I didn't. I just said that he'd be the one to choose."

"So . . . Devon made a bunch of predictions, hoping one would hit?" replies Gerald.

"That's the obvious answer to me. There could be hundreds of videos out there with him calling out earthquakes that never happened. When a major one did, whoever is behind this released the one that fit the most. We don't know about all the wrong ones. Until there's a video describing an event before it happens, there's no reason to think anything else is going on."

"He's been dead for years. That would mean thousands of videos," says Jennifer.

"Hundreds. Three hundred if you just want to cover the next ten years."

She gives me a puzzled look. "He said today's date."

"He didn't say today. He said within a six-day window of today. That could be six days on either side, covering thirteen days. That's less than thirty videos per year."

Jennifer acquiesces. "Fair enough." Clearly I satisfied her analytical side.

I turn to Ailes. "But you already knew this."

"It's fun to watch you perform," he replies. "And being fooled is healthy."

"I never admitted defeat," says Jennifer.

"That's why sports have referees," Gerald shoots back.

I think for a moment about why Ailes had me go through all that. "Wait a second. You're not worried about this video? It's what's next that has you concerned."

The smile fades from his face and he's back to looking weary. "If we've learned anything about people who like to do things in a dramatic fashion, they never lead with their strongest bit."

"They save it for the end," I answer. Grandfather's secret to winning over an audience was to promise them something really amazing as a finale, like vanishing a chorus line of dancers, but instead making an elephant appear. Never reveal the real surprise. *Save your powder* is what he used to say.

I wish we were only dealing with a cigar-chomping megalomaniac who just wanted a standing ovation.

"Precisely," agrees Ailes. "This video has everyone's attention. They'll be debating it for days. Eventually they'll reach the same conclusion you have: that this was just a magic trick. I think that's when the next one comes."

"The real prediction," I reply.

"Yes. The one where he tells us something is going to happen before it actually happens. It will be something even more terrible than this."

"But what?" I wonder.

"That's why I want you off McGillis for now and working on this. Hopefully it's nothing. But if it's not—"

"It will be big." I have to agree with him. I want to take McGillis down myself, partly for personal reasons. But this could be much more important. "Alright."

"And I have a favor to ask."

I know where this is going. He's broached this before, but he can tell from my reaction that it's the last thing I want to do.

"To anyone else, Blackwood, this would be an honor."

"I'm not a political creature like you," I shoot back.

"Maybe not, but you never know when you might need to call in a favor."

"Dr. Ailes." I shake my head. He's right and I just have to accept it.

"She's especially disturbed by the earthquake. She has asked to meet with you again. Please, do it as a personal favor to me."

Ailes isn't the type to pull that card unless it's absolutely necessary. I've watched him work the phone, getting CEOs and senators to assist us by subtly reminding them they owe him. Never calling in debts for personal gain, only when lives are on the line.

Asking me this way tells me it's critical I say yes. Things must be worse than he's letting on.

"Fine. Set it up while I get on the earthquake stuff. Any smart people I should talk to?"

"I have a couple in mind. And thank you, Jessica." I can tell he's relieved, because he used my first name. "The first lady will be very happy to hear you're coming."

CHAPTER SIX

NONLINEAR CALCULATIONS

ON A SATELLITE map, the Appalachian Mountains resemble a rumpled green blanket with long ridges stretching north and south along most of the East Coast. Standing on a cliff near Big Schloss overlook, Virginia appears to me as a relatively flat plain to the east, with DC itself hiding behind the distant haze. West Virginia, to the west of the overlook, is a series of valleys and mountains that seem to go on forever.

Professor Charles Kaur, our FBI expert consultant on all things earthquakes, has been giving me a crash course on the Virginia Seismic Zone—where continental plates collide, forming the Appalachian Mountains. An athletic man in his midfifties, he spends a good deal of his time hiking over these hills installing sensors and studying landslides. He has receding sandy blond hair, a tan complexion, and a boyish quality I notice in a lot of scientists and engineers. I can tell that the humanist in him is conflicted with his inner scientist over what happened. Washington, DC, and most of the East Coast is still reeling from the quake and the aftershocks.

He points to the rock below us. "The peculiar thing about East Coast earthquakes is that the rock here is much older than it is on the West Coast. It's had a chance to cool down."

"That's why we get fewer earthquakes out here?" Growing up in Los Angeles, I've gone through my share of earth shaking.

"Part of the reason. But it also means the ground behaves differently. On the West Coast, the rock is spongy and so it absorbs tremors, minimizing the impact area. Out here, the rock is harder and so the effects of an earthquake can be felt from Canada to the Florida Panhandle. Were you here for the twenty eleven quake?"

"No. I was still a police officer in Miami."

Kaur nods his head to the south. "Louisa County was the epicenter, but it cracked the Washington Monument."

"This one did even more damage," I reply, stating the obvious.

"That's because it was a hell of a lot closer to the city. Location, location, location." He points to a range to the west. "This quake knocked our reflector *six inches* out of alignment," he says, with the emphasis suggesting that six inches is quite a lot in his field of study. A few yards away, a stubby tripod is being secured firmly into the bedrock by a group of students. "The laser can correct for up to three inches either way. Not six. We weren't expecting that when we mounted it out here. Six inches." He shakes his head again in disbelief.

Scientists often get labeled as cold or unemotional, but I think the opposite is true for many of them. They care very deeply, only often about things most of us barely comprehend. It's easy to get excited about space when a television host shows you stunning pictures of planets and distant galaxies, but for a man like Kaur— whose area of study is miles below the surface of the earth, and whose most exciting visual aids are squiggly lines on a graph—the disconnect is tremendous. It takes a tragedy for people to appreciate what he's devoted his life to understanding.

The rural landscape is serene, a sharp contrast to the chaos of the city, but as I see the hills and valleys through Kaur's eyes I begin to appreciate the titanic forces at work beneath our feet. I glance over at the laser. "So despite all this technology, it's impossible to see an earthquake coming?"

"I wouldn't say it like that. I'm saying that even with the information I have available they are unforeseeable. I sure as hell didn't see this one coming. There were a couple of minor quakes a few hours before. Major quakes are often preceded by them, but are rarely ever followed by them. The East Coast has fewer quakes than the West—about a tenth as many—which makes it hard to get enough data to determine their source."

"So you think the Devon prediction is a hoax?" I've already shared with him my after-the-fact prediction theory.

"I'd say that's the most likely answer."

I nod my head. "Fair enough."

"But . . ." He hesitates. "It's not that simple. Some things are truly chaotic. We can't know what's going to happen because subatomic events can send an event in any direction. You see that cloud?" He gestures to a puffy wisp drifting over a distant hill. "A stream of cosmic rays could knock a few water molecules into each other at any given moment and start a cascade effect, leading to a downpour before the cloud even gets to the other side of the hill. There's no way for us to know if that's going to happen because we don't know what went on inside the sun eight minutes ago, which is when those particles would have been emitted."

"Chaos theory?" I had a mathematics professor at the University of Miami who loved to wax on about how small factors could influence big events.

"Or complexity. However, earthquakes present a different problem. Since we're dealing with massive slabs of rock that weigh trillions of tons as opposed to the fate of one little particle, it's more of an information issue. If you have enough information, you might be able to make a better forecast. But in seismology, most of our data is gathered after the fact. The hard part is knowing what's going on deep down. We discover a fault only if the fault makes itself known. We can then apply sensors to that fissure and watch for any changes.

"It would be nice to have a bunch of pressure sensors in the earth to tell us what's there, but the deepest hole we've ever dug is about eight miles. A shallow earthquake, like the one we just experienced, can originate about fifty miles below. Intermediates can be almost two hundred miles below, and deep quakes as much as five hundred miles. That's as far as DC is from Atlanta. Our only way of knowing what's going on that far down is by listening. But waiting for a signal to make it through a hundred miles of rock isn't the most precise method of measurement."

"So it's unknowable," I answer. I came out here to get Kaur to definitively sign off on the notion that there is no way Devon could have made that prediction with any foreknowledge, so we could focus on how whoever posted the video managed to make it *look* that way. Instead of shutting the door, he's revealing new ones.

"Well, that's where it gets tricky." He puts his hand on a metal box at the base of the laser. "Inside here is a sensor glued to the rock. It's extremely precise. If a butterfly landed on top here, it could count the wing beats. It's the most accurate civilian sensor you'll find outside a lab."

"Civilian?"

Kaur nods and looks frustrated. "This is decades-old technology. I can only guess what the folks at the NSA have down there so they can listen in on Pakistani bomb tests, or what gear they have sitting on the ocean floor waiting for a Russian submarine to swim by so when the captain flushes the toilet they can tell what he had for breakfast."

"So you're saying that an intelligence agency could have seen this coming?"

"No. They're not looking for this kind of thing. I mean, it could be in the data, but you have to know what you're looking for. But they do have access to all kinds of instruments that those of us on the civilian side can only dream about. Besides passive listening, they're researching quantum-entanglement radar, and a host of other things that might be bullshit, solely for the purpose of getting funding.

"I guess what I'm trying to say is that we've been attempting to predict these things for a while, and I think it's less and less likely that we can. Yet, like the weather, we still hold out hope that a better data set, a faster computer, or deeper sensors could tell us what we need to know. So, while I wouldn't bet on it, I wouldn't rule it out entirely."

I try to figure out how I'm going to wrangle that nonanswer into a report.

He sees the look on my face. "I'll throw you another thing to think about. Remember all the effort we went through to save the Hubble Space Telescope? All this fuss about what an amazing achievement it was? And then, a couple years ago, the National Reconnaissance Office calls up NASA and says, 'Hey, we got two spare spy satellites even better than the Hubble just sitting in a warehouse. You want them?' Makes you wonder what else they have up there in space. It also makes you wonder what kind of other equipment and technology they have access to that we've never even heard of.

"Scientists thought the bottom of the ocean was a desert until just a few decades ago. But if you look through old naval archives, you'll find out they knew a hell of a lot more about what was down there. The thing is nobody was paid to care. The folks listening in on Pakistan through the dirt might have a hell of a lot more information about what's going on under our feet than even they'll ever realize. They have access to supercomputers, maybe even quantum computers, which can perform calculations I could only imagine. Last year, roughly the same number of people were killed by earthquakes as by terrorism. Care to guess what the US Geological Survey's budget is compared to that of the intelligence community?"

I sense his frustration at being unable to answer my question. He's out here with a bunch of student volunteers trying to study science that affects tens of millions of people, while government spooks are playing with tens of billions of dollars to find out what's on our iPhones.

"I know. I know." He grins. "You were hoping I'd shut the door for you on this Devon thing potentially being true. That's the trouble with science. We can never shut the door completely. The debate, in fact, is never over. Some things just seem less likely than before."

I thank him for his help and head back to my car at the base of the trail. All I'd wanted was for him to laugh off the idea of the earthquake being predictable. I don't need a conspiracy theory to add to the already convoluted situation. The Peter Devon prediction is going to be harder to shut down than I hoped. I'm leaving with fewer answers than I had when I arrived.

Speaking of answers, I check my watch. There's barely enough time to go home and change before I'm expected to provide a few to a woman who wants more than I have.

CHAPTER SEVEN

1600

A s the granddaughter and former frequent assistant of a world-renowned magician who loves rubbing elbows with celebrities and politicians—even if it means barging his way into their circles—I'm no stranger to meeting famous people. The walls of Grandfather's house are lined with photos of all the different people we've encountered and accosted. My favorite one is of a nine-year-old me, full of awkward, pulling a coin from behind one of the Prince of Wales's famous ears. His broad grin is sincere. I still remember the way he looked at me, as if I were some kind of dwarf cunningly disguised as a young girl.

Many of these photos were taken in Hollywood restaurants, which is where Grandfather would go to seek out a particular A-lister he wanted to ingratiate himself with. He'd send me over to a table where Brad Pitt or Sandra Bullock was dining. Then as I walked by I'd pretend to find a hundred-dollar bill on the ground and ask if they'd dropped it. Half the time their managers would say yes, and try to reach for it, at which point I'd make it vanish in a snap of my fingers. This invariably elicited laughter, and Grandfather would rush over, profusely apologize, and manage to get us invited to sit down.

Growing up like this means I've never been intimidated by fame or power. But I also never developed Grandfather's gift for talking to people in those positions. He has a way of flattering them while elevating himself to their level. He has a sixth sense for spotting who the real kingmaker is. He'll often disappear at a party to smoke cigars with a Russian banker or the head of a film studio, regaling them with stories and making them laugh raucously the whole time. But I'm not sure what his connections and social skills actually got him. At best, the bankers might hire him for parties in Manhattan or their dachas on the Black Sea, and the studio heads might throw him a consulting job or give him an occasional development deal he'd never follow through on. One of our family's best-kept secrets is how many people he's hand doubled for, including two James Bonds. Although the reason this is such a secret isn't due to the actors or the studios. It's because Grandfather, full of ego, was always angry the rest of him wasn't playing the actual part.

In retrospect, I think for Grandfather these connections were the end goal. To be able to sit on a veranda with a bunch of powerful people and feel for a moment like a kind of equal—that was the prize.

COMPARED TO THE rest of the White House, the first lady's office feels like the waiting room in a medical clinic. Fluorescent light fixtures, white ceiling tiles, and a complete lack of decorative molding give it a blandness at odds with its location inside the most historic building in America, which largely serves as a museum of colonial-era design. I'd say my anxiety is about on par

with that of a doctor's visit. It reminds me of the hospital hall-
way I was standing in when the earthquake hit. Thankfully, the
DC metro police have told me the infant is back with her mother
and doing fine. This is one ray of light in an otherwise dark time.
Good thing the child will have no memory of that horrible day.
We should all be so lucky.

I focus on the present and look around. As far as I can tell, the
modern and comfortable couch and chairs are straight out of an
Ethan Allen showroom. The only sign we're someplace special is
the depth of the windowsills, a reminder that the exterior of the
building is made of foot-thick armor.

I wonder what it must have been like to be inside the White
House when the earthquake hit. The building and subbasement
probably sit on some kind of shock absorber designed to minimize
the impact of a nuclear bomb. But what about a shock from below?
While there are broken windows and cracked foundations just a
block away, the White House appears to have made it through un-
scathed. I'm sure there were people cleaning up any broken dishes
or tilted picture frames within seconds of the aftershock. The last
thing anybody wants is for the center of power for the free world
to appear to be in disarray.

First Lady Miriam Kent appears anything but disarrayed as
she walks into the room. In her late forties, the former competitive
swimmer still has the poise that helped her become an Olympic
alternate. Though she is confident in her walk, as her eyes dart
around the room I sense that underneath her smile she's still trying to get stable footing.

In interviews, President Kent loves to tell the story about a
night they spent near an air force base in Europe, when a pilot
did a low-altitude flyby while they were asleep. Miriam heard
the roar of the plane, shoved the commander in chief out of bed,
and covered his body with hers in order to protect him. The first

lady still blushes whenever the story is told, embarrassed because she thinks it makes her look foolish. But to her husband, to me, and to everyone else, it's the act of a devoted wife who was willing to put her life on the line to protect the man she loves—and to protect her country. One of her Secret Service code names is Tigress.

Ailes's urgency about this meeting has me concerned. I'm not sure what I'm supposed to say. I don't know what she wants. I frequently encounter younger agents at the bureau who sheepishly tell me how much I mean to them and ask me for advice, as if I'm a female Eliot Ness who has all the answers. Women especially are often stuck looking for role models in a world filled with statues of men. It's not that we don't admire them, but I noticed in Neil Armstrong and Winston Churchill biographies, the chapters on trying to find balance by thirty, and the pressures of trying to succeed, lack a certain female perspective.

The first lady has a warm, natural smile. Her brunette hair is bobbed to accentuate her strong cheekbones, and although she's in her late forties she looks years younger. Not because of vanity, but because of healthy living, good genes, and avoiding radical cosmetic procedures that tend to call attention to themselves.

I glance down at my navy-blue pantsuit, suddenly conscious that the first lady, in dark slacks and a yellow blouse, has managed to dress slightly more casually and yet more fashionably than I have. I bought this outfit three years ago, and I'm sure I didn't see a single person with the same lapel style in the entire FBI building in the last twelve months. It's stupid stuff like this that drives me nuts. I'm hung up on it because I think other women may be hung up on it. It's a vicious cycle.

Thankfully, the first lady isn't looking at my work clothes, my shoes, or my purse. She clasps both my hands and her assistant departs, leaving us alone. I take my seat, absentmindedly pulling my jacket over my hips as I sit down.

"Thank you again for coming to visit, Agent Blackwood."

"It's a pleasure, Mrs. Kent," I reply, trying to sound genuine. She's a likable woman. I just have no patience for politics or politicking. Grandfather would already be pulling a flower out from behind her ear.

"Miriam, please. May I call you Jessica?" Her voice is melodic. I would listen to her narrate audiobooks.

"Certainly." We're equals, right? Last night she had dinner at the Chinese embassy. I ate leftover Panda Express. Same thing.

The contrast between public and private personas is fascinating to me, especially because the private ones rarely measure up. In the security waiting room I saw a television feed of her handing out water bottles and meals in a neighborhood that's still without power. It was a photo op for sure, but she seemed sincere. I think I'm sitting with the same woman right now.

Her smile wavers for a split second. She's nervous about something. "I . . . I've wanted to meet you since the whole Warlock thing. And then the assassination attempt. All of it is so very impressive. You're quite a woman."

"I, um, have a very interesting job."

"Yes, you do. And an interesting family." Her eyes light up as she takes a photo album from the table. "I had our historian pull these from the archive." She turns the album toward me and opens it to a photograph of a group of children in their Sunday best sitting on a rug in a room of the White House, smiling together at the camera. One rather serious-looking brunette girl with a missing tooth looks very familiar. I'm off to the side of the image, but unmistakable. "This was taken at the Easter egg roll. Your grandfather was invited to perform. You were what? Six or seven?"

"Six," I nod. "I think I lost that tooth that day out on the lawn when I fell chasing after an egg." Actually, I'm pretty certain I was tripped by the French ambassador's nephew, but I didn't want to start an international incident.

"Oh, my! That's not a pleasant memory."

"I was fine." I remember it as a happy day. Grandfather and father were both there, although I'm pretty sure we couldn't get Uncle Darius anywhere near the White House due to his criminal record. Holidays weren't exactly a nonevent in my house, but they were never celebrated around so many other children.

We make more small talk for a little while. The first lady's very good at it, but after a few minutes she delicately changes the topic. This is how politicians work. I wonder if there's a timer in her head that tells her when she's spent a sufficient amount of time loosening up her subject, or if she just tries to read my visual cues.

"I thought about becoming an FBI agent, too," she says. "I even majored in criminal justice. I chose another path, obviously. But sometimes I wonder what it would be like."

"I have great coworkers, which makes up for the time I spend digging through mud up to my arms for clues that aren't there, without a change of clothes."

This is my stock answer. The real one involves me sitting in the bathtub while the shower rains down and spills into my glass of red wine, pretty sure I'm not crying because, you know, it's a shower.

I used to think this was a "girl" thing, but I've spotted Ailes in his car in the parking garage, not talking on the phone or listening to music, just sitting there staring at the concrete wall as if he could look through it at the home he has to return to and the problems he has to cope with. Once or twice, after Gerald has bid us a smiling good-bye, I've seen his face right before the elevator closes. It's blank, as if he can't bear being the happy-go-lucky one anymore. Even Jennifer, as emotionally unyielding as the Nebraska granite she was carved from, has her moments. She can drop twenty pounds faster than I can sink a Starbucks Flat White. Her stress relief comes from running marathons. Not the half ones I occasionally do, but full-on solo weekend marathons, where she just keeps going until her feet start to bleed and whatever she's running from has died from exhaustion.

"You're very modest," Miriam replies. "I have to know something. With all you've seen, do you ever get scared?"

"Scared?" I raise an eyebrow. "Are you kidding? All the time. Frankly, I'm a little terrified right now." Not so much because I'm talking to the first lady, but because I have no idea where this conversation is going.

She smiles and gives her head a small shake. "I mean about the kind of cases you're involved with. It all seems so . . . dark."

If I reply fast enough, I don't have to think about it. "Bad people are how I make my living."

"Sure, sure, but it just seems lately that people are acting so much more strangely. There was the Warlock, and now this earthquake and the Peter Devon prediction. Don't you worry about all of this?"

My mind flashes back to what happened the day before at the stakeout loft. I couldn't sleep last night thinking about that baby. I'm not sure when I will be able to sleep properly again. I don't think this is what she means, though, so I try to grasp what she's asking. "I think there have always been horrible people and horrible things."

"And these evil people coming out of nowhere?"

I try to channel my inner Ailes. "There have always been bad people. Now they all get their own miniseries and nonstop news coverage. People think they're in the last generation before it all goes to hell." I remember something I recently read in an article. "The fact is homicide rates keep dropping and life expectancy keeps increasing. I think we're just built to be pessimistic."

"And Peter Devon's prediction?" she asks again.

From the concern on her face, I can tell she's taking this video very seriously. The first lady wants answers, and evidently she's decided they should come from me. I'm here because I'm one of the government's experts on weirdos. I provide my rehearsed reply. "We only heard about it after the earthquake. He could have spent the last year of his life filling up tapes with predictions that never came true. He had to be right at least once." I don't tell her I'm hoping the earthquake prediction is the last time we hear anything from the departed professor.

"So these things don't keep you up at night?"

"No," I lie. I don't tell her about the new nightmare about the woman at my door, or the one I still have about falling from an airplane. Or how I go to bed earlier most nights now, knowing I'll spend several hours at the very least staring at the ceiling.

"Would you tell me if they did?" There's a vulnerability in her voice as she puts her hand over mine and clasps it. Just like when Sophie Gunnerson and I snuck into *The Blair Witch Project* at the ArcLight theater and she grasped my right hand in the middle of the movie. At first I thought she was being a little weird. Then I realized she was scared. John Carpenter once watched Grandfather cut my head off with a guillotine in our living room, so my sense of fear and Sophie's were calibrated differently. I just let her hold my right hand as I used my left one to feed myself Skittles.

Her question catches me off guard. "Sure. I mean, I don't worry about the supernatural things. *I* have no reason to believe in them." The real stuff is scary enough. I think about the woman who tried to kill the child. "What worries me are the people who believe in these things. They're what keep me up at night."

She nods reflectively as she thinks about this. "Do you attend church regularly?"

I think she's asking me politely if I believe in God. The answer used to be so much easier. "Not as often as I should."

"Well, if you get the chance, you're welcome to come with us sometime."

What? Did the first lady just ask me to pray with her? I'm taken aback. I'm not sure if this is some kind of token offer, or something else. I know Ailes is on friendly terms with the Kents, but he never speaks about their relationship. It's more of a golf game here and there, and an occasional phone call about policy when the president wants an outside voice who won't go running to the press. I begin to realize the first lady is a very lonely woman. Lonely and frightened. Is she a grown-up version of Sophie, who just wants a hand to hold? Then why mine? I'm just a worker bee. She could talk to anyone.

"That's very kind," I say, responding to the church offer. "I might enjoy it."

She smiles. "I'll have my assistant give you my personal number. Would I be imposing if I gave you a call sometime?"

"Not at all." To talk about what? If I had answers to any of her questions, I'd be getting more sleep and drinking wine that wasn't watered down.

We finish our conversation and I leave, not quite sure what just happened. She's obviously worried about the earthquake and the prediction. But there's something more to her anxiety. I wonder why she can't just talk to her husband about all this. Is she afraid of appearing scared after all the times he's told the story of her bravery? But that seems odd. They are obviously very close. The two of them are simpatico. I can't see them hiding anything from each other.

Maybe they don't.

It hits me. She *has* talked to her husband about this. She's not speaking with me discreetly about her fears. These are *their* fears. She's reaching out to me because they want someone outside their inner circle to put things in perspective.

While my case history may make it look as if I'm an expert on these kinds of things, I'm grasping for answers like everyone else.

WALKING BACK EAST toward the FBI headquarters where I parked my car, I try to figure out what I'm going to tell Ailes about this conversation. It's clear he thought it would be a good idea for the first lady to speak with me. I just wish he'd told me beforehand what she really wanted.

The crowds along Pennsylvania Avenue are thicker than usual. Not all of them are tourists. Clusters of protesters are holding up signs, many of them complaining that power still isn't on in much of the city. The fact that the White House was brightly lit last night while the surrounding blocks were in darkness didn't endear the mayor to the people dealing with the ongoing blackout.

As I cross Thirteenth Street, my phone rings. The number on the screen has a local 202 area code. "Hello?"

"Agent Blackwood?" a woman asks.

"Yes?"

"Hi, this is Detective Lewis with DC metro police. The Prince William County Sheriff's Office may have found the woman who kidnapped the baby and threatened you. Are you available to do an ID? It'll take an hour or so."

A thousand questions I want to ask that woman race through my mind. "Yes. Of course. Where?"

"I can pick you up at the FBI building. I'll drive us to the morgue."

The morgue?

CHAPTER EIGHT

TROUBLED

A LINE OF POLICE cars races down Pennsylvania Avenue toward the Mall as I wait outside FBI headquarters. Two crowd-control vans follow behind. I catch a glimpse of cops with riot gear through the passenger window. That's not going to be fun. I don't envy them.

Shortly after they pass, an unmarked police car with a blue light on the dashboard pulls up in front of me. "Blackwood?" asks the compact black woman in the driver's seat. Her piercing hazel eyes match those in the photo I had Ailes send over to me. I can never be too careful.

"Detective Lewis?"

"Aileen to my friends." She gives me a quick inspection. "I guess that includes the FBI. Hop in."

"Jessica," I say, offering my hand after climbing inside.

"I know all about you," she replies. Her tone is friendly.

She's stating an obvious fact. After the Warlock case, keeping a low profile within the law enforcement community became impossible for me. Even though the extent of my involvement in thwarting the terrorist attack on the Pope was largely kept out of the news, it's a poorly kept secret within law enforcement.

"So, you get a lot of nut jobs?" Aileen asks as we head toward Interstate 395, a trace of sarcasm in her voice. Almost like I've been asking for this trouble.

With cops you can tell pretty quickly if you're going to click or not. I get along best with the ones who say what they're thinking. Lewis is to the point. She's probably trying to figure me out. Am I some kind of showboating opportunist who happens to be in the right places at the right times? Or am I just another flatfoot trying to do my job? It's pointless trying to set people straight on what I consider being in the right place. Still, I can tell Lewis hasn't yet made up her mind.

"In my dating life, or professionally?"

She smiles at my joke. "I get the impression trouble follows you."

"I'm beginning to get suspicious myself."

I've dealt with creeps all my life. I'm just thankful my time as a teenage magician was over before the invention of Twitter and YouTube. I was uneasy with my stage attire of fishnets and sequined leotards even at seventeen. Other than when a classmate caught my appearance on some variety show, there was a solid disconnect between the girl who wore jeans and hoodies in trigonometry and the scantily clad girl escaping a straitjacket onscreen. My current social media footprint is effectively nil. I don't even spend a lot of time googling my name to see what comes up, other than to make sure whatever undercover disguise I'm using hasn't been blown. Not that the FBI would put me on an actual undercover case at this point, but in the field I still try to look different from the few photos of me you can find online. My least favorite, besides my teenage magician magazine cover, is the one taken on a windy Fort Lauderdale beach, where I was investigating the reappearance of a missing World War II plane. That one got me labeled as the FBI's "Witch."

Occasionally someone discovers my FBI e-mail address and I get unwanted messages. Thankfully I can send them over to a unit that handles this kind of thing, and contact tends to stop after the pervert gets a visit from a couple of agents who look like linebackers. Every girl should be so fortunate.

Lewis takes the on-ramp heading south, then shrugs as she looks at the city retreating in the rearview mirror. "Glad to be out of that mess."

"Is it getting better or worse?"

"Officially? The city is getting back online. They got those people out of the metro car. There's still no word on when we'll have full service."

"And unofficially?" I'm curious to know if what she's heard is different from what we know in Quantico. I don't spend as much time on the street as she does, and I can only imagine what she's thinking.

"Everyone is working double shifts," she explains.

"I guess that's to be expected."

"Yes, but we're not all doing disaster relief. Some are undercover. People are flooding into the city to protest."

"I imagine they're upset."

"But that's the thing. Many of them are out-of-town folks. This thing is barely twenty-four hours old and the street in front of the White House is already looking like Occupy Wall Street."

I sense her agitation. I would ask if there's something else, but I suspect at this point it's just her cop's intuition that's telling her things aren't looking good.

"Anyway. Back to our little case. A dog walker found the body near a culvert in The Plains a few hours ago. It looks like the killer tried to cover the body with some plastic bags and branches."

"So they didn't want the body to be found for a while."

"Bad luck for them. Good for us."

"How'd they connect the body to my case?" I ask.

"They didn't. I've been scanning arrests since I got assigned to it. This woman sounds a little more than unstable. Babynappers are usually in the middle of a downward spiral. I figured it was only a matter of time before she got popped for something minor, like shoplifting or throwing a tantrum at Starbucks. The signs are all there. Then this body came across the bulletins. It seemed like a potential fit."

We weren't recording the entrance to the safe house because we weren't expecting McGillis to come knocking. Fortunately, I was able to make a composite drawing using the FBI system. It matched the security cam footage of the woman stealing the child earlier in the day. "So you matched the face to the body?"

Lewis shakes her head. "Not quite. The face is a bit of a mess, but the body matches the general height and size you described, plus the hair and clothes. There aren't that many unidentified bodies we come across."

I guess that's better than no lead, and Lewis gets points in my book for paying attention to the bulletins in the midst of all this. Still, it's a tenuous connection.

"I know what you're thinking," Lewis says. "The reason we're driving out to the Plains is because of the way she was killed. The knife you described? Your drawing looked like a sashimi knife. This woman was killed by the same kind of knife. The medical examiner was able to spot the wounds right away. Either she's a victim of our kidnapper, or she's our kidnapper who became someone else's victim."

The idea that the woman who tracked me to the loft was murdered is still registering. This would mean someone else is involved. Her murder couldn't have been random. Damn. This thing is getting real complicated, real quick, and at the worst possible time.

Lewis thinks out loud. "So, if this is our babynapper, it raises the question of who killed her, and why."

I'm afraid I already know the answer, at least part of it. "Her accomplice. They killed her because she failed." There was a sense of purpose in the woman's eyes. I felt she was sent on a mission, and not acting alone.

Lewis nods as she studies the traffic in front of us. "This is the part that's still unclear to me. I've gone over your report several times. After she draws the knife, there's not a lot of detail. Was she trying to kill you? Or the child? Or both?"

"I don't know. All I remember was seeing the knife and reacting. It was kind of a blur." This is the difficult part to explain to people who aren't cops. They don't appreciate the fact that the hardest decisions we have to make are the ones we only have a fraction of a second to think about. In their minds it's like a TV show, where the bad guys tell us what they're up to and we get to have a long debate. It drives me nuts. I'm torn up by what happened, but I don't know what my alternative was.

"I understand. Not the time to ask her what her intentions are," Lewis replies sympathetically. "I wish just once other people could know that feeling when you walk up to a car in the middle of the night and see someone reaching into their jacket."

My thoughts exactly. "Or respond to a suspected burglary, climb through the bushes, and see someone pointing something metallic at you and there's only a moment to decide if it's a kid with a toy, a drunk, or somebody about to shoot you."

"I don't miss my days on patrol." She laughs. "I once used my stun gun on a goat."

"How'd *that* happen?"

"I got a call about a prowler. Turned out a Dominican family was raising goats in their backyard and couple of them got loose in the neighborhood. I loved filling out the report on that one. Kept finding gyros in my desk drawer for a month."

Cop humor. There's nothing quite like it. You deal with so much darkness you have to learn to find the comedy where you can. And if they sense you can't take a joke, they'll only make it worse. "First time I used my stun gun was on a judge."

She gives me a surprised sideways glance. "A judge?"

I still blush at the memory. "I was responding to a noise complaint. It was a group of guys getting their drink on before a bachelor party. So I show up in my patrol blues."

"Hah!" she cackles. "Let me guess. They thought you were a stripper!"

"For the record, that happens pretty equally to both rookie guys and girls in uniform in Miami! I'd been on the job for just a few months, and this was one of my first times out on a call without supervision. This middle-aged man with a beer in his hand answers the door of the townhouse, grins, and grabs me by the arm. I pull away and tell him to stand down. He's having none of it. He's convinced this is all some setup."

"So you tasered him?"

"After sufficient warning. Long story short, my supervisors told me it would be better to have a judge who owed me a favor than to take him in."

"I wish all altercations had such happy endings." There's a long pause before she speaks again. "By the way, good reaction on this one. I'm not sure what I would have done if I'd seen the knife."

It's always gratifying to hear another cop say you did the right thing, even if you have no memory of consciously making the choices you did. "Shooting wasn't an option. Not with the baby there. I'm sure you would have done the same."

"Maybe, but still. Every part of me would want to get the bitch."

"I didn't have time. If I'd chased her down, the baby probably wouldn't have survived." I still don't know what the right choice was. If I made the right one, like people are telling me, then why do I feel so horrible?

"Yeah. That'd be messed up. The child would be dead and the woman would still be alive."

"Maybe."

Maybe not. Was she murdered because she failed to kill me? Or because of something she knew?

Neither answer is reassuring.

CHAPTER NINE

CAUSE OF DEATH

FOUR RED LINES, sutured shut with forensic glue, crisscross the face of the woman who threatened me just a day ago. With the blood now washed away, she's unmistakable, except for one important difference. This woman's final emotion was fear, not rage. Her mouth is open, twisted in what looks like a scream. The medical examiner tells us she died coughing on her own blood as she fought for air while her punctured lungs drowned her from within.

I hate what she did. I should hate *her*, but I can't. I still don't know what drove her to kidnap that child and come to my doorstep, but I'm certain that ending up here on a cold metal slab wasn't part of her plan. Maybe none of this was. I've seen people be manipulated into doing things they'd never agree to willingly again and again. But what, or who, could cause her to do the evil she did?

"Is this her?" asks Lewis.

I want to see the body in person. The 4K monitor displays in the conference room show every horrifying detail, but still, I need to be in the room with her to say for certain. I've learned that looks can be deceiving. The investigation that launched my career with the FBI involved a series of misidentified victims, and I barely saw through that. There's no guarantee I would be so lucky again.

"Is the body in this building?" I ask.

"Yes. I can have them pull her out of the freezer." The medical examiner, Dr. Tuft, a serious woman with short silver hair, waves to the conference room screen. "We're not due for an autopsy for another day or so. We've got all the field photos and the preliminary lab images uploaded." She's telling this to Lewis, not me. This isn't my case. I'm a witness or a victim, depending on how you look at it. Tuft's only letting me see the forensic information as a professional courtesy.

"I'd like to look at the body."

"We will, but is this her?" Lewis asks again. She understands how difficult this is for me, but she needs her own legal closure on the issue.

I nod. "It looks like her."

As we walk down the corridor, a detective named Greer from the Prince William County Sheriff's Office joins us. Tall, almost stooping, he gives me a courteous nod but directs his attention to Lewis. "We found her partially covered in some trash near a drainpipe. It appears to be the spot where she was murdered."

"Did the concealment look rushed?" asks Lewis.

"I'd say so," says Greer. "It was an out-of-the-way place, but not that out-of-the-way. There are a few spreads of woods nearby that are farther away from the riding trails, but it would take another half hour or so to walk there, especially if you were avoiding the highway."

Lewis writes something on her pad, and I make a mental note.

This is her investigation. I can't go jumping in with my own questions. So I follow them closely, while trying not to step between them.

"Shoe prints?" she asks.

"We got some partials. Also some tread marks on the reeds. That would be consistent with the knife-wound angle and the bruising."

"Bruising?" I blurt out before I can catch myself. I may be used to sitting in on other agents' cases and keeping quiet, but I'm not usually this personally invested. Bruises, like a map of choreographed footsteps, can tell you quite a lot about how someone was killed.

Greer shoots me a backward glance, unsure if he should answer me directly. Lewis nods, telling him it's okay.

"Yes." He gestures toward his right bicep. "Here"—he points to his neck—"and here. Dr. Tuft will show you, but it looks like she was in a bit of a scuffle before she was killed."

"Both arms?" I ask.

"Yes." He turns to face me now, agitated. "I'm sorry, Agent, is this an FBI case now?"

Before I can speak, Lewis interjects. "Our Jane Doe may have kidnapped an infant from a DC hospital and threatened an FBI agent on duty there before she was then found dead in Virginia. You do the jurisdictional math, Detective. If they decide to step in, it's certainly within their right." She says this while still managing to be polite and professional. I'm not sure if I could have pulled it off nearly as well.

Lewis is right about the FBI having potential jurisdiction, except for one important detail: this wouldn't be *my* case. Never in a million years. I'm a victim and not impartial—if there really is such a thing. I'm just here to identify the body. Although Detective Greer doesn't feel the same sense of professional courtesy

Dr. Tuft does, I don't take it personally. The FBI has a reputation for taking over local cases and claiming all the credit. It's probably a bit exaggerated, but more than a few cops have done a lot of hard work only to see a news headline, months later, attributing the success to us. J. Edgar Hoover was a complicated man, but he certainly understood the value of PR.

Thankfully, Lewis is giving me some latitude. She can tell this is probably going to be a bureau case sooner rather than later.

"Do you have any idea who this woman was?" she asks, directing Greer's attention to something more important than a pissing match.

"Not yet. She's not local. We know that."

We come to a stop in front of the cold-storage room.

"I'll leave you with Dr. Tuft while I make a few phone calls." He gives me a hesitant look. "Agent, have your supervisor call me if you need anything."

Lewis's eyes flicker toward me, gauging my reaction.

I don't have one, because I can't tell if he is being polite or an ass. "Thank you for all your help, Detective."

TUFT LEADS US into a prep room. "Scrub up over there. There are some smocks and masks on the counter. I'll go get our Jane Doe ready."

Lewis waits for us to be alone. "I'm sure he means well," she says sarcastically.

"It's understandable," I reply as I pull a mask over my face. "This is your case for the time being and I'll respect that."

"Say it," Lewis orders.

"What?" But she's been watching me since we got here. I'm sure my poker face has slipped a few times. "Am I that obvious?"

"There's a tone. You want to say something." She nods to Tuft on the other side of the glass door. "You've been waiting for her to leave."

"The bruises on the arms. She was held."

"Yeah. One person held her. Another knifed her. I'm going to get on Greer about the boot prints. I think they may have more here than they realize. Anything else?"

Over the years, the FBI has collected millions of data points from crime scenes. Analyzing the location and angle of a knife wound can tell you if the murder was committed by a stranger or someone known to the victim, if it was premeditated, if it involved multiple assailants. It's not exact, but more often than not, pretty accurate. "If the ones on her arms and the neck are the only bruises . . ."

Lewis knows where I'm headed. I don't really need to lead her. Her instincts are as good, if not better, than mine. "How did she get down there? It doesn't sound like the kind of place I'd go willingly. The photos showed a lot of blood on the ground. I'm sure she bled out there." Lewis pauses for a moment, then adds, "It doesn't seem like her killers were strangers."

"Doesn't sound like it," I agree.

The look in her eyes tells me she thinks the same thing I'm thinking. Our Jane Doe wasn't acting alone. There are at least two others out there strong enough to overpower her, kill her, and then leave her there. They didn't even go to great lengths to hide what they did. Greer said the girl wasn't a local. Were they just passing through?

I follow Lewis into the examination room. Tuft unzips the body pouch. Jane Doe's face has the same expression of horror I first saw on the screen, but this time in 3-D. It takes me back to my introduction to the Warlock. But my gut tells me not to expect something so dramatic this time. That victim was murdered to make a statement to the world. This one, killed for what she failed to do or what she knew, is just a discarded body. She was just a prop.

Her skin is pale. Pale, like—like an orchid.

WHILE MY GRANDFATHER is the showman of the family, my father is quite clever in his own right, and he has one trick that's fooled me more than any other. It isn't from any book I could find, or a variation of anything else I've ever seen. I love it for its simplicity.

He would take an orchid from a bouquet, pluck its petals off one by one, place them into the palm of his hand, squeeze them, and then open his fist to reveal they had vanished. The most astonishing part was what would happen next: Father would take the bare stem, wave it in the air, blow on it, and the petals would miraculously reappear. Night after night, I would escape whatever dancer was babysitting me and watch his part of the show from the wings. Dad always winked when he caught me spying on him.

My curiosity finally got the better of me. I had to know the secret. After the performance, I grabbed the orchid as they swept up the stage and inspected it. I was hoping to see some kind of trick mechanism, maybe a silk flower with springs.

But it was real. The stem wasn't bruised, or even bent.

I became determined to find out how he did it. Every evening after he did the orchid trick, I'd wait until the curtains dropped to pluck it from the debris. My dad caught me sneaking around a few times, but he never said a word. It was a game. He is a quiet man, with nowhere near the bombastic personality of his father. He's subtle.

One night, not long after my obsession with the illusion began, we were caught in a rainstorm as we did a load-in, and half the props got stuck on the loading dock. Dad was still drying them out with a leaf blower minutes before his turn onstage. As soon as he'd finished his bit, he rushed back out to continue the salvage operation.

The orchid was in the sweepings, just like after every other show, but when I examined it this time I noticed there was something different about it. The green stem was in fact a piece of thin pipe. The white petals were made of thick silk. At the base of the flower there was a spring, painted green.

Dad found me later as I sat in the corner of the theater, looking at the mechanical flower and crying because the magic was gone.

"I'm sorry, Jessica," he said with a sad face. "I wanted you to believe."

Every night when he performed the illusion, he'd hide a fresh orchid in his pocket. After he made the petals magically reappear on the fake flower, he'd switch it for the real one and drop it to the stage in the blackout.

He did this to entertain an audience of one.

He did this for me.

You CAN TELL how much someone values a secret by how far they'll go to make sure no one, not even an eight-year-old girl, will find out. But sometimes the things we discard end up revealing what we work so hard to hide.

The secrets of our magic are hidden in the litter we leave behind us on the stage. Playing cards made of plastic, newspapers with invisible tape holding them together, fabric flowers that are supposed to be real.

This young woman was discarded. Not just because of what she failed to accomplish, but because of what her killers were about to do.

CHAPTER TEN

OUT OF STATE

Tuft holds up a clear evidence bag with a small bloody object inside. "Alright, ladies. You ready for your first clue?"

"Just a second." Lewis turns to me. "Jessica, still sure this is her?"

I gaze down at the body. "Yes. This is the woman who came to the loft."

Her eyes stare up at the ceiling. What was her last thought? Did she know the people who killed her? Did she feel betrayed? Did she see it coming?

I shudder at the thought that deep down she didn't want to kill me or the infant. What if she'd planned to fail? Did she hesitate long enough for me to draw my gun? It's difficult to judge her now. I'm alive. The baby is alive. She's not.

I have a thousand questions, and no answers.

"What's in the bag?" asks Lewis.

"Our victim had her monthly visitor," replies Tuft.

I glance over at Lewis. She gives me a small shrug, also unsure of the importance of this. By itself, it doesn't seem like much help, but I'm sure Tuft is just priming us.

"Tampons are like shoe prints and tire treads," she explains. "They can tell you a lot. This lot wasn't sold on the East Coast."

"Greer said she wasn't local," Lewis remarks.

"She wasn't recognized as being local, true, but it's a big county."

"So what are you saying?" asks Lewis.

"If she was staying near here, it probably wasn't going to be for more than a few weeks." Tuft takes another bag off the table and shows it to us. Inside it is a pair of generic black panties. "See the crease here? It's from a cardboard holder. She didn't have these on very long. Straight from the package. Never washed."

I get what Tuft is saying. This woman had time to grab underwear from a store and plenty of opportunity to grab a new box of tampons. Yet she did the former, and not the latter. She was probably living out of her purse, or was even on the run. God, I know what that's like. She just grabbed what she needed.

"One more thing." Tuft unzips the body pouch all the way and points to the feet. "I found some dry mud here. It's typical to this area. Probably a week old. She was walking around barefoot within twenty miles of here about seven days ago."

"So she *was* staying locally," Lewis replies.

"That's up to you to find out. I know Greer has been checking all the motels."

I don't know if her crowd is the motel type. On a whim, I pull out my phone and do a rental search, and I find over a dozen rental properties in the more rural areas nearby. I pull up satellite views of the listings to see which ones are the most secluded. I find six promising locations.

"What do you have?" Lewis asks me.

I hesitate for a moment. I don't want to start running her case. "This is your thing."

"Don't worry about hurting my feelings. If you got something, I'll just take the credit." She winks.

"Deal. How do you feel about checking on a couple potential places where she might have stayed that aren't motels? I don't want to step on Greer's case."

"He's an asshole," Tuft whispers under her breath.

Lewis laughs. "Well, that settles it."

"What about the clothes the woman was wearing?" I ask.

"Store-bought, like the underwear," says Tuft. "Same as the shoes. Like what you'd find at Walmart in a hurry."

"May I?" I gesture to the box of latex gloves.

"Hell, you can prep her too if you want," Tuft offers. She doesn't seem the least bit threatened by my meddling. Confident enough in her own abilities, she just wants the thing solved. Her ego isn't on the line.

I slip the gloves on and grab a lock of the girl's hair. It's still wet from the preliminary examination; they wash the hair to see what particles are in there. Dust, dirt, hair from somebody else— the tiniest clues can break a case. I notice there's still a red tint at her roots.

"Bad dye job," says Tuft. She raises a stained finger. "Done yesterday afternoon."

It looks like it didn't take all that well. I pull at the girl's hair, which barely reaches her collarbone. This is the kind of tiny clue that's hard to get from a photo. You need to be in the room to realize what's different. "She also cut her hair since I saw her."

Lewis leans in to get a better look. "She was trying to change her appearance?"

"Yeah. But you don't stop to dye your hair if you think some-

one is about to kill you. She probably did this right after our encounter, shortly before she was killed."

Where did she go after she ran from the loft?

Probably to a safe house of some kind, maybe one of the rent-
als I found, where she had some time to get ready before she hit
the road. I'd bet anything she was with her killers. Little did she
know she wasn't going to make it to the next stop.

They killed her because she was no longer needed, or because
she failed. Maybe both.

"Anything else we should know?" Lewis asks Tuft.

"I'll send you the formal autopsy report when we're done.
However, I'll just say this anecdotally." Tuft pulls the girl's right
hand from the bag. "See the fingernails? Notice the ridges? Also,
look at her skin." She's waiting for us to tell her what's supposed to
be obvious. But to me, our Jane Doe looks like lots of other young
women I see walking around the city every day.

"She's malnourished," Lewis observes.

"Exactly," says Tuft. "Like from some weird diet where you're
not hitting all the food groups. I have a niece who is vegan. The
first few weeks, she looked like death. I had to explain to her how
to be smart about it."

"You pumped the stomach yet?" I ask.

"Pumped, but not examined." Tuft points to a refrigerator.
"I'll get to it as soon as we can.

I strip off my gloves and toss them into a garbage can, trying
to distance myself from the touch of death. Most FBI agents go
their entire careers without ever seeing a corpse, much less having
to be in the room with one.

Tuft begins to zip the girl back into her pouch so she can be
sealed away in the freezer.

Something is missing.

I'm missing something.

"Wait!" I shout.

Tuft freezes.

"Is this exactly as she was found?"

"Yes, bar the dress, underwear, and shoes," she says defensively.

"Can I see one more thing?"

"What are you thinking?" asks Lewis.

"I'm not quite sure. I just want to see the back of her neck."

Actually, I have a hunch, but it's just easier to look than explain my reasoning.

"If you'll help me turn her?" says Tuft, her curiosity engaged.

The three of us flip the body over to reveal the woman's neck, which is bare except for bruising where she was held by one of her assailants.

"Is that it?" asks Tuft.

"No." I don't want to say it aloud, lest I jinx it. I change gloves and probe the hairline, where I find a tiny red mark. It could almost be mistaken for a freckle. I point it out to Tuft.

"Huh. I thought that was a scissor mark from the quick haircut," she says, leaning in.

"Can we magnify that?" I ask.

Tuft brings over a small camera connected to a monitor. Magnified on the screen, we can see the abrasion much more clearly. There's a defined edge to it.

"What's that look like to you?" I ask Lewis.

"Like someone grabbed her chain in a mugging."

"She was wearing a distinctive red necklace when she showed up at my door. It was a little unusual, and I think it was more than decorative. It was symbolic. But she's not wearing it now, and I don't think she took it off to hide her identity. I think it was forcefully yanked off her neck. Dr. Tuft, can you tell if this happened before or after she was killed?"

She examines the image on the screen and shakes her head. "It's too difficult to tell. Clotting can still happen minutes after you die."

I'm not sure if it matters. The important part is that it was forcibly taken from her. Our Jane Doe had probably already changed into her disguise when it was taken from her. It meant something to her and to her killers. And this act of violence was intended as a punishment, not as an act of concealment, similar to a cop's badge being revoked or a soldier being stripped of her rank.

What does that chain signify? What could mean so much to them?

CHAPTER ELEVEN

SHUNNED

SET BACK FROM a neglected road at the end of a gravel driveway, behind overgrown trees and a yard full of tall yellow weeds that's slowly being absorbed back into the wild, the house is a faded white single story with what looks like a large attic. Its weather-beaten exterior siding gives way to bone dry wood, and the rock foundation it sits on resembles something from the colonial era. It could be twenty years old, or a hundred. A dead, bloated raccoon lays by the mailbox, covered in flies.

"Well, this is pleasant," I say as I double-check that my service weapon is loaded before securing it in the holster on my hip.

"Country weirdos freak me out," says Lewis as she inspects and holsters her gun as well. "I prefer my city ones. They at least keep their yards nice."

The owner of the house, Thomas Zwingli, a tax attorney who lives out in Richmond, has given us permission over the phone to inspect the property. His tenants had paid cash up front for the month. Today was the end of last month's payment, and he hasn't heard from them.

On speakerphone, he described the occupants as rather odd. He'd thought they were Amish at first because the two men both had thick black beards. They looked alike, but only in the sense that they dressed in simple clothes and had similar hairstyles.

Zwingli never saw the girl up close. He vaguely recollected there being someone else in the car when he gave them the keys to the house, but he wasn't sure if it was a woman. He couldn't even give us a make or model for the car, other than that it was some old compact that may have been red or blue.

We exit Lewis's car and she reaches the porch first. The boards creak so loudly it's comical. She glances back at me, grinning, and shakes her head. "I guess the doorbell works."

I move to her opposite side, clearing the door and keeping an eye on the backyard, which is an untamed acre of weeds dotted with a few rusted metal drums.

Lewis knocks on the door. "Hello? Anyone home?"

There's no answer.

She gives it another minute. Still nothing. She reaches a hand out and turns the doorknob. It's unlocked. "I guess people are trusting out here."

"Or in a hurry to leave."

Lewis steps inside and I cover her flank. It's dark, except for a sliver of light from the gap between the drawn curtains.

She takes the flashlight from her pocket and searches the room. "Guess they forgot to pay the electrical bill," she says, flipping a useless switch.

My light lands on a melted candle stub on the fireplace mantle. "I'm not sure they've ever paid one."

The house is Spartan, lit only by faded sun streaming through slits in the curtains that cover its few small windows. The kitchen is empty except for a dining set that looks like it came out of a Depression-era Sears catalog. Besides the kitchen and the bathroom, there are only two other rooms. Each one is empty, not even a bed.

I get down on my knees and search the floor of the first of these rooms with my pocket flashlight. My fingers feel the wax droppings from a candle. I inspect the next room and find two more places where candles have been set.

"Hey, Blackwood," Lewis calls from the kitchen.

When I find her, she's standing in front of the fuse box. "What gives with this?" She flips a circuit breaker and the kitchen light comes on.

"Huh." I walk over to the sink and take a whiff. The disposal is dry. No scent of food or soap.

"Looks like they never even used the kitchen," Lewis observes.

"Yeah, why didn't they use it to wash spoons and store takeout containers like a normal human being?" I reply.

"Oh, you're one of those people," says Lewis.

"One of what?"

"When was the last time you cooked a meal in your kitchen?"

"I haven't had company." I also haven't unpacked my dishes since my last move.

She shakes her head. "You don't need company to cook. It's something you do for you. At the very least, invite a coworker over and cook for them."

"I like them too much to do that."

"You're impossible. You come over next week and we'll make up something."

I'm amazed at the effortless way she just invited me to hang out. It would take me weeks to ask someone I worked with to spend time together socially. I'm too much of a loner.

"Thank you. That would be nice."

"I don't want you turning out like these weirdos." She gestures to the curtained windows. "Should we be looking in the basement for three coffins from Transylvania?"

"You go down there first. I'll be at a Starbucks in Richmond."

She waves her hand in the air. "You're tougher than that."

I'm about to reply that it's not a conscious choice, but something catches my eye through the kitchen window: an odd dark area on the ground of the backyard. "I want to check something out."

Lewis follows me out the back door. "Okay, the basement can wait."

Directly behind the house in the middle of the dry brush, there's a patch of dirt with a fire pit in the middle. A couple of cut logs sit around it like seats.

"Did they eat their meals out here?" asks Lewis.

"Maybe." I walk through the brush to the other side of the pit. A few yards away, in another clearing, I come to another fire pit. Three charred mattresses lie in a heap.

Lewis joins me. "Were they trying to destroy forensic evidence?"

"Possibly." I go over to a couple of the oil drums I spotted earlier. Both of them have a layer of ash on the bottom.

"If so, it's not the most thorough job," says Lewis.

I agree with her. "This feels more like campers leaving an area, getting rid of any big traces, than killers trying to cover their tracks." I grab a stick and start combing through the brush beyond the second pit.

"Looking for anything in particular?"

"Yeah." I'm thinking about the orchid again. "What they didn't want us to find."

I spot a third fire pit, this one much smaller and deeper than the other two. There appear to be several layers of ash. Trying not to disturb it too much, I poke through and discover the burnt spines of three books. They are too charred to make out the titles, but I take a photo anyway.

Lewis walks toward me. "What did you—whoops." As she navigates through the grass, there is a crunch under her foot. She freezes, looks down, and with a gloved hand picks up a piece of black plastic. "It was broken like this before I stepped on it," she insists.

"I believe you." I know the feeling. When I was a Miami police officer I once came home from a crime scene and found a victim's blood on the cuff of my uniform. I don't remember coming anywhere near the body and it could have been an issue if I'd contaminated the scene. Thankfully, it wasn't a problem.

Lewis holds up her find to inspect it more closely. "I think this is part of a cell phone." She looks around the field. "A burner. We get them all over the high-trafficking areas in DC." She slips the piece into a plastic evidence bag.

"I'm sure the rest of it is out here somewhere," I reply.

"And god knows what else."

I eye the ground suspiciously. "Methane probe?"

"Yeah, I'll tell Greer what we found. But to be honest, we don't even have a connection to the victim."

"No. But I'd say the weird threshold has been crossed. If Greer doesn't want to come out here, I'll make some waves on my end. If he thinks the FBI is ready to swoop in, that might motivate him." I don't know what kind of weight I can pull in the middle of this crisis, but I've got a feeling this isn't something we should be sitting on.

Lewis calls Greer to fill him in on what we've found. From her side of the conversation, I can tell he's not too thrilled we came out here without telling him. Technically, we don't need to.

Well, at least Lewis doesn't. I'm just a bystander. If Greer wants to, he could give my supervisors crap, but I doubt it'll come to that. Lewis seems more than willing to run interference.

While we wait for him to show up, I try to figure out what the hell was going on here. We have three people who refused to use electricity. They didn't even use running water, as far as we can tell. Yet according to Zwingli, they drove a car, and from what Lewis found, used cell phones.

"So, are they some kind of cult?" she asks, trying to make sense of it all.

"Maybe. Heck if I can figure out the rules."

"Well, they all make exceptions."

I think I know where she's going with this. In some Amish communities, members rotate as designated drivers. One drives a pickup truck so the others can get around when need be. While he does this, they shun him. When his turn is up, another member drives the truck and gets shunned. It's a pragmatic solution to a problem imposed by their theology.

"So, were these the shunned ones?" I ask.

"Like the Amish? Actually, I was thinking of terrorists. When they're on jihad, the rules are different."

I know she doesn't literally mean these guys are Muslim extremists. What she means is they use technology when it serves a purpose.

The cell phone was important to their purpose.

"You okay?" Lewis asks me.

"What?" I pull back to the present.

"You have a lost look in your eyes."

"Sorry. I'm fine." But I'm not. Between the phone discovery and Lewis's mention of jihad, I'm starting to see something, and I don't like it.

A few days ago, my biggest fear was that a psycho would show up at my front door. Then that happened. Things got worse when it turned out she had two accomplices—accomplices she lived with, until they killed her.

But this is bigger than three people.

I think I see it now.

I'm not dealing with a couple of lone weirdos. They're part of a group. They needed phones so they could coordinate.

There's a word for the way they are organized. Like the jihadists Lewis suggested, they're part of a cell. One cell implies more. Maybe a lot more.

I don't think killing me was their primary goal. Otherwise the men who killed our Jane Doe would also have been at my front door, helping her.

They came here for a purpose. If murdering an FBI agent is just one small part of the plan, what's the bigger goal?

I turn to Lewis. "I have to call Quantico, right now."

CHAPTER TWELVE

PAPER CHASE

EVANS, THE SENIOR agent in the conference room, raises an eyebrow and asks, "A cult?"

I could have said we should all go picnic on Mars and received the same reaction. With graying blond hair and a coffee mug perpetually clasped in one hand, he's the kind of bureaucrat who tends to come preinstalled in government buildings, like office chairs and cubicles. For him, investigations are just things that exist on paper. The world outside is irrelevant if it isn't itemized on a form.

The FBI tends to hire people from three kinds of backgrounds: legal, accounting, and actual law enforcement. All have their value in an agency that prosecutes plenty of white-collar crime, but Evans—who is clearly the accounting type—is evaluating my report like it's my tax form and I've suddenly asked him for an irrational deduction.

Evans shoots a glance over at Agent Carr, a recent hire who is almost twenty years younger than he is. His expression, not exactly subtle, is one of disbelief. Not so much of what I just said, but of my written statements. I try not to take it personally.

This meeting had started out cordially enough. Evans and Carr are the agents assigned to investigate what happened at the stakeout loft. We exchanged pleasant courtesies; they praised my past work. But I knew things were heading south because of Evans's almost gleeful reaction when I told him the Jane Doe in the Manassas morgue was the woman who'd showed up on our stakeout doorstep. As I relayed to him the details of what happened at the loft, and my relative certainty that this was the same woman, he gestured increasingly enthusiastically with his coffee cup, like a conductor with his baton. He wasn't thrilled because someone who threatened a fellow agent's life is dead; he was happy because this could be an open-and-shut case for him. As far as he's concerned, solving her murder is a job for local police.

When I got to the part about it being a possible conspiracy, his animation came to a screeching stop, as if his orchestra had suddenly started playing a different tune than the one he was leading.

Carr has been quiet. He seems more focused on the details than how quickly he can punch out on the case. "Do you think there's more than the three of them involved?" he finally asks.

Evans turns to him with a death stare, willing the younger man to shut up lest I keep talking and make their lives much, much more complicated.

"Yes," I reply. "I don't think she was acting alone."

"Wait a second." Evans holds up his coffee cup, this time like it's a stop sign. "We don't even have a connection between this woman and the farmhouse. I think you're getting ahead of yourself."

"Prince William County forensics is out there now, pulling fingerprints, shoe impressions, fibers, everything."

Evans waves his coffee cup in the air again, trying to dissipate the dark cloud I've just conjured. "Let's just wait and see what they have to say in their official report."

I have to control my response. I can't afford to antagonize him. He's too senior. Too connected. "I see your point. In the meantime, what do you recommend we do before the trail gets too cold?"

"Trail? She's dead."

"I think she means the trail for the two men who may have killed her, and also been part of the attempt on Agent Blackwood's life," offers Carr.

Evans shrugs off the comment. "We don't even know there *was* an attempt on your life. You said so yourself. She may just have been trying to kill the infant."

"Possibly." I want to call him out for trying to take the easy way out, but all I need is one more person telling people I'm "diffi-cult." It doesn't matter if my file is great. Ailes has already warned me, more than once, that it's the off-the-record, behind-your-back comments that make all the difference.

Evans realizes how lazy that sounds—or he sees my redden-ing face—and catches himself. "Of course, we take any potential attempt on an agent's life very seriously. I'm going to give this my complete attention."

Translation: He's still going to do nothing. At best, he'll put out an FBI bulletin once the county sheriff finds something con-clusive.

He reaches a hand over to a stack of folders. "We've got a lot on our plate, as I'm sure you do. Right now there are about a thou-sand people at the White House gates protesting the earthquake response. Secret Service is swamped and we're out there looking for potential terror suspects."

Wow. He dropped the terrorism card on me? While he's telling me my case is a top priority, he's reminding me that of course the real top top priority is the terrorists. For me to complain would be just unpatriotic. I suppress an eye roll. "How do you know these guys aren't terrorists?" I reply flippantly.

Evans ignores my comment and retrieves a sheet from a folder. "We just got this back. It's a breakdown of the image of the burned books you found. One is on gardening. Another is a volume of poetry, and the third is about French literature. Not exactly ISIS reading material, is it? Or devil worship manuals?"

He pushes the paper toward me, but I'm too pissed to read it. Is he this much of an asshole to everyone? The vast majority of the agents I work with are supportive colleagues, but every now and then I run into one of the two types who can only acknowledge my achievements through gritted teeth: female agents who feel this is some kind of competition, and male agents who think my success is a threat to their masculinity. They'd never call themselves chauvinists—some will even actively claim to promote gender equality—but when they come across a woman who may actually be better at their job than they are, they can't handle it. They look for a catch, any excuse to explain why someone they feel is inferior has outshone them. Maybe it's preferential treatment; perhaps it's luck. If this were just a performance review, I could care less. Well, at least at this point in my life. But because this involves the lives of others, I feel myself stretching too thin as I try to contain my anger.

I'd love for Evans to tell me how preferential treatment helped me survive when a renegade Mexican militia was trying to gun me down in a Mexican grocery store, or when I was drugged and nearly shoved out of an airplane. Last I checked, bullets and gravity are gender neutral.

"We appreciate you taking the time to go out there and ID the body," Evans says, confusing condescension for grace. "If any more leads show up, like the farmhouse, just send them to us."

The farmhouse isn't a lead that just appeared out of thin air. I figured it out, with Lewis's help. We only found it because we persistently asked questions. Evans doesn't seem like the question-asking type. He doesn't even like answers.

Right now, I don't have many options. I can make a stink over this, but I'll look like a prima donna—like I'm begging for attention. The best outcome I could hope for is a supervisor saying he'll look into it. And all that means is he'll give Evans a few days, then call him up and ask for an update. Evans will repeat whatever the Manassas sheriff tells him and pass it off as overall progress in the case. Maybe the supervisor will see through it, maybe not, but he'll give him at least another week to have something new to say. If it stalls there, Evans will only get leaned on if there's an indication it might be a coordinated effort. Maybe. And that could take weeks.

Evans flips through a pile of notes, pretending to be diligent. "Are you certain the woman said your name?"

"Pardon me?"

"I'm looking through your case notes. It seems like it was a very frantic moment. Are you sure she said your name?"

"Yes." I'm about to ask why. But I know where this is going.

"Are you *sure*?" There's suspicion in his voice.

I'm at my limit and trying to control my mouth. He's saying he'll put his best foot forward on this, but right now he just wants an exit. He's telling me: *Fuck you and your attitude.*

My words come out faster than I can think, fueled by anger that's been welling inside me. "If I say no, would that make you feel better? Because then you can suggest this had nothing to do with me or the FBI. Wouldn't that make your life easier, if you could just toss this all over to metro police? Isn't that what you want me to say? Maybe I should. At least I know a real cop would be handling this." I turn to Carr. "No offense."

Now Evans turns red. He's a lazy ass and I've just called him on it. I can tell he wants to use a word that'll put him in hot water. This is going to haunt me.

Damn it. I still haven't figured out how to only speak part of my mind. I made this personal when I shouldn't have.

"Whoa," Carr calmly interjects. "Let's take a step back, folks. This earthquake and all the pressure has us on edge. We're all cops here."

Maybe two of us are.

Evans does some calculation in his head, maybe assessing how much shit I could stir up for him. I'm not that type. But he is, and so he assumes everyone else is that petty. He holds up his hands, still gripping the coffee cup in one of them. "I surrender. Last thing I want is your curse to get to me."

My *curse*?

Carr shoots him a frustrated look.

Evans flinches, then produces an insincere smile. "You're hard-core, Blackwood. No doubt. You made your point." He glances at Carr. "We'll take this seriously."

Translation: I'm Carr's problem now. Fair enough. One cop is better than none. But, while I mean no disrespect to him, Carr seems really green. I don't have a lot of hope he'll take this very far. I still might as well be at the bottom of the stack of folders Evans brought with him.

I realize now why they were there on the table in the first place. He wants to show me how busy he is. What a tool.

The briefing ends with all the friendliness of a handshake lineup after a high school basketball game between rivals. Evans pretends to take me seriously. Carr pretends this wasn't as tense as it was.

I leave the room wondering why people think I'm cursed.

Then again, maybe it's not so hard to see why.

CHAPTER THIRTEEN

MIMICRY

AILES PATIENTLY LISTENS to me unload on Evans like I'm talking about a bad day at school. Gerald and Jennifer, my surrogate siblings, sit on the other side of the large table where we work and shake their heads sympathetically. We may have some minor disagreements, and sometimes I do feel like the foster kid, but in this unit we have each other's backs. Part of the reason we do most of our work in this common area is so we can solve problems as a group, lending each other help on cases and setting aside egos. There's not much Ailes or the others can do at this point. But I know he'll use his soft but effective touch if things don't progress, and it's satisfying to know my coworkers share my frustration.

When I finish my rant, I notice a stack of papers and journals on the table. They have titles like *Elliptical Mathematics Quarterly* and *Quanta Journal*.

"I'm sorry I missed out on your book club," I reply, finally relaxing in my chair.

"No you're not," says Gerald.

"You're right." I pick up a printout of a research paper and see Devon's name listed as the author. About the only thing I understand is the word "abstract." I hold it out to Ailes. "What? You guys don't trust me on this?" It's a half joke. I wasn't aware they were also pursuing the case as well. The more the merrier. I guess.

"Let's just say if we see any more Devon predictions—" says Ailes.

"Post-dictions," I interject. It may be a nitpick, but I think it's important we don't start giving this guy too much credit.

"Yes. It seemed wise to do a little more background into his work. Since I left the academic world, there have been advances in a number of areas I'm not familiar with."

"Care to give me the BuzzFeed version?" I ask.

Gerald drops a journal he's been reading back onto the pile. "Devon went nuts."

"I don't think that's quite fair," says Jennifer. Other than when I melt her genius-level brain with a magic trick, she's usually quiet and nonconfrontational. Blunt, but not the type to interject if she doesn't have to. She's bothered by the idea that Devon, someone she respected, got posthumously pulled into this.

Gerald shakes his head. "This whole simulated strange attractor mimicry thing is like *A New Kind of Science* without the pretty *Game of Life* graphs."

"You're being too reductionist," replies Jennifer. "He's speaking metaphorically."

"Metaphorically, or abstractly? Is it a transitive observation or a reflective one?"

I interrupt them to bring the conversation back to earth. "Did I mention I saw the dead body of the woman who wanted to murder me?"

Gerald and Jennifer look at me, trying to grasp the relevance, then realize I'm making a morbid joke.

"Sorry, Jessica. Nerd argument," Gerald replies.

"If you want to talk Boba Fett versus Captain America, I'm your girl. But this is a bit beyond me. A lot beyond me." I turn to Ailes for the cable-documentary-level explanation.

"Devon was trying to develop a way to look at complex systems and make predictions. We do this all the time in investigations. We try to find hidden patterns in random evidence collected at the scene of a crime. Or in medicine, doctors look for warning signs in a heartbeat. Finding that signal in all the noise is how stock market computers work, not to mention weather and even earthquake predictions." He points to the stack of journals. "It seems that after Devon stopped publishing in the big journals, he was releasing papers in some of the niche ones. His focus was on signal mimicry in chaotic systems."

"Obviously," I sigh.

"When you try to predict something, you want to separate the signal from the noise. The problem is that not all signals are noise, and not all noise started out as noise. And when you want to influence something, you can mimic the signal and change the system. Devon was studying signal mimicry."

"Um, I think I understand the words, but I'm not sure I get the context."

I usually grasp more than I let on, but find it safe to play it slightly dumber, lest they get too enthusiastic and go too geeky on a topic.

"Imagine the stock market. It's thousands of fluctuating prices. If you're trying to play the market, you look for something predictable, like a proven pattern. When there's war in the Middle East, oil gets more expensive. In a recession, fewer people are buying cars. But these days, the market is much more complicated because most of the pricing is driven by computers looking for microfluctuations in the market. They're not looking at reality as much as the decisions other computers are making. The mimicry comes in when you decide to trick the other computers. If you realize they're basing their trades on a few different factors, like the price of industrial machinery dropping or an energy boom in Iceland, you do a number of trades to manipulate those factors and trick the computers."

"It's like bluffing at poker, only the other players don't realize you're even sitting at the table," adds Jennifer.

"Got it. Like the margay?"

"The jungle cat?" asks Gerald.

"Yeah," I reply. "It'll imitate the cry of a baby tamarin monkey to lure adult monkeys out into the open, and then pounce on them to get some delicious monkey meat."

Jennifer and Gerald stare at me blankly for a moment.

Ailes grins and replies, "That's exactly what signal mimicry is."

"I watch a lot of the National Geographic Channel," I explain, leaving out that I usually watch it for company as I drink a glass of wine and then pass out on the couch. "So what's this have to do with earthquakes?"

"We're still trying to figure that out. Devon became interested in mimicry when he realized that some systems were just too chaotic to predict. That's when he got the idea of influencing systems to cause major shifts."

"What kinds of shifts?" I ask.

"Think about a crowd of people in a stadium watching a football game. Assuming the scoring is random, there's no way to predict when the crowd will start to cheer. Despite that, crowd waves will spontaneously emerge, group clapping and stomping. All of these can be initiated by one persistent person. If they keep clapping, soon people around them will pick up. Or if they start the wave, you get the idea. One person can affect eighty thousand."

"And that many stomping people could cause a stadium collapse," I add. "So Devon was looking for ways to goose the system?"

"Sort of. Going back to the football game analogy, there's a small correlation between crowd behavior and scoring. That one persistent person might be able to have a slight effect on the outcome of the game. Devon was interested by how, in otherwise chaotic systems, you could create some predictability." Ailes suppresses a knowing smile. "Small advantages mean a lot in chaotic systems."

What he means is that this is how he made his own fortune. He found the signals within the noise of the stock market.

I survey the journals on the table and the realization that my one contribution to the conversation involved the phrase "delicious monkey meat." I think I'm out of my league. "I get the idea I'm the wrong person for this case."

Ailes shakes his head. "No. Quite the opposite. If someone walked in here with an antigravity machine it'd be up to Gerald, Jennifer, and me to do our due diligence on the science, but in the end, it'd be up to you to figure it out."

"*Me?*"

"Yes. You. Because antigravity machines aren't real. You're the only one here who knows how to make it look like things are flying. Same with Devon. He can't predict things the way he claimed. There's a trick to it. Figuring that out is your job. We've been spending the last few hours thinking about how signal mimicry could create an earthquake."

"Can it?" I ask.

"Maybe. But what does your gut tell you?"

"It's a trick."

"And that's why we need you and it's still your case."

I gesture to the journals. "So why all this?"

There's an uneasy silence in the room.

I answer for them. "Ah . . . external pressure."

Ailes nods. "I have to give a briefing to the president's science advisor."

"You?"

"Let's just say mathematics isn't his strong point."

"He hasn't published anything meaningful in two decades," adds Jennifer, dismissively.

"I guess politics is time-consuming," Gerald replies.

I pick a bookmarked journal off the table and flip through it. I point to the coauthor of Devon's article. "Does Dale Cyprian ring any bells? Where have I seen his name before?"

Ailes nods. "I think he was the last person to collaborate with Devon in the journals. I've seen his name in some econ stuff."

"Okay. Maybe I should talk to him? I haven't found any family or other leads for Devon. The video was made after he stopped teaching. To be honest, I got nothing else to go on right now. I can catch the shuttle to Boston and be back tomorrow morning." I'm not eager to hop on an airplane, but it's either that or obsess over the forensics on the Jane Doe.

"Do it," says Ailes. He holds up a finger for a moment as he thinks something over. "You didn't find any evidence of satanic or occult practices at the farmhouse?"

"No. They seem like Amish vegans."

"Odd. I'd figure the people out to get you would be more of the *Dungeons and Dragons* kind."

"That's just prejudiced," Gerald interjects.

"No offense, Gerald. You know what I mean. It just seems odd."

Does Ailes doubt the connection between the girl and the men who rented the house? Now I'm questioning myself. Was I a bitch to Evans for no reason? No, I decide. He was still an asshole. "Did I just chance upon a weird scene that had nothing to do with the Jane Doe?"

"I don't know. I'll put in a call to the Manassas sheriff's department and get put in the loop. You focus on Devon connections. We need something more than we've got, and sooner rather than later."

"You still think there's another prediction coming?"

"I hope not. But I want to make sure we've done our homework."

I HEAD FOR the airport with the unsettling feeling that somewhere in Ailes's head there is an equation involving me and Jane Doe, and he doesn't like the solution he's seeing. I'd hoped he'd get more bureau attention focused on her and her conspirators, but now I'm worried.

The stack of journals I saw on the table also makes me feel a bit guilty. While I was out chasing down a case that's not really my own and causing problems with Evans, my coworkers were back in the office covering my ass on something that was my responsibility.

I had one job, and nothing to show for it.

I didn't take Devon seriously. But Ailes did. Now I'm more than curious to hear what the dead mathematician says next.

I'm afraid.

CHAPTER FOURTEEN

CONTROL

PROFESSOR CYPRIAN, NOW a member of an academic think tank called the Spritzman Group for Advanced Mathematics, located near the heart of Harvard College, sits behind a desk covered with colorful toys and puzzles. He's got a Rubik's Cube with at least twenty-five blocks on one side that gives me a headache to even think about. His office shelves are lined with books on fractals, nature photography, and novelties relating to mathematics and patterns. The room looks like a nerdy kids' store.

Cyprian, a small bald man with thick black glasses, seems too small for his chair and more suited for Santa's workshop, where he'd be the elf in charge of fun educational toys. He recognized my name immediately when I called on my way to the airport, and readily agreed to meet with me.

"I've talked to your father a few times," he says, after guiding me into his office. "A clever man."

Sometimes people confuse my famous grandfather for my not-so-famous father. "He's quite a showman."

"I'm sure it runs in the family, although I've never seen him perform. But his informal talks at the Gathering 4 Gardner conferences are always illuminating. His puzzle boxes are quite exceptional."

Interesting. Cyprian *does* mean my father. One of dad's hobbies is creating intricate wooden puzzle boxes that are almost impossible to solve. Grandfather, who could never see much potential in them, regards them somewhat dismissively as bad magic and poor security devices, missing the point entirely.

Dad makes these boxes by hand and shows them to other puzzle and curiosity enthusiasts at conferences such as Gathering 4 Gardner, which is a biannual meeting of magicians, mathematicians, and scientists. I shouldn't be too surprised that he and Professor Cyprian would cross paths.

I tap the monstrous puzzle cube with my fingernail. "Unfortunately, that kind of smarts skips a generation."

Cyprian ponders this for a moment. "Huh. I would imagine you take after your father quite a lot, given your line of work."

Perhaps he's right. Sometimes I underestimate how much of my father is in me. We have such different personalities. He's nonconfrontational, whereas I'm blunt to a fault. But Cyprian has a point. Dad loves to create little puzzles, like he did with the orchid, and I used to love figuring them out.

I notice that Cyprian is watching me the way you might someone who is wearing a disguise, scrutinizing my face. It's a little unnerving. I call him out on it so I can keep the upper hand. I'm not the one that needs to be thrown off balance here. "Professor, are you studying me?"

He gives me a sincere grin. "I was, Agent Blackwood. I was looking at your microexpressions. The subtle, small reactions we make when people talk to us."

"Yes. They taught us about microexpressions at the academy," I reply.

"Probably so. But we've been using artificial intelligence and physiological data to discover new ones they probably didn't teach you. For some of them, there aren't even simple terms to describe the emotions. A lot of them are subconscious."

"So you're treating human emotions as a puzzle box?" There's a hint of disdain at the thought of being a lab rat that wandered into his office.

"Right now we're working with a children's hospital on finding ways to help diagnose pain and inner emotional states in children who have communication problems." He points to my face. "Just now you exhibited a slight shame response. A degree of reddening in your cheeks when I mentioned it was to help children. But even before I gave you that information, your forehead and chin muscles tightened. This is what we call the 'anticipation of an inverse response' reaction. Your mind was already reaching a conclusion that you might be embarrassed."

"Before you replied?" I ask, feeling extremely self-conscious. "Isn't that a little, um, fringe?"

"No. Not at all. You heard the tone of my voice. Our speech patterns are complex versions of warning calls, which by design need to be extremely efficient. Sometimes the first syllable is all we really need to hear."

"So your tone told me I was about to be mildly scolded?"

"Basically. And you were already preparing a response. That was your subconscious prepping your conscious mind. These tones are an important part of language. The lack of them is what makes written communication difficult."

"Especially online," I reply.

Cyprian lets out a small laugh. "Too true. But an old problem. Almost five hundred years ago, John Wilkins, a philosopher and bishop, pushed heavily for the written language to adopt an upside-down exclamation point at the end of a sentence to indicate irony. Think of how many online feuds that could have prevented."

Other than when he's embarrassing me a little, the professor is a likable man. I can tell he's a naturally curious person who wants to see how everything works, including the person in front of him. I have my little techniques to get people to talk. In this case, by being unguarded myself and letting him expound on his work, I'm making him more comfortable and hopefully more open to talking about his relationship with Devon.

"So you've been using mathematics to probe the mind?" I ask.

"To some extent. Looking for clues in a complex system."

"Did you and Devon work together on this?" I change the conversation to the subject of why I'm here.

"You've been holding that question in for at least two minutes," Cyprian replies. "It's in your chin. If it's not pointing at me, your eyes never let me leave your field of vision. Like you're a hawk waiting for the right time to pounce on a mouse."

I hold up my hands in mock surrender. "You're too smart for me."

"I seriously doubt that. Anyway, in answer to your question, Devon and I never worked on this particular area together. I was focused on individuals. He was thinking more globally."

"How do you mean?"

"He was really out to change the world."

"That seems noble."

Cyprian folds his hands. "So were Attila the Hun and Vladimir Lenin."

"Oh," I reply. Those comparisons certainly seem sinister.

He observes my reaction. "Oh, no. I don't mean anything so

tyrannical. Not overtly. I'm of the school that a scientist's job is to make observations and suggestions where invited, and not to let one's political or philosophical beliefs have undue influence. Peter felt like his job was to lead the way."

"Through mathematics?"

"Sort of. You know we started collaborating right out of college? We had some early successes using math to make some real positive changes. Peter liked to keep a count of how many lives we saved."

"Saved? How?"

"I'll give you one example," he replies. "We became fascinated by the rates of infections in hospitals. Peter and I did all sorts of measurements and surveys. We realized the single biggest thing we could change was to get doctors and nurses to wash their hands more. Simple. I know. But easier said than done. How do you do that? It's not like they don't know you're supposed to do that. So we tried to figure it out. Long story short, and this will sound sexist, it was decades ago, but we realized that the hospitals with the highest rates of infection transmitted by the nursing staff correlated with scrub rooms that didn't have mirrors over the washbasins. Add a mirror, and you give people a reason to stop at the basin. With doctors, we found that just adding a color dye to hand soap made them use more of it."

His face lights up as he recounts that discovery. "These are just some of the small examples. But for two aspiring mathematicians out to change the world, it was addicting. Hospitals adopted our suggestions and we saw statistically significant drops in infection rates. Peter added this to his scoreboard. Eventually he created an electronic spreadsheet that would tick every time a life was saved, statistically speaking."

"What about the earthquake revelation? Is this something you worked on?"

"No."

"But the two of you stopped publishing together. Was there a rift?"

"Our interests diverged. Peter chose a path that I think was greater than his intellectual capability."

"Was there a specific point where you drifted apart?"

"Cassandra."

"A woman?"

Cyprian grins slightly. "No. Not quite. Peter's passion project, named for the Greek prophet. He wanted to build the ultimate prediction system. Understand, this was back in the late eighties. Computers were making fortunes on Wall Street. Imaging systems were spotting tumors, and you could finesse static-filled sonar data for oil wells.

"Peter's idea was to build a universal prediction system that would tell you anything if you gave it enough data. It was a big, ambitious project. The problem was it was deeply flawed. Peter believed that with enough computing power you could find something he called the unified signal. He thought that just like physics has elementary particles the real world has some basic algorithms and if you figured them out, the weather, well everything, could be determined."

"That seems a bit extreme for a mathematician of his background. More like kabbalah, or numerology."

"Yes and no. There's certainly a supernatural stigma to it. The search for Ein Sof, god before form, what have you. But this was a little more complicated. Peter also believed there were driving signals. Things that influenced the randomness. After all, human history has been about determining them." Cyprian points to his desk calendar. "That's a prediction system. It tells you the lunar cycles, the shortest and longest days of the year. Almanacs tell you when to plant. All of this was noise at one point. Even after we figured out cycles of the moon and planets, the 'why' was a mystery until Newton came along and figured that out. Einstein clarified it even further, revealing truths that were right in front of us. What a really accurate calendar tells you is the theory of relativity. Right inside there is $E = mc^2$. One simple formula controls gravitation and our fate. Even now, we're looking for galactic events that may cause mass extinctions from cosmic radiation and solar cycles that bring deadly meteors toward Earth. A lot of the random things aren't so random. Forty-year blights can be tied to locusts that wait that long to come out of the ground or bacteria that only bloom when certain environmental things come together. My point is there are an awful lot of real signals we don't recognize. Peter initially wanted to find those."

"So what happened to Cassandra?" I ask.

"It was a big, dumb, overly ambitious project that promised too much."

"It died?"

"Worse. The government funded it. Some secret off-the-books agency that doesn't report what it does to Congress came along and gave Peter a lot of money to make it happen. He asked me to come on board. I declined. I want to help people, not fight shadow wars. And intellectually speaking, I think you have to solve a lot of small problems to figure out the big one and not vice versa. So that was it."

"You lost touch?"

"He disappeared into a black hole. I can't tell you the number of promising graduate students who vanish from academia and into the bowels of the NSA, NRO, and other agencies. Who knows what genius the world was deprived of so we could find a quicker algorithm to read an Afghan shopkeeper's encrypted e-mail?"

"So you don't give much credence to Cassandra?"

"No."

"So it's not connected to this prediction?"

"I didn't say that." Cyprian thinks for a moment. "My fear is that it became something else." His voice is grave.

"What?"

Up until now, I thought he was dismissing Devon's research as a fool's errand.

He shrugs. "I don't know. But I'll give you an example. Down the hall from me is a brilliant biologist, Dr. Andrzycki, originally from Russia. He went to Moscow State University to become a doctor and to save lives. His specialty was viruses. Two years after graduation he found himself in Southeast Asia, hunting for strains of hantavirus. Ostensibly, it was for humanitarian research, but every sample he collected was taped up and shipped back to an army base outside of Kiev. There was no known medical facility there. Just a semisecret weapons research center. Once he realized what was going on, Andrzycki defected to the West. Not that we didn't have our own programs for weaponizing those things, but at least most of the people we sent into the field were trying to save lives. Most military projects go nowhere. Sometimes though, they become worse than the problem they were trying to solve."

"And what do you think the worst-case scenario was for Devon's project?"

"It would never work. But when you can't predict what's going to happen, you do the next best thing: you find a way to force it."

"Artificial strange attractors." I recall the name from one of the easier-to-read research papers I'd taken with me on the flight.

Cyprian lights up. "Yes, that's it! Dumb name, though. It has nothing to do with strange attractors. It was just marketing to impress the people with the money."

"The government?"

"Yes. Government-backed contractors. Think tanks. Research firms, whatever. I've had two promising grad students erase their

LinkedIn profiles after they went to work for an obscure agricultural aid agency I'm sure is backed by the CIA."

Cyprian's theory makes sense. Devon vanishing into a government project would explain the lack of information we have on him. It also means it might be next to impossible to find out what he was up to. There are still files relating to 9/11 that involved agencies won't even release to the FBI—probably to hide their own incompetence. Something tells me the moment Devon came back from the dead, somebody started a paper shredder and began bulk erasing data.

When he was just a lone crackpot with a video camera, he was a joke to me. Now that I know he may have had access to unlimited funds and total secrecy, he's suddenly become a greater cause for suspicion.

"Thank you, Professor. If you could discreetly ask around about Devon, that would be appreciated."

"Of course. And please tell your father I said hello. And give him my congratulations on the Magic Castle nomination. That's quite an honor. You must be proud."

"I am," I reply, trying to hide the guilt on my face. I still haven't talked to my dad since Grandfather mentioned it.

As I leave I get a text message from Gerald: *Hurry back! New Devon video is online. This time it's an actual prediction.*

This is going to be interesting.

CHAPTER FIFTEEN

UNNATURAL DISASTERS

I N THE NEXT *seventy hours, it is with eighty percent certainty that I can predict a natural disaster will strike within a thirty-mile area of the coordinates mentioned, causing the deaths of between four hundred and eight hundred people. I strongly encourage local authorities to do their best to prepare for this catastrophe. The involved people have my sincerest sympathies. I only wish I had more time to provide specific details. Black Fall is coming.*

Twenty years ago, the dire predictions of a dead man wouldn't have garnered much attention unless his name was Nostradamus. In the Internet age, links to the video spread around the world like wildfire before there was enough time to watch it all the way through.

For the people in Yanoa, Bolivia, the video is more than a curiosity. They are right in the epicenter of Devon's prediction.

Compounding all this is the fact that a massive tropical storm is already headed their way.

"Anybody have any thoughts?" asks Ailes. He called us into a

late-night meeting at our office, and I headed here straight from the airport.

Gerald looks up from his computer, where he's been monitoring weather reports. "This is the first specific prediction he's made. And we have a tropical storm headed right for there."

"The video was released after the storm track was announced," I point out.

"Yes, but the predicted loss of life is specific."

"And it hasn't happened yet. All we have is a video identifying an area *after* the fact. We have no reason to believe anything has been predicted yet." I still smell a charlatan, and I can't let it go.

Ailes thinks this over for a moment. "What would you do if you were the president of Bolivia? How seriously would you take this?"

"I'd be afraid to not take it seriously," I admit. There's something going on here, something potentially dangerous.

"Even though you and everyone you've spoken to is skeptical of his predictive ability?"

"Yeah, but maybe he, or whoever is actually behind this, would try to find a way to force it. Psychics have been known to plant evidence, and sometimes even cause the event they claim to predict by force."

"How do you cause a natural disaster?" asks Jennifer. But it doesn't come across as a challenge, just a question for the room.

I give this some consideration. "What kind of disasters kill the most people?"

"Storms," replies Gerald. "Flooding. Earthquakes are a distant second."

"I'll quit my job and call this guy the Chosen One if this is another earthquake, based on what Kaur told me. As far as storms go, this isn't even a massive one."

Ailes seems distant. Something we've said has him thinking. "I'm going to make some calls."

"What would you like us to do?" By "us" I mean me.

"Let the wheels spin in the back of your head."

HALF AN HOUR later, my wheels are still spinning, but they aren't getting much traction. I keep going in circles about method. All I can do is try to focus on motive, and I still come up blank. Meanwhile, Devon is gaining more converts as news sites go crazy over the latest video.

My phone rings, distracting me from my research into Devon's contacts.

"Want an update on the Jane Doe?" asks Lewis.

"I'm not in the pipeline on this," I tell her. I have to be super cautious about not getting in Evans's way—if it's possible to get in the way of a tree stump.

"That's not my question. I spoke to your boy Agent Carr, by the way. He seems nice enough. Does he know you guys don't get merit badges in the FBI?"

"What do you got?" I ask, heading into the hall.

"County forensics officially confirms the boot print at the farmhouse connects to the murder scene on the Jane Doe. We're looking at tire tracks now."

The validation of my suspicions don't make me feel any better. It makes me feel worse, in fact. "Any word on an ID for her?"

"No. Although Dr. Tuft found something in that neck wound."

"What?"

"Nothing much, just some tiny red paint flakes. Mean anything to you?"

"She was wearing that red necklace."

"Part of the coating must have flaked away when the chain got yanked off her."

Something about her words gets me thinking. "Chain," I repeat. That's exactly what the girl's necklace looked like. A red chain. I open the door to our office and holler to Gerald. "Can you look up anything related to a 'Red Chain' in the cult database?"

"What are you thinking?" asks Lewis, overhearing me.

"There's something about the phrase, it feels familiar. 'Red chain'."

"Let me know if anything turns up. Meanwhile, how are things with you?" she asks, concerned.

"We're trying to prevent a natural disaster from wiping out hundreds of lives," I say, almost robotically, because I'm still thinking about the chain.

"Oh? Um, good luck with that."

"Yeah. And Aileen? Thank you for keeping me in the loop."

"No problem. Who knows when I might need a favor from you FBI people. And don't forget, next week we're doing dinner."

"Of course." I suddenly realize that underneath her easygoing manner Lewis might want someone to talk to as well.

I WALK BACK to the table and sit down. Next to my notes about disasters and failure points, I circle the words "red chain."

"It was an offshoot Christian cult in the fifteen hundreds," says Gerald. "They were vegetarians, basically animists. Excommunicated and pretty much wiped out by the Inquisition."

"Oh, guess that rules them out." I'm not ready to implicate a centuries-old cult in my attempted murder.

"For what?"

"Nothing."

"Huh. Well, that name pops up again. Turns out a radical environmental group used the name in the early nineteen eighties. Started by a couple of professors from Michigan."

I'm more chilled than elated that my suspicions were on the mark. "What happened to them?"

"One of them is doing time in federal prison not too far from here."

My ears perk up. "Really?"

"Yeah, Ezra Winter. He was convicted of sending mail bombs to nuclear power plant developers and agricultural tech executives. One of them killed a man. He's serving out a fifty-year sentence."

"Seriously?"

Gerald taps a few buttons on his keyboard. "I'm sending you everything. Is this related to the Jane Doe who showed up on your doorstep?"

"Maybe." This screams of a connection, but I don't want to jump too quickly to a conclusion.

When Ailes comes back into the room, I pull him aside. "I've got nothing on this natural disaster thing."

"None of us do," he says with a tone of defeat that coming from him sounds unnatural.

I feel guilty for what I'm about to ask him in the middle of this. "I may have a lead on the Jane Doe." I tell him about the Red Chain connection.

After hearing me out, he replies, gently admonishing me. "It's not your case, Blackwood."

"I know. But the men who killed her are still out there, and Evans and Carr aren't going to do anything with this lead."

"Do you think Ezra Winter sent the woman to kill you?" he asks me bluntly.

"I think he may be connected. That's all. I just want to see him face-to-face."

Ailes thinks about this for a moment. "This should be Evans's case."

"I understand that. But as far as he's concerned, there isn't a case, much less a connection to Winter. Do you really think he's going to follow a lead based on one fleck of red paint?"

He shakes his head. "No," he admits. "Be back here by noon tomorrow. Got it?"

"Yes."

Noon doesn't leave me much time, but I know he's pushing things as far as he can.

"I'm serious, Blackwood. I need your full attention on the predictions. We're going to have a lot of explaining to do no matter what happens."

"I get it."

"I hope so." He lowers his voice. "Right now, this woman is a distraction. An understandable one, but usually you're better at compartmentalizing."

"I know." But I can't get the image of that knife blade poised over the baby out of my mind.

"As your supervisor, the right solution is to ask you to take leave. Which you're entitled to. Which I *should* make you do after everything. Truth is, I would if we weren't short staffed with the earthquake and the protests."

We're all feeling like a lone sheriff in an indifferent town.

I steal a glance at the bullpen. "Don't take this away from me. It's not about me. It's about the child." As I say it, I realize why I've been so affected by the case. My obsession is driven out of guilt for inciting what happened, not self-preservation.

"I get it." Ailes calls to Gerald. "You and Blackwood have a field trip tomorrow."

Gerald gives us the thumbs-up, then returns to his computer screen.

"Why are you sending him? Don't you need him here? No offense, Gerald," I shout over to him.

"I need you both. But if Winter is connected to your Jane Doe, then it would be foolish of me to send you alone."

It was more comforting when Ailes regarded my fixation on the Jane Doe as a foolish whim. Now that he's taking it seriously, I'm getting even more concerned.

CHAPTER SIXTEEN

MASTERMIND

I'VE BEEN TO dozens of prisons, and talked to scores of inmates. From jailhouse snitches looking to get some leniency on an embezzlement conviction by ratting out a cell mate who has some information on a crime I'm investigating, to a serial killer I know would do anything within his power to hurt me, most of these encounters have been as dramatic as returning a book to the library. As the words flow out of Ezra Winter's mouth, I'm speechless. Gerald and I both do our best to hide our shock.

Winter is a slight man with a short white beard and prison crew cut. He sits across from us at the table with his hands chained through a ring. We'd come here to ask him about his little cult, and to see if he was still active with it, but instead he's just blurted out something that makes my heart jump a beat.

As soon as we sat down, he shared a knowing smile and then said, "I figured it was only a matter of time before someone came around to ask about me and Peter."

Peter.

Peter Devon.

I catch myself, and carry on as normally as possible. Right now he thinks we know something, and he's primed to talk to us, if for no other reason than to feel important. "How would you describe that?"

Gerald, to his credit, doesn't react. He makes a small entry in his notebook and pretends to only be half-interested. The kid is good. Real good.

"My relationship with Peter?" Winter says with a dramatic sigh. "Where to start? We had shared interests. We wanted to save the world from itself. I ended up here, and Peter, well, he died too soon."

"What about the predictions?"

"You mean, Black Fall?"

"Yes," I reply. I give Gerald a glance, but my reminder is not necessary. He's already got his phone out behind his pad, recording this.

"I'm the one who told him about it. He was too myopic to see the grand scheme of things. Too left brain. It takes a poet to look at all that data and see the trend." Winter is laying it on like a dinner theater actor who thinks he's finally got his big Broadway break, and is using all of his skills to make us appreciate how important he is. He wants attention and possibly some kind of leniency.

"Black Fall?" I repeat.

"Exactly. Unfortunately, Peter wasn't very good at explaining things to everyone else. I'm not sure he even got it, to be honest. I tried. God knows I tried." He looks off to the side, sighing to show us how exasperated he is.

I realize that what this man truly wants is an audience, so I play to this to keep him talking. "Could you explain it to me?"

Winter gestures with his hands, oblivious to the handcuffs

as they clang against the ring binding them to the table. "If you look at the timeline of history, I'm talking about all the way to life starting on earth, you see a series of rises and falls. Life builds up, then it collapses. Sometimes externally, other times internally. With human civilization, the greater the rise, the bigger the fall. We had a good run from the Greeks to the Romans, but then after the fall of the Roman Empire we had a thousand years of the Dark Ages. The Renaissance brought about the collapse of civilization in the Americas. Now, here we are at the highest point of history thus far, and inevitably we're going to have the biggest collapse. A dark age unlike any other. The Black Fall."

"Then what happens?" I ask.

"There are two outcomes," Winter replies, launching into his narrative. God knows how many inmates he's practiced this speech on. "The survivors, the ones who make it through the plagues, the riots, and starvation, foolishly try to rebuild the world that collapsed, or they find a better way to live."

"Like the way the Red Chain lives?" I throw it out there casually, so it doesn't come across as an accusation.

Winter flinches and stares down at his bound hands. "I don't have any association with that organization anymore."

It is a canned response, like one an attorney had him rehearse. But he wants to keep our attention. I just need to provoke him. "Is that what your lawyer told you to say? You're behind bars because you believed in the cause, yet I don't see anyone else here. They abandoned you."

He twitches, then smugly smiles. "Don't be fooled. I have my supporters. And they're very loyal to me."

"Loyal enough to show up at my door and try to kill me?"

I say this as lightly as I can. I don't want him to think I'm flustered.

"Pardon?" Winter gives me a confused look. "I'm sorry, but who are you?"

He's an arrogant man—full of his own bullshit and yet convinced of his own brilliance—but his reply feels utterly truthful. I had expected some kind of gloating hint, not an old man genuinely befuddled by this interruption to his diatribe.

I change the topic back to Black Fall to keep him focused. "What do you know about the predictions?"

He dismisses my accusation as quickly as I'd delivered it. "I wasn't directly involved. But I have information that could be helpful." He raises an eyebrow.

"Such as?"

"Look around you." He nods to his chains. "Maybe if some arrangements can be made, I'd be able to help you out. As it stands, I have nothing to gain."

"You would only be useful to us if you were still in contact with the Red Chain."

"To my knowledge that organization no longer exists." His eyes narrow. "But if it did, my influence extends well beyond these walls."

"But you can't explain why one of your cult members wanted to kill me?" I slide a photo of our Jane Doe across the table.

Winter glances at the photo, then shrugs. "I've made it clear I have no involvement with said organization." He overenunciates this in a way that suggests he means the opposite. "Some say they have many cells, acting independently. Obviously someone thought you were a threat."

"To you?"

"To humanity," he says with certainty.

"Me?" I turn to Gerald. "I don't always separate my trash into the right bin, but I've never been called a threat to humanity."

I have to treat Winter like a buffoon if I want to keep him talking. He's fighting for me to take him seriously, and I'm afraid he'll shut up as soon as he thinks he's won.

"You don't see it," Winter replies. "Or you pretend not to. But neither did the men who built nuclear weapons and engineered crops that were a crime against nature. We're all guilty. It's just that some of us see it as our duty to fix the harm."

Gerald interjects. "Have you had any contact with current or former members of the Red Chain?" He phrases the question as a formality, distracting Winter from our exchange.

"I'm not allowed to. My calls and communications are monitored."

"Do you have e-mail?" asks Gerald.

"Yes. And federal marshals get to read everything I send," Winter replies tersely.

"But you still have influence," I reply.

He doesn't actually answer the question about contact with the Red Chain. Gerald notices this too.

Winter gives me a smug smile. "You could say."

"Were you involved in the taping of Devon's predictions?"

"I've said what I can. If you have any more questions, bring a US attorney with a parole deal and I could be quite forthcoming." He leans back, satisfied he has our interest.

I stifle a yawn, feigning indifference. "To be brutally honest, we have a bunch of other people to talk to today. We're not calling anyone unless you give us something more to work with."

There's a twitch in his brow as he tries to decide if I'm bluffing. "I knew Peter Devon. Maybe better than anyone else. What more do you need?"

"We'll think about it," I reply, then nod to Gerald to signal it's time to leave.

"WHAT ARE THE odds that'll happen?" Gerald asks as we walk back down the corridor.

"Normally, I'd say zero. He's in here for murder. But if Devon manages to scare the right people, then who knows."

We pass a door marked INFORMATION SERVICES. Gerald comes to a stop. "Got a second?"

"What do you have in mind?"

"Research." He has the look on his face he gets when he has an idea.

Gerald knocks on the door, introduces us to the US marshal on duty who monitors inmate communications, and asks for a tour of the office.

The marshal, a stocky man named Hopkins with close-cropped brown hair, explains the communication system to us. Mostly to me—I'm sure Gerald knows it backward and forward. He points to a list of prisoners.

"Every inmate who is allowed computer access gets a correctional facility account to talk to his attorney and a list of other approved people. Some have different privileges than others."

"So even a killer like Winter gets e-mail?" I ask.

"Well, he was a mail bomber and not a hacker, so yeah. Is that who you want to look up? We can read anything that's not between him and his attorney."

"Mind if I look?" asks Gerald.

"Go ahead, but good luck with that. I think he's sent maybe two e-mails. I guess it's against his religion."

Gerald taps away at the keyboard and pulls up an access log. "You said two?"

"I think so."

Gerald runs a finger down a long list of dates on the screen. "Then how come it shows at least a few hundred sessions here?"

Hopkins leans in to look at the screen, confused. "What?

That's weird. Every sent and received e-mail gets dumped into my box." He leans over and taps away, opening Winter's Sent folder. It's empty. The Trash and the Inbox are empty as well. "See, nothing there," he says, satisfied. "Might be a glitch."

"A glitch." I can see the wheels turning in Gerald's mind. "Well, thanks."

"No problem," Hopkins replies as we head for the door.

"WHAT'S GOING ON?" I ask Gerald when we're back in the hall.

"Maybe I should have said something to Hopkins. I guess I'll e-mail him."

"What?"

"You don't need to actually be able to send an e-mail to use an e-mail account to communicate. If their system just monitors what's sent and received, then it's seriously flawed."

"What do you mean?"

"Want to see a magic trick?" he asks with boyish enthusiasm.

"What do you got?"

He types something on his phone, then hands it to me. "See my e-mail account? Check the Inbox and the Sent folder. Just remember what you see."

There's just a bunch of departmental e-mails. "Okay?" I hand him back his phone.

"Okay, take my word on this, I'm going to do something, but I can't tell you what just yet. I want you to give me a word. Any word."

"Like 'aardvark'?"

"Perfect." Gerald taps something into his phone.

A moment later I get a text on my phone from Jennifer. It says: *aardvark.*

"I don't get it," I reply.

Gerald shakes his head and hands me his phone. "Look in my Sent folder and my Trash."

I do. There's nothing there. "Did you erase it from the Trash?"

"Nope."

"Then how did you e-mail Jennifer?"

"I didn't."

"Text? Another app?"

He shakes his head. "I just used my e-mail account."

"Is this some techy hacking thing?"

"No. I can teach you in two seconds."

"Okay, what?"

"Can I just remember the moment I stumped the Amazing Jessica Blackwood?" He's trying to suppress a smile.

"If you don't tell me soon, I'll give you a bruise to help memorialize the moment." I'm not mad at him, just eager to find out what's going on.

"No need to get rough. You're very scary when you're frustrated. I gave Jennifer my account password, but I never sent her anything."

"You just used your Draft folder," I blurt out, suddenly getting it.

His smile fades as I steal his thunder. "Yes. I wrote 'aardvark' in a draft e-mail and then Jennifer erased it."

"So Winter could be talking to people all he wants. All they need to do is just read what he saves in his Draft folder then erase it."

"Terrorist cells were using this trick to bypass e-mail sniffers. They just needed the password to communicate." He looks back toward the office. I can tell he feels a little guilty for not telling the marshal. "Should we go back?"

I think about this for a moment. "Let's tell Ailes first. I'm afraid they might close this off before we have a chance to exploit it."

"You mean monitor what he's saying?"

"Exactly. If you've broken an enemy code, it's a good idea not to let them know you did so. You want them to keep talking."

CHAPTER SEVENTEEN

THE LINK

And you think he's still running the Red Chain?"

Ailes's voice echoes over the speakerphone in our car, which is still parked in the visitor lot at the federal penitentiary.

"Maybe. Gerald found a little exploit in the prison e-mail system."

"Odd for a Luddite to be that technologically savvy," Ailes replies.

I've been thinking the same thing. He doesn't seem like the hacker type, but who knows what hobbies he decided to pick up behind bars.

"His rejection of electricity didn't stop him from using batteries in his letter bombs. Either way, he couldn't wait to tell us he knew Devon."

"Doesn't that seem a little weird?" asks Ailes.

"Maybe. But he's quite full of himself. He wants to cut some kind of deal."

"That sounds more desperate than in control."

"Maybe he's sick of prison. Or he's bullshitting. Either way, he knew Devon at one point."

"Yes, that's interesting." Ailes goes silent. I can hear him tapping on his keyboard. "Okay. Against my better judgment, but speed is important, can you make a side trip?"

"Where to?" Gerald asks.

"A halfway house about an hour away from you. Belinda Cole. She's under federal supervision."

Yesterday Ailes was adamant we hurry back to the office. Now he has us running a side trip. "Okay. What's her story?"

"Belinda Cole, formally Belinda Winter. She's Ezra's ex-wife," he explains. "She was given a light sentence for her involvement in his mail-bombing case."

I flip through my printouts. "How could I have missed that?"

"The prosecutors probably gave her a sweetheart deal. She was tried separately."

Peculiar. Ezra never mentioned her once. That's more than suspicious.

THE SUPERINTENDENT, A middle-aged woman with a distrustful stare, greets us at the door of the apartment complex where the halfway house is located. It's near a truck stop and a row of motels. Down the street, children kick a ball around a sad playground with a broken swing and rusted monkey bars.

After we show our badges, she lets us inside. The first floor of the house has portraits of Jesus, with varied tortured expressions, on virtually every wall. Gerald and I avoid exchanging raised eyebrows over the décor.

"Belinda," she shouts upstairs. "You have visitors."

Belinda Cole is sitting in a chair near an open window, reading a Bible. She turns around to greet us, but stays seated. Her curly hair has streaks of gray, and with her reading glasses she looks like a hippie librarian. A silver crucifix dangling from her neck is her only jewelry.

"Hello," she says in a friendly manner. There's no trace of concern in her voice. She's probably used to court-ordered visits. "Have a seat." She directs us to the bed pushed against the side of the wall.

The room is small, barely large enough for the bed, a small dresser, and a writing desk. It feels like a transient motel room. When Gerald and I sit down, a metal spring squeals in protest.

She stares at me for a moment, ignoring Gerald. I sometimes get this from people who've seen me in a newspaper or online. "You're not from the US attorney's office, are you?"

"No. We're with the FBI. I'm Agent Blackwood, and this is Agent Turner." I almost call Gerald by his first name.

He takes out his notebook and pretends to be not fully engaged in the conversation, even though he's watching everything.

"How may I help you?" she asks, with the earnestness of someone talking to a parole board.

"Two things. First, you must be aware of the Peter Devon predictions." With all the coverage on the news, it'd be impossible not to know. "We were wondering if you had any connection to him?"

"Me? No. I've never met him. What makes you think I have?" She sounds surprised, maybe a little too much so.

"Your ex-husband."

"Ezra?" she says dismissively. "Ezra said I knew Devon?" She takes off her glasses and searches my face. "Why on earth would he say that?"

So far she's acting entirely consistent with someone who testified against her spouse for a lighter sentence. "No. Let me clarify. He said *he* knew Devon."

"I see." She nods in recognition. "Of course he did. I'm sure

the two could have met. I may have met him once, but I don't remember. You meet so many people, hard to remember them all.
Of course, Ezra being Ezra, he would tell you he was best friends
with Stephen Hawking or Mahatma Gandhi if he shared a time
zone with them once."

"You're saying he exaggerates?"

She rolls her eyes. "That's being polite. Lies is another word
for it. Ezra is downright messianic. Lord knows he had me believing him for the longest time. I take full responsibility for my
actions. But Ezra, he sure could tell you a tale or two."

"What do you know about Black Fall?" I ask.

"That nonsense? Only what I see on the news. If I have to hear
any more about that, I'll jump out the window." There's something almost rehearsed about the way she says this, almost as if
she'd expected the question.

"And the Red Chain?"

Her face slackens and she touches her crucifix. "Better left in
the past."

"You're saying it's no more?"

"Ezra is the last remaining member I know of."

"Nobody from them has contacted you?" I ask.

She shakes her head. "As far as I know, they are all gone."

"They? How many were there? What were they?" All my research so far has amounted to very little. Even the case against
Winter just mentioned it in passing. There was no conspiracy
charge or mention of collaborators other than his wife.

"It's just a name, really. Ezra used to hold these meetings and
people would drift in and out. It was nothing more than that. Just
a few people who shared the same concerns about the environ-
ment, civilization, and the like. Not much else."

"Just meetings?" I can tell she's not being as forthcoming as
she could be.

"We had a big house a while back, outside of Boston, and a farm in Michigan. We tried the commune thing. My ex-husband spent more time trying to screw any young thing that came through the door. It didn't last."

"And the letter bombs? That was just you two?"

"That was Ezra," she says adamantly. "When I found out, I tried to stop him. But he could be persuasive. I thought they were only going to scare people. I didn't know we were going to hurt anyone!"

I casually flip through my notes. "They killed an engineer and blinded another target's wife," I say, watching her reaction.

She grasps her crucifix again and touches her other hand to the Bible in her lap. "That was wrong. Don't think me an awful person. At the time, Ezra explained it to me like it was some kind of cruise missile diplomacy. When the president sends a Toma-hawk into a Middle Eastern country, we accept a certain amount of collateral damage. Every army base has secretaries. Every pal-ace has innocent maids and janitors. I know it's wrong to think that way. But I was in a different space then. Ezra's way of looking at the world was . . . persuasive." She lifts her hand from the Bible to her heart. "There's not a moment that goes by that I don't think about those poor people." Eyes to the sky. "And I know my judg-ment is coming."

She's told us as much as we're going to get using this line of questioning. I have to put her on the defensive, so I glance up from my notes and ask bluntly: "Did you have your religious conversion before or after federal agents placed you under arrest?"

Her eyes narrow. "Sometimes we need a wake-up call."

Gerald blinks.

I may have pushed her too much. I change my tone to one that's more matter-of-fact. "We don't want to keep you. Just an-other question. How did you choose the victims?"

"Pardon me?" she replies.

"For the letter bombs. How were they chosen?"

"I don't know," she shrugs, maybe exaggeratedly. "I think Ezra would just read a name in the paper or a magazine and decide that person needed to be taken out of the equation."

"Equation?" asks Gerald, looking up from his notes. He's been watching her as intently as I have, and I can tell he's curious about something.

"A figure of speech," she says sharply.

On my phone I scan the e-mail Ailes sent me about her. "It says here you have another four months to serve. What's next for you?"

"Someplace with a lot of trees and few people. Where I can pray and live in peace." She's trying to project as warm and friendly an image as possible. I'm not sure if it's an act for us.

I notice a photograph, of a man holding a fishing rod next to a cabin, on her desk. "A friend of yours?"

"Just someone who writes me encouraging letters." She picks up the photo and stares at it for a moment.

"A former member of the Red Chain?" I ask.

She lets out a laugh. "Lord no." She sets the photo back down, but curiously tilts the frame away from us.

It could be nothing. She might just want a clean break, but I'd love to know who the man is. I get a text message from Gerald, who's sitting less than a foot away: *distract her.*

He's thinking the same thing. I stand up and go over to the window. "That's quite a view you have here." I point to the playground in the distance. Children are chasing a soccer ball around, yelling and laughing. "Does the noise bother you?"

She has to move from her seat to see where I'm pointing. Out of the corner of my eye I spot Gerald reach out a long arm and snap a shot of the photo with his phone.

"No. Not at all. I quite like the sound of children. Ezra and I . . . well," her voice softens. "We never had kids."

Her eyes show the sadness of a woman who knows she's past the point in her life where that's going to happen. This may be the first genuine thing I've heard her say.

I feel a little numb myself. I could be in that same position one day. I sometimes joke that I don't need children to look after me when I get older, because I'll have Amazon Prime.

Now that I'm thirty, it's not as funny to me as it used to be.

ONCE WE'RE BACK in the car, Gerald shows me the photo he secretly took. There's nothing familiar about the man. He looks clean-cut and in his midfifties. It's the kind of image you'd use on a dating profile. "I'll run it through an image database."

"Alright. I'll ask the marshals if they have a log of her contacts. Maybe we should check back with the halfway house superintendent when Cole isn't around."

"You think she's still involved with the Red Chain?"

"I don't know. I'm not sure whose benefit that act was for. If she was up to something serious, I'm not sure why she'd stick around here. It's not like she can't just walk away."

"She did seem to be less than forthcoming about the Red Chain. She went from it being just a few meetings to admitting they had a compound with people living there full time," Gerald points out.

"True. Sounds like she wasn't too happy with how that turned out. She seemed very eager to put Ezra under the bus. Maybe she was just jealous about the commune thing."

"Maybe. But there's no reason to believe the free love only flowed toward Ezra," Gerald says with a smirk.

"Point taken."

CHAPTER EIGHTEEN

FORCE MAJEURE

I KNOW THINGS ARE kind of hectic, but Kylie and I would love to have you over soon," Gerald says, somewhat hesitantly, halfway back to Quantico.

Kylie is his new girlfriend. Well, newish. They've been seeing each other for six months now. She seems a little more adult than the college-age girls he usually dates. I guess my boy is growing up.

Should I be bothered that this is the second dinner "intervention" I've received in as many days? "That would be great," I reply, then return to replaying our conversations with Ezra and Belinda in my head.

"Maybe next week?"

"Let me check a couple things."

"Things are busy. I know. But Jessica, you got to have your own moments."

My own moments. I can't even imagine what Gerald would say if I told him about the moments I have been stealing away for. "That would be nice."

"Great. It'll be just me, Kylie, and a few friends."

"How few?" I smell a setup about to take place. Every now and then someone takes pity on me, or decides to settle a grudge with some available male, and attempts to arrange a blind date. It has a tendency not to turn out well.

Nadine, a fellow agent, once forced me to list what I was looking for in a mate. She'd read it through, then shaken her head.

"You described yourself, Jessica."

I can barely live with myself, so how can I expect anyone else to?

"It'll be an odd number," says Gerald, sensing my anxiety. "Don't worry."

My phone rings, saving me from the awkward situation.

It's Jennifer, with an unusual sense of urgency in her voice. "We need you guys to head to DC. Ailes and I are on our way there too."

"What's up?" I ask.

"Bolivia. They lost at least three hundred people. Devon has everyone in overdrive."

"So now it's a real FBI case?"

"It is, since his latest video says there's going to be rioting in DC, New York, and other major world capitals. Ailes wants you to make a case for the connection to the Red Chain."

"Whoa? That's just a thought. I've only got the thinnest proof."

"We need something," she says desperately.

Don't we all.

I TAKE MY seat next to Ailes and Jennifer in a large FBI conference room. Thirty people are arranged around the long table. Several different divisions are here.

At the far end of the room, an agent is walking through a

presentation of what happened in Bolivia. Someone calls him McAllister when they ask a question. I scan the hastily prepared document sitting in front of me and learn that he is a forensic meteorologist who helps us understand how weather affects crime scenes. With his jacket off and his sleeves rolled up, he resembles a harried weatherman as he shows us aerial photos of the flooding and video of dead bodies drifting down an engorged river like rag dolls.

I feel nauseous. This was my case. This was my responsibility.

I don't know what more I could have done. But maybe that's the problem. I didn't really try. I took Devon for a joke. I saw through the gimmick on the first video, and thought it was just a hoax. Now people are dead. Lots of people. He said it would happen. It did.

McAllister points to the screen. "Right now we don't have a lot of information. Tropical Storm Esmeralda wasn't particularly powerful. But it hit this region really hard."

A woman five seats down from me speaks up. "How exactly did these people die?"

McAllister's expression is anguished. "The river overflowed its banks. It wiped them away."

"They really didn't see this coming?" she asks.

He shakes his head. "You can usually predict how much rise you're going to get based on the size of the storm. The problem is they live in a deep valley where small changes in vegetation can affect how much water gets absorbed versus how much comes rolling down the hills. In this case it was a lot."

"It looks like a dam broke," says a senior agent from across the table.

"The upriver floodgates are intact," McAllister explains. "It appears the storm just dropped a lot of water in this area."

The agent who called this meeting stands up and thanks McAllister, then introduces himself.

"I'm David Collins. The assistant deputy has appointed me to head up this task force. Right now we're trying to wrap our heads around what this is about. The people behind the Devon tapes haven't made any demands or expressed any ideological aims outside of what we've seen. So we're in the dark for motive.

"Our computer forensics people are trying to find out the source of the videos. While we've now made it a priority to determine the method of the prediction, we already had an agent investigating. She's here to brief us on what we know so far."

Crap, he's talking about me! I wouldn't call this stage fright as much as stage terror. Usually, I'm much more prepared for this sort of thing.

Usually, there's not already a body count on my watch.

"Blackwood?" He nods in my direction.

I walk slowly to the podium and try to put together a presentation I didn't know I had to give. All eyes in the room are on me. The best I can do is give everyone bullet points of the facts.

"As you know, Peter Devon has been dead for several years. Before he died, he became something of a recluse. We haven't found anyone yet who had contact with him right before he passed away."

"Not even neighbors?" asks Collins, immediately putting me on the spot by letting me know this is *his* question-and-answer session, and I better have some answers.

"We're looking into that now." I'm planning to, so it's not a lie—not exactly. "I just spoke with three people who have worked with him in the past, two of whom are in federal custody. As far as how he's managed these predictions, bear in mind that the first prediction was released after the fact. We have no reason to believe he actually knew the time and date of the DC earthquake." I realize the images of the flood are on the screen behind me. "This instance is far more specific than we anticipated."

That's an understatement.

"How'd he do it?" asks Collins.

He's trying to keep the spotlight on me. "How'd he do what?" I ask.

"Know all the people were going to die."

I pause. "I don't know." Three words I hate to say. But it's the honest truth.

"No idea at *all*?" asks Collins, shooting Ailes a reproving stare. Don't pull him into this! That's bullshit. I can fight this battle. "I could only speculate."

"Well, then speculate. We're all dying to hear what our own expert has to say."

I get it. This fell into Collins's lap and he's trying to cover his ass by making me look incompetent. This way he can buy himself time by saying how much he's had to fix because of my meddling.

I throw the focus back on him. "The specifics of meteorology and hydrology are outside my areas of expertise."

"So, what *can* you contribute, Blackwood?" He rolls his eyes to show everyone he just landed a zinger.

What. A. Dick. He's trying to assert his authority by calling me onto the carpet. It's a show of force. It's weak. I'm being humiliated for not having the answers he knows I haven't had a chance to get.

Focus, Jessica. You've been through this before. You know how to handle it. Stay calm. Stick to the facts. If those don't work, baffle them with bullshit.

I change my tone, mimicking the professorial cadence Ailes uses. "There are only three possibilities as far as I see them. One"—I look around the room, making sure everyone knows I'm laying out the facts—"he got a one-in-a million lucky guess. I don't buy it, but it's possible. Two"—another dramatic pause, *write this down, kids*—"he really has some way to predict these things." I raise a very skeptical eyebrow, letting them know what I think of that theory. "Or three." I gaze above their heads as I say the words, because I don't want to face them for this part. It's too absurd, but the only other conceivable option. "He, or rather the people behind it, caused the flooding."

"God?" Collins scoffs.

"No." I stare right at him. "I mean they did something to make the storm deadlier."

"How in the hell do you do that?" he replies.

"Like I said, that's the question. If I had all those answers, we wouldn't need this meeting, nor would you be here." I see Ailes wince, but I can't help it. I don't want to be Collins's whipping boy. "What's your theory?"

He holds up his hands. "I've only been on this for two hours."

"If I may make a suggestion," Ailes speaks up. Thank god. "It's not as outlandish as it seems."

"Really?" Collins replies. He almost does a double-take. "Illuminate me."

I can't tell if he's a true jerk, or if he's just afraid of this mess falling in his lap.

"A large area of defoliated hillside would increase the likelihood of flooding or landslides," Ailes explains. "This is a common problem in third world countries due to deforestation or bad land management. A loss of vegetation increases the kind of damage you can get. A more extreme but still plausible explanation is cloud seeding. Someone could increase the hourly rainfall that way, overwhelming any kind of drainage. Or, on a simple level, you could have a problem like New Orleans did in Hurricane Katrina, where the levees just aren't able to support the surge."

"They said the floodgates were intact," Collins interjects.

"I know. I'm just illustrating that Agent Blackwood's observation was quite on the mark. I believe that's at least three man-made ways you could magnify the effect of the storm. But like you"—Ailes dramatically checks his watch—"we've only had a few hours since the storm hit to make our guess."

Damn. Ailes just put this jerk on the ropes and showed him for what he was. We're the ones trying to solve things, and Collins is the guy getting in the way. I still feel guilty as hell for not doing more, but at least Ailes has my back out here. This kind of shutdown is rare for him. But it only makes me feel worse.

Collins relents. "Fair enough. But we still don't know how Devon predicted the storm." He's trying to put himself back in charge.

I speak up. "He didn't."

"Can you clarify?" He seems frustrated that I haven't withered.

"Esmeralda had already formed and was on a track toward that area when the video was posted. Devon didn't predict it. In fact, if you listen to the video again, he didn't say *how* the people were going to die. He just gave us a number."

"A very specific number," says Collins.

"An approximate number. Based on the number of people in the affected area."

Ailes decides to preemptively move things forward. "Perhaps it would be helpful if we sent a team down to Bolivia to find out what we can? Maybe someone from the FBI and a liaison from FEMA?"

I try to figure out if I have enough clean clothes at home for the trip.

Collins nods. "I think that would be wise. I'll make contact with our Bolivian consulate. Who do you have in mind?"

"I know the perfect person for the job," Ailes says, as all eyes fall on me. He turns to Jennifer. "Agent Mathis speaks fluent Spanish and has a degree in engineering."

My first reaction is a wave of relief. Then, deep down, a bit of jealousy seeps in. Has Ailes lost faith in me? I did sit on this longer than I should have.

"Blackwood, do you have anything more to add?" asks Collins.

I suppress my fear that I let Ailes down, and remember why he wants me here on the case. "Yes. A few important notes. As some of you may know, on the day of the earthquake a distraught woman showed up at an undercover stakeout where I was working and threatened to either kill me or the abducted infant she was holding. We found her body the next day. She had been murdered with a knife similar to the one I saw her brandishing when she accosted me. We now have reason to believe that she and possibly her assailants are members of a group known as the Red Chain."

"How is this connected to Devon?" Collins asks, trying to understand where I'm going.

"It may or may not be. But the former head of the Red Chain, who claims to have information on Devon, is serving time in federal prison."

"Did he contact us?" asks Collins.

"No. I visited him to investigate his connection with the Red Chain."

"And did he acknowledge knowing the woman you had the altercation with?" Collins is sounding more skeptical.

"No. But, as I said, he claimed knowledge of Peter Devon." I know this sounds weak.

So does Collins. His voice now takes on a note of condescension. "Did this man ask for any kind of clemency?"

I know where this is going. "Yes." Collins is making me out for a fool.

And he's right to. I just told him I made a visit to a random felon who claims to have insight into the man all over the television. Now I sound like an idiot.

"I know it's specious. My point is there are two or more members of the Red Chain on the loose who may be acting under Winter's orders *and* possibly coordinating with whoever is behind the Devon tapes."

"Noted." Collins doesn't even bother with a rebuttal. "Anything else?"

I shake my head and leave the podium. I try to keep my composure. Some of the faces watching me seem sympathetic, others suspicious. They all know me, or at least my work. But they have no idea what to make of me.

Am I the real deal or someone who has luckily blundered through several high-profile cases?

I don't know the answer to that one, either.

THE MEETING ENDS with the assignment of people and units to different task forces. I'm left out. I corner Ailes outside the conference room once everyone has gone their way.

"Why am I being pushed out of this?"

"You're not. I'm sending Jennifer down there because this is in her area of expertise."

If it's rain gauges and levies, she's got the mechanical edge, but I still feel like I'm being sidelined.

Ailes can see that I'm hurt. "I need all of you doing what you do best."

"Okay. But what about the Red Chain? Do you believe the connection?" I nod to the conference room. "They looked at me like I was a lunatic."

"They don't know what to make of any of it, or you. I think there's reason to believe there's a connection. Gerald does too.

We all do. We just need more information. But you heard how it sounded."

I know. Crazy, out on a limb. My only saving grace is that they're even more clueless than I am, and have no idea where to even begin.

"So now what?"

"Get me more on Devon. He may be dead, but somebody out there knows something. Find them."

CHAPTER NINETEEN

PSYCHOMETRY

My LIFE WOULD be easier if magic were real. Standing in what was once Peter Devon's living room, located in a two-story house in a little suburb a few blocks away from the train line, I stare at the empty shelves and bare floors, wishing I could really just touch something and get an impression of its owner, like I'd used to pretend I could with a borrowed set of keys, or a ring.

Psychometry, the apparent ability to divine information from touching an object, is one of those "blurry tricks," as my dad used to call them. To half the audience, there was an element of truth. Unlike my grandfather's psychic occult pendulum that was a bit of winking comic book hokum, the idea you can use some highly developed sense to pick up information from an object isn't quite as farfetched. Any bloodhound worth her salt could take a whiff of my sneakers and know what park I run in, what kind of soap I use, and how much garlic I'd had for dinner the night before.

My own skills are considerably less developed. Devon's former home has had several new occupants since he died, and is now vacant once again. Whatever physical traces he left behind have long since been bleached, vacuumed up, and painted over. His body was cremated, and his assets divided to the winds. An estate-sale company auctioned off whatever else was left. The bookshelf he sat in front of to make his predictions is now just a stark white wall of dusty cubbyholes. The only thing that remains of him is his ghostly electronic image. Although that's quite a legacy.

Sure, there are plenty of little details around the house, but I think most of them were left by people who moved in later. I see an indentation in the hallway door frame from a childproof gate used to keep a toddler in her little prison yard. A patch of carpet in the corner looks as though it's been clawed by a cat. A nearby wall sports deeper furrows, probably left by a family dog. My guess is the dog moved in after the cat and, frustrated by the scent it left behind, constantly tried to find it. Searching for something he couldn't see.

I guess Devon is my invisible cat.

I came here to confirm that this is where Devon shot the videos and—a long shot—hopefully to find something else to tie them to him. I also want to talk to the neighbors, to see if anyone remembers him having visitors.

Nobody can recall the man.

Is this how I'll be remembered? Not at all?

Ever since I was a little girl I've been surrounded by the notion that I will never be complete if I don't marry. I reject this idea on principle. I see myself as fully realized, not needing someone to complete me. But in truth—as my footsteps echo around this vacant house—I think the idea of a partner isn't so much about wholeness, but rather about giving your voice, your steps, your life a witness. Proving you exist.

I can count in *years* the time I've spent watching television shows I can't remember, reading articles that don't make a difference, flipping through catalogs of things I'll never buy. Is that time wasted? I don't know. I'm not sure if having someone by my side in a normal relationship would make my life more meaningful. But maybe it would make it count a little more.

I wonder if the first person to realize I'm dead will be the mailman who sees Amazon packages stacking up on my doorstep. This scares me more than I let on.

What if my apartment was a crime scene? What would another investigator notice?

Why did she need two different sizes of the same pair of heels? Was she too lazy to send the other back? (Fact.)

Why was she stockpiling so much bath salt under her sink? Did she have some kind of addiction? (I stress buy salt and candles when I'm in the grocery store after work.)

How can someone have so many recipes taped to their refrigerator, but have a stove that hasn't been turned on in months? (Wishful thinking for an imaginary dinner party.)

I put aside my pathetic introspection and ask myself what I would like to find in Devon's house.

Not just information about him. A clue to the person who is the bridge between Devon and the videos appearing online. Our missing link. That's what I want.

But this person isn't here.

Okay, so what traces could they, or Devon, have left that would last this many years?

It's futile. But then, futility is my business.

My phone rings. It's Ailes. "How's it going?"

I was hoping to have something to report when he checked in. "I'm about to break out the Ouija board and try contact that way."

"That well? I guess the trail is a bit cold." He sounds sympathetic, not disappointed.

"The trail got bulldozed and paved over." I inspect the empty living room, trying to imagine Devon sitting at the desk where he made his predictions.

"Don't kill yourself. It's not realistic to expect to find something after so long," he consoles me.

"Yeah. Well. Sort of," I grumble, suddenly reminded of something.

"What do you mean?"

"After Houdini died, occupants of his house were finding little love notes he wrote to his wife, Bess, for years. Tucked away behind the radiator, wedged into window jambs, they were everywhere."

"Sounds like quite the romantic." Ailes is impressed.

"He was. He was also a compulsive cheater constantly apologizing for his transgressions. Later on it was revealed he'd been carrying on an affair with Jack London's wife, among others."

"Oh. What a guy," Ailes replies.

"Yeah. He's still my hero, just not romantically."

"Keep at it then. Maybe Devon left something behind that was overlooked."

"I will."

Ailes's pep talk convinces me I shouldn't give up. At the very least, he doesn't think it would be the craziest thing to keep searching.

I hang up and walk through to the kitchen. I pull out the drawer under the oven to look at the floor. Dirty tile and bread ties. No credit card receipts, matchbooks, or business cards with *I did it* scrawled on the back.

After I push the drawer back, I use all my strength to slide the refrigerator away from the wall. There I find a Chinese menu and a dead cockroach. The menu looks recent; the cockroach isn't talking.

I eye the radiator in the corner suspiciously. Did Devon have a secret lover? He never married. I'm not even sure if he was straight.

That's an interesting possibility. He may have led a double life. He was of an older generation that tended to keep their sexuality very private. If nothing else comes up, I'll ask Ailes if he's heard any rumors. If Devon was gay, a potential line of inquiry might be finding other closeted academics he may have known.

In the meantime, I have his empty house in which to ask embarrassing questions. I walk the floors again, hoping something sticks out at me. Nothing does. I even count my steps to see if there are any hidden passages. Sadly, this isn't a *Scooby-Doo* cartoon.

Before I give up, I close my eyes and try to think of the life cycle of a house.

First your realtor shows it to you. Then all your moving boxes arrive. Then you leave and have all your stuff packed up. The end.

But is it?

When I moved into my last apartment, the previous owner had left a fern on the balcony and a can of bug spray in a hall closet. They didn't take everything.

What would Devon have left? Or rather, what might the estate company have left behind?

The fern and the spray "belonged" with the apartment. What might belong to this house? Whatever it is, I would likely find it in the less-frequented places. The house doesn't have a basement, but there is an attic.

I find the entrance at the end of the main hallway upstairs. The narrow wooden steps unfold from the trapdoor, and disappear into a dark hole in the ceiling. The steps creak as I climb up. Predictably, the attic smells of insulation and wood when I poke my head inside. My flashlight illuminates bare plywood flooring that stretches to either end of the house. Other than rat droppings, there's nothing else here.

The quiet is discomfiting. The shadows of the beams eerily move along with my light, like they're trying to hide from me in the dark.

Hopes of a secret chamber dashed, I begin my climb back down the steps.

That's when my light catches it.

Sitting on the insulation, almost flush with the floor, the box is easy to miss despite being literally under my nose. Eight inches across, the faded cardboard is almost the same color as the wooden beam next to it.

Inside the box is an assortment of light bulbs and fuses. The bulbs are the old incandescent kind they don't sell anymore. But they're not what interests me. It's the name on the box: VIDEOPRO.

Dad used to order supplies from them to record our shows. They sold videotape in bulk.

My mind races. Devon had to have used a *lot* of videotape to make his predictions. It'd make sense he was buying it in large quantities.

I flip over a lid panel and check the address label.

This is where it gets really interesting.

The box isn't addressed to Devon.

CHAPTER TWENTY

MISDIRECTION

I'M BEING FOLLOWED.

I didn't notice him at first. As soon as I put the key to Devon's house back in the real estate agent lockbox and started down the sidewalk, I had my face buried in my phone, giving me poor night vision on an already darkened street. I don't know at what point the man started shadowing me, but it is his footsteps that gave him away. Walking down the block toward the commuter station, I noticed a distant echo almost matching the pace of my stride—almost.

It's easy to get paranoid, especially when you've been through what I have. I remind myself that lots of people take the train. It's not unusual that someone else would be heading the same way as me. But as a test, I go one block west then north, adding distance to the trip.

He does the same.

There are a thousand innocent explanations. He could simply be on the same path. All the same, I unbutton my maroon peacoat, so my hand can quickly reach the pistol on my hip.

His pace is measured. He keeps his distance, never getting close enough for me to casually turn around and look at him.

Psychologically, there's a game we're playing. If I turn back to look, he knows he has me unnerved. But if I keep walking straight ahead to the station, he has to wonder if I know he's behind me. If he assumes I don't, I have a small advantage. If he assumes I do, the fact I haven't nervously glanced in his direction should let him know I'm not afraid.

Or he's just some guy going to get pizza. I've played this mental exercise more times than I care to remember.

When I finally get to the station, I find that it's deserted after I step through the turnstile. Just a row of benches and public service posters. I take a strategic position against a metal pillar, putting it between myself and the entrance, which allows me to keep my eye on the platform.

The train squeals in the distance as it approaches. Behind me, I hear the gate turning as the man enters.

I stare down at my phone, let my eyes flicker up to acknowledge that someone else has stepped onto the platform, then go back to acting indifferent.

He's staring right at me. Intense eyes, unflinching. His face, unshaven. He's wearing a thick black coat, probably in his late twenties, and I've never seen him before in my life. But the way he looks at me tells me he knows exactly who I am.

The train pulls into the station and I step into the car in front of me as soon as the doors open.

The seats all face forward and there's no place to stand. I sit down a few rows away from the entrance so I can have my back to the window and watch the whole car.

The man enters from the front. He looks around, makes eye contact with me, and starts walking in my direction. Then he calls across the car: "Aren't you Jessica Blackwood?"

I feign a quick glance behind me, pretending I think he's talking to someone else. I've got a knit hat on and my hair is tucked underneath it. Nobody ever recognizes me like this. Still, it's a possibility.

I shake my head. He keeps walking toward me.

Exaggerating the movement as much as I can, I reach my right hand into my jacket and put it on my still-hidden gun.

He freezes.

If he were just some doofus who recognized me and decided to follow me, he probably wouldn't have realized I was one second from drawing on him. The fact he stopped tells me he knows what's going on. Unfortunately, I still don't.

He regains his composure and drops down onto a seat three rows ahead of me, facing forward but watching me in the reflection of the window.

A chime announces that the doors are about to close. A Hispanic man, also wearing a thick black overcoat, dashes onto the train and takes a seat at the back, boxing me in.

I could be trapped, or in my already anxious state I could be jumping to conclusions. As a cop, you only get one chance to get things right. You don't get a redo. You don't get to second-guess something you saw on an out-of-context YouTube clip. If you draw, you have to be ready to pull the trigger. If you pull the trigger, you have to be ready to kill.

The Hispanic man gets up and starts to walk down the aisle toward me. I push my back against the window and turn to him.

"Something wrong with your seat?"

It's overly aggressive. Fine. If I'm wrong, he can think I'm a bitch for all I care.

He gives me a cold grin and sits down two seats back. The other man watches me—only me.

I keep my hand on my pistol and my eyes on the two of them.

They know I'm ready to draw. I have to come up with a plan, soon. I have a feeling they're not going to let this last until the next station.

The man in front looks behind me as the doors between the cars open. I glimpse an older woman as she enters.

Perfect. Just what I need, an innocent bystander.

I've been calculating how to take down both these guys the moment one of them shows a weapon. My math doesn't involve a little old lady in a frayed winter coat.

She walks down the aisle, oblivious to the tension, and stops at my row.

Not here. Please not here!

She starts to sit down.

I try to stop her. "Ma'am, someone spilled coffee on the seat."

She doesn't seem to care, or even understand. She nods warmly, then slides in right next to me, her body momentarily blocking the elbow of my gun arm.

The man in the front is the first to bolt from his seat.

Before I can draw, I catch a flash of reflected light to the side of me as the woman pulls a knife from her pocket.

I recognize the type of blade immediately.

CHAPTER TWENTY-ONE

ASSAILANTS

IN ACADEMY TRAINING, you practice various forms of self-defense. From hand-to-hand combat all the way to the proper technique to crash your car into a bad guy's vehicle. We almost always practice on people physically bigger and more threatening than ourselves. What you never fully prepare for is how to deal with a violent suspect who is much less imposing. We're only minimally trained to deal with violent children and women, or handicapped aggressors. This is a thorny area, and it's all theoretical anyway until the old woman pulls a knife and tries to shove it between your ribs.

I let instinct take over. Second-guessing right now will get me killed. My elbow comes down hard on her wrist. I feel the slightest stab into my side, but ignore it. My hand snaps up, the back of my fist hitting the woman square in the nose. There's a crack and she howls, then falls between the seats.

I grab my pistol and yank it free, just in time to hit the Hispanic man on the side of his head with the barrel.

"Fuck!" he yells, spinning away.

Two hands on the butt of the pistol, I wheel around and aim it right in the face of the other man, who is now inches away and pulling a knife from his jacket.

"Drop it!" I scream.

He wavers, trying to figure out what to do next. I push the gun closer as I step over the woman and into the aisle. She's clutching her bleeding nose.

In the reflection, I see the Hispanic man regain his balance and come at me, knife in hand with the blade facing down, special forces–style. He raises it for a strike.

I try a side kick to his knee and miss, striking his shin instead. It's enough to send him backward, but the blade narrowly misses my thigh. I use my momentum to twist around toward the first man, the one who followed me. I shove the gun ahead of me like a spear. He tries to grab my wrist, but I kick him in the groin and bring the butt of the pistol down on his head—hard.

"Goddamn bitch!" he snarls as he stumbles backward.

I spin around him, putting them all in my line of sight. Then I step toward the front door. The man from the back looks like he's weighing whether or not to rush me, but he's leaning heavily on the leg I didn't kick. His partner has one hand in the air as he uses the other to get the old woman to her feet. He's either helping her or using her as a shield.

The train jostles as we come to a stop.

I follow his footsteps like a boxer would. They tell me where his center of gravity is and what he plans on doing next. He's thinking about making another run at me.

The doors open and people start to file onto the train.

"Stay out of the train!" I shout, but I'm ignored by a rush of college kids.

My assailants push past, using the students to retreat.

"Get out of my way!"

People suddenly realize I have a gun and freeze in stunned panic. They part as I scramble through them, but not fast enough. My three attackers have already exited and are vanishing into the mob.

I race to the platform. But the crowd is a tide I can't fight against.

I can't keep up.

My vision begins to narrow.

My legs give out and a man catches me.

"Lady, are you alright?"

By the time I get to my feet, they're gone.

I run to the nearest ticket counter and flash my badge, demanding in halted breaths that they call the police.

MINUTES LATER, I give my descriptions to the transit police captain. He calls them in and makes me sit down.

"Are you sure they were trying to harm you?" he asks for the third time.

I glare at him.

"Sometimes these things can be misconstrued," he says defensively.

I shake my head. "I'm positive."

"But you didn't fire your gun?"

"No. I said that." I'm angry at myself. Angry at him. And angry at the people who came after me.

I stand up and look down the platform at the other cops who've gathered to stand around. None of them have a sense of urgency. They're looking at me like I'm a hysterical woman who almost had her purse snatched by a joking teenager.

The captain senses my frustration. "We have units looking. We're on this. We just need to be clear it was an actual attack and not a misunderstanding. I don't want a bunch of SWAT guys pouncing on folks who just wanted an autograph."

"A misunderstanding?" I ask him incredulously. "They weren't after an autograph." I pull my coat around my body. It's so damn cold out here.

"I know. I know. They may have been muggers."

I shake my head again. "No. This was planned." They'd been waiting for me at Devon's house. It was the the Red Chain. Maybe not the men from the farmhouse, but others sent to find me. How many are there?

"We'll get this sorted," says the captain. "Can I get you coffee?"

I'm so cold right now. Coffee sounds good. "Yes. Thank you, yes."

"We can go to a shop across the street."

I take two steps then stumble.

I hear my name being called.

"Agent Blackwood?" The captain is standing over me. Fluorescent lights make a square halo around his head.

So cold.

I touch my side. It's wet. My fingers come away covered in blood.

The old woman's knife got closer than I realized.

"Get a fucking ambulance here!" screams the captain. "And find those assholes!"

I try to stay conscious.

It's hard as all the warmth leaves my body.

CHAPTER TWENTY-TWO

ORDERLY CONDUCT

I REMEMBER THE AMBULANCE and a light being flashed in my eyes. Someone told me to stay with them. My side felt cold, like an icy finger was pushing into my flesh. Now it's all a dull roar as I slowly wake up.

"Jessica . . ." Someone calls my name.

It's a familiar voice that used to cause me so much anxiety, but I've made my peace with it.

When my eyes open I see the outline of a man illuminated by moonlight coming in through the window. He wears a blue nurse's uniform and he's checking a machine by my head. But he's no nurse. Through the shadows I can make out the shape of his jaw and the mouth I know so well. His gray eyes dart toward me and catch me observing him.

"There's my girl," he says with a casualness that drives me nuts, but that I secretly miss when I don't hear it for stretches of time.

"Damian . . ."

My own voice is so weak I don't recognize it. I sound like a child.

"Sorry, doll face. I came as soon as I could."

How do I describe Damian Knight? Stalker? Sometimes lover? A friend in college invented the term "serial personality disorder" to explain his proclivity for popping up in my life with different identities. He likes to reinvent himself, not just through a different hair color or style of dress, but by changing his voice and his expressions like a skilled actor. Why he does this is a mystery to me. His only explanation is that he wants to "avoid boredom."

Our friendship is hard to explain. We dated when I was a college student, and then I discovered that the Damian I'd known was just one of his many personas. Ever since, he's been a shadow looming in the background. For a long time I feared him, and with good reason. I suspect he killed a man who injured me back when I was a cop in South Florida.

Brilliant, mischievous, and dangerous, I don't trust him, but I trust he'll usually be there when I need him—eventually. I always push Damian away, only to open my door when I realize yet again that sometimes only a misfit can understand me.

What that says about me, I don't even want to get into.

I slowly regain my senses and realize this isn't a dream, although my brain still isn't fully alert. "Did they find them?"

"No." His warm fingers grasp my wrist and he gently pulls an IV from my forearm.

"What are you doing?" I try to sit up but only succeed in lifting my head an inch off the pillow.

"Getting you out of here." His casual, almost flippant tone of voice is gone. There's a sense of urgency. "They missed your vital organs. But you lost a lot of blood. Good news is they got you almost topped off." He sets the IV needle to the side and makes an adjustment to the heart monitor attached to my chest. The machine keeps blipping, but he unhooks the connection.

He clearly knows what he's doing, but his actions have me baffled. However, I can only maintain one train of thought at a time. "Why are you here?"

He sits down on the edge of the bed and puts his hand on my cheek. "Call it a lack of faith in the local authorities. That's two times these people have tried to kill you. You know what they say about the third."

"Thank goodness you were here in the nick of time," I mutter sarcastically.

His eyes drift to my side and the exposed bandage. "Uh, yeah. Well, we talked about boundaries."

"How long have I been here?"

"Four hours. Hold steady. I'm going to sit you up." He reaches around my shoulders and supports my back, carefully helping me upright. "That's my girl."

The wound hurts, but I know it's only a fraction of the pain I'd be feeling without medication. My head feels like a seashell half-filled with sloshing water. "What are you doing?"

"Taking you someplace safe." He sets a duffel bag on the end of the bed and starts pulling out clothing. I know better than to ask where he got them from.

"Safe? We're in a hospital," I reply.

"I got in." He arches an eyebrow.

"But you're you."

Damian is a force of nature. God help us all if he ever shifts his focus to anything more sinister than alleviating his boredom.

"I know. Feet over the edge." He helps me turn sideways. "Good girl. Can you slide into these sweatpants?"

I let him guide me into them. Even though we've been far more intimate than this recently, his manner is entirely clinical. Almost insultingly so.

"I'll tie your shoes." He kneels down and slides on a pair of sneakers.

"Damian, what are you doing?" I still feel so passive from the drugs.

He stands up and rests his hands on my knees. "The people who are after you. Their leader, Winter?"

"Probably."

"Why did he go to jail?" he asks.

"For killing someone."

"Right, how?"

"A bomb."

"A bomb," Damian replies.

"You think he might try that next? We need to tell Ailes."

Damian shakes his head. "There's nothing to tell right now. All I'm saying is that it's only a matter of time before they stop coming after you with knives. The sooner we get you out of here, the better."

"I don't think they'd come anywhere near here. The police have their descriptions."

"Yes, of the ones on the train. What about the girl in DC? Was she working with others?"

"We think so. We found a farmhouse. Two men lived there."

"Were the ones who attacked you from there?"

"No. Probably not."

He looks up at me, his arms still resting on my knees. "Three people in DC. Three people here. Plus at least one calling the shots. That's seven people, Jessica. At least seven that we know of. How many are in this cult?"

"I don't know."

"Any idea why they want to kill my favorite FBI agent?"

"No." I shake my head. "Last time it was for something I saw."

"That bitch, Marta," Damian snarls. "I've been thinking. Maybe she put a contract on you before she died."

"These people are environmentalists, not hit men. It doesn't make sense."

I let Damian slide my hospital gown over my head without hesitation. In our infrequent rendezvous, we probably spend more time together naked than dressed.

Reaching to my side, I feel the bandage. I pull it free and see the puffy skin and stitches. It's not that big a gash. The surgeon did a pretty good job from what I can see. I'll have a scar, but not a bad one.

"Three pints." Damian kneels back down to look at it in the moonlight.

"What?"

"That's how much blood you lost. Any more and you would have gone into cardiac arrest."

He places a new bandage on the wound while I try to clear my head.

"It doesn't add up," he says. "Going after you is attracting attention they shouldn't want. And they're environmentalists? Not some voodoo cult?"

"No. But they're weirdos, for sure."

He helps me put on a bra and a hoodie. I try not to tear up as the wound begins to sting. "Are you good to go? There's a guard at the door. I'll distract him."

"FBI?" I ask.

"No. They've got their hands full. Only local. Thus the urgency."

"Isn't Ailes coming, or Gerald?"

"No. It's complicated." He takes my arm and helps me to my feet.

"Complicated?" I feel reasonably steady, but I let him brace me for a moment.

"DC is in lockdown."

"Lockdown? What happened?" I stumble, but manage to grip the edge of the bed and steady myself.

"Rioting. Very bad. They've shut down the airports and train stations."

My head clears. "What's going on?"

Damian steps back to see if I have my footing. "There was a shooting."

"The president?" I immediately think of the first lady.

"No, no. He's fine. Nothing like that. Capitol Police shot into an unarmed crowd on live television. At least four people are dead. Several more are wounded. The whole town is going crazy."

I feel like I'm going to throw up. "They shot into the crowd?"

"They killed one protestor almost point-blank. A teenage girl."

"All of this over the earthquake?" Nothing makes sense.

"Now it's a civil rights thing. The rioting has gotten much worse. People are converging from all over. They've shut down the roads into the city. Protests are breaking out in New York and here in Boston too. That's why you've only got one sleepy guard."

"Damian, what's happening?"

He checks the door, anxious that we're being too loud, but knows me well enough to understand that I won't relent until I have some answers at least.

"Well, if you watched the news over the last few hours, you'd think we were on the verge of civil war. People are shooting at the cops in DC. The White House, the FBI building are surrounded.

It's a mess and it's getting worse. Police have had to pull back. Marines are inside the gate of the White House holding the line along with the Secret Service uniformed division. Martial law is going to be declared any moment." Damian walks toward the window. "Crap!"

"What?" I lean over to see what he's looking at. There's an orange glow in the distance.

He nods to the conflagration. "It looks like they set fire to Schroeder Plaza. The police station is there. It's starting here too."

"Rioting?"

He moves away from the window and takes my arm. "Rioting. The fires. In DC they're even shooting at firemen."

"But, I was just there a few hours ago."

"Twitter, babe. People were primed for this."

I'm still trying to understand the world I woke up to. "They shot at protestors?"

He leans me against the wall by the door and peers into the hallway for a moment. "Clear as day and in four K. Even the Iranians are condemning us. That was just a few hours ago. It's going to be even worse tomorrow when word spreads. Nothing like that has happened in this country since Kent State. And that wasn't broadcast live."

"Can I at least tell Ailes I'm okay?" I ask as we head out the door.

"No need."

"Why is that?"

"He's the one who told me to come get you."

CHAPTER TWENTY-THREE

THE INFORMANT

Traffic leading into the city is at a complete standstill as police direct cars toward on-ramps and away from the chaos downtown. Damian listens to updates on a police scanner and takes us around the congestion through center aisles, side streets, and occasionally sidewalks. He's acquired a large black SUV it would seem expressly for this purpose.

The cars on the road begin to thin out the farther we go. Occasionally an emergency vehicle, lights flashing and siren blaring, races past us. He takes the entrance to I-95 and starts driving southbound. I dig through the duffel bag at my feet and find my phone. There are several text messages from Ailes telling me to call him.

"What have I missed?" I ask after he picks up.

"For heaven's sake, Jessica!" His voice is full of surprise. "Let's start with: How are you?"

"Fine. Fine." I touch the bandage at my side. It's beginning to itch. "I was careless."

"I'll say," Damian mutters.

I glare at him, but he ignores me as he studies the road, keeping a watchful eye on the rearview mirror.

"I hate to ask you this, but when you feel up to it, come into the office."

"I'm up to it." My head is groggy, I can still feel the knife in my side, and I'm half-convinced this is a nightmare, but there's no way I can sit still.

"Well, you have to give us mortals a chance to sleep. It's four in the morning." He sounds tired, but not sleepy.

"I'm sorry. I didn't mean to wake you," I reply.

"Are you kidding? I should have come straight to you."

"Stop," I cut him short. "We've got a lot to deal with. It's under control." I throw Damian a sideways glance. "And I'm in, um, capable hands."

"Yes. He was closest to you. I would have come or sent Gerald, but Dulles and Reagan National are shut down."

"That bad?" I ask.

His voice sounds distant, almost defeated. "The panic is always the worst part. They're telling people not to go into the DC office."

"You're kidding." The FBI headquarters is shut down in Washington? What the hell?

"No. I wish I was." This must weigh even more heavily on Ailes than it does on me.

"I guess that's why you've resorted to unusual methods," I say, referring to Damian.

"He is unusual." Ailes lowers his voice. "I was afraid of the Red Chain getting to you first. Boston PD was overstretched."

"I'm sure I'm safe. If he wanted to kill me, it'd have happened by now," I say, glancing sideways for Damian's benefit.

"Don't worry. It'll be a murder-suicide, with you doing the killing." Damian's wink is more chilling than comforting.

"I was able to push through a temporary authorization for him as an informant," Ailes explains. "That'll make it easier on our end when we have to explain why you're in the presence of an FBI person of interest."

Person of interest. That's one way to sum up Damian. With a knack for getting involved in cases in the most suspicious ways, there are more than a few people in the FBI who would like to get him into an interrogation room.

"Have we had a chance to follow up with Boston police about my attackers?" I ask.

"We've sent out your descriptions. You think these are the two from the farmhouse?"

"No. My gut says it's a separate group. Maybe a Boston cell."

"Hmm." There's a pause as Ailes thinks this over. "Different cells with three people each?"

"Well, the DC one was until they killed the woman who failed to get me. Maybe they're recruiting. I should check Craigslist for Psycho Hell Bitch Wanted ads."

I see a grin at the corner of Damian's mouth. Eyes forward, he reaches one hand over and squeezes my left knee.

"Never change," he whispers.

"Interesting," Ailes says.

"What?" I can tell when he's on to something. Processing takes him an instant; conjuring up entire theories and explanations takes a few seconds longer.

"I've been reading up on cult structures. It's kind of fascinating. We think of the classical cult where they brainwash members into staying. But some cults maintain devotion by expelling people. Rather than convince you to stay, they make you afraid you'll be forced to go. It's a little more complicated than that, but the threat of excommunication can be very powerful.

"There's also a third way that's even more powerful. And that's making you loyal to your subgroup. Like a military platoon. Your loyalty is to the people immediately around you. You stay because of them. It's one of the reasons cults are quick to sanction their own marriages.

"Three is an interesting number. Too small to be a platoon or even a family unit if they're all adults. But there is an exception. When Pol Pot and the Khmer Rouge took over Cambodia, one of the things they did was break apart families and force people into three-person units. Each one was pressed to inform on the others. It became easier to have them self-manage. There weren't any secrets."

"So is this a political group or a religious group?" I ask.

"Probably the worst of both. The IRA, Hamas, Al-Qaeda, ISIS were all aligned on religious and political axes. The Red Chain may have a similar structure."

"If they're that internally sufficient, it would be easier for Ezra Winter to pull the strings."

"Maybe," Ailes replies. "There are lots of instances where cults kept going while their leader was imprisoned, but there was usually someone on the outside vocally supporting them and directing the group. With Winter, there's not a visible connection."

"What about the e-mail hack?"

"For sure. That doesn't surprise me. We're all but certain the major skinhead gangs have been operated by guys behind bars serving life sentences. It's not out of the question here that Winter could technically be issuing commands. It's just that there's not much of a Free Ezra Winter movement. You'd expect that if he had legions of devout followers."

"Maybe anonymity is more important to the cause?"

"Possibly."

"But you're not buying it. Me neither, I guess. I think he has a lieutenant, someone who is really running the show. But Ezra is too arrogant to let on he's not directly running the Red Chain."

"That'd make sense," Ailes replies. "I'm going to dig into his visitor records and see if there's someone who doesn't raise any red flags, but might be worth investigating." He continues, "So, if it's not too soon to ask, find anything at Devon's house?"

I'd almost forgotten. I was in the process of sending the address from the box when I'd realized I was being followed. "Yeah. Let me text you an address I found on a videotape box in the attic." I send the message through. "Got it?"

"One second. Citizens Communication Agency?"

"Yeah. Heard of it?"

"No. Let me do a records search." Ailes stifles a yawn. It's late, but I know neither one of us can sleep without an answer. "Nothing. Hm. I can make a few calls in the morning when the rest of the world is awake."

Damian takes an exit off the highway. Quantico is almost a straight shot down 95 from here. "Where are we going?" I ask.

"An airfield outside Providence. I'm not driving you all the way back to Virginia." Although he's kept a careful watch in the rearview mirror, I know he's still concerned we might be followed.

"Great. A small plane."

I've had a particularly bad experience in one that involved almost getting thrown out of it a thousand feet up, and then crashing. Of course, the crash was technically my fault, since I shot the pilot on account of not wanting to be thrown out.

"It's an FBI pilot," says Ailes. "He'll take you to Alexandria. Agent Nadine Cox will be there to pick you up. We can't get a proper safe house set up just yet. So she'll take you to the dorms at Quantico."

"Great. I should just buy a mobile home and park it there."

Going after the people I do, I frequently make it onto someone's hate list and find myself needing to put a barrier between them and me. Often just to prevent bystanders from getting hurt. The dorms are usually where I end up.

"Wait here." Damian pulls my gun from the duffel bag and lays it on my lap. He then climbs out of the cab and walks over to the plane to talk to the pilot, checking to make sure everything is legit. He gives me a thumbs-up.

I say good-bye to Ailes. "See you in a few."

Damian puts his hands on my shoulders and kisses me on the forehead when I reach him midway between the SUV and the plane.

"You're not going with me?" I'd been kind of expecting him to make the trip all the way. To be honest, kind of hoping.

He shakes his head. "I think you'll be safe until you do something stupid again."

"Again?"

He points to my side. "Yes. You were a centimeter away from an artery."

I avoid eye contact and look across the dark airfield. "I don't need a lecture. I know how close I came."

"Twice," says Damian, holding up two fingers.

"What?" I shake my head, confused.

"Twice. You were dumb to find yourself cornered on the train. Then you were dumb for ignoring your wound and deciding you can just troop through it. You were real close to cardiac failure."

"I don't need this from you. You're not my grandfather."

"Father," he replies.

"Excuse me?"

"People normally say 'father.' You said 'grandfather.' That's my point. You wouldn't listen to your father, your grandfather, or anyone else. You won't even listen to yourself. Jessica, you got to be smarter."

"What's that supposed to mean?" I reply tersely.

"You're a target. You're always going to be one. Every room you walk into, you have to assume someone is out to get you."

"That's no way to live." The truth is it's how I've been living, but I've been denying it's a permanent way of life.

"You're right," he says. "We can get back into the car and just drive away from here. Leave all this behind. You've done your part. More than that."

So much of me wants to just go away with him. We could do whatever the hell we want, and stay far away from people who want to shove knives between my ribs or hurt others around me.

"I can't." I think of Ailes and the others. I think of my sense of responsibility.

"I know," he replies. "That's why you have to be even more paranoid than ever. Be careful."

I get the sense he's not sending me to safety as much as sending me away from him. "What are you going to do?"

Damian avoids my gaze. "Look for your friends in Boston."

It's pointless to tell him not to do anything rash. "We need information from them." It's the only way I can tell him not to kill them.

"I understand. Like I said, be careful. It would be bad if we lost you."

"Bad for who?" I reply.

His face grows serious. "I'm one person with you in this world. Without you . . . I'd be another."

Of all the personalities I've met—geniuses like Ailes, psychopaths like the Warlock, and master manipulators like Marta—Damian has the greatest potential of any of them. Like any other kind of raw power, that potential could be used for good or for bad. I'm both frightened and to be honest attracted by the thought I'm the one guiding light leading him toward good.

I hope.

CHAPTER TWENTY-FOUR

CITIZENS COMMUNICATION AGENCY

WHEN I WAS a student at the University of Miami, I went through a few different roommates. Some I still talk to, and others I've lost touch with. In weird dream logic, Nadine Cox, the ever-cheerful FBI agent who's the sunny yin to my dark yang, is the college sorority sister pulling me out of bed in the morning and dragging me from party to party at night, never relenting in some kind of happy-go-lucky torture.

Right now I'm dreaming she's brought a whole party to our dorm room and everyone is drinking coffee. I can smell it like it's right in front of me.

My eyes focus and I see a strange man looking down on me. Nadine's bright grin beaming from her too-cheerful face, framed by her dirty-blond hair, is the only thing stopping me from pulling my gun from my purse by the bedside.

She waves a latte under my nose. "Don't shoot the nice doctor. He's only here to check on your wound."

"It'd be better to do this in the clinic," says the doctor. I recognize him as one of the staff physicians at Quantico. In his midthirties and very tan, he's on call to treat the numerous injuries that occur as students climb through obstacle courses, undergo firearms training, and do all the other dangerous things we practice for, but rarely witness outside of action movies.

"We can't all get what we want," replies Nadine sweetly. "Now lift your shirt so he can inspect the damage."

"Good morning," I reply groggily, turning on my side and lifting the hem of my shirt.

He lifts the bandage and examines the wound. "Not too bad. I'm going to change the dressing. I hope you're going to stay in bed today?"

"I once had hope," I grumble darkly.

He sighs. "In that case. I have some glue to put over the stitching."

I take the coffee cup from Nadine. "Thanks." I see a sheet and pillow on the couch. "You stay here all night?"

She shakes her head. "No. Gerald came by and watched so I could get some stuff from your apartment and grab coffee."

I'm very lucky to have people like Nadine and Gerald looking out for me. It's above and beyond the call of duty. "Did he head back to the office?"

"He's bringing the car closer."

Oh, jeez. I am pathetic. "Where we going?"

"Nowhere, if I have a vote," the doctor protests.

"You don't," Nadine says in a manner so cheerful I could never imagine being able to master it myself. "Your address from Devon's house. The Citizens Communication Agency. It's in Alexandria."

"What's there?"

"That's the mystery. Just an industrial park according to Google Maps. I should tell you to stay here while Gerald and I go investigate, but I know you won't sit for that."

"Damn straight, sister. What do we know?" I sit up and stifle a groan, but my pained face gets a rebuke from the doctor.

"Easy." He shakes his head.

Nadine sits on the edge of the bed. "Records searches came up almost blank. No Virginia business license. No IRS information. It's just a name and an address. Which is kind of odd. Who pays the rent? Especially at that address?"

"What do you mean?"

"Like I said, it's an industrial park. Tenants are a mapping agency, some think tanks, and other companies that are either intelligence contractors or outright fronts for CIA, NSA, and NRO projects."

"It's government?" I ask.

"Well, Gerald did a search of Government Accountability Office records. The lease is paid up for another twelve years."

"So it's active?" This is getting interesting.

"We don't know. There hasn't been a safety inspection in years. Ailes asked some of his intelligence contacts, and nobody had even heard of it. The only mention we found is a nineteen eighty-five intelligence briefing for a congressional committee. That's it."

"Nineteen eighty-five? Have we reached out to the CIA or NSA?"

"No official response. It's possible they don't even know. There are a lot of off-the-books projects that only have one or two points of contact. Sometimes the Pentagon funds stuff and forgets it."

"Our tax dollars at work," I reply. "So what's the plan? We just go down there and knock on the door?"

"It's government property, so we can take a look if nobody answers. You might want to bring your bag of tricks." She nods to my purse.

Nadine has seen me open a lock without a key on a few occasions. Being raised by a master magician and escape artist can teach you a few things.

"It'd be easier if they just let us in."

Her eyes drift down to the bandage the doctor is dressing as she has second thoughts. "You sure we want to meet these folks face-to-face?"

"We're all on the same team, aren't we?"

THE CITIZENS COMMUNICATION Agency is located in a two-story building at the far end of the industrial park. We don't have to pass through security to get there, but the moment we pull up, a private security patrol stops us as we get out. I flash my badge and start questioning the security guard, a fiftyish man with a belly from sitting down too long.

"Have you seen any people coming in or out of here?" I ask.

He takes a look at Gerald and Nadine, trying to make sense of what we're up to. "Not a one. You're the first. I stopped you because we have a lot of government stuff here."

"We know," I reply. "Anything you can tell us about this building?"

"FBI?" he says, deciding we're okay. "It's been here longer than me."

With almost no windows, the brown concrete structure looks more like an elongated pillbox than a public-facing agency. I imagine some architectural firm got paid tens of millions of dollars to pull the blueprint for Bland Government Complex #2 out of their files and dust it off.

His eyes dart to the side of the building, then back to me. He steps forward. Nadine and Gerald protectively close ranks. The guard ignores them, assuming they're trying to hear.

"What I can say is that not all these buildings are what they look like." He points to one down the street. "It goes five stories underground. It was supposed to be a CIA mapping facility until the *Washington Post* leaked that information. This one"—he nods to the CCA—"I've always wondered about."

"But you've never seen anyone go in there?" Nadine asks.

"No. But that doesn't mean anyone isn't in there," he responds in a hushed tone.

Gerald speaks up. "How do you mean?"

The guard leans even closer. "Some of these buildings are connected underground. That way you don't know who works where or at what time."

Well, that makes things complicated. "Wonderful. Any idea which ones?"

He shrugs. "I just mind the surface and keep anybody out who doesn't belong. You belong, right?"

I eye the CCA suspiciously and wonder if I know the answer to that question. "Well, we're supposed to be here. Are you guys plugged into an alarm system?"

"At the guard hut."

"The door alarm is about to go off, just so you know." Better to warn him now.

"Understood. Mind if I call in your badges first, then? So I don't have to call the police?"

Gerald hands him his information while Nadine and I walk around the building. There are several fire exits and a loading dock in the back. Security cameras from the Flintstones era are mounted on all the corners.

By the time we get back, the security guard is waving good-bye. I stop him. "A quick question. If the alarm goes off, you're supposed to call the police?"

"Of course."

"Could you check if there are any other numbers on an emergency list?" When I was a street cop, every bank, store, or any other business always had a twenty-four-hour contact. I'd love to know who that number connects to.

"Will do." He eyes the building before getting back into his truck. "I'm dying to know what's in there. To be honest. It kind of spooks me out."

Me too. I stare back at the security cameras, wondering if someone is watching from inside.

CHAPTER TWENTY-FIVE

E-TICKET

Barely lit by a dirty skylight, the atrium is a wide open space of dull earth tones. Colorful tiles form images of satellites, Earth, and smiling people. In front of the largest mosaic sits a welcome desk with rounded corners and a smoked-glass top. Plastic ferns in planters divide soft cushioned seats that form small waiting areas. Dust is everywhere.

"I feel like I just stepped into a forgotten Epcot ride." Gerald hits the nail on the head as we enter the lobby after I spent all of five seconds jiggering the lock.

The only thing I'd add is that it feels like a ride after a zombie apocalypse. It's some kind of corporate tomb that looks centuries, not just decades, old. The shaft of light from above only reinforces the lost-tomb analogy.

I put my lock-picking set back in my purse and suppress a wince as it hits my side.

"You okay?" asks Gerald.

"I think the stiches hurt more than anything else. I'll be fine."

"Um, okay," he says, still looking a little unsure.

"Don't worry, I'll let you know otherwise. Let's see what we have here." I aim my light into the hall and begin exploring.

Behind the desk, large tube letters, like the old NASA logo, spell CCA. Off to the side is a small plaque:

THE ONLY WAY TO DISCOVER THE LIMITS OF THE POSSIBLE
IS TO GO BEYOND THEM INTO THE IMPOSSIBLE.
ARTHUR C. CLARK

"What did I say?" Gerald replies. "Are we taking bets if this is a dark ride or a movie with chairs that shake?"

"I've never been to Disney World," says Nadine, as she uses a gloved hand to inspect behind seat cushions.

"Never? What about Disneyland?" he asks, with the shock of someone who just found out their friend is a Martian.

Nadine shakes her head. "Nope."

She had a rough childhood, basically raising her brothers and sisters. But to meet her, you'd think she was a little preppy raised by two loving parents in the nicest house in the best part of town.

"We're going," Gerald and I say at the same time. We laugh, because it's the kind of thing teenagers say, not FBI agents.

"You'd go?" Nadine looks at me, surprised.

"Hell, yes."

"Really?" Gerald blurts out, equally amazed.

"Why are you surprised? I used to take the bus to Disneyland when I was eleven. In college we used to go to Orlando for study breaks."

"I, uh, never took you for the type," he says as he taps the dust off a fern.

"And what type is that?" I ask in an exaggeratedly terse voice. Gerald and Nadine exchange glances, too nervous to reply.

I roll my eyes. "I like to do fun stuff too."

"Does she?" Gerald asks Nadine.

"Um." She thinks for a moment. "We once looked at shoes after going to the shooting range."

"Wow, Blackwood, you know how to live it up."

"Considering most of my clothes come to me on a UPS truck, that's living on the edge." I aim my flashlight at my wounded side. "And in case you haven't noticed, extroversion can be painful for me."

"Ah, good point," he replies.

We turn our attention back to the lobby. It really does feel like the start of some kind of futuristic theme park attraction, albeit one designed in the late 1970s.

Gerald opens a drawer under the reception desk and shines his light around. "Empty. Not even a phone book." He cranes his head inside. "Looks like a computer monitor is under the glass, but the computer itself has been yanked free." He slides open another drawer, finds a phone with an array of buttons, and picks up the receiver. "I have a dial tone. Looks like they paid their phone bill."

Nadine traces a finger across the glass, creating a furrow in the thick dust. "But not the cleaning crew."

I step to the dark glass door at the back of the lobby. There's a magnetic card slot to the side. Fortunately, the lock is a standard government facility tumbler like the one in the front, and it opens without much effort on my part.

Gerald looks at me, bemused. "I guess it was pretty pointless of me to give you a key to my place to look after it while I'm out of town."

"Pretty much," I hold the door open for them and follow.

THE HALLWAY ENDS in darkness. Nadine steps in front of us with her comically larger billy club flashlight. It cuts through the dark like a spotlight and illuminates a huge room filled with cubicles.

Gerald flips a row of switches at the end of the wall without any success. There's not even a glowing exit sign to be seen.

"Guess they didn't pay the electric," Nadine observes.

"Maybe. Maybe not," says Gerald. "It's not uncommon to just throw a master switch when a building like this is mothballed. The phone system had power. Let's keep an eye out for an electrical room."

We walk through the maze of cubicles. Each one is identical to the others. There's a desk, a chair, and a faint outline in dust where a computer or typewriter sat. The filing cabinets are empty and the drawers don't contain anything other than rubber bands and pencils.

The whole building looks wiped clean of any actual information. I shouldn't be too surprised. There are contractors that specialize in doing just that when an agency moves or gets shut down.

On the first floor we find a break room, several cleaned-out offices, and a mail center. There's absolutely no trace of what this facility was for. It could have been anything.

Gerald flashes his light down the hall. "Shall we try the second floor? Stairs, or take our chances in an elevator that hasn't been inspected since Tupac was among the living?"

"Stairs," I reply. "And he's coming back."

THE SECOND FLOOR consists of corridors of more private offices. All the doors are open. They've been cleaned out too.

"Where did the people go?" asks Nadine, after we've made it down another empty hallway.

Gerald puts his light under his chin, casting himself in a ghostly glow. "Maybe their mother ship took them home?"

"Jealous they left without you?" I ask.

"I'm here by choice."

"Theirs," Nadine shoots back.

After the fifth or sixth office I notice something lurking at the back of my mind.

"Can you guys do me a favor? Let's grab all the chairs in this section and bring them into the hallway."

"You got it," Gerald answers, used to my harebrained ideas.

We drag a dozen chairs into the middle of the corridor. I line them up against the wall. "Gerald, would you sit in one?" I direct my flashlight toward the middle.

He looks at the chairs then back to me. "Okay, now I'm scared." He takes a seat anyway.

"Comfy?" I ask.

"Well . . ." His heels are off the floor. "One second." He reaches underneath it and makes an adjustment. The chair drops two inches with a pneumatic sigh. "That's better."

"Okay. Try the next one."

"Hold on." Gerald gets in the chair to the left and makes the same adjustment.

"They've never been used," Nadine realizes.

"Yeah. I was totally going to go with that, and not that this place was run by giants," Gerald remarks. He shines his light along the row of chairs. They're all the same height.

"I don't know what's creepier," I think aloud. "That this place was abandoned, or that it was never even occupied."

"Or only partially occupied. We haven't checked all the chairs," Nadine, the stickler for details, points out.

WE CONTINUE OUR search on the second floor and end up finding at least three offices that appear to have been used. We compare notes in a small classroom marked ORIENTATION on the outside.

Gerald scratches his chin as he paces the room. "So not a whole lot of people worked here. That'd explain why nobody heard of it."

"It could still be a front," says Nadine.

"A front for what?" I reply.

Gerald notices a fuse box on the wall and turns a switch. The lights come on in the room. I look into the hallway. The lights are still out in the rest of the building.

"Interesting," he says. "Local shutoffs. You use that in some buildings where you need to conserve power in emergencies." He walks over to a television on a mobile cart and investigates a machine below it.

I'm getting frustrated by the fact we've found next to nothing. "The building is an empty mausoleum. There *has* to be a way to squeeze something out of it. Maybe we should have the used offices dusted for fingerprints? If they were government employees, we should have them on file. Especially if they had security clearances."

"We could also see if the phone system has any numbers saved," Nadine suggests.

"That's a great idea. It would be helpful to know who they were talking to, at least."

"Yeah, and maybe we can find out why they were such Beatles fans," Gerald replies.

"What?" Nadine and I turn toward him, confused.

He's holding up a large format videocassette he pulled from the machine. On the spine is a label that reads: PAUL IS DEAD.

Nadine shakes her head. "'Paul is dead'? I don't get it."

"Beatles reference. Before our time," says Gerald. "Maybe this will explain it. Should I play it?"

It's the only piece of information other than the tile mosaic and the seat heights we've been able to find.

"Heck yeah." I reply.

Ten minutes later, we're even more confused.

CHAPTER TWENTY-SIX

PAUL IS DEAD

THE FIRST THING that comes to mind is the industrial films by Saul Bass my father used to show me. Designed to be part art house short film and part propaganda, they used bold images and text to drive home a point, which could be why the AT&T logo was so clever or why you should drive a Volkswagen.

An unseen male narrator, straight out of an educational documentary, begins talking over a vaguely sci-fi soundtrack of synthesizers played alongside images and clips.

For the entirety of human history, man has resolved violent conflict through destructive physical force. From the first rocks and club weapons to space-age guided missiles, man has waged war using weapons made of matter. But now, an even deadlier weapon is on the horizon. One whose devastation can't be measured in kilotons or body count. A weapon so powerful, its impact can change the course of history both future and past.

"My money is on lasers," Gerald quips as we crash zoom into a photo of the Earth.

We've seen forms of this weapon in use behind the Iron Curtain. En-tire citizens wiped clean from the face of the earth. In Red China, towns, villages, and entire ethnic groups have been erased as if they never ex-isted.

The film illustrates this with names of towns vanishing from maps and people disappearing from photos. The examples are all places in the United States and Europe. Chicago disappears. People on a city street, dressed in late seventies and early eighties clothing, are erased one by one from the still image until the block is empty.

In flash points around the world, this weapon has been used in tar-geted measure, resulting in civil unrest and overnight political upheaval.

Stock footage of nameless rioting mobs in cities around the world. It makes me feel a little uncomfortable, given what's hap-pening in the world.

This weapon is now a thousand times more potent in the electronic age. Its impact can be felt around the world at the speed of light. Its effect is so damaging, no retaliation is even possible.

"Computer viruses?" Gerald wonders aloud.

Wars can be fought and victors declared at the press of a button. This powerful weapon. This destructive force. Is . . . the Information Bomb.

Nadine mouths "information bomb" to me. I shrug.

The video cuts to photos of Orson Welles speaking into a microphone and a montage of the alleged panic over his *War of the Worlds* broadcast. Next, a newspaper with the headline IS PAUL DEAD? fills the screen, followed by images of the Beatles and the rumor that one of their albums hid the message that Paul McCartney had died.

"I get it," says Nadine.

The narrator continues:

In the electronic age, warfare isn't fought with bombs dropped from the sky, but with information cruise missiles flying through the telephone lines, radio waves, and the digital communications of tomorrow.

"Information cruise missiles?" Gerald shakes his head at the clumsy phrase.

The ammunition is rumor, innuendo, misinformation, and leaks. More biological than mechanical, the delivery vehicles are ordinary citizens, journalists, media personalities, and politicians.

He snorts. "Even better!"

The Citizens Communication Agency is at the forefront of safeguarding our nation and our allies from the spread of information warfare.

"Thank god," Gerald says sarcastically.

Our goal is round-the-clock monitoring of news media and other forms of information dissemination. Our first line of defense is information countermeasures working hand in hand with trusted news agencies, local authorities, and citizens dedicated to preventing information age warfare.

I think of the empty building we're in and whisper, "Well, I feel safer knowing the hardworking men and women of the CCA are protecting us."

The video ends and Nadine turns away from the screen to face us. Her expression is one of shock. "What the hell was that?"

"At least half a million dollars if you ask me," says Gerald. "I can only imagine what the rest of this boondoggle costs."

"Yeah, but can you explain to me what this was supposed to be?" No nonsense, and not afraid to sweetly tell someone when they're bullshitting her, she's having a problem with this. We all are.

"A government public relations office?" Gerald asks.

"Why would a public-facing PR office be a super-secret government agency? It kind of doesn't make sense," I observe.

"Maybe this is a front for something else?" Nadine replies.

Gerald points to the television. "That's a lot of effort for a smokescreen. This is something you show employees to get them psyched about their mission."

"Or to convince a senator to keep funding you," I add.

Nadine now seems confused. "Fund you for what? It's just an empty office. What were they supposed to do here?"

"Protect us from information cruise missiles. Isn't it obvious?" Gerald answers drily. "I mean, there are a lot of agencies that don't make sense. The more secretive they are the less oversight they have. This could have just been some NSA idea that went nowhere."

"We're asking field agents to cut down their gas mileage and we've got the money for this?" Nadine is getting more incensed by the whole concept as she ponders it.

"Protecting democracy isn't cheap. Or efficient," Gerald replies.

"Maybe there's more to this place?" I think of the security guard's talk of underground levels. As a little girl I lived in a house with secret passageways and rooms. I was six before I found out that wasn't normal.

"We didn't see anything else," he says.

"We weren't exactly looking," I explain, thinking of all the times guests walked right past hidden doors in our mansion. "Maybe we should look again?"

Nadine is staring at her phone. "Southeast corner."

"What?" I look over her shoulder. She's pulled up a Google Maps aerial view of the building.

"See that?" She gestures to a metal box on the roof. "That's an elevator housing."

"We looked inside the elevator. It only had two floor buttons." Gerald had made a point of inspecting it.

"That was the one in the front." She shows us the entrance.

"Notice on the image how there's no motor box? That's because it was a piston elevator. It only went up one floor. This one is in the back, and it has a machine room on the ceiling because it probably goes much deeper."

I'm amazed at how she knows this. "You can tell that from a photo?"

"I once wanted to work with the CIA. This is the kind of thing they look for."

Gerald and I nod with approval, impressed by her yet again.

A FEW MINUTES later, we're in a conference room at the back of the building knocking on wood paneling, looking for a secret passage. Counting strides and comparing it to the aerial photo, we've narrowed the possible section down to just a few meters. Nadine taps the butt of her flashlight against the wall right in the middle, and it sounds hollow.

Gerald pulls out a pocket tool and uses the blade to pry open a hidden door being held shut by a magnet. When we swing it aside, there's an elevator behind it.

"Holy crap," he mutters. "This is some *Mission: Impossible* stuff!"

"I guess this makes sense," I reply. "If you want to go to the secret section, just call the people into a conference room and lock the door." I use my lock pick to activate the call button. A moment later, the doors open.

We nervously eye the interior. I wonder if one of us should wait behind, but we all step inside. There's no way I'm not going down there, and I'm sure they feel the same way.

"Are we taking bets on what we're going to find?" Gerald asks as he presses the only button.

"Sex dungeon," says Nadine sweetly, shocking Gerald and me a little.

"It'll be spiders. Lots of spiders," I groan.

A few seconds later, the doors open. None of our guesses are even close.

CHAPTER TWENTY-SEVEN

THE BRIDGE

My GRANDFATHER TAUGHT me a lot about suspense, expectation, and surprise. One of the most important lessons was that to truly enthrall your audience, you need to exceed whatever it was they were imagining was behind the curtain.

What's on the other side of the elevator is going to have us talking for a long time.

Nadine is the first one to speak as we try to process what's in front of us. We all want to say the same thing, but she's the only one fearless enough to just put it out there. "Is this supposed to be a spaceship?"

It's an absurd question, but a spaceship is exactly what comes to mind as the lights flicker on at the end of the corridor and we step into a chamber that resembles the bridge from an old *Star Trek* episode. The walls are all curved metal panels. A large metal chair sits on a riser in the middle, flanked by two sleek workstations with large CRT monitors. Headsets rest on the consoles alongside an array of buttons.

Directly in front of them is a huge video projection screen, the kind of thing you'd expect to show alien spacecraft or planets right before phasers start firing. Smaller monitors line the walls over workstations with plastic signs saying things like: INFORMATION BALLISTICS and COMMUNICATIONS TRAJECTORIES.

The expressions on Nadine and Gerald's faces are of confusion and wonder. What the hell have we stepped into? Our initial assessment of this being something like an Epcot ride is only reinforced. Clearly we're not on a spaceship, but this thing has some purpose beyond just entertainment.

We spend the next few minutes silently exploring the room. I take a seat in the central chair and try to understand what this is all for.

Whoever sits here is meant to direct the action of everyone else in the room. There are jacks for audio equipment, but no display. On the right armrest there's a clunky keypad and an LED display. Possibly for entering some kind of authorization codes, or maybe just to make phone calls?

"Is this a war-gaming room?" Gerald asks, ready for us to start guessing.

I point to a plastic sign that reads: DEMOGRAPHIC ANALYSIS. "That doesn't sound like something you'd find in NORAD. Maybe this is some kind of emergency response center?"

"For what?" Nadine replies.

I shrug. "Information cruise missiles?"

She sighs. "Whatever those are."

Gerald slides his hand along an aluminum panel on the wall and gives it a push, revealing a hidden compartment. There's a bank of switches inside. "Should I turn it on?"

"Why not? What's the worst that can happen? We start World War Three?" I say halfheartedly. Although this place has power, it's been sitting dormant for decades. "Just don't press anything that says 'Launch,'" I add, only partially joking.

He flips a switch. "Well, if that's all that's at stake."

Old computers whir to life all around us. The CCA logo appears on the main screen—a little hazy and pixelated, but still clear enough.

Gerald takes the right workstation, and Nadine sits in the left.

"Where to?" I ask.

"Mars?" Nadine suggests.

"Nineteen seventy-two?" Gerald counters. He types into the keyboard on his station. A simple green text menu appears before him. "Is there a selector knob on your captain's chair?" he asks.

I look down on the armrest and see a rotating knob that corresponds with the layout of the room. I turn it toward his workstation. The CCA logo vanishes, replaced by his computer screen.

"I guess my job is just to decide what channel we're watching," I reply.

Gerald reads the list of menu options aloud. "System Check, Simulator Options, Command Mode, and Archive. What do we want?"

"Let's try Simulator Options." That sounds reasonably safe.

The screen fills up with a list of odd titles:

Cleveland Initiative
Ohio Compromise
Chicago Fallback
Niagara Switchback
Los Angeles Heat Wave
>More

Well, that's helpful. "Okay? Something tells me these aren't folk music groups. Any suggestions?"

"Did you see the movie *WarGames*?" Gerald asks.

Nadine pulls her hands away from her console. "The one where Ferris Bueller almost starts World War Three?"

I give my buttons a nervous look as well, afraid to touch anything. "This is a simulator, right?"

"We're in the simulator mode," Gerald says hesitantly.

"So we can't do any harm? Can we?" I ask, hoping he has some insight I'm not privy to.

"Well, even a nuclear submarine has a simulator mode. It's your call, Captain."

"Why did I have to choose this chair?"

"Like any of us had a chance," Gerald replies.

"Ohio Compromise," says Nadine. She makes a hesitant smile. "Come on. It's just a simulation. We're not really going to nuke Ohio. Or info bomb them. Right?" Her curiosity seems to have overcome her initial fear.

I wish I had her confidence. I suddenly feel silly for being so nervous about the room. "Go for it. At least we're in a bunker."

"Here we go." Gerald presses a button.

The screen vanishes and is replaced by a new list of menu options.

Philippine Destabilization Initiative:
Time to live: 5 hours
Phase 1:-5 hour mark
Media pre-seed
Phase 2:-4 hour mark
Broadcast interrupt
Phase 3:-3.5 hour mark
Proxy initialization

Phase 4:-2 hour mark

Capital blackout

Phase 5:-1 hour mark

Civil defense communications disruption

"Um, okay?" This looks like some kind of old-school computer text adventure to me. "Does this make sense to any of you? We went from Ohio to the Philippines."

"Press another button? Phase One?" Gerald asks.

"Sure," I reply.

To our right, a loud printer that was probably built during the Nixon administration begins to fire off. I climb out of my chair to get a better look. It's actually an old-school telex machine wired into the command center.

I rip the printout off the feeder as soon as it finishes.

"Well?" Nadine asks.

I show her the page. "It's an Associated Press report. It says that a Philippine senator has been placed under house arrest after pushing for a probe of the president's finances. It goes on to say the presidential administration has issued a denial."

Nadine reads the news report for herself. "They don't name names."

Gerald leans over her shoulder. "I guess it's supposed to be a generic situation. They don't want this to feel too dated."

I take the captain's seat again. It's an odd room. I can't quite figure out the purpose of the simulation but a hazy picture is forming. "There's something we're missing here. Press Phase Two," I instruct Gerald.

"You want to see how we manage a broadcast interrupt?" he asks.

"Yes." I don't tell him what my hunch is. I could be way off base.

The monitor on a workstation to our left glows as it turns on. A video map of the Philippines appears on the screen with red dots and lines that connect them. Each dot has a number. Another screen lists names next to the numbers.

1. DZBB
2. DZWET, etc.

Below the screen is a keypad that lets a user select one of the numbered dots.

Nadine leans in to look at the map. "Well, that explains nothing."

"Select a number and press the red button next to the pad," I tell her.

"Okay." She chooses DZBB. A third monitor flickers, showing a Samsung phone commercial.

"That's certainly not prerecorded," Gerald points out. "At least not when this was made. I guess this must be a live feed."

Nadine presses the button and the screen goes blurry, wavy lines turning to static.

"Did I break it?" she asks.

"Let go of the button," I reply.

The moment she does, the video comes back as clear as before.

"There must be a short," says Gerald, his fingers about to tap the keyboard.

"Crap! Nobody touch anything!" I shout, suddenly sick to my stomach. "There's no short. That's what's supposed to happen. This isn't an emergency response room. *This is for creating emergencies.*"

Nadine glances at Gerald, then back to me. "I'm not getting it."

I point to the screen. "Those simulation options, they're all real situations. If we go into the active mode, everything we just did would actually have happened." I point to the telex. "We weren't receiving a news report. *We were sending one.* A fake one. A report designed to get people angry. The broadcast interrupt, that's connected to some kind of jamming device. Or would be if they ever finished this place. The power outage option? They might have equipment in place to cause blackouts. This *is* a war room. It's what the film upstairs described. Only the CCA isn't meant to prevent these information bombs, it's meant to launch them."

"What's the Peter Devon connection?" Gerald asks.

I get a sinking feeling in the pit of my stomach. "He wanted to predict the future. When he realized that was impossible, he decided he'd try to control it instead. This is the project his former partner, Professor Cyprian, told me about. He got the government to fund his mad mission to try to influence people, and change history."

"So this is like a big psychological warfare control center?" Gerald lifts his hands from the console in front of him.

"Exactly. Only most of it is push-button tricks and sabotage. Nineteen eighties style. And the riots, the flooding, are all some newer version of this." I slap my palm on the armrest. "This is where it started!"

"But it didn't end here," says Nadine.

"No," I agree. "It morphed into something even worse than trying to foment a coup d'état by interrupting international television. They actually figured out how to cause disasters."

CHAPTER TWENTY-EIGHT

ESCAPE VALVE

WHEN WE GET back to Quantico, the assistant director of the FBI, Breyer, is waiting in our bullpen. Jennifer, fresh off the plane from South America, is walking him through a PowerPoint presentation on the overhead projector.

Breyer and I have our own history. He seems to regard everyone as either a zero or a one. While my results speak well of my methods, he's constantly watching for me to screw up so I can go back to the zero column in his ledger. In an agency filled with cynics and skeptics, who are mostly men, a woman who's unintentionally become a rising star has to expect to encounter an undue amount of scrutiny. But still, can't a girl get a break? He looks in our directions as Gerald and I take a seat at the back of the table near Ailes, who has been sitting quietly as Jennifer details her findings.

We'd filled him in briefly on the way back and he told us about Jennifer's harrowing journey. She'd made it into Bolivia with a group of Red Cross disaster response workers, and an FBI agent

stationed there had escorted her to several of the locations she'd
wanted to investigate.

For the first day, they were able to get around fairly trouble
free. The people were still in shock over what had occurred. The
death toll began to climb. Then rumors began to spread. Blame
started to fall on the government, and foreigners were considered
suspicious.

They'd had rocks pelted at them in one town, and were forced
to leave their hotel in another when pickup trucks with angry men
began to pull up outside.

Jennifer, who unsurprisingly looks rather unshaken after her
experience, displays an image of a metal cylinder surrounded by
a torrent of water. "This is a rain gauge next to the main source
of flooding. It's operated by the Bolivian weather service." She
points to a smaller gauge mounted on a post near a tree. "This
one belongs to an agricultural research team from Caltech.
Their project ended two years ago, but they still collect data. It's
also connected to a moisture sensor. The readings between the
official sensor and the Caltech one don't match up precisely, but
are fairly close."

"No evidence of tampering?" asks Breyer.

"I don't think so. We have satellite estimates of how much
water fell. The gauges are within the margin of error." She's direct
and doesn't seem intimidated by Breyer.

"So, it's just a freak accident?" he asks.

"Well, that's what it looks like on the surface. But then I pulled
up the moisture data and found that it wasn't out of the ordinary
for that season. So I did a little more investigating and found some
satellite images."

She pulls up a photo of a pale brown hillside with sparse vegetation. Rivulets of muddy water are streaming down the side of
the hill.

"The prevailing theory is that vegetation loss caused more water to slide downhill than be absorbed."

"That looks pretty credible to me," Breyer replies, not sure where this is going. But I know Jennifer well enough to know that when she says something like "prevailing theory" she's about to demolish it.

"It would, except this photo was taken three years ago." She cycles through several more images showing roughly the same amount of change in foliage. "Every year, this happens. Maybe in different places, but overall approximately the same amount of precipitation and erosion. I could find no evidence that there was a greater amount this year. This isn't my area of expertise, but it simply doesn't add up."

"But the storm? The flooding? That doesn't happen every year. Why now?" asks Breyer, trying to comprehend what she's telling him.

"The rainfall was normal, but the water level wasn't," Jennifer says. "The river overflowed its banks by several meters. Locals claimed the dam overflowed, but the water level was at least ten feet below the top."

I'm impressed by her ability to matter-of-factly respond to Breyer without getting frustrated. She knows she's the authority here and has the facts to prove it.

"I'm confused," Breyer presses. "Where did the extra water come from?"

"This is where it gets difficult. I was only given limited access to the dam and looked at some of the equipment. The likely ex-planation is that the water came from the dam, but was released through an overflow valve, either accidentally or intentionally. So the excess water came through the dam, not from the storm. That's what caused the river to overflow its banks."

The import of what she's saying hits him. "The flood was intentional?" Breyer asks, surprised.

"I don't know who we mean by 'they.' But it wouldn't have been terribly difficult for anyone with technical knowledge to have caused this. In examining the equipment that controls the secondary release valves, I saw things that were . . . suspicious." Jennifer displays an image of a cable going into the concrete. "This is marked as a ground wire. I traced it to the surface of the dam. It's actually an antenna."

"A remotely controlled floodgate?" says Breyer. He's trying to reconcile the full force of what Jennifer is saying with her dry delivery.

She nods. "That's what it appears to be. Someone could theoretically control a release off-site, remotely causing a flood. They don't have anywhere near the security controls we have in place here, but I wouldn't take too much comfort in that."

Breyer shakes his head in disbelief. "What did the Bolivians have to say?"

Jennifer stares at the floor for a moment and her voice changes. "They were not very receptive to this. I was told our services were no longer required. At that time, I decided it would be expedient to get out of the country."

Holy hell. Jennifer narrowly avoided a political catastrophe. I can only imagine their reaction when she told them their natural disaster was human caused.

Breyer was clearly not expecting this turn of events. "Is this a cover-up?" he asks Ailes.

"An embarrassment. I doubt they know what happened. But at this point they don't want to be culpable for what is still considered a natural disaster. That could affect disaster relief funding, not to mention destabilize the region."

I've seen this before, firsthand. In Tixato, Mexico, where I unknowingly encountered the narco-terrorist Marta, an entire town became a recruiting ground for anti-government and anti-church gangs after a failed disaster response killed scores of residents. To this day, the United Nations tries to downplay a cholera epidemic they created in Haiti by sending sewage downstream from a base after responding to the earthquake.

"So who is controlling this?" Breyer asks.

Clearly he thinks Jennifer has made a solid case. I got to hand it to home girl, she knows how to walk a room through a PowerPoint.

Her eyes catch mine. Now that she's done with the facts, it's time for me to interject some half-baked theory. Lucky me.

I speak up. "I think it's clearly the same people behind the Devon videos. Likely the Red Chain."

Breyer scrutinizes me for an awkward moment, probably thinking *zero or one?* "The Red Chain? The people who assaulted you on the train?"

"And the ones who helped the woman track me to our stakeout." And the reason my side feels like a steak knife holder at this moment.

"All of this is connected?" The way he says "all" is as though I'm attempting to tie the Federal Reserve, the Moon landing, and Elvis into one vast plot.

I point to the image of the floodgate. "We just came from a defunct government facility that was Peter Devon's brainchild. They had simulators for causing blackouts, jamming communications, and misdirecting media. Some of the equipment looked like it was ready to be wired into an actual electronic sabotage weapon."

Breyer throws Ailes a skeptical look. "What's this?"

Ailes nods. "It's an actual facility and former agency. I've seen the photos. It's real. I'm sending Gerald and a team back to make a more thorough investigation."

Breyer processes this new twist. "I don't get it. TV broadcast jammers and blackout generators?"

"Probably installed on location by independent contractors," says Gerald. "The same way we tap foreign embassies. And compared to the cost of a cruise missile, cheap. You just need some people who know what they're doing. The CIA managed to bug most of Eastern Bloc Europe at the local level in the sixties and seventies. These are the same kinds of dirty tricks. Just . . . more elaborate."

He ponders this bombshell. "We'll table that for a moment. Explain the Red Chain connection," Breyer says to me.

"They're a cult tied to the ecoterrorist Ezra Winter. Interestingly enough, I spoke to some of our agents who deal with those types of groups. Dams are a frequent target."

"But the Red Chain didn't take credit," he points out.

"No. That's not their primary goal."

"What is?"

With Breyer you have to phrase things succinctly through a framework of motivation and consequences. "Why are you here in Quantico, instead of in DC? Collapse of government. Panic. They use Devon's predictions to instill fear and tell people how to respond. First he says he foresaw the earthquake, then the flood. When he says rioting is next, people fulfill the prophecy. He primes them, then gives them a target." I let that sink in for a moment then hit him with my other thought. "I believe the police shooting in DC was staged." I'm jumping into this blindfolded, but my gut tells me it's related.

"Staged?" His face can't contain his surprise at my allegation. "You think the officers were in on it?"

"I don't know. But I believe that the Red Chain was involved in causing it to happen. They needed an antigovernment spark to turn public opinion. Coldly speaking, this was perfect."

"The drone too?" asks Breyer.

"Drone?" I haven't heard about this.

"A police drone fell out of the sky in Chicago and landed on a group of people, sending several to the hospital. We suspect it was hacked."

This keeps getting worse and worse. "That would certainly serve their purposes."

Evidently, the drone incident has already raised Breyer's suspicions about outside actors. "But you still don't have any hard evidence that links these incidents to the Red Chain?"

This comes across as more desperate than challenging. I've been preparing for a fight, but it seems that in the middle of this storm, our team is the only one with answers.

"We could lean on Ezra Winter more," I suggest.

Breyer shakes his head. "That's going to be difficult. Department of Justice lawyers have informed me he just acquired the services of a new attorney, Samuelson Gray."

This isn't good. I know Gray by reputation because he has represented foreign leaders and the heads of billion-dollar drug cartels. He is a formidable opponent who can throw more lawyers on a case than even the Justice Department could muster.

"How did he afford that?" I ask.

Breyer throws up his hands in frustration. "They aren't talking. So what do you need to make the Red Chain connection and take it all the way back to Ezra?"

Wow. He's just offered support instead of antagonism. Now I should *really* be scared.

There's another angle for me to make a connection, one where the Red Chain may be directly involved. "I want to look into the police shooting at the White House."

I can read his face before he even speaks.

"I can't do that. We already got a hundred Justice Department people all over that, plus the Capitol Police are pretty wound up."

"Okay. But have they found the cops who did it yet?" If they had, it would be all over the news unless they are keeping it quiet.

"No. We're looking into the possibility they're being sheltered by family or other police."

I have a hunch and decide to make a gambit. I need to give him something they haven't thought of, or at least show him I'm a step ahead. "Have their cell phones recently been used outside a hundred-mile radius? Maybe Atlanta?"

Breyer raises an eyebrow, surprised. "Who have you been talking to?"

"A lucky guess." Actually, I've just worked backward from a theory and hit the nail on the head. "It's a ruse. Whoever is using those phones *isn't* them. Someone's activated the phones far away from here to mislead the chase. As long as we're acting under the premise that the cops from the shooting are working alone, with minimal help from family, we wouldn't expect assistance on a larger level."

"Are you saying the fugitive cops are part of the Red Chain?"

"I don't know. I need to get more information. My instincts say no. Maybe they were coerced. But right now, neither the Justice Department nor Capitol Police are looking for a Red Chain connection. That could be key."

Breyer weighs this over. "If I let you look into this, how do you propose to find that connection? Capitol Police isn't being super cooperative right now."

"I have a contact in Metro who knows some officers in Capitol Police. She might be willing to work with me if I can make it clear there's a scapegoat here other than her fellow cops."

CHAPTER TWENTY-NINE

VIGIL

MY SENSE OF dread builds as I move toward the center of the protests. It's one thing to see them on the news, but it's something else entirely to be on the ground.

Beyond the abandoned barricades, I see more shattered windows, more graffiti. A vandalized BMW is still spewing black smoke toward the night sky as its interior smolders. People walk past, indifferent to the wreckage. Occasionally someone picks up a rock or a bottle and tries to smash any remaining glass. There's no sound of a fire truck within miles. Authorities have given up trying to respond unless a building is burning.

Three young men with shaved heads, black denim jackets, and angry expressions almost collide with me as I walk down the street. There are a lot of scowling faces around tonight. If Ailes knew where I was right now, he'd kill me himself. But for me to understand what happened during the shooting, I have to get a look at where it took place.

This neighborhood near the White House has become a

no-go zone for uniformed cops, and those who do venture into the vicinity are subject to a barrage of insults, rocks, and worse. A consulate worker from the German embassy was attacked, almost killed, when someone announced to the mob that he was an undercover officer. But there's definitely a police presence here. I can spot undercover law enforcement a mile away, watching and only discreetly intervening when absolutely necessary. When violence does flare, backup units in riot gear can scatter the crowds with tear gas. But they keep flooding back in even larger numbers.

Those who are in this for the long haul have erected tents on sidewalks. I spot a group of college-age kids camping in a burned-out Starbucks. Convenience markets are being looted for toilet paper and food. Concrete barriers and portable fences have been put up around the Treasury, Senate, and Congress buildings, and a line of civilian volunteers at the Castle has been pleading with people to leave the Smithsonian's museums alone. So far, that seems to be the one line nobody is trying to cross. There are reports that curators have been putting the most precious artifacts in their basement vaults and barricading the doors.

Outsiders watching all this on television news keep asking why they don't just arrest everyone. Pundits have to point out that there are five hundred people to every police officer. Beyond that problem is the question of where to house them. On the police scanner I listened to on my way here, I overheard chatter about prepping Nationals Park as a holding facility. Attempts to shut down the entire DC metro area have been met with several problems, both legal and practical. Civil rights attorneys from all over the country have filed petitions with the courts to allow the protests to continue.

Part of the problem is that this isn't just a bunch of millennial barbarians storming the gates. A number live and work in Washington themselves, so it's a protest, at least partially, from within.

Whether it's based on genuine grievances, or just locals' desire to be part of the scene, I'm not quite sure. But I'd wager that 90 percent of the people here could give a damn about some greater cause. There's a lot of laughing as they move toward the White House, like they're on their way to a concert. They're here because they feel a sense of self-worth by instagramming and Facebook updating that they were part of whatever this is.

WITHIN THE CROWDS, fleet-footed journalists try to do standup interviews with iPhones to avoid calling too much attention to themselves. There have been several instances of assault on reporters, and of million-dollar news trucks being firebombed and tipped over.

The safest places for them to cover the story are from helicopters and the rooftops of secured buildings. The lights of at least five choppers are visible overhead: far enough away not to call attention to themselves, but close enough so they can use advanced optics to follow individuals in the sea of humanity.

"Where you going, white girl?" someone calls out from behind me.

My hand goes to my waist. I've got my sidearm in a quick-draw position, and a can of mace in my pocket. And my side still aches from two days ago, when I last let someone get too close.

I steal a glance over my shoulder and do a double-take. It's Detective Aileen Lewis in street clothes. Emphasis on street. Her hair is tucked under a knit cap. She's wearing a gold jacket, and as much makeup as a showgirl.

She sizes me up. "You look like a Georgetown postdoc doing fieldwork. The blond wig and glasses are a good touch, though."

"You still spotted me." I get a nervous thought about what

would happen if someone recognized me here who I *didn't* want to see me. I took all the right precautions, but . . .

"True. One, you told me where to meet you. Two, you're the only girl other than myself dumb enough to be alone out here."

Like me, she's out here unofficially. Her dedication is admirable—and borderline suicidal. Which sounds familiar.

We walk toward the White House keeping the conversation light, in case anyone is listening. Groups of people are going around trying to sniff out anyone they think doesn't belong. In some cases, they're getting women to scream for help to see who comes running with a gun drawn.

The tactics being used to ferret out the police make me suspicious. College protests and other riots are never this strategic, and undercover cops rarely have difficulty infiltrating them. Here, it's more like a counterintelligence agency is pulling the strings.

As we head toward the White House, I piece together the story of Tia Connelly in my head. A nineteen-year-old artist studying at the Corcoran School of the Arts and Design, she'd joined the protest when some friends of hers decided they were tired of sitting in a dorm without electricity.

They pushed their way to the front lines. Tia had brought her camera to get photos of the action. She'd raised her lens to take a shot of one of the masked police officers trying to keep the mob from pressing against the gates. And that was when—point-blank—he raised his pistol and shot her in the face. The officer to his right fired several rounds into the crowd, scattering them. The two cops then pulled back, and haven't been seen since.

Hundreds of cameras were videoing as the shooting transpired, some even live. There was no ambiguity about it. Talking heads on television have tried to attribute it to stress, and the pressure of being in what's essentially a war zone. But until police officers Eric Bogden and Hef Steadman talk, we won't really know why this happened.

As far as victims go, Lieutenant Bogden couldn't have chosen someone more photogenic, sympathetic, and ready for a cause. Besides being pretty and conveniently white, Tia's parents own an art gallery in New York City and have Oscar and Nobel Prize winners on speed dial.

As we get closer to the scene of the shooting, I see banners and signs emblazoned with Tia's image—a self-portrait pulled from her Instagram account that's become an icon overnight—along with the hashtag #VictimZero.

"Here." Aileen takes two candles and a lighter from her pocket. "Better to look like we have a purpose."

We light our vigil candles and work our way through the crowd to a line of people slowly moving alongside the White House fence. Thousands of people have come here to where Tia was gunned down to pay their respects. The mood is more subdued now that the weight of what transpired beneath our feet sinks in.

The bars of the White House fence have been covered on the other side with camouflage netting and canvas, hiding the most famous home in America from view up close. Several portable watchtowers have been stationed on the other side. There are no Secret Service or military figures visible, but it's clear we're being watched.

Aileen whispers, "They're getting several jumpers an hour. A small group tried to scale the fence together. Their screams changed the other's minds."

"What'd they find?" I look at the barrier.

"Besides a platoon of marines? Probably a pain-field generator, tear gas, and snipers with rubber bullets. Beyond that, I'm told there's barbed wire. The word is that under no circumstances are they to let the lawn be overrun."

Better to spill blood than let the White House fall, I think to myself. It may just be a symbol, but in America, it's *the* symbol.

Right outside the no-fly zone, news helicopters hover. I realize they're not here for the riots and protest, because they've got tons of footage of that. They want to be here when the angry mob finally storms the gates and tries to lay siege to the White House. That would be a futile effort. The sharpshooters, machine-gun nests, and other countermeasures will keep the building safe. However, the image of civilians being gunned down on the White House lawn is one we'd never be able to erase from our collective conscience. Governments have fallen over incidents like that.

I get a chill as I finally see what we're up against. It's not just a plot to make Devon into some kind of prophetic leader of a fringe terror group. These people are trying to create their own flash point, like the assassination of Archduke Franz Ferdinand or the Reichstag fire. The former led to World War I, the latter, World War II.

We shuffle forward, and Tia's memorial comes into view. Flowers litter the sidewalk and cover the fence. Thousands of candles light the memorial as if it were a Hindu shrine.

As the crowd shifts, we move away from the sidewalk. The flowers form a barrier around a circle of pavement. In the center is the chalk outline of Tia's body. Where her head lay is a pool of dried blood.

Everywhere around me, people are sobbing. Mostly young men and women. I can see the look in their eyes: if my government would do this to her, what's to stop them from doing it to me?

The meme is that Tia just went there for answers. She wasn't a protestor. She wasn't political. She was just a teenage girl with a camera and she was gunned downed by a man in uniform.

It's heartbreaking.

I want to cry.

But now that I'm here, seeing it for myself, I know that it's all a calculated lie.

CHAPTER THIRTY

OPTICS

Tɪᴀ'ꜱ ᴍᴇᴍᴏʀɪᴀʟ ɪꜱ deeply moving and brings nearly everyone around us to tears as we move past. Beyond the candles, people are listening to a woman with frizzy hair and horn-rim glasses urging them via a handheld microphone not to take it anymore. She points to the security towers beyond the White House fence and makes a passionate speech declaring that our government has failed us. It's disturbing to see her manipulating everyone's grief.

"Who is that?" I ask Aileen.

"Probably some cultural studies professor waiting for her moment in the spotlight," she says, rolling her eyes.

Behind the speaker, a video of protests from around the world projects onto a bedsheet stretched between two trees. A midtwenties man sporting a man bun and a camo jacket and holding an iPad calls out the latest updates on global protests from Twitter.

People spread through the crowd handing out pieces of paper with #BlackFallNOW written on them, admonishing everyone to follow on social media.

A college-age girl with auburn hair, wearing a T-shirt that bears Tia's face, walks up to us. "Are you guys ready to make a stand?" She clutches a clipboard under her arm.

"Damn straight," Aileen replies, fully in character.

"Then you should sign up." The woman turns the board toward her.

Aileen holds up her hands, refusing to touch it. "Whoa, how do I know you're not a cop collecting names?"

The girl reacts with shock. "Do I look like a cop?"

"I'm not signing anything." She grabs me by the arm and pulls me away. "Neither is she."

"This feels like some kind of recruitment ground," Aileen whispers to me when we're out of earshot.

Exactly. Tia's memorial is intended to get us worked up emotionally. As our anger and sadness peaks, we land right in the arms of organizers trying to recruit us. It's pure showmanship. Somebody set this up like a play. The first act, approaching the memorial, is the buildup. The second act, the memorial itself, reduces you to tears. The third and final act incites you to anger so you'll sign up for whatever the opportunists have planned.

Get a few thousand phone numbers and send a group text—STORMING THE WHITE HOUSE FENCE—and all hell breaks loose. Not everyone would follow such a suicidal call to action. But seeing all the angry and disillusioned faces around me looking for a way to channel their frustration, I'm convinced a few would. Personal judgment goes out the window in the face of mob psychology.

"What do you know about the cops involved in the shooting?" I ask Aileen when we're off to the side from everyone else.

"Not much. They weren't standouts. Not *known* hotheads. But that doesn't mean they weren't."

We grab a spot where we can watch the line. A news truck is

turned on its side, windows smashed. The interior has been gutted, its black cables and electronics spilling out like the entrails of a butchered animal.

I survey the area, noticing how people are being funneled through like a line at an amusement park. "I think this whole thing is a setup."

"What do you mean?" she asks.

"I think this was orchestrated by the Red Chain."

While I'm certain that antigovernment groups were ready to jump into action at this crisis, the skill with which it is being pulled off implies forethought. Somebody had a plan to stoke these flames. Prior protests, like Occupy and Ferguson, certainly had opportunists who were ready to grab attention for themselves. But on the whole, those protest organizers were disorganized and fought just as much with each other as with the power they were challenging.

Aileen's gaze drifts to where Tia was killed. "Are you saying Steadman and Bogden were in on it?"

This is a pretty heavy accusation, but she's not rejecting it outright.

"I don't know. Maybe they were forced. Maybe something else . . . The shooting was too perfect."

"Perfect?" She searches my face for context.

"I mean, it's exactly what the Red Chain wanted." I take out my phone and pull up a photo. "See this frame grab?" It's a high-resolution image of Tia with the gun pointed at her. "This was taken from a press photographer standing on a news truck over there." I point to the corner where the truck had been. "See this one?" It's a photo from a different angle. "Taken from over there on the other side. This spot was probably the most watched point in DC. In the world. More cameras there than anywhere. Professional, amateur, international. There have been hundreds of flash points. But two cops decide to lose their heads right here? It's too suspicious." The phrase comes to me. "It's a photo op. When Grandfather wants to sell more tickets to a show, he'll stage an event and stop traffic, literally. He's gone to the middle of an intersection and levitated one of his dancers right in the middle. He made sure to do it in front of the biggest paper in town so they could get a photographer there before the cops showed up."

"To avoid getting arrested?" asks Aileen.

"No. To make sure the photographers were there when the cops arrived. It turned a stunt into an *event*."

She responds to my weird family anecdote with a half smile. "Maybe. But there have been news crews everywhere. This could just be a very unfortunate event. Maybe Bogden didn't mean to fire? And Steadman panicked?"

As a fellow cop, I understand her need to rationalize what happened. It's scary to think two of our own could do something so awful.

"Maybe they were forced to," I offer.

"When we find them, they can tell us." There's a sense of resolve in her voice, implying there better be a solid explanation. If not, the backlash from the police might be even worse than the one from the public.

I'd been thinking that over. "Aileen, I think he and Steadman are dead."

"Dead?" She repeats the word, making sure she didn't mishear me.

"Assuming this is all staged, an attempt to manipulate the public, the Red Chain doesn't want them talking. It could ruin everything. I think that's why we haven't found them."

She stares at my face, trying to decide how seriously to take my allegation. It's a lot to absorb. I've asked her to make a number of leaps, and now I'm telling her that her fellow cops have been killed.

After some consideration, she asks, "So, was Tia a plant?"

I hadn't thought about that. "I think she was just a victim of opportunity. Young, female," I hesitate before adding, "white."

"I couldn't imagine a better victim," Aileen replies.

"It's got the suburbs up in arms. People who dismiss minority shootings are looking at this differently." Tia really is the ideal victim. Aileen may be on to something about Tia being chosen beforehand, or involved with the Red Chain. I make a note to tell Ailes to have that looked into. I've seen bad guys maneuver their victims into position before. This wouldn't be a first.

We move away from the White House and cross Lafayette Square. The grounds are filled with tents and lawn chairs, as though this were a folk music festival. On Andrew Jackson's statue, someone has scrawled in red paint: HE KILLED AMERICANS TOO.

"Yikes," mutters Aileen. "First he loses the twenty, now this."

My mind is elsewhere. "Do you think you could get us into Bogden or Steadman's homes? Did they live alone?"

"Both were single. But maybe. Why?"

"I don't know. There might be something there." If they were approached by the Red Chain, some kind of physical evidence tying them together could be crucial to making the case.

"Their places have been searched since they disappeared."

"I know. But it might be something unconventional." I recount how the box in Devon's attic led to the underground command center.

Her mouth is open, but she's speechless as I describe the spaceship-like room. "Holy crap. That's just plain insane!"

"Government accounting," I reply.

She gives me a hesitant look, as if she wants to say something, then clearly decides not to.

I think I sense what she wanted to ask. "No, I don't think this is some kind of government plot. Not an intentional one at least. It appears as if the people that funded the CCA decided it was a bad idea. My guess is the contractor wanted to keep it going."

Aileen taps me on the elbow. I turn to the side and see two men following us. Both white and scruffy, they're wearing patched jackets and appear like they're here for trouble.

We veer to the right and cross the street. The two men keep pace, but don't stare at us directly. Their eyes are on the crowd.

"Shit," Aileen whispers. "This could get ugly."

I can feel my stitches start to itch from all the walking. This is all I need.

A woman wearing a half coat, her messy brown hair sticking out from under a knitted cap, sneaks up on my other side. Short, she barely reaches my shoulder. I wait for the glimmer of metal, ready to draw. I see Aileen in the corner of my eye, ready to back me up.

"Are you lost, Agent?" the woman asks in a hushed tone, taking me by surprise. "Tell Detective Lewis to stand down. We're on the same side."

"Are we?" I reply. I'm not taking any chances. There's something familiar about her, maybe her cheekbones, but I'm not taking any chances.

"Dr. Ailes told me to tell you: eight zero eight."

Eight zero eight is a simple code Ailes and I came up with. It's the number on every ace of spades and the joker in a deck of Bicycle playing cards. Ailes wouldn't give that up, even under torture.

On hearing the woman say this, I relax slightly. "Okay. What can I do for you?"

"Follow me, while the men to your left track your tail," she says, indicating that the two degenerates who have been following us are actually on her side, and presumably ours.

"Tail?" I avoid looking over my shoulder. *Crap.* I can't be getting this sloppy.

"Yep." She heads across the park and through the crowd, not checking to see if we are following her, but confident we will.

WE REACH A row of brownstone townhouses. Some of the windows are broken. Others have boards or shutters over them, protecting them from rocks and other projectiles.

A man is leaning on a railing next to a flight of stairs that leads to a basement apartment. Unshaven, in a long coat, and smelling like alcohol, he resembles any number of faceless bums you walk past in a day. As we pass him, I spot a small earpiece in his ear and realize he's keeping guard.

Aileen follows me down the steps. Someone opens the metal door from inside and lets us through. Our escort turns to me once the door is shut. Although she's shorter than I am, she has a fierce expression.

"Alright, genius, care to tell me what you're doing out here?"

"Paying my respects."

I'd told Ailes I was going to meet Aileen. I didn't tell him where, specifically. He'd have gone through the roof.

"Uh-huh," she says, calling bullshit. "You know there's a bounty on uniformed cops out there."

"Good thing I gave up my dress blues years ago."

She turns to Aileen. "Does your captain know you're out here?"

"Do you know you're rude?" Aileen then looks at me. "Why are we standing for this?"

I finally remember where I know this woman from. My visit with the first lady. She had been carrying file folders and kept to the background. I also think she had short blond hair then. "Because she's White House Secret Service."

"Well, she's on the wrong side of the fence," Aileen replies, not having it. She doesn't appreciate the little power trip this woman is on.

"My job is to keep things on the outside of there. Right now that's difficult enough. Having two potential hostages traipsing through isn't making my day any easier."

"Hostages?" I ask.

"Or victims," she says sharply. "Your guess is as good as mine. What I know is that you were being followed by at least three people. They were very interested in you."

Yeah, stupid, I know. I suddenly realize this could be a lead. "Do you have photos?" I ask excitedly. "And what's your name, by the way?"

"Marisa Vachon, and we're looking into it. In the meantime, why are you here?"

"Like I said, Tia Connelly."

"Yes, and . . . ?" She knows there's more to it.

I exchange a glance with Aileen. She shrugs.

"I think the murder was a setup. There's something fishy."

"The Red Chain?" Vachon asks.

I'm surprised, but I don't reply. The Secret Service keeps track of any potential threat that comes to their attention. As they monitor what's happening outside the White House fence, they're probably running down every lead.

"I've been following your reports," she says. Then she adds, "It's a bit sketchy."

"So I've been told." But not too sketchy to catch their attention.

"But it would make sense." She nods.

"It would?" I wasn't expecting her to say this.

"We've been seeing some very coordinated activity. Unlike in any other protest we've ever covered. There are at least a dozen people out there arranging things, organizing sign-ups, and keeping watch on who enters the area. We haven't traced them to any foreign intelligence agency. So far we haven't even been able to get an ID on any. We're hoping to get fingerprints. But as you can imagine, we can't just pull them in off the street."

"That didn't stop you from grabbing us," Aileen replies. She's still trying to assess Vachon.

Vachon turns to her. "I think there was a credible threat to Agent Blackwood. Seriously, it's dangerous for you to be out here." She's scolding us like we're a couple of high school kids caught in the park after midnight.

I'm not in the mood for a lecture. If the Secret Service is aware of this threat, they're still not doing enough. Turf wars aren't going to help.

"Why don't you put your badge on your chest and we take a walk outside and see who's the first one to get assaulted? Right now, we're all targets."

"Some of us are special targets." She glances down at my side. "I heard you had an encounter already."

"How is trapping us in a basement in the middle of DC going to help?" asks Aileen. She points to the door. "Whoever was following us could be waiting for us to leave your little clubhouse."

"Trapped?" snaps Vachon. "I pulled you in here to get you *out* of here."

"Well, unless you got some Harry Potter shit up your sleeve," Aileen replies, "I don't see how you're going to manage that one."

Vachon smiles at me. "It turns out I'm not the only one here who knows a trick or two."

CHAPTER THIRTY-ONE

WORMHOLE

MARISA VACHON'S TRICK was an impressive one. If our pursuers had the benefit of a bird's-eye view, they would have seen us enter that brownstone just down the street from Lafayette Square and never emerge.

Her method was behind a secure door in the basement. On the other side stood two marines and a golf cart at the entrance of a narrow underground corridor that stretched for several blocks. Vachon turned toward L Street before we got to see how far it actually goes.

The White House tunnel leading to the Federal Reserve is a well-known piece of history. It was excavated during World War II so President Roosevelt could be wheeled to his bedroom inside a vault. It was the safest place in the city for him to wait out a theoretical Nazi bombing raid.

In the years since, the White House has dug deeper basements and created a labyrinth of tunnels below the city. I briefly dated a software consultant who once showed me an infrared map of DC.

You could see the well-known tunnels leading from the White House to the Federal Reserve and the Capitol Building, but there were also several others leading off in various directions, including what looked like a small subway line straight to Andrews air force base.

If it sounds like an extravagant effort, it's important to remember that this is the federal government we're talking about, where a few billion dollars can represent a rounding error on a defense appropriations bill.

"I guess this makes getting to work a little easier," I joke as Vachon takes the corner.

"That would not only be a firing offense, it's probably also a federal crime," she replies, with a small sigh. "I'm sure the Russian and Chinese have maps of these tunnels, so keeping it a secret is really just a bureaucratic formality. You guys get a free pass, given the circumstances."

As we drive down the tunnel I see basement entrances to other buildings at intersections that follow the street map above.

"How do they keep landlords from digging through their basements and into here?" I ask.

"We're under the sewage lines, mostly."

"Well, that makes sense," says Aileen, under her breath.

"I heard that," Vachon shoots back. "Sometimes we need to move the president and other officials around more securely than we can on city streets. We've expanded on the tunnels recently given changes in technology. It's the cost of living in an age when, for under a thousand bucks, you can buy a remote control drone that could deliver a half pound of C4 faster than you shout, 'Get down.'"

I've had my own run-ins with bad guys using the devices. It's scary to think we're only just scratching the surface of what can be done with technology. The future is frightening.

"You guys can jam those kind of things?" Aileen asks.

"We have countermeasures . . ." She doesn't elaborate as she brings the cart to a stop in front of a metal door. "Here we go."

I stay put. "Are you going to level with us?" I ask flatly.

Clearly the Secret Service has its own intelligence about the Red Chain and what's been going on. I'm getting a little sick of the interdepartmental territorialism. Vachon doesn't seem like the type to tolerate it either. I get the sense she's trying to level with us, but doesn't know how, or is under pressure not to.

Aileen gives me a confused look.

"I'm sorry?" Vachon acts genuinely bewildered.

I gesture to the corridor. "Why expose all this to us?"

"I'm sure you can be trusted with a secret."

"Of course. But there were other ways to get us out of there."

Vachon fiddles with the keys on her chain. "Speed is critical."

"What's going on? Is there something we need to know?"

She nods toward the street above. "We think things are going to blow up pretty badly out there. We're about to have several platoons of marines stationed in the tunnels ready to protect federal buildings at all costs."

"What's changed?" asks Aileen.

Vachon weighs something in her head for a moment. "I can't say, but could either of you pull the radio transcripts for Capitol Police?"

"We have overlap. I could," Aileen responds. "What do you need?"

"I don't need anything. I just don't want to be telling tales out of school. It's going to leak any moment, and that's what we're preparing for."

"What?" I implore. She's testing my patience.

"Bogden and Steadman, the two officers involved in the shooting? One hour before it happened, they were dispatched to meet with Senator Friedkin. He's the head of the domestic surveillance appropriations committee. That was the black-budget committee the public only found out about a few months ago."

That caused yet another public privacy outrage, because this was the group that voted in secret on how much to spend tapping our phones and reading our Facebook posts.

"If you were into conspiracy theories and wanted a bogeyman, Friedkin would be it," Vachon says. "Obviously, it's just a coincidence. But that's not the way the less stable people are going to see it. They *want* to believe the shooting was a planned government plot. You've seen the news. It's one thing when we have two random cops acting out of line. It's another when they were allegedly just with the one man who oversees the NSA and CIA's secret budgets beforehand. The one guy who could lead a coup."

"You sound like one of the protestors," I reply.

"I have to understand how they think. I have to be even more paranoid than they are."

"What do you mean when you say they met with him?" Aileen asks.

"Capitol Police provide a protected escort, in between reinforcing White House Police and Metro at federal buildings. They were sent to get him out of the Capitol."

"He's still here?" I ask, surprised that someone this high up would still be in the city after the protests.

Vachon shakes her head. "No. It was a scheduling screwup. An old appointment on his calendar. Apparently Bogden and Steadman never actually met him. But the conspiracy theorists won't see it that way. They'll spin them as his own hit squad or something equally ludicrous."

"But the radio transcript has them meeting with him?" I ask.

"Yes. Their badge numbers are called out and told to go to

that address to pick him up. They use a code for Friedkin, of course. But it's a thinly held secret. The media is already suing for the transcripts. It's only a matter of time. Like I said, things are going to get real ugly. That's why I need you ladies out of here."

"What address?" I ask.

"For what?" Vachon holds open the door.

"What address were they sent to? Is it in or out of the protest zone?"

"Outside. Why?"

I turn to Aileen. "Because we're going there." I can tell she's with me on this.

Vachon groans. "Whatever you two do away from the White House is your business. But it's not safe anywhere near here. Especially for you." She looks right at me. "There are people out to get you."

"It's not safe for anyone. And has anyone looked into the pickup request? Doesn't that sound weird?"

Too many coincidences are piling up. A pattern is emerging. Vachon and everyone else's problem is that they're too cautious to call it what it is—a conspiracy.

"People kind of have their hands full. Besides, it was a non-event. Unless you think Friedkin really was there." She considers us for a moment. "It's on Ninth near the Convention Center."

"I don't think he was there," I reply. "But the call is suspicious. And right now, we shouldn't let anything like that go by us without looking into it."

We haven't been able to crack the Red Chain yet, and I'm desperate for anything that could tie it to the protests. The Friedkin connection could be something.

We follow Vachon up a flight of stairs and through another

door to emerge into the back of a post office on L Street. She walks us to a side exit.

"Don't do anything stupid."

"Too late for that," says Aileen. She glances at me. "We're full of stupid. No point changing now."

CHAPTER THIRTY-TWO

LINE OF SIGHT

BOGDEN AND STEADMAN were supposed to pick Friedkin up at a brick building next to a dry cleaner and a print shop. The businesses are all closed in the event that the protest expands even farther outward.

A front doorway leads up a flight of stairs to two offices. One belongs to Friedkin's accountant, the other to an attorney. Both of them cleared out of the city when the protests started getting violent.

Aileen called the building superintendent and got permission for us to take a look at the common areas. He offered to bring us a key, but I told her to decline once I saw the lock. A simple tumbler, I have it open in five seconds. Aileen, still on the phone, scowls at me like I'm a delinquent teenager. I take notice of the fact it wouldn't have been difficult for someone less skilled than me to trip the latch with a piece of thin plastic.

As she finishes up on the phone running down some leads, I stand in the doorway and think things over. Assuming the dispatch was intentional but they never met Friedkin, what was the purpose?

Did they meet with someone else here? Were they threatened? I've seen something like that happen before. But Bogden and Steadman were single and childless, and not the kinds of guys who would easily be threatened.

Were they blackmailed? Did the Red Chain have something on them?

Aileen puts her phone away. "The dispatcher said the call to pick up Friedkin was booked several days prior. There's no information besides that. Friedkin has three secretaries. One of them says she could have made the request."

"'Could have'? That doesn't sound too sure."

She shrugs. "They make a hundred calls a day."

"Still." I walk up the flight of stairs to the accountant's office. "It seems like a clever way to pull two cops from a war zone."

Aileen steps into the hallway and scans the names on the directory. "And do what? Ask them to commit murder?"

"I know. I know." I take a seat on the top of the stairs and stare down at her.

"What would make you shoot at an unarmed protestor?" she asks, trying to put herself in Bogden and Steadman's shoes.

I can't think of a single reason. But I'm sure we all have our limits. "I couldn't even take the shot when that crazy bitch was about to kill the infant . . . I don't know."

"Me neither. I keep telling myself the gun went off accidentally and Steadman was just reacting to that."

"But why did Bogden point it right at her face?" I ask, more to myself.

"I know. I know," Aileen says, echoing my thoughts.

I survey the small hallway and the staircase. "Did they meet with anyone after they were here?"

"Not that we know of. After here, they were called to the White House perimeter. It was really chaotic. They had to back up White House uniformed police."

"So they were in riot gear already?" I'm trying to imagine what the hour before the incident was like for them.

"Probably. Lots of us are reporting straight from home to the front lines. We're stretched thin."

Until they left, Bogden and Steadman were considered fine upstanding law enforcement officers working for Metro Police, skilled enough to assist other Washington, DC, law enforcement agencies on special details. Nothing about them raises a red flag until the shooting. After that, they both go on the run—almost as if they'd planned an exit strategy.

Why? What did they stand to gain? If they were coerced, then fleeing would be the dumbest thing they could do. The only alternative, assuming premeditation, is that they were bribed, but even then I can't imagine a price high enough to persuade someone to commit a public killing like that. Especially if they are police offers with everything to lose.

On my phone, I pull up the image of Bogden in riot gear, pointing his gun at Tia. She's ten feet away, but the angle and focal range make them seem much closer. In all the photos, he looks cool and dispassionate behind his face shield. Headlines describe him as "unemotional" and a "monster."

"What do you have?" Aileen asks, noticing the expression on my own face.

Damn. We may have been looking at this the wrong way.

"Hold on a second." I lie flat on the top of the landing, facing down the stairs.

"Are you feeling okay?" She starts up the stairs.

"Yeah. One second. Back up a foot. Don't move." Behind Aileen's head I can see the street a foot beyond the sidewalk. "Come up here."

She stares at me, unsure if I've gone insane.

"Seriously, woman?" She shakes her head and joins me, giving me a skeptical glance as she lies down next to me.

"Indulge me." I pull out a laser pointer from my purse and hand it to her. "Aim this at my head," I tell her as I get up and go down the staircase.

She's humoring me like I'm a crazy person, but she shines the light right at me, as asked. "Better hope this is all I'm pointing at you."

I stand at the bottom of the stairs with the green dot on my forehead. "Just a little higher. Maybe over my head?"

Aileen raises the light. When I turn around, the green dot is roughly where I was looking at outside from the top of the stairs.

She lowers the laser. "You're not thinking . . . Seriously, what are you thinking?"

I think she knows where I'm leading her with this, but she doesn't want to say it out loud and look like the mad one.

"I don't know. Hold it up again?"

I step outside the entrance and search the street around the green dot. I move a stone to where the green laser dot lands. "Okay. Come down here."

Aileen descends and hands the laser pointer back to me. "I only see two problems with your theory."

"I didn't say I had a theory," I reply, examining the asphalt at our feet.

"Well, it doesn't take a genius to see where you're going. As I said, two problems. The first being that there are no bullet holes here. The second is if Bogden and Steadman were killed, then it'd be damn hard for them to have killed Tia too. Ghosts can't kill."

"But people impersonating them can."

"Impersonating?" she asks, surprised.

I pull out my phone and show her the image of Bogden right before he shoots Tia. You can make out his face, but sunglasses cover his eyes.

"Why do we think Bogden killed her?" I ask.

"Because it happened in plain sight."

"Let me play defense attorney for a moment. We have a man with his face obscured by sunglasses and a face shield. I can have a silicon prosthetic made that would look real in those conditions. In all the photos and video of the shooting, neither Bogden nor Steadman move their mouths. In fact, the press called them sociopaths because of their lack of expression. What if they really couldn't?"

"Are you saying they were impersonated?"

"You know why everyone thinks they did it? *Because the Capitol Police think they did it.* Bogden and Steadman show up for duty, go on a fool's errand, and the next time they're seen, an hour later, they murder a girl in public and vanish under the noses of the Capitol Police. Why couldn't they find them?"

"It was chaotic."

"Maybe so. But I think it's time we start asking if that's really Bogden. Were any of the men on the line friends of theirs? Did they talk to them?"

"I don't know." Aileen shakes her head. "But you still have your second problem." She points toward the ground. "If they were shot entering this building by someone at the top of the stairs, chances are there would be a bullet in the ground here. Now, I know it can be impossible to find one without a metal detector, especially in asphalt, but this surface is smooth. Real smooth."

"Yeah. I know how it sounds." I was hoping to find some kind of ballistic evidence. Rain would probably have wiped away any visible blood spray.

"It was a clever idea," she consoles me.

"Maybe too clever." Sometimes I make things more complicated than they need to be.

"I doubt they got rid of the bodies and the bullet holes at the same time . . ." Aileen trails off then glances at me sharply.

"Unless they did," I reply, the other piece of the puzzle falling in place.

Her eyes light up as she whips out her phone.

"Hey, Jackson, I need a favor."

FORTY MINUTES LATER, an older Metro cop who looks to be on the verge of retirement unlocks the gate and lets us into the police impound yard, which overlooks the Potomac River at the south end of the city. He leads us through rows of cars with his flashlight and fills us in.

"The van was stolen about a week ago. They found it yesterday in a parking garage near Union Station. Plates were gone. A quick field fingerprint inspection didn't find anything, but they only check the steering wheel and the door handles in a case like this." He stops at a blue cargo van. "Here we go."

It's about as anonymous looking as you could imagine. I inspect the side door with my light while Aileen has a look at the driver's seat. The Metro cop leans against a Cadillac and has a smoke.

If Bogden and Steadman were killed, the convenient thing would have been to have a van parked right near the building to haul them away. Immediately across from the entrance to the building would be best. That way, their murderers minimize the number of witnesses and are able to move the bodies quickly.

If that was the setup and they were shot with a high-powered rifle from the top of the stairs, the bullets would have gone straight through and into whatever was behind them. In this situation, the side of the van. Unfortunately for my theory, the exterior is intact.

So far, all I have is a stolen van. It was a little optimistic of me to think the first stolen vehicle we inspected would be the actual one we're looking for. I lean against the door and try to think of some other solution.

Aileen raps on the window from the inside, startling me.

"Hey genius, you know these things can move?" She points to the door.

I grab the handle and swing it open. Her flashlight is aimed at the floor. There are two distinct holes about a foot apart.

She taps a gloved finger next to one. "If the bullets aren't in the undercarriage, I'll bet you anything they ricocheted into the street outside of where we were looking."

I suppress a grin. It's good to be right, but being right also means that not only are two men dead, they've been wrongly maligned by the rest of the world.

To be sure, I inspect the holes in the van more closely, making sure they're not just rust stains. I know not to touch them. There could be flecks of blood we could match to Bogden and Steadman. If we can find their DNA in the van, then maybe people will start listening to me.

I give Aileen an approving nod. "Still think I'm crazy?"

"More than ever. Now I know it's contagious."

CHAPTER THIRTY-THREE

SNARE

AILEEN AND I are sitting in an SUV on a road near the industrial park where the CCA building is located. There's a highway a few hundred feet away and a line of trees off to the shoulder. The moon is hidden by clouds, so the only light is from the street lamps, which are stretched a little too thinly to provide full coverage. I keep a steady watch on the road ahead of us, as well as the rearview mirror.

Aileen taps her passenger window. "Did you know President Roosevelt used Al Capone's car to get around after he made his Pearl Harbor speech announcing we were at war? It was the only armored car the Secret Service could find."

"Really?" I reply.

"No." She shakes her head. "People say that. But it's an urban legend."

"That Capone had an armored car?" I ask.

"No. He had one. Three thousand pounds of armor. The man was paranoid."

"I can relate. I wouldn't mind having one for personal use. I imagine the gas mileage is rough, though."

"You ever thought about a different line of work?" Aileen asks.

"I like this work. Mostly." I keep telling myself this. "Why do you ask?"

She turns to me. "Well, it's not normal to have this many people want to kill you. You know that?"

"I've met some DEA agents at a survivor meeting I sometimes go to who'd say otherwise. I know some cops in Mexico who won't even let other members of their department know their faces. But yeah, I get your point. I never expected to be *this* in the thick of things. Marta, the woman behind the gang X-20, it was never really personal with her. I was just a badge that saw something. After we ID'd her, that was the end of it."

"You sure about that?" asks Aileen.

"No," I admit. "At the time, I was worried that the Warlock, I mean Heywood, was after me. His psycho buddy tried to push me out of an airplane."

"I heard. I read up on you."

Gerald interrupts us over the open radio. "Black Rabbit, we have a silver Prius coming your way. Out-of-state plates. We're running them now."

Aileen and I both tighten our grips on the guns in our laps.

Three hours ago, I had Gerald leave a message in Ezra Winter's Draft folder as bait for Bogden and Steadman's shooters, who we think are also the killers from the farmhouse. It's a long shot. But right now, we'll take any chance we can get. Even if it means using me as a prize.

The message said I was on a stakeout without backup. It's a gamble, but hopefully one they can't risk not taking. Our goal is to get them to make a move while we can still control things.

Aileen had insisted on sitting in the car with me. She said it'd be more realistic if I was on a two-person stakeout than if I was by myself. I feel horrible putting her in harm's way. It's a dumb plan, but we're shorthanded.

"It's clear," says Gerald.

Gerald is in another unmarked car hidden at the far end of the road. His job is to look for any cars with stolen plates, or that fit descriptions of recently stolen vehicles, and run them through a computer before they get to us. He's set up a license plate recognition camera to track everything that drives by. Nadine and Jennifer are at the opposite end of the road, doing the same. If they see a suspicious car, the plan is for them to intercept it before the suspects reach Aileen and me. We're here just for show. If the shooters are smart, and so far they have been, they'll try to spot us first, probably from the highway, and then decide if they're going to get closer.

"Yeah. I kind of pissed him off," I say, retracing our conversation back to the Warlock. "He didn't like me spoiling his game. When X-20 tried to kill me, he went out of his way to tell me it wasn't him."

"That was nice of him," she says drily.

"Yeah . . ." I think about the fact we haven't heard anything from him lately. I'd like to believe this is because the Texas prison he's in has him locked down good. But I know that's not true. If a Luddite like Ezra Winter can get messages through to the outside, Heywood shouldn't have a problem. It'd be easy for him to communicate without us or even his attorneys knowing. And it's not like it's hard to find a guard in those prisons who's willing to smuggle in a cell phone or carry out messages.

This is what's really frustrating to me. We work hard to lock the bad guys up, but all it takes to make our lives complicated is one crooked prison employee to poke a hole in security.

"So you don't think he's involved in this?" Aileen asks.

"I don't know. It'd mean I have one less person trying to kill me. But there's no connection between him and the Red Chain. What makes Heywood interesting is that as intelligent as he is he just doesn't have the charisma of a guy like Ezra Winter. Heywood had to pull off big spectacles because nobody would pay attention to him otherwise. He's smart, real smart, but he's really just a sociopathic nerd." I go back and forth on this argument every ten minutes in my head.

"Who wants to kill you." Aileen says sympathetically. She's trying to wrap her mind around all this. For her, being a cop is supposed to be a job you do, then go home. It doesn't follow her. For me, it's consumed my life.

I sigh. "Pretty much."

"Like I said, you ever think about a different line of work?"

"Think they'd let me be?" I ask, genuinely curious to hear her point of view.

"Maybe Heywood has it in for you for a different reason than revenge," she says.

"How's that?"

"I'm just a city detective, not a fancy-pants FBI agent, but even I know some killers are strategic. Like that X-20 bitch. Maybe Heywood just wants you off the chessboard? More a tactical than personal motive?"

I've heard the chessboard description used before. Back when I first went after the Warlock, he'd attempted to manipulate the media to draw attention to me so my superiors would pull me from the case. When that didn't work, and we caught him, he flatout tried to have me killed. I'm not sure what advantage he would gain by having me murdered now. He would still be in jail, and prosecutors don't need me to build their case.

"Well, he's in prison. Not sure what the point now would be. They don't really need me for a trial."

"I'm sure he doesn't plan on staying there," Aileen replies.

"We've got enough to tie him up in court for years on appeals."

"Maybe he's not looking for a legal solution. Either way, if I were him and I got out, I'd feel better knowing you weren't on my tail."

Aileen makes sense. I've thought this over a lot, but I've avoided expressing it because it makes things . . . complicated.

"Yeah, well we don't have much indication he has any personal pull outside of prison. Like I said, he'd love to be a cult leader, but he lacks the talent."

"Black sedan going fast!" Gerald shouts over the radio. "No plates!"

Aileen and I scoot lower in our seats and crane our necks to see behind us. The road is still empty.

"We're going to flash the blues," Gerald says. "Snare Two?"

"We're heading toward you!" says Nadine.

A half mile ahead, I spot the blue light on their dashboard as it flares on and they roar out of their hiding place. Behind us, the lights of the sedan race down the road. Farther back, Gerald and his pursuit cruiser give chase.

"They're not stopping!" he shouts.

The sedan quickly closes the distance between us. It's almost parallel. Aileen and I pull on the bulletproof helmets that go with the Kevlar we're wearing, and I draw my pistol.

All I can think about is how I don't want to shoot my gun in here. It'd be loud. Real loud.

But the sedan takes a slight turn to avoid us, and keeps going. Its windows are too dark for me to see through them.

It skids across the asphalt and heads straight on toward Nadine and Jennifer's pursuit car. At the last second, the driver swerves onto the easement and goes around them.

Gerald flies past. Nadine and Jennifer do a U-turn, and chase after them.

"Should we pursue?" Aileen asks.

I have a horrible feeling the sedan was a trick. Something inside me screams to get the car started and moving.

It's too late.

Before I can get the car in gear, a man dressed in all-black body armor runs from the bushes into the middle of the road aiming a high-powered machine gun at us. He tosses a smoke grenade under our car, and we're engulfed in darkness.

Then the shooting starts.

CHAPTER THIRTY-FOUR

SEIZURE

B ULLETS SHOOT THROUGH the windshield in a burst of automatic gunfire. Shards of glass rain down on Aileen and me, angrily striking our exposed faces like hail. The noise is deafening, like being inside a garbage can with a brick of firecrackers.

She and I exchange glances, hoping for a pause long enough to return fire. But the shots are unrelenting, and we're trapped. This was not the plan.

"Black Rabbit, are you under fire?" Gerald calls out.

"Affirmative!" I yell over the sound of bullets and breaking glass.

"Snare Two, we're going back to Black Rabbit!" Gerald shouts to Nadine and Jennifer.

"Roger. We've got a bailout!" says Nadine. "Pursuing on foot!"

"Mother Ship? Are you there?" Gerald asks.

"Affirmative," replies the pilot of the FBI chopper that is holding back from our location.

"Please assist Snare Two!"

"Roger that."

Christ. This is a fuckup.

Finally, the shooting stops as he reloads. I reach for the door handle, ready to bail out and create a distraction so Aileen can get away. She sees what I'm about to do and grabs my wrist, stopping me.

Two seconds later, he's shooting at us again. The bullets come from a different angle, through the side windows to hit the body of the car with a metal *ping*. The only reason we're still alive right now is that Aileen had a brainstorm in the police impound yard. The SUV we're in isn't standard police issue. It's one they seized from a drug dealer. The body is made of reinforced armor and the glass is bulletproof—up to a point. We're moments away from him figuring out our little survival trick, because the rounds are going to make their way through real quick as soon as he finds a weak spot, or gets a higher angle. If he's as smart as they've been so far, then Aileen and I are going to die.

Something hits the back of my neck as the gunfire stops, and I flinch.

Aileen doesn't.

The split second the glass in the back window starts to shatter, she pops up and fires her whole magazine through the now-open rear, then ducks back down to reload.

"You okay?" I yell.

"Far as I know!"

Shots continue to echo from outside the car, but they're not hitting us. She may have got him.

The rearview mirror sits on the center console, and I use it to see over the dashboard through the dissipating smoke. The man in black armor fires at me again, then staggers toward the blue lights of an oncoming police car. But before he can raise his rifle, he's struck at about fifty miles an hour. He slams into the hood with a *thunk*. As the cruiser skids to a halt, the shooter flies off the bumper and rolls across the highway like a discarded toy.

"God*damn*," Aileen says, peering out of the window.

"It's the fall that gets you," I reply.

"Our suspect just got onto a motorcycle and is heading westbound on the highway," Nadine calls into the radio.

"Mother Ship is in pursuit. Did you say westbound?" asks the pilot.

Crap. They already lost the other man.

I open the door and crouch low. Gerald has swung his car around, aiming his headlights at the crumpled man on the ground. I have my gun pointed at the body, but I'm keeping my eyes open for a third shooter. Anything is possible at this point. Another police escort rolls to a stop exactly where the man had stood a few seconds ago. Gun held tightly in my hands, I approach. His rifle lies in the grass.

"Stay back," Gerald says as he gets out.

It takes a moment to realize he's talking to me.

I hold up, and keep a paranoid watch on the trees as Aileen pulls the magazine from the machine gun and clears the chamber.

The man on the ground twitches.

"Face down!" Gerald screams.

The man moves his arm weakly.

Gerald closes the distance between them and aims his gun at the man's face. With his left hand, he rolls the man onto his stomach. The police officer from the other car runs over to keep the man covered as Gerald pulls a pistol free and searches him for other weapons. He then cuffs the man, and rolls him onto his back.

Normally you wouldn't touch somebody in a situation like this, but normally your accident victims haven't just fired a machine gun at an FBI agent, and don't have what look like grenades strapped to their chest.

"Ambulance is four minutes away," says the police officer.

Gerald pulls the shooter's helmet free and checks his pulse. "He might make it."

I run back over to the SUV and pull out the bandages I keep in my purse. It's become a habit of mine lately to have medical tape and gauze there, just in case.

Aileen managed to shoot the man in the neck. Gerald is pressing his hand on the wound to keep the man from bleeding out. There's another wound in his shoulder, which I grasp with my left hand. My gun is still in my right.

The man looks up at me. His eyes are glistening. A terrible wheezing is coming from his lungs. God knows what the impact did.

"Is this the man from the train?" Gerald asks.

I shake my head. "No."

The man coughs up a bubble of saliva and blood. I don't know if he'll make it to the hospital.

"Why are you trying to kill me?" I ask.

His face spasms.

"Why are you doing this?"

His eyes begin to focus, and he looks at me.

More coughing.

I don't ask him any more questions. I don't want his last breath to be a lie.

A paramedic steps in to take over. Gerald and I go to the side of the road to keep watch.

"The other man?" I ask.

"The helicopter lost track of him. Jennifer says they found another bike in the woods near the highway here."

"How did we miss that?"

"We were looking for parked cars. My mistake," he says, ashamed.

I put a hand on his shoulder. "Don't be stupid. You did great. If I hadn't listened to you and Aileen, I'd be dead right now."

I move away to give him some space and realize Aileen is standing by herself at the back of our SUV. She's staring at the ground, watching the paramedics work on the shooter as they get ready to put him on a stretcher. I know that feeling. I go over to her.

"You saved our lives," I tell her.

"Then how come I feel like shit?" Her eyes are welling up.

"Because you have a soul." I wrap my arm around her shoulders and squeeze. "You did real good. I froze. You didn't. You saved our lives. Between taking the shot and suggesting we use the tank, you're a heck of a cop."

I continue to hold her, never taking my eyes off the shooter.

"How do you get used to it?" she finally asks.

"You just do," I lie. "You just do."

As I pull away, I notice Gerald is looking at the man on the stretcher with the same expression as Aileen's. I don't know if I should hug him or high-five him because we got a bad guy. I'm not sure how men really feel about this kind of thing.

I'm not sure I do, either.

"I'm going with him to the hospital in case he makes complete sentences," Gerald says, straightening up.

"Are you okay?" I ask.

He shakes his head. "No. Hell no. But I'm just going to Blackwood through it and figure out my feelings later." He gives me a lopsided grin. "Could you, uh, call, my girlfriend and tell her everything is okay?"

"Sure." I think he's afraid he'll break down on the phone. *Blackwood through it?* What the heck?

Aileen turns to me. "Look at us." She wipes away at her eyes. "If only we were made of the same stuff as you."

Yeah, the same stuff I'm made of. Maybe the next time I can't get to sleep, or I take a shower just so I can tell myself I'm not crying, I'll give you guys a call and let you know what I'm really made of.

But I don't tell them this right now.

"You guys are going to be fine. We got our first bad guy. We're catching up." It's the best pep talk I can think of. No wonder I'm not a leader.

CHAPTER THIRTY-FIVE

WHITEBOARD

My HAND TREMBLES slightly as I try to hold the black marker. I tell myself it's the three cups of coffee I drank to wake myself up, and not my nerves. It was a long night. I got about two hours of sleep—technically, two hours of staring at the ceiling.

"Tell it to me real simple," Breyer says.

Ailes, Gerald, Nadine, and Jennifer are hovering toward the back of the room while Breyer and his aides sit at the bullpen table trying to make sense of what's happened. He knew about our honey-trap operation, and gave it the okay mainly because he doubted it would work. With one shooter in the hospital on life support and no agents injured, despite the bullet-ridden SUV Aileen and I had, the mission wasn't a *complete* failure. Although there's little chance we can use the same trick with Ezra Winter's Draft folder again.

I write *"Devon"* on one end of the whiteboard. At the other I write *"earthquake video,"* *"Bolivia dam sabotage,"* and *"White House shooting."* In the middle, I draw a circle.

I take a breath and remember to speak slowly. It's the best way to hide how agitated you are. I think part of the reason Gerald and the others think I'm so calm and aloof is because I've been dealing with stage fright since before I could walk. I've gotten real good at burying my true emotions.

"Three major events have led to the current crisis. We have no reason to believe Devon actually predicted the specifics of the DC earthquake. Regarding the loss of life in Bolivia, Jennifer makes a very strong case that this was an act of sabotage intended to coincide with a general Devon prediction."

"But Devon is dead," Breyer interjects.

I'm not sure how many of the reports we've been filing he's had a chance to read. I sense the purpose of this meeting is for us to tell him everything we've been telling him already.

"Yes," I reply. "But before he died, we think he recorded hundreds of hours of video making predictions."

"Why? Was this his hoax?"

Like a lot of people in the bureau, Breyer tends to think like an accountant. He has difficulty seeing beyond the spreadsheet and into the real world, where people are more than numbers in a report.

"I don't know his intentions. I suspect it may not have been a hoax on his part. Think of Siri on your iPhone. She's just a collection of words and phrases said by a real woman. You can use her voice to say anything. In Devon's case, he may have been trying to cover every situation for some kind of computer program he hoped one day could really predict these events. Something that could live on after him.

"What we think ended up happening is someone got hold of those videos, maybe the person who helped him make them, and decided they could be put to use in another way. Instead of predicting the future, they could be used to influence it."

"Self-fulfilling prophecies," he says, surprising me with how quickly he gets it. "Propaganda in a way. Like Soviet newspapers."

"Essentially. What's really important is the 'who' and the 'what.' Who is behind this and what are they up to? The who is a group known as the Red Chain, which we believe is being controlled from behind bars by Ezra Winter. The what is some kind of civil collapse. They're trying to scare us into an apocalypse and aren't afraid to nudge us."

"Why? What's their goal?" Again, he's a practical man looking for practical answers.

"What's the point of jihad, or of Seventh-day Adventists knocking on your door? Their reasons are tied up in their belief system."

I write *"Red Chain"* in the circle. "We haven't tied them to video uploads or the Bolivian dam breech yet. But we have strong reason to think they were anticipating the riots, and had a plan in place to capitalize on them. Forging a pickup in the Capitol Police calendar and impersonating officers aren't things they thought of last minute. Either they're the ones behind the release of the videos, or they're in contact with the people who are."

Breyer studies the board, as if there's some hidden truth to be found there. "And you think this all circles back to Ezra Winter?"

"We caught one of the two potential shooters last night when we used Winter's e-mail account to send a message to them. The man we took to the hospital was wearing a red chain, like the one around the neck of the woman who attacked me. We've ID'd him as Karl Gunther."

A video screen next to the whiteboard displays a Colorado license plate and hospital photo of Gunther.

Gerald holds up his finger to get my attention.

"Yes?" I reply.

He gestures with his phone. "We just got a preliminary forensics report. Gunther's boots match the prints found at the murder scene of the Jane Doe that attacked you, and the ones from the farmhouse."

That's some relief. The sickening fear that this was all a goose chase on my behalf abates a little.

"Well, there you go," I say to Breyer. "That settles the question. These men have been in the DC area for some time."

"Waiting for the earthquake?" he asks. He's still hung up on the prediction part.

If my grandfather stands onstage and asks if there is an "Angela" in the audience, that woman would go home telling her friends he had no idea she was going to be there that night. She was right. He didn't. He just knew that in an audience of a given size, there'd be someone there with that name. When someone else's name is called, it's a coincidence. When it's yours, it's a miracle.

Breyer is still trying to look at this from the wrong angle.

"No," I explain. "Waiting for something. Anything to happen. I was assaulted by three people in Boston. I'd assume there are at least three more in New York. Maybe in a few other capitals. At some point, something is going to happen for them to exploit. Ideally, something natural, like an earthquake."

"But you haven't proven they were the actual shooters at the White House," Breyer points out.

He's not challenging me as much as hoping I'm going to put something else on the whiteboard that will clarify everything. I wish it were so easy.

"No. We're looking into the van for forensic evidence. Gunther's build matches Steadman's real close. But the mere existence of the van where Bogden and Steadman were seen prior to the shooting is proof enough for me."

"Not for court," says Breyer.

I'm taken aback by his answer. Court? Are we even on the

same planet? People are threatening to storm the White House over all this.

"Assistant Director, right now our primary goal isn't to build a legal case. It's stopping them from whatever they have planned next. I can stop and build a legal case against Gunther, but that leaves his accomplice out there and the rest of the Red Chain."

Breyer thinks this over for a moment, assessing the larger picture. "Yes, of course. Understood. What do you need?"

Just as his court comment caught me off guard, I'm surprised by this question. I was expecting pushback. I'm not prepared to answer this intelligently, so I start talking and let my mouth catch up.

"We need to go public with the Red Chain. We need to announce them as persons of interest and ask anyone who knows anything to step forward."

"Such as?"

"Former cult members. Neighbors. We run Gunther's photo everywhere we can," I reply.

"Oh nuts," Nadine blurts out as she looks up from her phone.

"What?" I ask.

"It'll wait," she says, realizing everyone is staring at her.

Breyer goes into a huddle with his aides, so I walk over to Nadine. "Tell me now."

She hesitantly hands me her phone.

Ugh. It's a headline from a tabloid news site:

BREAKING!!! FBI'S WITCH STRIKES AGAIN:
BLACKWOOD TAKES DOWN ROGUE DC COPS

Unnamed sources in the FBI are saying that Agent Jessica Blackwood shot and killed the two Capitol Police officers implicated in the killing of Tia Connelly.

There are so many things wrong with this I don't know where to begin. We've tried to keep the whole situation out of the press. I grab Nadine's phone and go over to Breyer.

"What's this about?" I ask him.

He groans. "Ask your boss."

"Dr. Ailes?" I give him an incredulous look.

"I was going to tell you after the briefing."

Confused, I point to the screen. "You did this?"

"The press got wind of something. They knew you were involved."

"But this isn't even true!" I growl. "We got one of the shooters and that was thanks to Aileen and Gerald's quick thinking. We could at least have said as much."

Ailes shakes his head. "No. We couldn't. Not to the same effect. Right now nobody trusts us or any other agency. We're all part of the same government that killed the girl."

"Then tell them we found the real killer!" I protest.

"They wouldn't buy it. They'd think it was another conspiracy to cover it up."

"It's the truth."

He sighs. "Nobody is interested in the truth right now."

"But it says I killed another cop. I didn't even fire my gun!"

"I know. We have to walk the public through this slowly. In a few hours we're going to deny Steadman and Bogden were shot or captured." He nods to Gunther's photo. "We're going to release that image and ask for information about him as a person of interest in Tia's killing."

"And tell them he's the one who did it?" I ask.

He has a pained look on his face. "No. We have to let the talking heads in the media reach that conclusion first. If we go out and say he did it, we'll just be accused of using him as a patsy. We have to make the case this is a conspiracy by getting the press to connect the dots."

It's so manipulative. I remember being disgusted by what I saw in the Citizens Communication Agency control room. This doesn't feel any different.

Ailes is seeing the bigger picture. I get that. But right now, I just feel like a number in one of his equations.

"Why me?" It's a pathetic question. I'd never wish this on any of my coworkers, but I hate the attention.

"Isn't it obvious by now?" Breyer answers, overhearing the conversation.

"Isn't what obvious?"

"Blackwood, nobody believes the government. We have marines on the White House lawn preparing for an invasion. Congress has been recalled. People are throwing Molotov cocktails at street cops. We're at the edge of anarchy."

"And your point?" I demand.

"People want leaders. That's why they're paying attention to Devon's videos. They want someone above it all. Someone who isn't tainted by government or power. You're probably the most famous active-duty law enforcement officer there is. Right now people are cheering at the idea that a heroic FBI agent killed the bad cops."

"But I didn't and it's a lie." I think of the families of the police officers. I can only imagine what they're going through.

"A useful lie. For the moment they see us, at least you, as the good guys."

I try to respond as calmly as I can. "I think you two are overestimating how much you can control the message."

"Maybe so," says Breyer. "But I know if that crowd climbs the fence and makes it to the White House lawn and we start shooting unarmed citizens, it won't much matter."

The marker makes a cracking sound as I snap it in my fist. Ink spills on my hand. I walk over to the sink and wet a paper towel to wipe it off.

Breyer keeps talking, ignoring my Hulk-out. "In twenty-four hours the story will change. Just endure it for the moment. In the meantime, tell me what you need."

I take a deep breath as I face away from the room and scrub away the ink. I calm down slightly.

"We need to catch them. All of them. This doesn't end with them trying to incite people to riot. We have to treat this like we have several dozen enemy saboteurs inside our country. This isn't a criminal gang. This is terrorism, and the clock is ticking."

I dry off with a paper towel and then survey the people in the room, not sure I really want to take this where it's about to go.

"I want you to imagine this is September tenth, two thousand and one. Knowing what you know now, what wouldn't you do to stop this?"

Ailes and Breyer are both staring at me.

My words catch up with me. Crap.

I just made their argument for using me.

CHAPTER THIRTY-SIX

SERIAL

NADINE FINDS ME in a side room we use for private conferences, hunched over my laptop going through the forensic data. My eyes are occupied by the images, but my mind is still stewing over how I've been used like a prop.

"Any word from Aileen?" she asks.

Although she's not assigned to our unit—Nadine isn't anywhere near dysfunctional enough for that—she works with us a lot and has a pretty good grasp of the dynamics at work. Ailes sometimes pairs us because we complement each other nicely. Okay, and her pleasant disposition makes up for my sometimes too blunt manner.

"She's home today because of the shooting. She offered to help us, though."

Aileen is a trooper. If she hadn't been there . . .

"She going to be okay?" Nadine takes a seat next to me at the table.

I think she's really asking about me. I close the lid of my laptop. "I'm sure she'll manage."

"I know you like to internalize stuff, but if you just need an ear," she offers.

"Internalize." I repeat the word a little too sharply. "I'm beginning to think that's how people who know how to communicate what they're feeling describe those who don't. I'd *externalize* if I knew what the hell I was thinking. The problem is I don't." I point toward the bullpen. "Right now, I want to strangle Ailes. He's like a . . . He's a role model to me, I guess. And now I feel used." I let out a sigh. "The fact is I would have made the same exact decision. It was the right move."

She touches my forearm. "Maybe that's why he went along with it. Just so you know, I think it's Chisholm's idea. I saw them talking together earlier."

"Really?" This takes me by surprise. Chisholm is the bureau's chief headshrinker and strategist in matters like this. "So why is Ailes taking the fall?"

"Guess he's just taking a dose of his own medicine. Maybe he believes in the end you'll trust him."

"Yeah, well, that can only go so far. What am I saying? I'm being selfish." I notice the folder in her hands. "What have you got?"

"When we ID'd Gunther I started making some calls in Colorado about our Jane Doe. The Colorado Bureau of Investigation and a few other places."

"Anything?" I ask.

"Not from them. Then I took a different tack. I called a cult information center and asked if they ever deal with missing persons."

That was smart. "And?" My eyes are scorching the folder.

"I got our Jane Doe." Nadine slides out a missing persons' flyer. "Heather Dryl. She was a community college student in

Grand Junction. One day she just stopped talking with her parents. The police couldn't do much because it was clear she'd moved out and broken contact. Her parents said they heard reports there had been some men around campus with an environmental group that sounds a lot like the Red Chain."

"How long ago?" I take the missing person file from the folder.

"Eighteen months ago."

I study the photo. Oddly, I don't have the gut reaction I expected. Heather looks so different. She's smiling. Her features are as I remember them, but her expression isn't anything like that of the woman who showed up on my doorstep threatening to kill a child she'd kidnapped from a hospital. What the hell happened to her? *Who* happened to her?

"This is great work, Nadine."

She gives me a small smile of acknowledgment. "Ready for more?"

"What else you got?"

She hands me a copy of a driver's license for an Amelia Hamilton. The name is different, but the face is Heather's.

"What's up with this?" I say as I examine the image.

"Amelia Hamilton was pulled over for an expired tag near Denver. She was driving a car registered to Heather Dryl. Nobody caught it at the time."

"Fake license?"

"Nope. It's in the Colorado DMV database."

That's strange. "So what happened to Amelia Hamilton?"

"I don't know. The Social Security number belonged to someone else. She doesn't exist."

"Interesting," I reply. It also makes things more complicated. "It's safe to assume all of the Red Chain members are going to have fake identities."

"They've been planning this for a while," says Nadine, gravely.

My phone rings, showing an unfamiliar number. "One second . . . Hello?"

"Good thing I never believe anything I read in the papers," Damian says on the other end of the line.

"No kidding. Did you call for comment?" I mouth to Nadine: "Damian Knight."

"Just use the speakerphone, for heavens' sake," Damian replies. I press a button so Nadine can hear him. "I've been looking into the people you met on the train."

"And?" I'm afraid to ask. The last time Damian encountered people who wanted me dead, it didn't turn out so well for them. Soldiers in the Mexican army, who were also members of Marta's cartel, had tracked me down to a little market in Mexico. While I did a pretty good job of fending them off, at some point during their long siege, a Good Samaritan separated their heads from their necks. While it looked like the work of a rival gang, I'm pretty sure my dark guardian angel was somehow involved.

"I found an apartment near Boston College," Damian explains. "Three people had been living there. Lots of candles, and a few books that would make the Unabomber's reading list look as conservative as Richard Nixon's. Sound familiar?"

"You said 'had'?" I pray he didn't do anything . . . proactive.

"Unfortunately, they seemed to have skipped town. No trace of where they went."

"Can you give me the address?" I ask.

"I'll text it to you."

I forward the address to Nadine's phone and ask her to send the Boston FBI office to check it out. Damian is thorough, but there is a chance they might find something. She leaves me alone on the call to run down that lead.

"Thank you, Damian. We finally got them to see the Red Chain as a real threat around here."

"Better late than never. Any progress?"

"We identified the crazy woman who showed up on my doorstep. Amelia Hamilton, aka Heather Dryl. Turns out she was using a fake ID."

"Not too surprising," he replies.

"It's not much of a lead, yet."

"I hear someone was shot last night?"

Other than the tabloid leak about Bogden and Steadmen, we've kept our efforts out of the news. Not difficult, given the other crisis. "Yes. A member of the Red Chain."

"Does he have a fake driver's license?" asks Damian.

I pull up the file. "Karl Gunther. We've got other information on him. He's actually got a prior arrest for a DUI. I'm pretty sure he's a real person."

"That's not what I asked. Does Gunther have a fake driver's license too?"

"Probably. I guess. Maybe?" It would make sense and wouldn't come as a surprise—unless Damian is going in a different direction.

"Can you find out?" he asks.

"It might take a while. Colorado doesn't use facial recognition software in their driver's license database."

"Fine. Hold on." I hear Damian typing. I don't know what he does when he's not making my life complicated. Besides access to large amounts of money he acquired, god knows how, he has a very deep knowledge of computing.

Nadine steps back into the room and sits down. A minute later, a text message pops up on my phone with a photo of a driver's license. It's Gunther's face, but a different name, Jason Chulick. "How the hell?"

"Long story short," says Damian, "I looked up Gunther in the DMV records and pulled his photo. I then used *that* photo to search a different database of every misdemeanor arrest in Colorado. Chulick is the best match. I then went back and pulled his DMV license."

I show the image to Nadine. Her eyes widen.

"Well, that's a heck of a stunt," I reply. "It would have taken the FBI computer days to sort through. Now we have two aliases to look into. Thank you."

"That's not all you have." he replies in his familiar, playful tone.

"Pardon?"

"Poor girl, you must be tired. Look at Chulick's license number and then Hamilton's."

I compare them side by side. Nadine looks over my shoulder. Her mouth makes an *o* shape when she recognizes it too.

Son of a gun. Like many other states, Colorado driver's license numbers contain the date of issue and the order in which they were processed on that day.

Hamilton and Chulick were processed the same day. The license numbers are only twelve digits apart.

"They got their fake licenses on the same day."

"Exactly," says Damian. "And that means?"

Oh, crap. It hits me. I feel butterflies in my stomach. "The other members of the Red Chain probably did the same thing. Maybe all in the same batch."

"Thanks to the help of a corruptible DMV employee," he adds.

I poke my head out of the door and shout into the bullpen. "We need to pull a series of Colorado driver's licenses!"

"What do you got?" asks Ailes, looking up from his computer.

"Possibly photos of every member of the Red Chain!"

"Seriously?" Gerald's face breaks into a grin.

Nadine departs for the main records building to see what they can find. I retreat into the office. "Damian, I could—"

"I know."

Suddenly everything goes black, except for the glow of my phone. "What the—"

A few seconds later, the emergency lights flicker on.

"Black out?" Damian asks.

"Yeah." Hesitantly I ask, "Are you in the building?"

"No. I'm still in Boston."

"How did you know?"

"Because the power just went out here too."

Oh shit.

I can't even enjoy a lucky break for a second before everything hits the fan. Christ. "Damian, I think Black Fall has already started."

CHAPTER THIRTY-SEVEN

CODE

GERALD AND JENNIFER'S faces, illuminated by the ghoulish blue halo from their laptops, stare back at me from the dark. Only the emergency lights in the hallway, hooked to a battery backup, are on.

"I'll call you back," I tell Damian before hanging up. "What the hell happened?" I ask, stepping into the bullpen.

"Wi-Fi is down," Gerald says, looking up from his now-useless laptop.

"Hold on." Jennifer types into her phone faster than I can speak. "Outages all along the East Coast. Several in Europe too."

"So . . . the power grid has been compromised?" It's more of a genuine question than a rhetorical one. Gerald and Jennifer are far more technically inclined than I am.

"Maybe." Gerald follows Jennifer's lead and starts using his phone for information. "Ugh. Internet just went down on LTE."

"I thought we had backup power and our own Internet connection?" I ask.

"We do," Jennifer replies. "But not in this building. Obviously." She rolls her eyes in frustration, not at me, but at the situation. I've had to learn how to parse Jenniferese. She only expresses annoyance at situations, never people, although sometimes it can feel like she's directing it at you.

Our ancient building doesn't exactly have the latest in technology infrastructure. There are even parts of the bullpen where you can't get a cell phone signal.

Gerald stands up. "I'm going outside. We can probably get the campus Wi-Fi signal from the front of the building."

We regroup on the front steps. The buildings at this end of Quantico are completely dark. The main facility and the dorms glow in the evening fog, their emergency lights powered by a generator we can hear humming in the distance. Oddly, there's some comfort in knowing that I'm only a few hundred yards away from a working vending machine.

"Don't tell me my FBI agents are afraid of the dark," says Ailes, as he joins us.

"Life without Wi-Fi isn't worth living," remarks Jennifer.

"How bad is the situation?" Gerald asks.

If anyone knows what's going on, it's Ailes. "Officially, or unofficially?" he says.

"I didn't even know we had an official yet," Gerald replies.

"An hour ago, a solar observation satellite spotted a flare building up on the sun."

"This is because of a flare?" Jennifer seems skeptical.

"I said that's the official story," Ailes replies. "The flare is real. But this outage isn't because of that."

"We've been hacked," I state flatly.

"Yes. A well-coordinated, well-planned attack on the energy

grid. We haven't figured out how, yet. But I think we can guess who. The good news, if you can call it that, is that we've known for years this kind of thing could happen. It just required a player with enough malice and resources to pull it off. And it looks like we have that in the Red Chain."

"How exactly do you hack the power grid?" I ask.

"You look for a point of vulnerability," Jennifer explains. "Last year there were seventy-nine serious attempts on the US grid. Hackers in the Ukraine took down the national grid for six hours by targeting several points. There are hundreds of different systems involved in a power plant. You could start at the source, and make the generator think it's overheating so it shuts down. You could do it at the end point, and make the system think transformers have blown, cutting off power to a region. You could attack it from the middle and make it reroute power so it overloads. If you are sufficiently evil, you can get the grid to damage itself by burning out power conversion stations and blowing entire lines. Is that what we're looking at?"

"Maybe. We're getting reports of physical damage," says Ailes. "Simply restarting the system won't work. It could have been attacked at the root level. Something planned in advance."

"Stuxnet for power grids," says Gerald.

"That's the virus we used to shut down Iranian nuclear facilities?" I ask.

"Yeah. That was a worm designed to target a few points of failure. It spread from system to system and kept hiding. A power grid worm could hit hundreds of points of failure."

"And keep attacking us," Ailes adds solemnly. "That's the biggest fear right now. This kind of attack might be part of a series of assaults."

"What about the rest of the country?" I wonder if this is nationwide.

"Just the East Coast, right now. If I had to guess, they're waiting to one-two punch us with more."

"So this is pretty sophisticated?" Obviously, it is, but I'm trying to grasp the level.

"Yes," Ailes replies. "It'd be more than one hacker. Someone would have to have some high-level understanding of how the grid works. It's a team project."

This doesn't quite make sense to me. "And up until now, the Red Chain has been pretty antitechnology? That's what has me curious. We know Devon embraced it. And we know they were somehow in collusion with Devon, or at least with someone who knew him. Which brings us back to the CCA project. The people behind that had no problem with computers, and what's happening now sounds exactly like the kind of thing they'd want to be capable of pulling off."

Ailes takes a seat on the steps next to me. "Unfortunately, the CCA project is something even I can't get information about. It was a deep, deep black project."

There has to be something for us to find. Some lead. Heck, I found out about the CCA from a mailing label in the attic of Devon's old house.

"Okay, I may sound stupid here, but we couldn't find much of anything in the CCA building, right? Just a prototype of their computer system?"

"It was standard hardware for that time period," says Gerald. "Some fancy cabinets and projection equipment, but it was all running on a VAX cluster."

"Yes, um, whatever that means. But the software? Who wrote that?"

"Government contractors. Probably the same people who write stuff for the NSA and CIA."

"But a company, right? This may sound very naive, but could we look at the source code itself?"

Gerald exchanges glances with Jennifer. "There might be something to that. Even if we can't find notation, certain scripting styles might imply specific contractors, maybe even actual programmers."

Jennifer mulls it over. "I can get a copy of the hard drive and make an emulator that should let us look more closely."

"Let's get on that," says Ailes. He turns to me. "You made any progress?"

"Me?" I think for a moment. The blackout made me forget everything that had just happened. "We got a lead on the Boston cell."

"Good. Good."

"Oh, and I think I have photos of at least seventy or so members of the Red Chain."

"Pardon me?" His voice raises in surprise.

"It was Damian's suggestion, really. Fake driver's licenses. We found a batch made at the same time as Gunther's and the Jane Doe, whom Nadine tracked down. We were in the process of contacting Colorado authorities and running a VICAP search when the outage happened. Nadine was going to the main computer center here to check up on that."

"I suggest you head over there too, and see what they can find. I'll call them and explain this is a priority."

As I start to leave, my phone rings with a DC number. "Hello?"

A frantic woman asks, "Is he dead?"

"Pardon me?" The voice is familiar, but I can't place it.

"Nobody will tell me! Is my husband dead?" she pleads.

All of a sudden I recognize her voice.

Oh, god.

The first lady is asking *me* if the president has been killed.

CHAPTER THIRTY-EIGHT

COMMANDER

O NE SECOND, MIRIAM." I press the Mute button on my phone. The words sound crazy as I hear myself say them aloud. "The first lady is asking me if her husband has been killed!"

Ailes matter-of-factly replies, "On it." Then he pulls his phone from his pocket.

I unmute the phone. "Miriam." I feel weird using her first name, but I need to calm her down. "What have you heard?"

Gerald furiously types away at his laptop, which he'd dragged out to the steps and connected to Wi-Fi. He pulls up a headline:

AP REPORT: PRESIDENT KENT KILLED IN EXPLOSION IN ATLANTA

"Are you still there?" asks Miriam.

"I'm here." I keep my voice calm and measured. She's border-line hysterical, understandably so. "This is the first we're hearing about it. What are they telling you?"

"Nobody knows anything," she says, frustrated. "I thought maybe . . . I don't know. I thought maybe you might know something."

She's asking me? The first lady of the United States is coming to *me* for answers? "Miriam, right now you shouldn't believe anything you hear. This group, the Red Chain, we think they hacked the power grid. We also have reason to believe they're spreading false stories in the media to ignite panic."

Of course, they've also been known to kill people in public.

"You mean he's alive?" She wants someone to tell her everything is alright.

"I don't know. It's just that right now, I wouldn't assume anything."

Ailes holds up a finger. I put Miriam on mute again.

"Atlanta is in a blackout. There were reports of Dumpster explosions on social media. We can't reach anybody there," he says.

"In Atlanta?" I ask.

"Downtown."

This is beginning to sound worse and worse. "Like a bomb strike?"

"One second." Ailes listens to his contact on the other end. "Got it." He hangs up to explain what he knows. "We can't contact the president's convoy directly because their radios are being jammed. Not just by one jammer, but by hundreds of small jammers that all turned on at the same time as the explosions. Normally, they'd take him to a secure location or helicopter him out, but the explosions were all outside the Secret Service security corridor and they have the president boxed in. Because of the jammers, communication has been difficult."

"What about the president? Is he okay?" I ask.

Ailes has a pained look on his face. "I don't know."

I unmute my phone. "Miriam?"

"Yes? Have you found out anything?" she asks, hopefully.

"It seems like someone is making it very hard for us to communicate with him. I think he might be okay." But I'm worried I'm giving her false hope.

"Now they're saying Senator Friedkin has been killed," Gerald whispers.

I mute my phone. "Friedkin, again? First his name comes up with the DC riot shooters. Now this?"

"I know," he replies, then points to his screen:

REPORT: SENATOR FRIEDKIN SHOT IN COUP ATTEMPT

"Coup!" I blurt out loud, then double-check to make sure my phone is still on mute. "That doesn't even make any sense."

"No, it doesn't," he agrees.

I return to my call. "Miriam, I'm going to look into this. I'm sure you'll hear from your husband soon."

"Promise?" Her voice is quavering.

I can't lie to her, but my gut is telling me this is all smoke and no fire. "I'd be surprised if you didn't."

"You handled that well," Ailes tells me after I hang up.

"What if he *is* dead?" asks Jennifer. "I mean, you did the right thing. But what if he is dead?"

"I'm not buying it," I reply. "If they could get to the president, they'd have released a Devon prediction saying as much. These jammers, they're not like the Russian one used during Marta's assassination attempt on the Pope?"

Ailes shakes his head. "No. These are handheld. The size of a phone. Cheap. Very short range. Easy to hide."

"And a few hundred of them." Gerald adds.

"Exactly," Ailes agrees. "Getting to the president is hard, damn hard. The Secret Service works at keeping any potential threat as far away as possible, and they react quickly. They scan for explosives, and always have a secure spot to pull him into."

"It sounds like the Red Chain counted on the Secret Service response to create a panic."

If you can't kill the man, make it look like you can come close.

"What's the point?" asks Jennifer.

"Fear," I reply. "Hysteria. Even the first lady is shaken by this. A constant state of fear."

"Distrust," says Ailes after thinking it over. "They've damaged the credibility of the government, and now they're going after the media, which is of course all too happy to run anything that trends."

"And Friedkin? Why does his name keep coming up?" I reply.

Gerald nods to his computer. "I think he may actually be dead. This looks authentic. Not the coup part. But there are eyewitnesses saying he was shot in front of his house in Virginia."

"It's such an odd thing. He's not even that well-known a politician. Just one of those people whose names you occasionally hear on the news over the years."

Then why him? Hold on.

Something comes back to me. "Hey? Remember how we couldn't find out anything about the CCA? Except for that one mention in congressional testimony?"

"Yes," says Ailes. "Wait a second." He starts typing on his phone. "Interesting . . . Friedkin was on the Senate public surveillance committee back in the early eighties. Hmm . . ." He sends a text message to someone. "Interesting," he says again, lost in thought. "It seems likely that Friedkin would have been the one to give the sign-off on the project. Maybe he's the one that shut it down too."

"And now he's probably dead," I reply. "And we're supposed to think there's some kind of internal power struggle between him and the president. I can only imagine what stories are going to come out next. If they can make us think Friedkin had some deliberate reason for wanting the president to step aside, then that moves us from just distrusting the government to thinking it's illegitimate."

"But people aren't that stupid," says Jennifer.

"It's not a matter of being stupid," I tell her. "It's just sowing paranoia. Some people think September eleventh was an inside job, for reasons I still can't understand. Same with the JFK assassination."

"This could incite the other radical groups," Ailes suggests. "From the White Power Nation to the New Black Panthers. They're already showing up in droves at the riots." He checks his watch. "I'm going to put the pressure on some of my contacts. I want you guys to get on a helicopter and get to the CCA building now. Let's start digging through that computer system."

We're in the air thirty minutes later.

CHAPTER THIRTY-NINE

VAX

GERALD AND JENNIFER have the guts of the main computer spilled out on the floor of the control room, and they are on their hands and knees going over every part as I sit and watch from the command chair. The DEC VAX machine that served as the central processor was built into a cabinet behind the back wall, accessible on the other side from a service tunnel that wraps around the seventies-era futuristic room.

I don't know what to make of the parts, but Gerald and Jennifer seem to have no trouble figuring things out.

"Looks like we should have borrowed some caveman flints from the Smithsonian," I joke.

Without looking up, Jennifer replies, "It could be worse. The original Apollo source code was stored on hard disks the size of a washing machine. At least this still works."

"Why not just try to get the code from the computer directly? Can't you guys hack it or something?" Even as I say it, it already sounds stupid.

"It could be booby-trapped," says Gerald as he inspects a large motherboard.

"Do we need the bomb squad?" I ask half seriously.

"No. Nothing like that." He points to a keyboard workstation. "I just mean if we start trying to get into the code from this computer, it might erase itself as a self-destruct. A lot of government hardware is designed to do that." He holds up a small cable. "What we're doing is connecting to the hard disk cable so we can copy the main file as it gets loaded into memory during boot up."

"What about encryption?" I ask.

Jennifer snorts, then catches herself. "Sorry. It's a good question. It's just that this thing is from the early eighties. Your iPod could run a decryption algorithm that could break it."

"Good to know." I decide to keep my helpful tips to myself. Jennifer and Gerald never try to make me feel stupid, and to be honest, I rarely do. I've seen them run circles around expert FBI technicians, so I don't feel all that bad.

Gerald stands up and checks his laptop, which sits on a console. "I think we're ready. Jennifer?"

She flips a switch, and the ancient computer's huge disk drive whirs to life. The main screen flickers, and lines of code start to scroll upward.

"Now what?" I ask.

"We wait," she says, taking a seat at an empty console to watch the code fly by.

The last time we started the system, it took forever. I lean back and try to imagine what it would be like to run an actual operation from here. Was there a team of information warfare specialists all trained and waiting on standby for orders to go to war with whomever? Did they have uniforms?

The idea of drone pilots sitting in dark rooms thousands of

miles away from the battlefield is strange enough. What's it like when you're trying to be the puppet master of civil unrest?

Do you high-five your teammates when you cause a blackout and rioting starts?

How long do you just sit here waiting for something to happen?

Or is this whole command center a delusion? Maybe Friedkin was the driving force behind it, and therefore profoundly upset when it didn't meet his expectations? Could his murder be a delayed act of revenge?

I swivel my chair around and tap my fingers on the armrest. I notice for the first time that the thing is made of fiberglass, like the seat on an amusement park rollercoaster, not actually of metal. Sheesh, this whole thing is a sham.

"I think we got the whole code," says Gerald as the screen goes blank.

"Well?" I ask, expecting something to happen.

He starts typing on his laptop. "It's not like an HTML file where they put everything in a header for you to read."

"Oh. I was hoping for a copyright or something. You, know, Evil Computers Incorporated, and their home office address."

"That would be convenient," says Jennifer. "Unfortunately, code like this often leaves documentation out because they're really limited by storage space. One photo on your phone takes up more memory than this whole system. The instructions are only in the manuals."

On our first visit, we'd found a cabinet that seemed like a good candidate for manual storage, but all we discovered was dust.

"So what are you hoping to find?"

"Code sections that we can trace to other projects," she explains. "Like a recognizable database structure, but with alterations. That might tell us who was contracted to make it. If the company is still around, they might still have billing records even if they don't know who they really built it for. Heck, Bill Gates could have made this for all we know. They certainly weren't stingy with money."

While they focus on the ones and zeroes, I turn my attention to the room itself. The space-age décor really is something else. It feels like a movie set—which makes me think. I take out my phone to see if I can at least send an SMS text message down here.

Grandfather replies almost immediately. The old guy sure has caught on to technology. Maybe faster than I have. I text back and forth with him while Gerald and Jennifer dig through the lines of code.

"I found a code block that matches up with something from a code repository," Jennifer calls out in what could be, for her, excitement.

Gerald leans over to see her screen. "What am I looking at?"

She indicates some Martian characters. "I was seeing how they did image handling. Back then the only people who could handle really large photo files were spy agencies. There were a few proprietary image formats. I found a code library for making thumbnails customized to the limitations of the database. The same method was used in a system for a JPL probe launched in the seventies."

"Can you get me a list of the software engineers?" asks Gerald.

"Sure. What do you got?"

"I've actually been doing some patent searches on multimedia servers from that period. I'd bet anything that whoever made this wanted to protect it."

They type away on their computers, trying to connect the code to something outside the secretive world of government black projects. A few minutes later I get a text from my grandfather at the exact same moment Gerald speaks.

"Found something!" he says.

"Desert Sun Consulting?" I ask.

He turns toward me, his mouth open. "Yeah . . . How?"

I do my best to hide my delight. I tap the chair. "I was thinking they spent a lot of money on this. I was also thinking it felt familiar, like a movie set. If you had a ton of cash and you wanted to build something that looked like the bridge of the *Enterprise*, who do you go to?"

"NASA?" asks Jennifer.

"No. Hollywood. I asked my grandfather if he knew the set builder for the first *Star Trek* movie. Turns out I've even met him. He'd built some magic props that ended up getting us tied in with the mob. It's a long story. Anyway, I had my grandfather ask him if he's ever made anything for a movie that never got made, or for a group he never heard from again. He's done lots of industrial work too, and remembers making something that sounds somewhat like this for a Virginia company."

"Desert Sun Consulting," Gerald replies.

"Yep."

Jennifer looks up from a keyboard. "I can't find anything about them after nineteen eighty-nine. Maybe we can look for articles of incorporation?"

"I have another suggestion," I reply, looking at my phone. "It turns out two sets were made. One was sent here. Another elsewhere."

"Two?" she says, glancing around the room. "There's another?"

"Yes. This may have been the prototype. The other was sent to Colorado."

"Same as the fake driver's licenses," Gerald replies.

"Exactly."

"Where?" Jennifer asks.

I do a quick Google search. "Some town called, Moffat. In the middle of nowhere."

"Never heard of it."

"Me neither, it's barely on the map."

CHAPTER FORTY

WHIRLWIND

I'D BEEN WAITING for your call," says Sheriff Boyer as he greets Nadine and me at the bottom of the staircase leading down from the FBI jet. An olive-skinned man with a thick black mustache, he wears a cowboy hat and gold-rimmed aviator sunglasses. I hope some things never change in the West.

"Sheriff, I'm Jessica Blackwood, and this is Nadine Cox," I say, shaking his hand.

We'd left the airfield near Quantico early this morning and flown directly to this small airstrip, miles from anywhere, as soon as we heard about Moffat. Even after Ailes and I talked to Boyer on the phone, we still could not wrap our heads around the extraordinary connection between Peter Devon and the bizarre story of what happened in—or to—Moffat.

Nadine and I managed a few hours of sleep on the plane, but I still have trouble stifling my yawn. The hangars and small control tower that make up the airport are surrounded by thousands of acres of grazing land. The Rockies form a bluish gray wall in the distance.

Boyer introduces us to the man standing next to him. "This is Deputy Eric Cranston. It was his mother-in-law who noticed Moffat was missing."

Cranston is in his early thirties, and his tanned face is shaded by his sheriff department baseball cap. He's got a military demeanor about him. "Missing?"

"I tried to tell you on the phone," says Boyer. "Gone. I can take you to a car rental, or straight to Moffat. It's about an hour from here."

I have to know what the hell is going on. "Let's go to where Moffat *was*."

Sheriff Boyer leads us to his SUV, which is parked on the edge of the tarmac. Deputy Cranston gives me the front passenger seat and climbs into the back with Nadine.

As he drives, Boyer fills us in on how they found out about the Moffat "situation."

"Olivia, Eric's mother-in-law, called in with the strangest thing. As you can guess, we didn't know what to make of it. Moffat is in an unincorporated part of our county. We've got a few different communities that like to keep to themselves. Fundamentalists and the like. We took it to the Colorado Bureau of Investigation and spoke with your Denver office. It was a big deal for a hot minute, then all the trouble broke out in DC and elsewhere. We've been dealing with our own riots in Denver and Boulder. Anyway, we sent a forensics team. The truth is people think it's kind of a joke. A few of these towns are trailer parks. Folks seem to believe they just drove off."

"What do you think?"

Boyer shrugs. "Eric knows the area better than me. It's a big county."

"Moffat wasn't a trailer park," says Cranston. "I mean, some of it was. But they had half a dozen real buildings. They're just gone."

"What did your forensics team find out?" Nadine asks.

"The only thing left is the road. It's like everything from the ground up just vanished."

"We didn't even know about Moffat until last night. Not even a blip on the news," says Nadine.

"Like I said, even people here think it's some kind of joke."

"I can see why," I point out. "The alternative is terrifying. Is anybody missing?"

"Other than the fifty-eight people who lived there?" Cranston says drily.

I quickly try to explain myself. "I mean, have there been any missing persons reports? Do you have names? We couldn't find any in the FBI database."

"These people are off the grid for the most part. Mail delivery was once or twice a week. The only person anybody is missing that we know personally is their regular mail carrier, Charles Pastorali. The only reason we know Moffat itself is missing is because Olivia had to do his route."

"So it could have gone away sometime before Olivia appeared?" I'm trying to find a satisfactory explanation for what sounds just bat-shit crazy.

"I don't know," replies Cranston. "Same day Olivia found it, or rather couldn't, I had a truck driver get lost trying to make a delivery. I'm sure we would have heard something from somebody in the last few days if it had already vanished."

"So it happened overnight?" I ask incredulously.

He stares ahead at the road and shrugs. "Maybe."

NADINE AND I spend the rest of the ride to Moffat trying to get as much information as we can about its inhabitants from Sheriff Boyer. He'd started digging into the town history after the disappearance, but doesn't have a whole lot to show for it. Still, it's more than what I knew.

"About fifty years ago, a preacher with a group called the Sons of Christ started buying up buildings in town. They started the trailer park," he explains.

"Was it only men?" Nadine asks.

"No. It was just a name. Maybe twenty or thirty people. They'd been living out there, keeping themselves pretty isolated. Then, about twenty years ago, younger people started moving in from out of state. Apparently, there was some kind of changeup. The Sons of Christ sign was taken down from the church. There was no more mention of that."

Nadine leans forward with her own questions. "What about the new people? What were they like?"

"Olivia could tell you better than I can. Some of them seemed like hippies. We get a lot of them out here now. They leave California to come here."

"Was it another religious group?" I ask, trying not to let my anxiety get the better of me.

"I don't know. I mean, is being a vegan a religion?" he asks earnestly.

"Depends on who you ask," I reply.

"Well, I did hear some reports that they'd drive into Boulder and other places and hand out literature on campuses. Nothing too crazy, as far as I know."

"Interesting," says Nadine. "We have a murder victim who may have been recruited in Grand Junction. We'd love to have a look at your missing persons files."

"For anything in particular?"

I speak up. "Young men and women who are into extreme environmental causes. The more estranged they were from their families, the better. So to speak."

"Also the less likely to flag anything," says Boyer, pointing out how hard they could be to track down.

"True," I agree. "We suspect they recruit people based on ideological beliefs and seek out those already estranged from their families. They're easier to indoctrinate."

"You keep saying 'they,'" Boyer snaps. "Can you tell me who the hell they are supposed to be?" His voice is raised, clearly frustrated from the lack of help from the FBI and other agencies.

I give it to him bluntly. "They're a medieval environmentalist death cult trying to enact the apocalypse through a strategy of murder, sabotage, and mass panic."

He glances at me for a moment to make sure I'm telling him the truth, then returns his attention to the highway. "Oh . . . I thought we were dealing with something dangerous."

"I'm not joking, Sheriff."

"I know you aren't. I see the news. I know how people are acting. None of this surprises me. And when you see what happened to Moffat, you'll feel the same."

I'm afraid I already do.

CHAPTER FORTY-ONE

GONE

MOFFAT IS GONE—GONE.

The gravel road ends and then there is nothing to see but dry dirt and tumbleweed. I only know Moffat is supposed to be here because of my phone's GPS, and because I believe Boyer and Cranston.

I get out of the SUV and kick the dirt with my sneaker, hoping that's all it will take to reveal the lost town. But I just kick up more dirt, covering the black canvas in pale dust.

Sheriff Boyer crosses his arms and leans on the hood, clearly having done more than just stick a toe in the dirt.

"We've been out here with metal detectors, rakes, you name it."

"And?" Nadine asks as she kneels down and lets some earth slip through her gloved fingers.

"Nothing. Barely even a cinder block," he replies.

Deputy Cranston walks over to a metal sign and leans down to dust it off. "My mother-in-law found this."

WELCOME TO MOFFAT, POPULATION 58

"This is all that's left, other than the road."

I scrutinize the sign, trying to figure out why it was left behind. It was pulled from the post—and whoever or whatever happened here left it as a calling card. They want us to know there was a town here. It's a little theatrical for my tastes, and suspicious.

"So, you think these folks might be your folks?" asks Boyer.

I stare out to the horizon, searching the brown rocks and pale green brush for something, anything.

"Maybe. One of the men who tried to kill me was from here. We've also traced a bunch of fake IDs to this area. These people had to come from somewhere. I guess Moffat makes as much sense as anywhere else."

Cranston abandons the sign to stare into nothing, like me. "So they just took over the town?" He's an intelligent man trying to make sense of madness.

"It happens. You get a cult group moving in and the balance begins to shift. After Ezra Winter went to jail, the rest of them probably wanted a place to hide out. Of course, there weren't that many members back then. The people here, they'd mostly be the second generation. New converts. Children of the originals."

Cranston glances over at Nadine. "You said they were recruiting?"

"On campuses," she replies. "We know that's how they got to at least one of our suspects. Cults are known for preying on marginalized young people, who are especially vulnerable if they're isolated from their families and having trouble fitting in."

"Recruiting for what?" asks Boyer.

"All this anarchy," I explain. "That was their plan. Or at least part of it. Starting riots, the blackouts, trying to make us all panic."

I sense Boyer is having trouble understanding what the Red Chain is about. I can't blame him. "Yeah, but then what?"

"I don't know. It's why we came here."

"I've got some aerial photos," Cranston says. Tired of looking at nothing, he takes a tube from the back of the SUV and slides out several large prints onto the hood.

From above, Moffat—at least the Moffat that used to be here—is a collection of rectangles around a small open center. It's a blown-up, higher-resolution version of what you'd see on Google Maps. There are several dozen concrete buildings, at least three dozen prefab homes, and other similar structures.

I trace my finger across the town. "Some of these buildings had to have foundations."

"We looked," Boyer replies. "Ripped up, disappeared, or pulled into a black hole. It's like the town never existed. We even asked a physicist at Colorado State if that was possible. He laughed it off, said it was probably a twister. Only, the meteorologists said that was even less likely."

"Isn't it possible they just hauled everything somewhere else?" Nadine asks, looking at me.

"Yes, it is," I reply. "But I can't imagine them doing it that quickly and without leaving behind some evidence."

"True. But the million-dollar question is why?"

"Rapture," says Cranston with a sigh. "That's what folks around here are saying. At least some of them, the ones who don't believe it's a joke. They think this might be some kind of divine act."

I turn to him, curious. "Do they take that stuff seriously out here?"

"Some more than others. The possibility certainly makes these people more interesting. Folks want to know what they were doing."

"Too bad they're not here to tell us," replies Nadine.

"But you can't just disappear a town!" Cranston protests.

"Yes, you can," I murmur to myself as I think it over.

"What's that?" Boyer glances up at me as he overhears my not-so-inner monologue.

"Sorry. I was just thinking. The answer is yes. You can vanish a town. This was done a lot in World War II, to hide cities and other strategic locations from bombers. There was a Lockheed factory in Burbank they covered with netting and tents so it would look like farms and houses from the air. The British used lights to create false cities on the coast. Of course, all of this was designed to fool people from the air, not the ground."

Cranston dismisses the theory with a shake of his head. "We can't even find a septic tank."

"So, is this an FBI case now?" asks Boyer, who clearly wants our help.

"Well, the post office isn't here. That makes it a federal case. So I guess, yes. The trouble is with everything else going to hell, I don't know how much help we can get for you." I nod to Nadine. "I was barely able to get her assigned here. My colleagues are back in Virginia taking apart a seventies-era computer in search of more clues."

"I could care less about jurisdiction and who gets credit," says Boyer. "I just want to know what happened to the people here. Maybe they're your Red Chain, but some of them were children. Tell me what you need and I'll see what I can do."

He's looking to Nadine and me for answers, but we don't have any. There should be a whole FBI forensics team out here as well as field agents. But all the ones in Colorado are tied up, and there's no way Quantico can spare the resources while state capitals are under siege from every crackpot group we've ever encountered.

I've just got to make do with what we have available here.

"You have an RV we could use? I'd like to be able to spend some time out here without having to traipse back and forth to town."

"You got it," says Boyer. "I'll even stock it up. Anything else?"

"Horses," replies Nadine.

"Horses?" I ask.

"To cover the ground," she explains. "We'll be able to do a better search that way."

"Good idea." Although I haven't been on one in years. Ugh.

"My brother and his wife have some," offers Cranston. "I'll get them trailered and bring them out here."

"Thank you," I reply, appreciating his eagerness to help. "I'll be honest, though. I don't know what we could find that you couldn't."

Nadine glances over my shoulder, toward the horizon. "Sheriff, are you expecting company?"

"No. Why?" he asks as he turns around.

We all squint to see what Nadine is staring at. A long plume of dust is coming from the road that leads off the highway. We passed nobody on the way here, and it seems odd that there would be traffic now.

"Hold on a second." Boyer reaches for a pair of binoculars on his center console and rests his elbows on the hood. After a moment, he mutters, "Jesus Christ."

"What is it?" I ask, holding my hand out for the binoculars.

He hands them to me without saying anything. I adjust the focus knob and the head of the plume comes into view.

Crap.

"Well?" says Nadine.

I give them to her. "It looks like Moffat isn't a minor story anymore."

"Seriously!" she exclaims. "I count at least three news trucks. Two local and one from Fox."

"Perfect," I groan. Just what we need.

When the first van comes to a stop and the reporter comes running toward me with his cameraman right behind him, I'm not even remotely prepared for the first question that comes out of his mouth.

CHAPTER FORTY-TWO

THE PATTERN

THE REPORTER'S NAME is Quint Trenton. I've seen him on cable news before, chasing after the latest scandal. With jet-black hair and a touch of "trust-me" gray at his temples, he's the kind of guy who reports on a hurricane while pseudo-bravely standing in knee-deep water, or who shoves his microphone into shocked refugees' faces to ask them how they feel about their lives suddenly falling apart.

He's no better or worse than any other TV journalist I guess. I've done my best to stay clear of them. Having your face on the news doesn't help if you're a career FBI agent who still wants to do undercover work. Plus, I know they'll twist whatever they can into a story, even if it's not quite the whole truth. Maybe I'm biased, but after the press gives you a nickname like FBI Witch you tend not to think too positively about any branch of the media. While I've never had a bad interaction with Trenton, he's here right now—the last place I need to deal with someone like him, or the other two that came in the convoy.

But it's not his presence itself that grates on me the most. It's the question he just asked me. It stings. It *burns*.

"Agent Blackwood!" He shouts, his cameraman lumbering behind him. "Are you here in connection with the Warlock case?"

I turn away and pretend to focus on the aerial image while I wait for Boyer and Cranston to get the journalists to back the hell away. When I spot cameras aimed at me, I sit down in the passenger seat of the SUV, facing away from the gathered news crews.

Nadine walks over and rests a hand on top of the open door, shielding me.

"Those assholes." She's pretty stingy with her expletives, so I can tell she's just as miffed as I am, maybe more. "Bringing up Heywood, sheesh." She rolls her eyes.

"Dumb," I reply.

Or is it?

Something that's been lurking in the back of my mind finally breaks free. I consider myself a great critical thinker, but I've been blind.

So damn blind.

"Why the hell would they come out here now? Boyer said they couldn't be bothered to care before. What gives?" asks Nadine, trying to sympathize.

I take my phone out and load a map of the United States into a drawing app. "I'm so stupid and stubborn," I mutter to myself.

"What do you mean?"

I nod in the direction of the news crew behind us. "Somebody must have heard I was coming here. They made the connection, but we should have seen it first."

"What connection?" she asks. "You mean to the Warlock?"

Hearing her say it is like a knife twisting in my side. Well, another knife. I take a deep breath as the reality sinks in.

"Yes. The Warlock's three crime scenes formed part of a pattern. That cemetery in Michigan, New York City, and Fort Lauderdale. Remember we picked him up at a fourth location in South Texas, where he was about to abduct a girl? We still don't know why. What we do know is that he was making a geopentagram with the crimes. Each location was a point." I jab a finger at the ground. "Here, right here. We're only twenty miles away from the fifth point."

Saying it aloud makes me numb. I don't want there to be a connection. *I resisted it.*

Nadine stares at my little map. "It's got to be a coincidence."

"No. It's not. It explains so much. I wanted to ignore some things about the case that didn't fit. I was afraid of where they'd lead me. Ezra Winter and his cronies are technophobes, so they must have had help hacking the electrical grid. The Warlock, I mean Heywood, that is his kind of thing. And now this?" I wave a hand toward the empty desert. "A whole fucking town vanishing in some kind of rapture? *Tell me* that's not his deal." My voice is raised, and I have to take a breath to calm down.

Her mouth slackens before she finds the words. "Are you saying . . . are you saying he's part of the Red Chain?"

"I don't know. Maybe he just offered up his services for a few favors . . ." My voice fades at the realization.

"Like, like trying to kill you?" Nadine replies hesitantly.

"Yes. None of this made much sense, until now. Ezra Winter was sending mail bombs, but not doing much else. Then suddenly he's able to pull all of this off while behind bars? What he has, Heywood wants more than anything."

"A following," she replies.

"Exactly." Heywood is brilliant, but his people skills aren't his strong suit.

Nadine gets out her phone and starts dialing. "I'm calling Heywood's prison. You call Ailes."

I take a moment to calm myself before speaking to Ailes. I don't want him to pick up on the distress in my voice. This is the last thing I want. I should be off this case and doing paperwork in some forgotten FBI office in North Dakota, not here, not in the middle of another one of his damn stunts.

"Blackwood? How's it going out there?" Ailes asks when he picks up.

"Not good."

I spend the next few minutes going over everything we've learned so far.

Nadine mouths "still in jail" after she gets off the phone with the warden.

At least there's that. Although it's only a small consolation given how much he's been able to orchestrate while allegedly having no computer access. He's shown us before that he has no problem reaching out to me when he wants to. Now it's clear he's been doing something far more elaborate.

"Well?" asks Nadine after I hang up with Ailes.

"He's sending a team in from Quantico and some people from Denver to help us out."

"Help us do what?" She gestures to the empty landscape. "We need to have a scene for a crime scene."

"Don't forget about the CCA equipment that was sent here," I point out. "They wanted it for something. There's more here."

"At least they're leaving," says Nadine as the crews start climbing back into their trucks at Boyer's request.

After they depart, Boyer walks over to us. "I told them to clear out, with this whole area being a crime scene. We're going to have to give them something, though."

"I know," I reply.

This story is going to get big, regardless of what else is going on in the world—and if they make a connection to the riots?

Chaos. I don't have a lot of time to act. There's so much at stake.

"Can we get a map showing who owns what parcels of land around here?"

"You looking for something besides Moffat?" asks Boyer.

"Maybe." I look through the driver's side window at the re-treating news vans. "Are we going to have them lurking around all the time?"

"I think I can get them to keep clear if we throw them a bone. Maybe have the FBI make a statement."

I shake my head in protest. "Don't look at me. I'm not autho-rized to talk to the press." That's not totally accurate, but close enough.

"I'll handle that," offers Nadine. "The talking-to-them part. I just need something to say."

"We can tell them this isn't Moffat," I suggest.

"What?" Boyer looks at me like I've gone mad. "We can't ex-actly lie to them."

As terrifying as the thought is that the Warlock has his hand in this, it also clarifies things for me. I know how he thinks. I un-derstand what really happened here.

All I needed was context.

The town vanishing is just a prelude. Now that I know who's pulling the strings, it actually seems like a simple trick. Just a dis-traction.

The real show is about to happen.

CHAPTER FORTY-THREE

LEY LINES

I WAIT FOR THE news teams to retreat over the horizon, then step out of the SUV and survey the landscape. Right now I can't obsess over what Heywood is or isn't up to. I have to stick to the facts and what's in front of me, or in this case, what's not.

"Why do we think Moffat was here?" I ask our small group.

Boyer cocks an eyebrow, trying to figure out if this is a serious question. The look on my face tells him all he needs to know. "Well, the road, for one reason. This is the road to Moffat."

"Okay. You can't destroy a town overnight. At least not easily, and without leaving a mess. But you can *bury* most of one."

"Bury one?" He kicks the toe of his boot into the dry ground, sending up a small cloud of dirt that's carried away by the wind.

Deputy Cranston points to some scattered holes that look like they were made by a meticulous gopher. "We brought out a post digger. Nothing doing."

"Of course not," I reply, as if that should be obvious. "Can I check that aerial map again?"

I compare the image to a scalable one I've pulled up on my phone. It's hard to tell anything without surveying equipment because there aren't any landmarks nearby. Still, I've got a hunch.

"You got a shovel in here?" I ask.

"Yeah," Boyer replies. "You plan on digging up a town?"

"Basically," I say matter-of-factly.

He gets the shovel out of the back and hands it to me with a grimace. "Do your magic."

"We'll see." I start walking north, feeling their eyes on my back. Even Nadine is trying to figure out what the hell I'm up to.

I guess I am too.

"The town is this way," Boyer calls out to me, probably convinced I'm insane.

I glance back over my shoulder. "Is it, Sheriff?"

I sound far more confident than I feel. I really don't want to look like some dumb girl in front of these guys. They're earnest and counting on the FBI to help them out. But instead of a forensics team, they got me.

I reach a berm beyond a small incline at the far end of where the town is supposed to be.

Nadine strides up until we're shoulder to shoulder and hands me a water bottle. "Please tell me you haven't gone crazy."

It's cool, but the air is dry. I take a swig then reply, "I don't think so." I speak louder so that Cranston and Boyer can hear. "The Warlock has a particular way of problem solving. A kind of "tell," a way he does things. He likes his mysteries to be TV friendly. Also, he wants them to be foolproof. Even if you think you know how he did it, there's always a bit of uncertainty. He'll hide the evidence. Which reminds me of a trick my father used to do involving an orchid. To hide the secret from me, he'd hide the evidence. The Warlock—Heywood—he wants this to appear to be supernatural."

"What's his connection to the Red Chain?" asks Boyer.

"I don't think we are supposed to know there's a connection between them. I think he just wanted a town to disappear, not necessarily a town full of religious zealots. I don't know. I haven't figured that part out. Maybe he hasn't either. He could be improvising, and just leaped at this chance when he had it."

I reach a patch of tan dirt with a clump of dying shrubs. Using the tip of my shovel, I dig at the root. It only takes me one push to set the plant free and send it tumbling in the wind, off to become tumbleweed, I guess.

With more force, I stab the shovel into the ground and throw the dirt aside.

"Want some help?" asks Cranston, clearly uneasy watching me work.

"Let the lady do her thing. Equal pay, equal work," replies Boyer.

"Spoken like a real feminist," jokes Nadine.

He offers her a smile. "I have three daughters, as tough as nails."

I make a small hole, large enough to reach my calf. "So the question for you all is: Why do you think Moffat is back there?"

"On account of the road," replies Boyer. "I thought we covered that." I can tell he's thinking I may be losing it.

"You mean the paved road that ended in nothing?" I ask.

"Yes. That would be the one. The only one off the highway for miles." There's an edge to his voice. He's not enjoying my Socratic method.

I jab the shovel into the ground again. The metal clangs against something solid. I feel a tingle of relief as I realize I might actually be on to something. I hurriedly scrape along the object with the shovel, scooping away more dirt from it until it becomes visible.

"You sure that is the only road to Moffat?"

I step back and reveal a small patch of asphalt.

Boyer squats down and touches the surface of the road like it's a religious artifact.

He looks up at me, his face almost white. "Holy shit."

I hand him the shovel. "Keep digging, and I think you'll find a demolished town buried at the end." I point to a small rise in the landscape, then bend down and yank away another loose shrub, holding it up for them to see. The roots are only an inch or so long. "This brush was planted only for appearances and never had much chance to take hold."

Boyer uncovers more road, revealing a white line, then he hands the shovel to Cranston so the deputy can start widening the hole. He wipes his hands on his jeans and then crosses his arms, ready for an explanation.

"Care to elaborate?"

"The road back there, the one we thought lead to Moffat? They probably made it a little bit at a time overnight. It wouldn't take terribly long, maybe a few weeks with the right equipment. They then buried it as the pavement finished cooling." I place my palm on the asphalt below us. "If I wanted to get rid of a town, I'd use some bulldozers to dig trenches I could push the buildings into. The dirt from those holes got spread out over the road here."

"That sounds like a hell of a construction project," says Boyer, not fully convinced.

"They could have dug the trenches in advance and then covered the road all in one night. A hundred people, less than a quarter mile? Doable. I think."

Boyer nods his head. "That makes sense. I'll buy it." He looks in the direction of the buried town. "This road and the other one are only a few hundred feet apart. Easy to miss." He shakes his head in disbelief. "All this time, we were looking in the wrong place."

"You didn't know someone was actively trying to deceive you. The landscape is pretty similar from the air. Moving any little landmarks would be a cinch. And the GPS is close enough. As long as we kept looking for Moffat in the wrong place, we'd never find it."

"Why do it?" asks Cranston, leaning on the shovel.

"I don't know. Knowing the Warlock?" I groan. "We'll probably find an exact copy of this town on the other side of the earth, in the Gobi or some bullshit."

"Really?" Nadine blurts out.

"Maybe. Who knows with him? The sooner we tell people we've found Moffat, the more it will deflate his little moment."

"Well done." Boyer tips his hat to me.

I shake my head. "No. This isn't the real problem. You asked me why he'd go through all this. That's not my concern right now. We may have found the town, but we haven't found the people. One hundred dedicated zealots willing to pull off a stunt like this? They are what scares me. We've seen how much damage just a few of them have been able to cause. Our capital is burning, and half the nation is rioting in darkness. Where the hell are the assholes who started this, and what are they up to now?"

CHAPTER FORTY-FOUR

RETREAT

I'VE GOT TWO dozen deeds spread out over the table in front of me in the RV. Nadine and I are taking turns poring over county records looking for clues as to who or what else may be out here. Through our window we can see the construction crew uncovering what's left of Moffat.

On a muted TV over our heads, scenes of fires and rioting play out in major cities. It's strange. Out here in the desert, it feels a million miles away, hardly connected. But it all ties together. The sooner we can figure out the why and how, the sooner we can stop the anarchy—if it can be stopped.

The door opens and Nadine and I scurry to keep the dry wind from blowing away the papers. Agent Nesbitt from the Denver office appears. She's a healthy fortysomething, with short hair and the physique of someone who runs marathons on weekends. To the point and a solid investigator, we are lucky to get her out here in the middle of the crisis.

"Sorry," she says, apologizing for the disruption. "We've had cadaver dogs all over what we've dug up, and they haven't found a thing. But that could be because any bodies are buried deep, and haven't decomposed enough yet to smell."

"I'm not surprised. Still, we should be trying methane probes and excavating septic systems." Over her shoulder, I spot a bull-dozer pouring dirt back into a hole. "For fuck sake!"

I barge past Nesbitt, storm out of the RV, and stride across the site to the hard-hat-wearing foreman. "What are you doing?" I shout over the sound of diesel engines.

"Ask her." He points behind me to Nesbitt as she comes run-ning out after me.

"What's going on? Why are they covering it up?" I demand.

"I'm sorry. Orders from above. We're being sent back to Den-ver. We're supposed to preserve everything until later."

"Until when? This is an active crime scene!"

Nesbitt nods. "I know. But we've got a lot of active crime scenes. The rioting is getting worse. We're being redeployed."

Nadine jogs after me with a defeated look, holding up her phone. "I just got an e-mail. I'm supposed to head back to Vir-ginia."

Everything is collapsing around me. "This is bullshit," I mut-ter to my feet, taking out my own phone to call Ailes.

"What the hell?" I blurt into the receiver.

"Remind me to talk to you about how to address your superi-ors," he reprimands me, although not too angrily.

I catch my breath and remember who I'm talking to. "I'm sorry. But jesus. They're pulling everyone out of here!"

"No bodies, Jessica," he says sympathetically. "There's noth-ing to actively investigate."

"The 'no bodies' part is what scares me. If we found a ditch of a hundred dead people, I could rest easy."

This remark earns me aghast looks from the construction

foreman and Nesbitt. Nadine knows me well enough to understand what I mean.

"I know. I know," says Ailes. "But there's nothing we can do.
Half our field agents have been assigned to provide protective
services. The other half are out chasing leads and trying to track
down the rest of the members of the Red Chain your driver's license trick revealed to us."

"That was Damian. But this place is a lead. This is *the* lead."

"I know you feel that way," he says patiently. "What have you
and Nadine found out so far?"

I think of the RV table covered in property records and deeds.
"Not much . . . yet. But it would make sense if they had some
property out here somewhere. A place to keep construction equipment. A place for the other CCA setup."

"That thing was ancient. You could do it all from just a laptop
now."

"Yeah. But—"

"What?" he asks, waiting for me to make my case.

Which I can't.

"I don't know." Everyone's looking at me, so I turn away and
talk lower. "It's a gut feeling. An instinct. They chose here for a
reason."

"To be away from everything."

"Maybe. But we still don't know when Heywood first made
contact. Hell, he could have been in the Red Chain."

"Don't make this personal, Jessica."

"I'm not! Okay, I am. But you can't pull us out of here," I plead.

"Breyer's orders. We're spread so thin."

I can tell Ailes is agitated by this too, but he has to follow orders.

"Yeah, but . . ."

I give up protesting. I can tell which way the tide is going.

"However, I made a compromise with him."

"What was that?"

"Since he doesn't think the place is an immediate threat, you can stick around. Although I'm personally uneasy with that."

"Then let me keep Nadine," I ask.

"I wish I could, but I can't. It's not under my control."

"Send Gerald or Jennifer!" I beg.

"They're busy working on a system to look for software vulnerabilities that could be set off by a CCA two point zero. The floodgate tampering has us very concerned."

Their work is too important. I get it. "Fine. Fine."

"I can give you two days, then I need you back here. Understood?"

I scan the desert and watch shimmering heat waves distort the distant Sangre de Cristo Mountains. "Alright."

"Jessica, don't do anything rash."

"Me?" I say innocently.

"Yeah, you."

We both know there's going to be no way to avoid that.

CHAPTER FORTY-FIVE

SILVERBACK

A BLACK AZTECA WITH a white-tipped mane, Silverback trots up the slope as I tightly grip the pommel. Deputy Cranston had said this was his most well trained horse—subtly suggesting that would make it the best one to handle a rusty rider like myself. The last time I spent any serious time on a horse, I was eleven and at a summer riding camp in Los Angeles.

A dozen other eleven-year-old girls and I would groom our rented horses then take them up the trails through Griffith Park, even trotting within view of the Hollywood sign. While we never got to break loose and run free across open pastures like I'd hoped, slowly riding nose to tail across dusty paths where the sprawling city could vanish for entire minutes at a time was still an exhilarating experience. Riding camp was supposed to be two weeks long, but we had to go to Ohio so Grandfather could perform in the state fair.

"There will be horses at the fair," he'd said when he saw the frustrated look on my face after Father told me I'd have to say good-bye to Popper, the old gray nag that had carried me around.

Grandfather was right, sort of, but it seemed cruel to ride the sad fair ponies that walked circles inside a closed pen while screaming children pulled their ears and kicked their flanks. I'd seen a horse as some kind of symbol of empowerment until then. That just seemed like torture.

The original plan had been for Deputy Cranston to ride with me as I checked out the surrounding bluffs and arroyos, but it fell apart when he got pulled into providing backup in town when the locals started stealing generators and fights began to break out. He reluctantly left me, but not before lending me one more cherished possession, a pistol grip tactical shotgun.

I feel slightly absurd atop a horse with my shotgun by my side. Switch my University of Miami baseball cap for a cowboy hat and I'd look like something out of a bad postapocalyptic Western.

I mapped out a path for Silverback and me to follow. Too spread out to travel to by the gravel roads that link them, horseback seemed like the most efficient method to explore the various parcels of land. Well, actually, a helicopter would be, but there was a fat chance I was going to get one of those out here. If I called Ailes asking for one, I'd have to explain that I was going this far out alone, and he'd lynch me himself.

Silverback and I ride along the ridge, past the first place I want to inspect. It's an open quarry where someone has tried to make a go of digging up marble. They mined what they could, then abandoned the site, and the dark blue granite walls go down thirty feet to a chalky brown floor that's slowly filling up in the desert breeze. An ancient fence lines the edge of the property on the southern face. Half the enclosure is collapsed as erosion has undermined the supports and they've given way to fierce winds.

There's some rusty equipment and a pile of discarded circular saw blades that trigger flashbacks to my days of being sawed in half. On a tour that took us to Greece, our host gave my family a tour of an ancient marble quarry. It looked a lot like this, even the tools. The only difference was the ancient one was made by human power, not the engines that carved this one.

Just as I couldn't at that quarry, I can't spot any tire tracks or other signs of human habitation here. A wooden shack the color of old newspapers—the lone standing structure—leans at an odd angle, its corners looking as though they've been gnawed by giant rodents.

"You smell anything, boy?" I scratch Silverback behind the ear and he responds with an indifferent blink.

Whatever, you crazy broad. When do I get to eat?

I gently nudge him and he trots to the top edge of the quarry. We start our descent down a small canyon onto the next parcel. The deed to the parcel said "mineral exploitation." The aerial photos showed some covered buildings and a few roads worn into the ground. It takes us about thirty minutes to get there, most of it over a slight upward grade.

"Sorry, pal," I mutter to Silverback, feeling guilty.

He continues to plod along without protest. While I don't think he's unhappy like the fair ponies, I get the sense that he too has resigned himself to the fact that his lot in life is to endure selfish mercurial monkeys asking him to go from point to point. I try to stroke his mane reassuringly like I'm throwing tips at a harassed waiter. I'm pretty sure he'd prefer the edible kind of reward.

The landscape of low brush and the occasional tree bent like some kind of desert bonsai would be more serene if I wasn't so focused on spotting something that stood out. To be honest, I haven't quite figured out what I'm looking for.

The last time I dealt with the Warlock, he had an entire warehouse where he planned and practiced his sick schemes. He'd even marked out a mock-up of Times Square on the floor for one of his more heinous acts. Discovering that was like finding a blueprint.

This time, with the Red Chain involved, I have no idea what I'm expecting. A giant building labeled: EVIL LAIR?

What Ailes had said—about the CCA dirty tricks system being able to work from a laptop anywhere in the world—got me thinking I might be barking up the wrong tree. The Red Chain folks could be long gone to some criminal island paradise, planning their next phase.

Their next phase.

What exactly *is* the next phase for a death cult that's already started a global panic? We've run through all kinds of scenarios, from dirty bombs to high-profile assassinations.

Like the things they've already done, I suspect it's something meant to incite a kind of panic: they want to get us to destroy ourselves. Just like the blackouts. We supplied the rioting and the looting. While messing with the floodgates and murdering hundreds of people is certainly vast in scope, I think it may also suggest they realize that the old CCA tricks won't work as well on a more modernized infrastructure.

Of course, that's discounting what they could do with the help of Heywood. He managed to hack the FBI's computer system. Technically just the home page, but still, a system more secure than those of many other vital facilities. According to Jennifer and Gerald, there are thousands of vulnerabilities open to a hacker with this kind of capability. Waiting to see what happens next is not an option.

On the ground, I can see that the buildings in the overhead photos I examined are actually just sheds, where a few trailers and oil drums are shielded from the sun. The tall weeds sprouting around the central yard suggest this place hasn't had many visitors either. After a few minutes of careful scrutiny, I decide to move on.

Next on my map is a piece of property listed as being owned by Triple Star Construction. Silverback takes us up a ridge and down a slope, then finds a very narrow trail that leads to the top of the hill. The ground levels off and we reach a flat parcel nestled between two high ridges.

Weathered water tanks and machine parts I can't identify are strewn about the lot. This place doesn't look like it's had much attention.

Silverback starts chewing on some grass. I decide he knows better than I do if it's harmful, and hop off so I can rest my sore ass. I find a rock that overlooks the valley, including where Moffat was. I guess *is*.

It's a great view. The valley floor is an undulating blanket of brown and bronze that grows progressively more wrinkled as it gets closer to the mountains. Slate-colored storm clouds hover in the distance and rain down over distant hills. I sip some water and try to forget the craziness going on in the world.

Up here, with her loyal steed and full canteen—actually a water bottle—a girl could get by just fine, assuming she doesn't need to eat, or sleep on anything with a decent thread count.

I enjoy the breeze and the sound of the horse munching on his high desert salad. As the wind drifts through the dry brush I listen to the crickets chirp. Silverback's ear twitches and he stares at something off to the side of the hill. He determines that it's just a normal bush, and returns to his buffet. But my own ears tilt as I notice the noise Silverback picked up. A whirring tone, mechanical.

One that's very out of place up here.

CHAPTER FORTY-SIX

THE BUSH

Had it been hidden out in the open, disguised as an electrical transformer for an underground power line or a pipeline, I'd have been less suspicious, maybe even just noting it down on my map to be checked later. But when the whirring sound leads me to a bush—a large and unusually round bush that on closer inspection resembles a fake Christmas tree, complete with humming and blowing air through metal branches—I get a teensy bit curious.

I'm immediately grateful I didn't have access to a helicopter, because I would have flown right over this.

Of course, I don't know what "this" is. But it sure as hell looks like something somebody doesn't want to be found. Through the metal and plastic, I spot a cylinder about two feet across, with a metal grate over the opening.

I drag the fake shrub away and uncover the rest. It's a tube going into the earth like a pipe from Super Mario Bros. Silverback wanders over to this new discovery, sniffs the fake shrub, then turns his attention elsewhere.

The metal grill is held in place by a padlock. I scoff at the puny thing and, before I even consider the legal ramifications, I have it open and toss it aside. Silverback inspects this as well, then dismisses it before shooting me a glance that tells me the next thing I send his way better be edible.

I peer into the pipe and see only darkness. But the upward draft blowing my hair tells me something's down there. It's clean air, not the noxious exhaust of a machine.

This is something. This could be it.

Whatever "it" is.

To no great surprise, my cell phone has zero bars. Calling this in means over an hour of trekking back to where I started. It could be nighttime before anyone gets here. And if we need to get warrants to inspect the property, hell, it could be days.

I look at my useless phone and get a sudden burst of inspiration. With the rope from the saddlebag, I'm able to make a tiny harness for it. Camera and light turned on, I lower the device into the hole.

Silverback watches me intently, trying to comprehend what the crazy woman is doing now.

"Take notes, kid," I tell him.

After about twenty feet, I feel the line go slack as the phone touches solid ground.

A dormant childhood fear surfaces as I remember a nightmare I had after watching the movie *Tremors* with my dad. I quickly reel in the line lest I attract a Graboid.

There's a sickening feeling in my stomach when the line suddenly slackens again. Damn it! From deep below I hear my phone hitting the floor and what may be my screen cracking.

"Oh shit," I growl.

The self-proclaimed World's Greatest Girl Escape Artist just lost her phone because she couldn't tie a proper knot. I'd instinctively made a false knot, designed to easily come undone.

Silverback, convinced I have nothing useful to teach him, turns his head to sniff at some weeds.

"I'm good at getting out of knots, not into them," I protest aloud, as I squat down with my back to the tube. Crap.

That is my government-issue phone—the one that has my business card laminated to the back of it. The business card that says FBI in huge letters.

Damn it. Of all the stupid things. If someone is down there, the element of surprise is gone if they find it.

Now isn't the time to sit here cursing myself out.

I have to act.

I have to get my phone.

CHAPTER FORTY-SEVEN

RESCUE OP

I TIE A DOZEN knots in the rope, spaced about two feet apart. Although I can do more chin-ups than most men, I'm not going to try to pull myself up with a bare grip. I double-check them to make sure I didn't pull a Tricky Jessica again and accidentally make magic knots. Dying at the bottom of a well because I fooled myself would be too humiliating a way to go.

I toy with the idea of tying the rope off to Silverback, but decide that wouldn't be the smartest thing to do given his penchant for wandering, not to mention whether or not he'd even decide to pull me back up. I can very easily see myself reach the bottom of the well only to have the rope vanish when he finds a particularly tasty patch of grass to munch on. And to be honest, given the disdainful looks he's been giving me and the hole, I'm not sure if he's fully on board with this plan. To him, this is yet one more silly thing monkeys do.

Silverback may not be game, but the U-shaped staple the grate was locked to is nice and thick, welded into the metal tube. It provides a firm place to tie the end of the rope.

"Okay, pal. You first," I say to Silverback as I dust the dirt off my hands. He blinks at me.

I get a thought. "Actually . . ."

I take a business card from my wallet and write out a short note.

EMERGENCY!!!
If you find this horse, call the number on this
card! I'm stuck in an underground vent at
Triple Star Construction!

I think that gets right to the point.

Using my spare hair tie, I wrap the card around the pommel. "Alright, boy. If you don't hear from me in ten minutes, go get help."

Silverback stares at me blankly.

I give the tube an anxious look and attempt to bury my anxiety.

"And get me a grande latte . . . um, and a cowboy . . . blue eyes, independently wealthy, not too rustic. Preferably educated in an out-of state-school. Maybe working finance or a hard science."

I pat Silverback on the flank, which he interprets as a signal to start walking.

I chase after him and grab the reins. "Wait! Hold up. Not yet."

Silverback stops and gives me another of his looks: *Seriously, lady?*

"Okay. Wait here for now. I'll be right back."

I wait to make sure he doesn't trot off. Obediently, he stays put and observes me as I stick my foot over the edge of the pipe and begin my descent.

He does a tiny two-step backward at the thought I might be asking him to follow me down, even thought that would be a physical impossibility. Given how narrow the tube has suddenly become, I'm not sure if I'm going to have an easy time of it either.

Gripping the knots with my fists and feet, I lower myself down. The butt of the shotgun, which is slung over my shoulder, scrapes the metal side as I descend and I cringe.

Silverback trots over to the mouth of the shaft and looks down at me. I think, although this could be wishful on my part, he actually has a look of worry on his long face.

Horses are quite brilliant when they just have a narrow set of things to consider. Watching a crazy human climb into a mysterious hole in the ground is outside of their set of experiences.

"Don't worry. I'll be okay. I've gone down tighter passages. Someday I'll tell you about the time a Jarrett Pedestal refused to widen for me."

His head is a black silhouette against the shrinking blue sky. His dark eyes reflect flecks of light as he stares down, confused and potentially concerned.

I look up at him and smile with false reassurance.

"I'll be okay. We'll ride again soon. Don't forget the cowboy. Um, maybe one with a tow hitch?"

I decide to stop talking when I get lower into the tube, afraid my voice might carry.

As I descend, the updraft maintains its steady flow, bringing with it the distant sound of machinery. I try not to think about my last experience going underground.

Less than a year ago, a corrupt Mexican cop tried to kill me by throwing me to the jagged bottom of a cave. But I got the better of him. I sent that asshole to the hospital—and, when his superiors found out he'd screwed up, his eventual demise. I've now nearly died in Mexico three times. Once, when I was a teenager performing an underwater escape on live television. Then with the cave. And last, but not least, the ambush at the grocery store.

I remind myself this isn't Mexico. Technically, this isn't even a cave. Or is it?

All I can see beyond my feet is a black void.

Anything could be down there.

Hell, I could be lowering myself feetfirst into a giant juice blender. Or maybe a feral rat breeding experiment.

I mentally cycle through the possibilities.

This could even be some kind of government installation that has nothing to do with the Red Chain. Maybe they're weaponizing Ebola down there.

Delightful.

But if this is a government facility, private security would have stopped Silverback and me from getting so close. It would be designated with some banal name, like US Department of Geology and Paper Products. Something designed to induce a yawn and encourage you to take your curiosity elsewhere.

My biggest mistake—I realize as I reach the end of the shaft—was not looking for another entrance. Assuredly, somewhere around the hilltop, maybe in an arroyo on the other side, a gravel road must lead to some kind of opening. Maybe a metal building up against the rock face, or a sloping driveway that leads down here.

Nice to think of this now. Brilliant, Jessica!

No. I decide if there is another entrance like that, I can count on it being under surveillance. They'll want to know who's knocking on their front door.

This air vent could be watched too, but I didn't spot any high masts on which a camera could be mounted. That's not saying there couldn't be a rock cam, or a rubber lizard with a sensor built into his head. But this entrance is probably the least guarded. Assuming there *are* even guards?

I reach the end of the pipe and my feet swing into free space.

It's still totally dark. I avoided using my flashlight for my climb down because this is supposed to be a stealth job.

Below me I see a faint rectangular glow, which I recognize as my iPhone, its flashlight facing downward.

I release the rope, and my shoes immediately touch the ground. I crouch down low and listen for a moment before turning off the video recorder on my phone, which now has captured eight minutes of black.

I only hear the whirring of a distant air handler.

Moving slowly, hand on the butt of my pistol, I grip my phone to turn the light on the chamber, ready for any movement. Spinning it around for a quick look reveals that I'm in a long tunnel, the farthest ends of which are in darkness.

I shut off the light and slip the phone back into my pocket.

Silverback's head is just a tiny shadow in the circle of light far above me. I'm deep down in whatever this is.

The sensible thing now is to climb back up the rope.

"Just give me another minute or two before you get that cowboy," I whisper, before doing the opposite.

CHAPTER FORTY-EIGHT

SECRET CINEMA

THE CORRIDOR STRETCHES to infinity in either direction. I decide to move toward the source of the flowing air, because it makes about as much sense as any other plan. The walls of the tunnel are cinder block, and they have that new-construction concrete smell that can linger in an enclosed space for years.

It takes me back to when I was thirteen and my classmate Fiona Schnell's older sister got a job working at a big Cineplex in Calabasas. One night after we came to see an *X-Men* movie, she took us on a little tour.

"Want to see something cool?" she'd asked, pulling a large set of keys from her pocket.

We walked around the outside of the building. I remember the heat coming off the walls after they'd baked in the sun all day. Halfway down the impossibly long wall of the theater, we stopped at a metal door.

"This place was supposed to have twenty-four theaters. They only opened with sixteen," she told us.

I wasn't sure what that meant, but I could tell from her tone this was something cool, if not downright spooky. She opened the door and ushered us into a dark space. Cutting through the pitch black, the light from the entrance revealed a dirt floor.

I was struck by how much cooler the interior was.

With a loud *thunk*, the door slammed shut and we were in total darkness.

"This is freaky," Fiona whispered.

"Check this out," said her sister as she turned on her flashlight.

The beam shot across the cavernous interior, barely illuminating the far wall.

"This is what a movie theater is like before they build the separate screens." Her light passed back and forth, revealing a vast football-field-size chamber with high ceilings and boundaries that seemed to go on forever.

It *was* spooky. It was surreal.

I felt like we were on an alien planet.

This massive empty space, with a half-man-made, half-dirt floor, was inside a movie theater I'd visited dozens of times without having any idea it existed.

It was almost like stepping into another dimension.

Being in this tunnel feels like that. Above me are parched desert, rusty hills, and hopefully a patient horse. The question on my mind is how forgotten a place this is.

As I walk toward the end of the corridor, the whirring grows louder. Cold air blows past my ankles and I catch two vents, as tall as me, in either wall.

This must be some kind of outflow chamber.

Just past the vents is a metal door, not unlike the one that led to the empty cinema. The lock is a small tumbler, but it isn't latched so I don't need to use my picks.

Carefully, moving the handle just a millimeter at a time,

I slowly open the door. Giving myself enough room to slide through, I step inside the next darkened chamber after listening to make sure it was empty.

Although my flashlight is turned off, this corridor feels different than the last one. The sound behaves differently. Besides the whirring having diminished, there's also less of an echo as I walk, even though the floors and wall are concrete.

When I reach the end, only about ten meters from the entrance, I notice the reason. Instead of a metal door, this side of the corridor has a thick black curtain.

I reach out and feel the texture. Heavy, like a theatrical curtain, the material is slightly coarse and woven from thick fibers. Like a bathroom towel, it absorbs much of the echo.

I stand still and listen before pulling the drape back and stepping inside the next room. My light is still off, so I wait again to make sure I'm alone. As an added precaution, I step away from the doorway in the event I'm being observed.

My unease is only increasing. I should have left as soon as I retrieved my phone. The churning pit of my stomach tells me I shouldn't be here. I feel as if I've ventured too deep into a predator's cave, and realize it might still be home.

This room feels different from the first two corridors.

I can still hear my clumsy feet shuffling as the sound bounces around, but the reverb has a different quality to it. Each scrape triggers my flight reflex. I should turn around.

I take out my light again, keeping my other hand on the butt of my pistol.

The acoustics of the room remind me of a . . .

I flick on the light when I'm certain no one else is here.

A church.

It's a large chamber, about twenty meters across and forty long. What gives it that church-like feeling is its very high ceiling, and the hundred or so mats lying on the floor in a grid. At the far end is an elevated platform.

Other than the mats, the only objects are ten wrought iron candle stands spaced around the perimeter. There aren't even pews.

The lack of ostentation chills me. This is exactly the kind of place I'd expect members of the Red Chain to gather.

Back at the farmhouse, they eschewed the relative niceties for a fire pit and mattresses on the floor. I'd expect the way they worship isn't much different.

This isn't a fun church with a born-again rocker strumming an electric guitar between sermons. They take their beliefs, whatever they may be, very seriously—more seriously than creature comforts.

I step up onto the small stage and scan my light across the floor.

From the entrance, I'd noticed a dark spot. Up close I can see it more clearly.

The foul copper scent tells me what it is before my eyes do.

Black, with a hint of maroon, it's a dried pool of blood.

CHAPTER FORTY-NINE

ADVOCATE

THE FRONT OF the church, or whatever they call this chamber, is a disturbing place to find a bloodstain. I can tell from the different shades that the blood is in layers, and some are much older than others. The most recent additions are lighter, almost glossy. They could have happened just days ago.

I move my hand away from my pistol and swing my shotgun around to my hip as a precaution. In the darkness, with potential assailants coming at me from any direction, I don't want to waste time aiming.

Technically, I'm trespassing.

Technically, this is fucked up.

My first thought is that I'm standing over a spot where they murdered people in some kind of ritual. But there is no drain and the puddle just isn't large enough to account for an adult bleeding out from an artery.

Then what?

Was this some kind of crazy blood brother ritual where they sliced their palms and slapped hands?

No.

I study the stain for the telltale patterns that can reveal how the wounds were made.

Something else about the dark stains stands out as I look closer; the flecks of blood radiate away from the center. It's a spray pattern, but not the kind that occurs when you slice a major vein, or stab someone.

I think about the stained floor of the workshop where my dad painted his props. I'd sometimes help him out, whether he wanted it or not. My clumsy strokes would send paint flying, splattering everything around in a fine mist.

I don't think someone was painting with blood. But they were doing something similar.

I take a few steps to the side of the stage and face the empty room. On impulse, I squat into a kneeling position, almost as if I'm in prayer.

Glancing over my shoulder on the concrete wall, I spot more drops of blood. If I . . .

I move my arm up, and over my shoulder. That's it!

When I stand up to examine the back wall, I notice that the black thing I'd initially thought was an electrical cable is actually a whip.

Not a long one. The short kind you'd use on yourself.

Ugh.

These people were into self-flagellation. That's their thing. The blood splatter is what you'd see if you knelt down here and whipped yourself.

Lots of extreme religious movements use this technique, but that doesn't make it any less shocking or disturbing and I'm not familiar with anywhere the one decoration in the entire church is a bloody leather whip.

Who decides which members get up here and whip themselves? Is it a punishment or a reward?

Our Jane Doe, Heather Dryl, didn't have any visible trauma to her back. Not recent, at least.

Maybe this is a special thing. Maybe it is just for the men. Even just the priests, if they have them.

What happens to your sense of identity when you kneel here naked and draw your own blood in front of others? I'm reminded that a cult isn't just a group of people who share different beliefs. They *think* differently. How do you get a nice, if misguided, girl like Heather Dryl to show up on my doorstep with a kidnapped infant and a murderous look in her eyes? Make her spend some time in this hellhole degrading herself physically and mentally. That's how. The combination of pain and psychological conditioning literally can rewire your brain.

I go to the opposite end of the chamber from where I entered. A small breeze is blowing under a black curtain. I spend a minute next to the curtain, listening to detect any movement on the other side.

More silence.

I switch off my flashlight and walk beyond the curtain, then wait again before turning it on. So far, I've just been going in a straight line, but this hall leads to a junction. Between the entrance where I'm standing and the intersection, there are several doors.

I go to the first one and slowly open it, making sure it doesn't squeak. On the other side are dozens of sleeping mats in a bare concrete room. At the foot of each mat is a pile of books. At the head is a snuffed-out candle.

The books are about exciting topics like botany and mathematical theorems. It's the kind of salacious reading selection you'd expect from a bunch of medieval monks. Math and plants may be the *only* acceptable topics around here, similar to what I found at the farmhouse.

I don't know what creeps me out more, the bloodstain in the church or their idea of an exciting night of reading in bed.

At the other end of the hallway beyond the intersection there's another room just like that one, also littered with mats and books. Girl and boy dorms?

I kneel down to pick up a copy of a book on mountain flowers. Tucked into the middle of the black-and-white pages, behind a scrap of paper, is a pressed purple Perry's Bellflower. Stashed away like a porn magazine, I wonder if this was a private pleasure. Late at night when all the candles were put out, did the occupant of this mat open their book so they could take in the forbidden scent?

I don't know if I want to run into him or her down here to find out. As it is, I'm pushing my luck.

What started out as a stunt has led me foolishly deep into the bowels of this place. A place where I shouldn't be. Every instinct is telling me to get out quickly. I decide it's time to back my curiosity off and make my retreat.

I step into the corridor. As a precaution, I kill my light. Just running my hand along the wall to guide me, I retrace my steps.

Suddenly, my skin begins to prickle. I get the feeling I'm not alone.

A gust of wind chills my cheeks and I hear a sound I'm never going to forget—footsteps running toward me in the darkness.

Small footsteps.

CHAPTER FIFTY

STRANGERS IN THE DARK

My body freezes. I turn toward the sound, which I think is coming from somewhere behind me. My right finger slides over the trigger to the shotgun.

The steps get louder as they grow closer. Closely paced and light, I can't tell if they belong to an animal—or to something else. My imagination goes to wild places in the dark. Stories of secret government experiments and strange creatures from conspiracy theories fill my mind.

I tell myself this is just crazy talk, but I've already been inside one secret government facility that bordered on science fiction. Now I'm not sure where to draw the line. It takes every ounce of effort for me not to fire into the dark at whatever's running toward me. My skin is flushed, and all my animal instincts are telling me to fire or flee. I'd call out, but I don't want to draw attention to myself.

As the sound comes straight toward me, I remember my flashlight. Right hand still firmly gripping the shotgun, I use my left to retrieve it.

The moment my fingers touch the switch, the footsteps stop. I can feel my heart beating in my chest as I listen. Something bumps into my arm, and I nearly drop the light as my right finger almost squeezes the trigger.

I recover and spin around quickly, but the beam only catches the empty far wall as the footsteps fade down the corridor.

What was that? Who was that?

Leave. It's time to leave. The voice in the back of my head is screaming at me to get the hell out of here.

But I can't.

I won't. I'm so close. There's too much at stake.

I have to know.

I chase the steps to the junction and down into the corridor.

This could be a trap. It has to be.

A metal door appears in the middle of the hall. I swing it open, light blazing, shotgun aimed forward, only to find rows and rows of canned food. The shadows from my light dance around menacingly as I frantically search the pantry. There are a hundred places to hide, but I didn't hear the door open and shut. I assume whatever it was didn't go in here.

I go back to the hallway. In a horror movie, I'd be yelling at myself to go the other way.

But I'm an FBI agent. *I'm* the one who chases after scary shadows.

I think for a moment about Aileen and the goat she tasered, and take a deep breath. Whoever is down here with me is probably just as scared as I am.

Yeah, right.

That's why they ran *toward* me.

And past me, I remind myself. If they wanted to hurt me . . .

The corridor leads to another, and then another, each one a long, musty tunnel of cinder blocks with a concrete ceiling and no light switch to be found. I start to lose track of which way I came.

I take another turn, and begin to fear I'm getting lost down here. These tunnels don't seem to be built in any orderly fashion.

Oh shit! What if this is a goddamn maze?

Maybe not an intentional one, but this is the haphazard layout of an ant colony.

E. E. Holmes, our nation's first truly prolific serial killer, built himself a murder house on an entire city block complete with a labyrinth and abattoir for human victims.

I don't think this structure is meant for that. At least, I hope not. I've been in bunkers that made about as much sense before. Of course, if the footsteps are intended to lead me deeper . . .

I clench the shotgun tightly. If a minotaur is waiting for me, I hope he likes buckshot.

I reach a metal door at the end of the passage, and I'm fairly certain the footsteps ran toward it.

Beyond thoughts of caution at this point, I grip the knob and fling the door wide open. My light catches row after row of tables and plastic chairs, those funky candelabras everywhere. This must be their dining room. I search back and forth with my light, but can't find anything lurking in the shadows.

I kneel down and flash the light under the tables. Nothing peers back at me.

I stand up, decide to hold my ground.

"I'm an FBI agent, come out with your hands up!" I say, with all the confidence I can fake.

No response.

"I'm armed and I need you to identify yourself for your safety!"
Nothing.

I jerk my light to a corner where I think I see a flicker of movement.

There are only the shadows of tables and chairs.

The furniture strikes me as odd: cheap plastic lawn chairs and card tables. For a sophisticated secret underground facility, they seem rather . . . temporary. And the pantry isn't all that big considering the number of people who are—or were supposed to be—down here implied by the quantity of mats. This doesn't feel so much like an underground bunker awaiting the apocalypse as it does a hideout.

I go toward a door at the opposite end of the room, keeping careful watch from the corners of my eyes. As I get closer to the wall, the back of my neck prickles. I sense something observing me and I whirl around, shining the light on a cluster of tables.

Nothing.

I reach the door and grab the knob.

That's when I hear plastic scraping across concrete.

I spin and walk to the source of the sound. I'm beyond terrified, but I have no alternative. Cowering isn't an option. I stride back across the dining room kicking over the flimsy tables, ruining any possible hiding place.

I give the edge of the last card table a powerful kick, sending it high into the air where it crashes against the wall. My finger is already digging into the trigger of the shotgun, which is ready to blast at whoever or whatever has led me on this chase.

Underneath where the table had stood, I see the shadow I've been chasing.

Oh, god.

CHAPTER FIFTY-ONE

ELIJAH

TWO EYES PEER out at me from the unkempt face of a frightened little boy. His hands are held high in the air, and he's frozen at the sight of the shotgun and the blinding light in his face.

A moment ago I was about to pull the trigger on him in the dark. I can feel the blood drain from my cheeks as I realize how close I came to firing out of fear. I lower the barrel and carefully retract my hand from the trigger, afraid that I might slip.

"Who are you?" I ask, letting the shotgun fall back on the strap, but not letting the light waver.

"E-E-Elijah," he stutters, terrified.

The child looks like he's about to piss himself, but I'm not going to let the Red Chain use another kid to get me to lower my defenses. I keep my attention on the shadows, wary of being blindsided.

Maybe seven or eight, he's got dirt on his face and stains on his white T-shirt and pants.

"Are you alone down here?" I ask.

"Y-y-yes," he replies.

"Where is everybody?"

"They . . . they . . . they left."

Crouched on his knees, hands still raised, the boy is trembling.

My pulse begins to slow down. I'm still on guard, but no longer in a panic state. My police training takes over.

"Turn around, Elijah."

He slowly gets to his feet. "Are . . . are you going to shoot me?" His question has a note of resignation to it.

"No! I'm here to help. I just have to make sure you don't have a weapon."

"Oh." He lifts up the hem of his shirt and spins around, revealing a too-prominent rib cage.

I wouldn't put strapping a bomb to a child past the Red Chain, but he's not hiding anything.

I pick up a chair I knocked over and set it upright.

"Have a seat."

He pulls himself into the plastic chair, his feet dangling over the cliff-like edge. It's easy to forget what it's like to be a small person in a big person's world.

Elijah is still scared witless. So am I.

I decide on a bit of a compromise. I take a seat with my back to the wall and set my light on a table to my left, facing away from us. This way, anyone entering the room will be blinded. It also gives Elijah a chance to see my face. As his eyes adjust, he studies me. His attention lingers on the shotgun that's sitting across my lap, aimed at the entrance.

"What's your name?" he asks, slightly less frightened of me.

"Jessica."

"Are you going to take me there?"

I keep an eye on the entrance, trying to figure out how I'm supposed to proceed. "Where is that?" I ask.

"Where they all went. I was supposed to go, but 'cause my mommy wasn't here they said I couldn't 'cause there would be nobody to take care of me."

I pull a clean tissue from my hip pouch and wipe away the crusted peanut butter and jelly at the corners of his mouth. "Did you find any bread for that?"

He shakes his little head. "I made a hand sandwich."

"A ham sandwich?"

"No." He holds out his palms, which are smeared with peanut butter and jelly. "A hand sandwich. That's when you put all the things you want in your hand."

The innocent answer makes me grin. "Oh, I get it." I take out another tissue and start to scrape away the grime. "Is it okay if I see if there's a little boy hidden under all this?"

He stoically remains still as I scrub away. I use hand sanitizer to get the more stubborn spots.

"Elijah, where's your mommy?" I ask after he's slightly cleaner.

He gives me a shrug. "I don't know."

"When did you see her last?"

"I don't have a watch."

"Was it days?"

"I don't know. Maybe?" he answers hopefully.

I realize that down here he might not be fully aware of time passing. The poor thing. "How many times have you slept since you last saw her?"

His eyes go up and to the side as he tries to make the calculation, before raising his hands and opening and closing them several times. At least fifteen times. Maybe two weeks.

"When did the people leave here?"

He opens and closes his index finger five times. That could be five days or less, given his nap schedule.

"You've been all alone here? Nobody to look after you?" I ask.

He nods his head.

I'm still wary that this could be a trick. "Are you sure?"

He nods with more certainty.

I ball up the tissues I'd cleaned his face with, and pass them into my other hand. "Elijah, blow a puff of air at my hand."

He exhales and I unclench my fist, revealing that the tissue has vanished.

His eyes widen. Not just like an amazed child's, but *real* wide, almost shock.

"Are . . . are you a seraphim?" he stutters.

"You mean an angel?"

"Yes?" His mouth is also wide open.

"Do you always tell the truth to angels?"

He furiously nods.

"Is there anybody else here? Did anyone else tell you to say you were alone?"

It's a dirty trick to play on a child, but I have to do it.

Elijah shakes his head so intensely I'm afraid he'll hurt himself.

"No, Elijah. I'm not an angel. I'm just a girl." I reach behind his ear and produce the ball of tissue. "A girl who does magic."

"Like God?" He stares at the ball as if it were a heavenly revelation.

"No. Tricks. Like you see magicians do on TV."

"I'm not supposed to watch TV."

"Oh. What about movies?"

He stares at me, confounded.

"No movies? No cartoons? Do you go to school?"

"I go to church school," he replies.

"With other children?"

"Yes, with Sara, Ezekiel, and Joshua."

This poor sheltered kid. Three friends? "Where are they?"

"They left with the others."

"But not you?"

"No. They wouldn't let me go because my mommy didn't come back."

She didn't return.

I get a chill down my spine and hesitantly ask, "Elijah, what's your mommy's name?"

"Rebecca."

I relax in a wave of relief.

Then Elijah continues: "But she used to be called Heather. Mommy's name used to be Heather Dryl."

CHAPTER FIFTY-TWO

UNDERCOVER

IN UNDERCOVER SEMINARS they train you how not to let your reactions show on your face. You focus on the plant in the corner of the room, a coffee mug, the funny joke you heard the other day. Don't react. Don't process. Store it all up and think about it later.

Elijah has just told me his mother is the crazy woman who showed up on my doorstep and attempted to kill me, not to mention the baby she'd abducted. The same woman I saw days later, on an autopsy table.

All her life, gone. Her last expression, a painful mix of confusion and terror.

He has her eyes.

"Do you know my mommy?" Elijah asks.

Try not to react.

Try not to wince.

Try not to turn your head away, or contort your face in pain.

I can't lie to the child. I can't tell him the truth.

I stand up. "Let's take a look around here."

With my back toward Elijah, I sling the shotgun on my shoulder and pick up the flashlight, moving the beam away from me. He can't see me right now.

He can't see my face.

Tiny fingers clasp my left hand tightly. "Could you help me find her?"

My heart is ripped out of my chest. I feebly hold on to his hand, trying to be strong. "We'll see, Elijah. We'll see."

It's like he's a ghost, sent to torment me because of my role in this series of awful events. I may have saved the little girl who was stolen from her hospital cradle by Elijah's mom, but in so doing I orphaned this child who was abandoned in the dark.

What monsters would do this? What evil fucks would hurt children like this?

Do I have to ask?

We live in a world where terrorists proudly strap suicide vests to little boys. A world where warlords put AK-47s in the hands of kids who haven't even reached puberty. A world where parents let their children die instead of getting life-saving medical treatment, because that goes against their belief in a God who, like a narcissistic tween demanding you hit "like" on every Instagram post, needs to be loved above anyone else.

I try to avoid defining my own religious beliefs, but if in this moment I saw Abraham raising his knife over his son Isaac, as God had instructed him to do, I'd unload my shotgun into his chest.

ELIJAH AND I walk along a corridor I haven't traveled down before. I distract him, and myself, with questions.

"How many rooms are here, Elijah?"

"Um," he thinks for a moment. "Dozens?" He seems unsure of what the word means.

"What's behind the doors?"

"Stuff."

"Food?" I ask.

"A couple places. Not much."

"How did you get down here?"

"Through a door."

His answers are typical for a child who assumes you already know everything. "Is the door you came through locked?"

"I don't know. There was a 'splosion."

"An explosion?" I ask. "Can you show me?"

He takes me through another long hallway, away from the main corridors. At the end of it is a massive rock fall, with boulders piled all the way to the ceiling.

Jesus. They sealed the place after they left.

"Where were you when this happened?"

"Sleeping," he replies, and points back down the way we came.

"What about everyone else?"

Elijah shrugs. "I was sleeping. Then I heard the 'splosion. It woke me up."

Those assholes, leaving the boy down here to die. I hate them. I hate them like I've never hated before. I will hunt them down. I will chase them.

Badge or no badge, I will find these fuckers.

"Ouch!" Elijah jerks his hand away from my tight grip.

I kneel down. "I'm so sorry."

He shrugs it off, then brushes a hand against my cheek and tells me: "It's okay to be scared. I'll protect you."

He'll protect me? After everything he's been through, he wants to help me.

Sensing the effect his promise has on me, he throws his arms around my neck and hugs me.

"It's okay," he whispers. "Don't be scared. I cried too when they left me. Don't tell Mommy, but I cried a lot."

"You're a brave little boy." I wrap one arm around him and return the hug, then stand back up.

"I found things to do."

"With no light?" I still haven't seen a single working source of light.

"Can you keep a secret?" he asks quietly.

I kneel back down. "Yes."

His voice is hushed. "I found some matches. I'm not supposed to use them."

"I think in this case it was okay."

"I ran out."

"What did you do then?" I ask, trying to fathom how he didn't go crazy.

"I watched TV."

"TV?"

His eyes flash open and, realizing he's done something wrong, he clamps both hands over his mouth.

"It's okay, Elijah. Don't you know that when grown-ups leave you all alone, you're supposed to watch television?"

He lowers his hands. "Really?"

I nod. "It's practically a law."

"Oh . . ." He nods at the revelation.

"Where's this TV you were watching?"

Hopefully this could lead to another way out.

He points down yet another corridor. "That way. There are lots of them. But I can't change the channels. Mostly boring stuff. People fighting and yelling."

"News?"

"Yeah."

"Sounds boring to me." I try not to let on how interesting this actually is.

"There's one really boring channel. Although sometimes I liked to watch it the most. It helped me practice my counting."

"Like *Sesame Street?*"

He shakes his head. "I don't know where that is. This is just a really long number that keeps changing into a smaller number."

I try to make sense of what he means. "Like ten, nine, eight, seven, six, five, four, three, two, one?"

"Yeah," he smiles. "But bigger."

"How much bigger?"

"A little, not a lot."

I try to keep calm. "Has it reached zero yet?"

"Not last time I checked. Maybe. Is that important?"

I try not to let my fear show. I force a smile. "Let's play a game, Elijah. Show me how fast you can run to the TVs, and I'll try to follow!"

CHAPTER FIFTY-THREE

GROUND CONTROL

WHEN I FINALLY catch up to Elijah, he's waiting in another concrete room.

"See!" he says.

His TVs are actually a wall of monitors, reminiscent of the setup we found in the CCA—in the same way an iPhone is reminiscent of an old brick-size cell phone. Instead of clunky CRT rear-screen projections, two rows of four large screens show CNN, Fox, MSNBC, BBC, Al Jazeera, and several other regional news stations. Below them is another similar screen with multiple terminal windows open. Six of them show countdowns that have completed. Two others are still ticking down.

I check my watch and do the math.

The first one has five hours left. The other, several months.

Counting down to what?

I realize that the finished countdowns have a "date of completion" at the bottom.

The first one is the same date as the dam break. The second

one coincides with the shooting at the White House. The others
match up to the dates of the blackouts.

Elijah leans over the controls, his small fingers about to press
the keyboard. I gently pull him backward.

"Want a granola bar?" I take my lunch from my pocket and
hand it to Elijah. "Have a seat by the wall for a second, okay?"

"Can I hold your gun?" he asks as sweetly as possibly.

"Not happening. Now have a seat."

"I just wanted to protect you."

"You do that by being a lookout. Okay?"

He takes the granola bar from me and squats down by the
wall and watches. I make sure I can keep an eye on him as well. I
trust him—to a point.

I don't know if the countdowns are passive, or if they are controlling something. If they are, then what is it?

Staring at the lines of mysterious commands, I wish I'd spent
less time palming silver dollars and put more effort into program-
ming. If Gerald or Jennifer were here, I'm sure they'd know what
to do in a cinch.

Hopelessly, I check the signal on my cell phone.

No Service. Obviously.

Thinking wishfully, I check the Wi-Fi in the event these backward, Luddite, floor-sleeping, candle-reading assholes happen to
make an exception for checking Facebook and have an open network.

Nope.

But what about this computer? What about the screens? They
have to be getting a signal from somewhere.

I crouch down and look behind the monitors. There are some
power plugs, a coaxial cable, and what looks like an Ethernet jack.

Okay. This thing is networked. That's something. In theory, I
could use this setup to talk to the outside world. That's if I knew

what the hell to do in a Linux or Unix or whatever the kind of system this is.

"You know anything about command prompt interfaces, kiddo?"

Elijah shakes his head. "I'm not supposed to touch commuters."

"Hah, when we get out of here I'm buying you an iPad and an Xbox."

He makes an excited squeal then asks, "What's an iPad-box?"

This is worse than child abuse.

"I'll show you later. Do you know if the people down here had a way to talk to people outside?"

"I don't think so. Sometimes people would come here to send messages, I think. I heard people saying they was going to the commuter room to send something."

"It's okay. We'll figure this out," I say, more confidently than I feel.

The countdown clock keeps whirring away.

I check my watch again. I have to decide if I just want to get out of here with the kid and call for some tech support when I get into cell range, or if I should stay and try to do something now. If I leave, it's going to be too close. Assuming a best-case scenario, I'd be on the phone in two hours.

And then what?

There's no chance in hell I'd be able to get anyone who knows what to do down here before the clock runs out. God knows what happens when it does.

I brace myself and type "help" into a command prompt.

A star (*) next to a name means the command is disabled.
JOB_SPEC [&] ((expression))
. filename [arguments]:

[arg . . .] [[expression]]

alias [-p] [name[=value] . . .] bg [job_spec . . .]

bind [-lpvsPVS] [-m keymap] [-f fi break [n]

builtin [shell-builtin [arg . . .]] caller [EXPR]

case WORD in [PATTERN [| PATTERN]. cd [-L|-P]
  [dir]

command [-pVv] command [arg . . .] compgen
  [-abcdefgjksuv] [-o option

complete [-abcdefgjksuv] [-pr] [-o continue [n]

declare [-afFirtx] [-p] [name[=val dirs [-clpv] [+N] [-N]

disown [-h] [-ar] [jobspec . . .] echo [-neE] [arg . . .]

enable [-pnds] [-a] [-f filename] eval [arg . . .]

exec [-cl] [-a name] file [redirec exit [n]

export [-nf] [name[=value] . . .] or false

fc [-e ename] [-nlr] [first] [last fg [job_spec]

for NAME [in WORDS . . . ;] do COMMA for ((exp1;
  exp2; exp3)); do COM

function NAME { COMMANDS; } or NA getopts opt-
  string name [arg]

hash [-lr] [-p pathname] [-dt] [na help [-s] [pattern . . .]

history [-c] [-d offset] [n] or hi if COMMANDS; then
  COMMANDS; [elif

jobs [-lnprs] [jobspec . . .] or job kill [-s sigspec |-n sig-
  num |-si

let arg [arg . . .] local name[=value] . . .

logout popd [+N |-N] [-n]

printf [-v var] format [arguments] pushd [dir | +N |-N]
  [-n]

pwd [-LP] read [-ers] [-u fd] [-t timeout] [

readonly [-af] [name[=value] . . .] return [n]

select NAME [in WORDS . . . ;] do CO set
  [—abefhkmnptuvxBCHP] [-o opti

shift [n] shopt [-pqsu] [-o long-option] opt

source filename [arguments] suspend [-f]

test [expr] time [-p] PIPELINE

times trap [-lp] [arg signal_spec . . .]

true type [-afptP] name [name . . .]

typeset   [-afFirtx]   [-p]   name[=valu   ulimit
   [-SHacdfilmnpqstuvx] [limit

umask [-p] [-S] [mode] unalias [-a] name [name . . .]

unset [-f] [-v] [name . . .] until COMMANDS; do COM-
   MANDS; done

variables-Some variable names an wait [n]

while COMMANDS; do COMMANDS; done { COM-
   MANDS; }

So much for that. I type in *"e-mail"* and get an error message. *"Browser"* gets me nothing either. I might as well be poking the thing with a stick and hooting at it.

"Are you talking to your friends?" asks Elijah.

"No, hon. I'm trying to figure out how to use this thing."

"Oh. Are your friends nice?"

I think of Gerald and Jennifer. "Yes. I think you'd like them."

"I miss my friends," he says softly.

"Me too."

"Sometimes we'd stay up after dark and whisper to each other. Do you do that?"

"Sometimes."

His question reminds me of how Gerald and Jennifer make each other giggle in the bullpen. We all keep an instant message screen open, but they like to use one of their geek things to talk as well. Jennifer had shown me once, so I could be in on the joke, but it was too complicated for me. What was it?

IRC. Of course.

They keep that open all the time. Hmm.

I type "Open IRC" into the terminal.

Damn. Nothing.

The countdown timer keeps dropping. I've still got hours, but it's stressing me out all the same. If this is like any of the other countdowns, people are going to die when it's done.

I take a deep breath. Let me think this through.

This isn't some magic box I can just shout commands at. I have to be specific.

open /Applications/IRC.app

Nope. Don't they call it something else?

open /Applications/IRSSI.app

Boom. I've got an IRC window in front of me!

What the hell did we call the channel we used?

Right: *#Misfitgmen*
Password: *PrincipalAiles<>*

GMANCER: Pepperoni

NOTACATLADYYET: Again? What about Hawaiian?

GMANCER: No dice. You and MagicWoman always gang up on me when it comes time to choose. I hate pineapple.

What name would you like to use to enter the chat room?

Seeing my coworkers bantering away about a pizza order makes me grin. I furiously type: *MagicWoman.*

MOD: *MagicWoman has entered the chat.*

MAGICWOMAN: Sorry, Gerald. It's going to be Hawaiian pizza again.

GMANCER: Jessica!!!!!

NOTACATLADYYET: Where the hell are you?

MAGICWOMAN: Deep underground in the Red Chain's subterranean evil torture lair with two countdown clocks and a scared orphaned boy.

GMANCER: Hah!

NOTACATLADYYET: ROTFL

MAGICWOMAN: No. Seriously.

GMANCER: FUCK!

NOTACATLADYYET: Why am I not surprised?

CHAPTER FIFTY-FOUR

SUDO

GERALD AND JENNIFER patiently walk me through the steps to give them control of my computer. It takes about twenty minutes for me to find the ports and enact other mysterious wizardry they need, but when it's done I watch as they rapidly open and close programs and scan through lists of text almost faster than I can see.

Occasionally they update me on the IRC channel.

GMANCER: *You have your phone?*
MAGICWOMAN: Yeah?
NOTACATLADYYET: We found a Wi-Fi network. We can turn it on and talk to you.
MAGICWOMAN: Great!

A few minutes later, I'm patched through to them.

"Jessica? Can you hear me?" asks Jennifer.

"Right here!" I say over speakerphone. Hearing their voices

makes me feel like things are going to be okay. "Say hello to Elijah."

"Hey, Elijah!" Jennifer says, revealing a much softer tone she must only break out in the presence of children.

He looks down at the phone in bafflement. I realize he may never have made a phone call before.

"That's my friend Jennifer," I explain.

His eyes widen. "Hello!" he eagerly shouts.

"Are you keeping my friend Jessica safe down there?"

"Yes." He pats me on the arm. "She was scared of the dark but I told her it's okay."

"You're very brave."

I'd filled them in on who his mother was and the current state of things down here via IRC.

"Hello, Elijah. This is Robert. I'm Jessica's boss." His voice is upbeat, but I can tell he's doing that to put Elijah at ease.

"Are you in trouble?" Elijah whispers.

"Always," I whisper back.

"Hello, Robert," Elijah says.

"Elijah, I have a very special job for you. Can you help us?" asks Ailes.

"Yes, sir," he answers, his back suddenly straight.

"Is there a chair where you can sit and watch the screens?"

"He can have mine."

"Okay. Elijah, I need Jessica to do some work. While she does this, I want you to sit right there and watch all the TVs. Can you do that?"

"Okay," he replies.

"Do you know your ABCs?" asks Ailes.

"Uh-huh. Not always in order."

"That's good enough. If someone comes into the room other than Jessica, I want you to type H for help. Can you do that?"

"Yeah. Is Jessica going away?" Elijah asks, worried.

"I need her to go down the hall to check on something. That's all. Tell you what. Why don't we play a game on the little screen. Alright? I'll give you a letter, and you try to type in as many animals as you can think of that begin with that letter. Can you do that?"

"Okay. What if it's H?"

He's a clever boy. I pat him on the head and he beams up at me.

"You're very smart, Elijah," says Ailes. "If you need help, type a lot of H's and then hit the Return key. Got it?"

I put Elijah in my seat and make sure he understands how to use the computer. The kid takes to it quickly. In an hour he'll be showing me how to run the thing.

I ruffle his hair. "I'll be back. Stay put. Okay?"

"Okay." His eyes are glued to the screen as he tries to think of animals that begin with B.

Out in the hallway I switch off the speakerphone. "Is he going to be okay with the computer?" I don't want him accidentally blowing up the facility.

"Yes. Only that chat window is working. He'll be fine," Ailes answers.

"So, what's going on?"

"We have the sheriff's department on the way, but they're still over an hour out. We've also been able to dig a little into the code on the system. It's the CCA two point zero, as we feared."

"Can't we just shut it down?"

"We need to know what it's doing first. It might have a dead-man's trigger."

"Christ." Just when I thought we had things under control. "What can I do?"

"We still don't know what the hell this place is. I was able to task a military satellite to get some thermal images of the complex. There are two tunnels longer than the rest, which radiate in different directions, and one of them leads to a large area that seems to have some industrial air handlers near the surface. I need you to check it out."

"What are you thinking?"

"We don't have a clue. Finding out what's in that room will help us figure out how to respond. We think the timer is connected to some kind of location, and the contents of this room could tell us what it's for."

I glance back at the control room where Elijah is dutifully trying to think of animals. I hate to leave him there, but I don't know what I'll find at the other end of the complex.

I FOLLOW AILES'S instructions and find a metal door I'd passed by before. Beyond it is a corridor that stretches farther than any of others I've been in down here. At the end of it is another door, which is locked.

"You there?" asks Ailes as I study the door.

"Yeah. I didn't realize the Wi-Fi would work all the way in here. Door is locked. Give me a second."

It takes me forty.

The beam of my flashlight bounces off metal counters and cabinets. At the other side of the room I see myself reflected in a large interior window.

"What do we have?" asks Ailes.

"Hold on. Maybe a kitchen." I fumble around for a light switch and find a box on the other side of the door. I flip the switch, and the overhead lights blink on one by one. It's the first source of illumination I've seen down here besides my flashlight and the glow of the monitors. I squint to adjust to the brightness.

"Jessica? What is it?" Ailes is anxious to know what's going on.

"Fuck."

"Blackwood?" he says, worried.

"All I know is that whatever it is they need a bunch of hazmat suits and a sealed lab to work with it."

CHAPTER FIFTY-FIVE

HAZMAT

THE LAB IS divided into two sections. On the side closest to me are workbenches and mostly empty shelves. On the other side, through an airlock, is a clean room with racks of test tubes, rows of refrigerators, and an entire shelf filled with binders. The facility is made up of white floors and gleaming metal walls. Unlike the sparse concrete interior of the rest of the compound, this looks futuristic and expensive.

"Jessica, I need you to hold tight until we can get a hazmat team in there," says Ailes.

"You're kidding, right? You've seen the clock. We don't have time."

I'd love nothing more than to get the hell out of here and take Elijah to Disneyland to deprogram him. But that's not the hand I've been dealt.

I set the phone down on the counter and grab one of the blue suits.

"Agent Blackwood, it could be anything in there, explosives, ricin . . ." He's using his serious tone to tell me I don't have a choice.

"Exactly," I reply as I find the zipper and step inside it. "We need to know now."

"You're not trained for this! I can't have you going in there."

But, like me, he knows we can't risk any alternative.

"Dr. Ailes, I'm the best trained person for this down here."

Considering the only other person down here is a child, that's not saying much.

"Fine," he relents, knowing we're out of options. "Let me loop in a couple of our people on our end."

"Get them on the line fast, because I'm stepping into the airlock."

"Is there a hose for you to plug the suit into?"

"Hold on." I look around and spot a coil of plastic tube. "Yeah. On the other side."

"All right. There should be a panel near the door. Make sure the air is flowing. You need to keep positive pressure in the suit, as that keeps whatever is in there out of you."

"Got it."

With no place else to put my phone, I slide it into my bra.

"Can you hear me?" I ask.

"You sound muffled."

"Don't ask. How's Elijah doing?"

"Right now he's given me six different animals that begin with G."

"I don't think I can name three."

"You also can't follow instructions."

"Obviously."

I swing open the steel door to the airlock and step inside. It's daunting to close it behind me and hear the hiss of air moving through the small chamber. This is not a happy place.

After a deep breath, I open the inner door and step inside the mysterious lab. It takes me a moment to get the hose hooked up to my suit. Once it clicks into place, I begin to fill up like a balloon.

"How you doing?" asks Ailes.

"Feeling bloated. I'm inside."

"Okay. I have Dr. Stiller on the line. He's one of our biowarfare experts."

Jiminy Cricket. My stomach sinks.

What the hell have I gotten myself into?

"Hello," says Stiller. "Thank you for doing this. I'm going to need you to just look with your eyes. Okay? Can you do that? Don't touch anything." His voice is calm and patronizing.

"Is he talking to me or to Elijah?" I snap.

"What's the difference?" Ailes responds.

"Sorry, Jessica," says Stiller, somewhat apologetic. "It's a habit. Sometimes I get gung-ho agents who want to open and taste everything."

"That's not me, Doc." Well, not always.

"Alright. Can you describe the equipment? Have you had much training for these situations?"

"Minimal. There is a thing for spinning test tubes. Lots of pipe work."

"Pipes? Glass ones?"

"Mostly."

"Are they climate controlled?"

"No. Hold on." I inspect a device at the base of the contraption. "I think there's a cooling unit at the very end."

"Okay. I think that's a good sign."

"How's that?"

"It's probably not a bacterial or viral agent."

"Well that's a relief."

"Um, sort of . . ." He pauses. "I should have had you use a Geiger counter first. Did you see one in the other room?"

"Nope. Too late now."

"Okay. I want you to look inside a refrigerator and tell me what you see. Remember, look, don't touch."

I go to the nearest one and swing the door open.

It's empty.

"Nothing."

"Nothing?"

"Nada. Zilch. Next one?"

"Hold up, can you tell me what the temperature is?"

"Uh . . ." I look around and find a control panel. "Two degrees."

"Celsius?"

"Yes, sir."

"Okay. That would appear too cold for bacteria. Just above freezing. I think we're dealing with a chemical agent. Possibly a high explosive."

At least I'm not going to die of a flesh-eating disease. "Great."

"The question is how much of it? Is there a storage unit near where you are? That would be a separate room."

"There's another chamber at the far end of the complex. Should I go there?"

"No," says Stiller. "This would be close by. Possibly with a loading dock."

"Nothing like that."

"Alright. It might be something they just need in small batches. We'll have a bomb squad take some field samples as soon as they get there."

"Doc, that's still going to take some time."

I'm worried that there's something else we're not noticing. The Red Chain doesn't seem like the old-school bombing types anymore. "There's a row of binders here. Should I open them?"

"I guess that's a good idea."

He *guesses?*

I grab the one at the end, which has several bookmarks sticking out, and flip it open on the counter.

"What do you see?" asks Stiller.

The complex molecules and chemical names I can't pronounce mean nothing to me. "Um, maybe see if Bill Nye the Science Guy can come down here and explain this."

"Can you read me some of the names?"

"I have a better idea."

"Jessica, what's that sound?" asks Ailes.

"I'm taking off the suit."

"Don't do that, Jessica!" Stiller protests.

"We don't have time." I pull the helmet back and let the torso drop to my waist. "Something nasty is about to happen. Either it happens to me, or to a hell of a lot of people. If I start gagging, I'll do my best to describe the experience."

I slide my phone out from my bra. "Can we FaceTime on this thing?"

"I can," says Ailes. "Dr. Stiller, I can probably relay what I see."

He leaves out: *Better than my idiot agent.*

Ailes's concerned face appears on the screen.

"Hey, boss." I give him an uneasy grin, then turn the camera toward the binder and start flipping through the pages.

Ailes calls out the chemical names to Stiller. Occasionally Stiller asks him to repeat one. I pick up one word in particular: *"Psychotropic."*

"Crazy juice, again?" Various mind-altering chemicals had been involved in my last two cases. The first one was an unknown, probably devised by Heywood himself. The second was a natural one, found in a fish that lived in a cave in Mexico.

"Yes, Agent Blackwood," answers Stiller. "That appears to be some kind of drug. Oh, one of your coworkers has sent me a video feed."

I keep turning the pages.

Stiller continues, "I don't see why they'd build a drug lab . . . Hold on. Turn back a page."

I flip back to the prior sheet.

"Oh my," he says. "You see that, Robert?"

"Indeed."

It's just a large dodecahedron or whatever to me. "Guys? What's up?"

"It's a kind of polymer," says Ailes. "Designed to protect a chemical from breaking down under certain conditions."

"And not in others," Stiller adds.

"Water supply!" Ailes shouts away from the phone, probably into the bullpen. "They're going to put something into water supplies. Lock down all the reservoirs and plants within the range we found."

"Dr. Ailes?" I'm not sure what's going on.

"They're trying to put some kind of psychedelic into a water supply. Maybe in a couple major cities. We think we know where, based on the source code. We already have the water utilities online."

"What do I do?"

"You did it. This is what we needed!"

"That's it?"

"For you," says Ailes.

"What about the other room at the end of the complex?" I ask.

He hesitates. "Yes. Yes, of course! That could be important."

I rip off the rest of the suit and exit the airlock, then hurry like hell down the hall.

CHAPTER FIFTY-SIX

THE DOOR

I RACE TO THE other end of the complex and find an identical steel door. I get a sick feeling at the thought that on the other side is another nasty surprise.

I pick the lock as easily as I did the first one, swing open the door, and step into a dark room. There is a light switch in the same spot as the one I discovered in the lab, but when I flick it on, I'm not greeted by scientific equipment.

This is something completely different.

A massive steel door, like a bank vault, wide enough to drive a car into.

What the hell is on the other side?

"Dr. Ailes?" I call into my phone.

There's no Wi-Fi signal. Damn it!

I take a photo of the door and then run back toward the middle of the complex, stopping just outside the room where Elijah is playing his animal game.

"Ailes?" I call again.

"Here," he says. "We have some dive teams heading for the LA and Chicago reservoirs. We think they want to cause a massive panic, maybe even religious hysteria."

"That's, um, nice. But there's something else."

"What's that?" He finally gives me his full attention.

"The other end of the chamber, it leads to a vault. Like in a bank. They've got something locked inside."

"Such as?" he asks, realizing the new mystery means this may not be over just yet.

"I don't know! L. Ron Hubbard's masterworks? I just know they've got a big-ass door designed to keep people out."

"Do you think it might be tied to one of the other countdown clocks?"

"Maybe. Do we want to wait that long?"

"I can have a team there in a few hours to get it open."

That's not going to cut it. "What if it has to do with the shorter clock? There's only a few hours left."

"I'd rather just get you out of there."

Me too. And there's something about his voice. "What is it?"

"We just found out two of the people who had fake driver's licenses were stopped six days ago in Colorado and then let go."

I shake my head. "Damn. They got away."

"No, Jessica. That's just it. We found out they weren't leaving Colorado. They were heading back."

"Back?"

"Yes. Back toward Moffat."

My skin starts to crawl. I'd thought they were running away based on Elijah's story. Something about this doesn't add up.

"The sheriff should be there shortly. Just hold on," says Ailes.

"I can't." I run back down the hall.

"Jessica . . . Don't go near the—"

His voice cuts out as the signal fades.

I know what he was about to say.

It doesn't matter. I have to know.

This isn't about my safety. No more deaths. No more waiting for things to happen.

I REACH THE vault door and stare at it. It's made from thick steel, the kind they use for Class 3 safes that are designed to take hours to cut into.

I look for a combination lock, or a mechanism to pick. There's nothing. This is some kind of custom job. Maybe all electronic. Parts of it are exposed, which is kind of weird. It somehow looks familiar.

Then it hits me. I'm looking at the vault from the wrong direction.

Grandfather would be laughing his ass off at me right now.

I can open it, no problem.

The smile fades from my face.

This vault is meant to keep something *inside*.

CHAPTER FIFTY-SEVEN

SANCTUM

HARRY HOUDINI WAS once challenged in court to escape from a safe. He did so easily, and when the judge demanded an explanation, he simply replied, "Safes were meant to keep people out, not in."

I don't think. I don't speculate. Time is ticking. I just use my multi-tool to unscrew the bolts holding the Plexiglas cover over the machinery of the vault.

The large sheets fall to the ground and I kick them away.

Getting the door open means pulling the rods back. To accomplish this, I have to disable the springs. Again, my multi-tool makes short work of that.

Now I've got all the pistons disengaged. The lower ones need to be pried back to stop them from dropping back down. I pull them free and set them aside.

Last, I have to pull back the main bolt. This takes some effort, as the metal is well lubricated and it resists my initial efforts.

After some persistence: *click*. It's done.

When I try to open the door at last, I confuse myself for a moment. It won't budge.

I push again. Nothing.

I check that all the rods and pins are out.

What did I get wrong?

Then I realize I'm an idiot.

It's supposed to swing the other way.

Using my back, I push against the door as hard as I can. It has to weigh over a ton. Eventually it gives way and slowly begins to open inward. I strain until there's enough of an opening for me to slide my body through.

On the other side, it's pitch black. My footsteps echo around the chamber as I fumble for my flashlight. The sound behaves differently in here than in the other chambers in the complex. There isn't an echo from the ceiling.

I take my light from my pocket and sweep the space, which is much larger than the antechamber.

It's empty. There's nothing here.

All that anticipation. All that adrenaline. All that fear.

And nothing.

I don't know what I was expecting on the other side, but I was expecting *something*.

Then my light catches something in its beam.

Not this.

I collapse to the floor, too numb to move.

A voice in the back of my head reminds me: *Be careful what you wish for.*

You just might get it.

CHAPTER FIFTY-EIGHT

ASSEMBLY

It's them.

It's the Red Chain. All of them.

The object that my flashlight caught in the dark was a shoe. To be more precise, a foot.

Over a hundred pairs of feet dangle from the bodies hanging overhead.

This is what it was all leading up to. This was their endgame.

At the far end of the room, underneath the last body, a ladder lays on its side.

They locked themselves inside here and then, one by one as the others watched, they hung themselves.

I muster the strength to raise my light all the way up to the ceiling.

Hundreds of hooks mounted to the concrete ceiling hold red metal chains that are locked around pale necks and tortured faces.

Most of their eyes are open. Some still clutch at their throats with white-knuckled fingers. These weren't quick, hangman-style executions in which their necks snapped in an instant as the floor dropped out below them.

These were long, agonizing deaths as they twisted and thrashed, gasping for breath while everyone else watched.

How could they do this?

I don't know.

Locked in the vault, it was their only way out. They sealed themselves in so they couldn't escape. At least not alive.

I pull myself to my feet and walk underneath the bodies, scanning the faces with my light.

So much pain.

This . . . this is madness.

It's a dark mirror image of how their praying mats were laid out. A fucked-up symmetry between heaven and hell.

I notice a space between several bodies and move to investigate the gap.

God, no.

Tiny feet. Children's bodies. A girl dressed like—

A small hand grabs mine in the dark.

"Don't be sad," Elijah whispers. "When Mommy comes, we can go with them."

CHAPTER FIFTY-NINE

INQUEST

A WEEK LATER, ELIJAH'S words still chill me as I sit in a deposition a thousand miles away. I'm not sure how his grandparents, people whom he never really knew, will explain to him what happened. I'm not sure they can. Or should.

The bodies in the vault aren't the only victims of the Red Chain's death pact. Other members, who weren't able to make it back in time for the sealing of the vault, and didn't show up in our driver's license search, also committed suicide. Ezra Winter was found dead in his cell from an overdose of painkillers he'd had smuggled into prison.

There was no note, although investigators found what may have been traces of one in his toilet. Maybe he couldn't find the right thing to say. In the end, his silence speaks louder than words, and raises more questions. I didn't think he had it in him.

People can surprise you.

Once the Red Chain was no longer around to throw gas on the fire, attempts to overthrow the world order fizzled out. People may say they want a revolution, but they also crave stability and things like pension plans and Starbucks with working Wi-Fi. You can try hitting that reset button, but all it's going to do is change the names of the players, not their actions.

We're still trying to figure out the roles everyone played in this fiasco. Belinda Cole, Ezra Winter's ex-wife, eyes me from across the table in this conference room in the Virginia district attorney's office, probably wondering why I've been silent throughout her entire deposition. Her hair is neatly combed, although grayer than I recall, and she's dressed in a jacket and skirt. She looks more like a senior executive more than the hippie librarian from the half-way house.

I haven't said anything because I'm watching her, studying her reactions, trying to understand what's really going on inside her head. In the aftermath of the riots and the Colorado suicides, there have been a lot of questions swirling around, and too few answers.

One of the victims found in the underground complex, Christof Belichick, has been identified as the de facto leader of the Red Chain for the last dozen or so years. A technical writer for the software industry, he fell in with the group at some point in the 1990s and eventually became the head of the commune.

"And you've had no contact with Belichick?" asks Laney Tierney, one of the Justice Department attorneys attempting to put a case together around what happened. She looks to be in her midthirties, with short dark hair and a champion poker face. She's burdened with the insurmountable task of trying to find out the truth even though all our chief suspects are dead.

Belinda waits for permission from her attorney, then answers. "Not that I recall."

"Not that you recall?" inquires Tierney.

"Correct," interjects David Lee, Cole's counsel. A senior partner at his firm, Lee had a successful career as a prosecutor before jumping the fence to the other side.

Tierney slides a sheet of paper across the table. "Do you recall this? While you were in custody, Mr. Belichick sent you this letter."

Lee takes the sheet and reads it over before commenting. "My client receives a lot of unsolicited letters and communications."

"And your client is adamant she has had no conversations with members of the Red Chain?" asks Tierney.

"My client is adamant that she's unaware of any such conversations."

His is careful phrasing. Lee knows that the Justice Department wants to find a living suspect whom they can attach to the case. Proving Belinda Cole and a high-ranking member of the Red Chain had some kind of correspondence she's failed to disclose could allow them to charge her with conspiracy. This could prompt her to turn state's witness if she has more information and other names.

Finding a connection is difficult. We've been going through her visitor logs from the last two decades, trying to find anyone we can tie to the Red Chain. The problem is that it would have been very easy for a member to meet with her at the halfway house, or the minimum-security prison she was in before, under an assumed identity.

As long as Belinda doesn't implicate herself, or talk herself into a corner, there's not much we can do. And with Ezra dead, we can't pit the two against each other.

The question burning in my mind is whether she had any contact with *him*. Heywood. The Warlock. We asked at the beginning and received a flat-out denial. Not that I should be surprised. She would have to lie to protect that relationship, if it exists.

THE DEPOSITION CONTINUES without any revelations. Belinda's
answers are carefully scripted and she follows her attorney's lead,
not letting Tierney trip her up.

With only a few minutes left, her inquiries exhausted, Tierney
turns to me. "Agent Blackwood, have anything to add?"

This is more of a courtesy than a Hail Mary pass on her part.
Belinda Cole has been circumspect, but not evasive. The real work
is going to be tracking down all of her contacts, hoping for a lead,
assuming the Justice Department gives us the resources to do so.
Chances are they might just be happy closing the case by saying
all guilty parties have been accounted for and hope the public goes
along with that narrative.

As a cop, you hope for that TV-style, one-liner question that
makes the suspect crumble. Sadly, that rarely happens unless
you're dealing with someone stupid. Belinda Cole is anything but.
She's smart, incredibly so. Much smarter than Ezra.

If I were the Warlock, Belinda would be the one I'd want to
work with, not Ezra.

Wheels turn in my head. We've been approaching this as if
Belinda were a potential accomplice. But as I sit across from her,
watching her watch me and everyone else in the room, I'm very
aware that she's calculating everything. She's smart enough to use
her attorney as a shield, and not to be drawn into anything that
might cause an emotional response.

She also could be smart enough to position her ex-husband as
her patsy. Maybe from the beginning. I nod to Tierney, letting her
know I have a question.

"Ms. Cole, when was your last contact with your ex-husband?"

Lee answers on her behalf. "We've already stated the two
haven't exchanged any communication in at least two years."

"I'd like to hear your client say that," I reply.

Lee shoots a glance at Tierney. "Is this necessary?"

"Your client is still under deposition."

"Fine," he mutters dramatically.

"At least two years ago," says Belinda.

"Two years?"

"Yes."

I play my wild card. I look right at her and say, knowingly: "Not even a note?"

She hesitates. A tiny gesture, but a telling one.

I follow it up. "Would you be willing to provide us with some handwriting samples?"

For the first time, her façade falters. She looks to her attorney before he can even respond. We've just moved the pieces in the middle of whatever chess game she's playing out in her head.

"I'm not sure why that's necessary," he replies, confused by the question.

Tierney jumps in. "Is that an official refusal to comply? Will I need a court order?"

Lee checks his watch. "It appears our time is up. Feel free to send my office any official requests and we'll give them due consideration."

After that, he stands up and escorts Belinda out of the room.

Under her breath, her face turned away from us, I hear her mutter, "Fucking idiot."

TIERNEY WATCHES THEM leave, then faces me.

"Not a good way to build trust with your attorney."

"She wasn't talking about Lee," I reply.

"Who then? You or me?" she asks.

"Neither. Her husband."

I'm going on instinct, a hunch that was reinforced when I saw Belinda again. She's a chameleon. A very clever chameleon who adapts to the world around her. In the halfway house with all the tortured paintings of Jesus on the walls, she played the part of the repentant Christian. Here, in the Justice Department office, she knew to show up looking like an intelligent, competent person who easily blends in. She looked like one of us. She has far more social acumen than her husband.

"We'll never be able to prove it," I sigh, frustrated. "But she was the mastermind behind all of this. I'm sure we'll find some kind of tenuous connection, maybe an intermediary, but nothing we'll be able to implicate her with. She's too smart."

"Catch me up here," says Tierney.

I've been putting it together in my head, and speaking without much context. "The fragment of the note we found in Ezra's cell. That was from her. She probably supplied him with the pills too."

"That's why you mentioned handwriting," says Tierney, getting it. "You wanted to see her react to the possibility that Ezra had left the note behind? Why would she handwrite it? That would implicate her."

"Because she knew the only way he would go through with it was if it was actually her doing the asking. She had to write him a letter. It was a risk."

"And unless you have some forensic magic, Lee will see through this." Tierney shakes her head. "There's not much to go on. I don't know what we can do next."

"We can't let it go." What I saw in the vault haunts me. "She's at the center of this."

Tierney sits back in her chair, defeated. "Maybe. But she didn't actively do anything. Others were the ones who did. And they're dead. There's nobody left to point a finger at her. It's difficult enough to build cases around mobsters with living witnesses. This . . . this may end here."

"It can't."

It can't end here, because I know where all this leads.

She offers me a sympathetic look. She doesn't understand.

He was frightening enough when he could hack computer systems and pull off theatrical stunts.

Now he's figured out how to manipulate entire religious movements.

CHAPTER SIXTY

PLAYGROUND

THE MANAGER OF Belinda Cole's halfway house greets me at the door.

"She's not here."

According to the terms of her parole, Belinda was due back right after the deposition. She's not in hard violation just yet, but I was able to beat her here.

"Mind if I wait for her upstairs?" I ask, doing my best harmless smile.

The manager shrugs and holds the door open for me. As I pass, Jesus gives me a pained expression, woefully looking up from one of the many crosses he's nailed to around the house.

Belinda's room is exactly as I remember it. Checking the hallway to make certain I'm not being watched, I slide open a dresser drawer. Her clothes are still in there. It doesn't look like she grabbed anything to go on the run.

If she is spooked, then I don't think she'd come back here. She'd just get the hell away as quickly as possible. That's assuming she actually fell for my little ruse.

Tierney didn't think Lee would, so I guess it's hopeless for me to expect Belinda to either. Although her own smugness might be used against her. She has so much contempt for her ex-husband it might overcome reason.

I check the desk and poke through her books, looking for something, anything, that would tie her to everything. I come up short. Everything is as boring as she wants it to appear.

I take a seat at her desk and survey the room. The laughter of children on the playground carries through the closed window. In the corner of the room, under her bed, I notice a thick King James Bible poking out. I kneel down to pick it up.

It feels lighter than it should.

When I open the book, I see that half its pages are carved out, creating an empty hiding spot. It's a classic ploy that wouldn't fool a middle school math teacher, but an effective one if the book is well hidden.

I set the Bible back down exactly where I found it. It may be nothing, but it is probably something. What?

I stare out of the window as children take turns sending a blue kite into the air. It smashes nose first into the brown grass before taking flight to their cheers.

A solitary figure sits at a picnic table, watching them. The streaks of gray in her hair are unmistakable. I rush down the stairs and push past the manager before she can ask me what's wrong.

I APPROACH BELINDA from behind. Her right hand is resting on her knee, but I can't see her left.

My hand is ready to go to the gun at my hip, but I'm wary of the children.

"I know you're there," she says at the sound of the dry grass crunching under my feet.

The children are at least a hundred feet away. Far, but still close.

"Let me see your hands, Belinda," I say calmly.

She shakes her head. "Come sit next to me," she says casually, not turning around.

"Let me see your hands," I repeat, this time more forcefully.

"See the little one in red? The one that keeps tripping?"

A small boy, maybe six or seven, dressed in a red jacket, chases after the tail of the kite every time it scrapes the ground. He stumbles, then picks himself up, laughing as the others run ahead.

"My gun is aimed at him," Belinda says coldly. "I probably won't make the shot, but you can't take that chance. Come." She pats the spot next to her. "Sit next to me."

I approach her from the side. If I rush her, I can tackle her to the ground and probably keep the gun from going off. Probably.

Right now, she's waiting for me to do that.

The smarter move is for me to distract her, making it difficult for her to aim at the children.

"Drop your gun, Belinda."

"Not right now," she replies, as if it were a polite request. She thinks for a moment, then adds, "Aren't you supposed to ask me why I did this?"

"I don't care."

All I care about right now is the gun in her pocket.

"Don't you want to know how?"

Her eyes are fixed on the children as she speaks.

"Give me your gun and you can tell me everything."

"I was visiting India when the idea first hit me."

She sounds almost like she's in a trance, like she's not talking to me, but making a case to the wind. "It was the nineteen seventies. Their population was still exploding. I was with a group trying to advise them. We tried everything, even getting the Catholic

Church to relent on birth control. So many people . . . I volunteered in the hospitals." She shakes her head. "Hospitals . . . covered in blood and sickness. Flies everywhere. And people, so many people. Then I saw it." She gazes over at me for the first time. "This was where we were heading. I saw the future. We had to stop this."

I step forward. "By killing people and sending letter bombs?"

"By any means necessary. China understood. They began to realize."

"And now there are far more boys than girls there," I reply.

She shrugs. "The alternative is worse."

"I'm not here to debate your population doom and gloom. Give me your gun." I take another cautious step, trying to put myself between Belinda and the children.

"I suspect you don't really care about anything else. You just want to know if he was involved."

I play coy. "Ezra?"

Belinda makes a condescending smirk. "Ezra was useful for getting followers. He was a charismatic blowhard that lost souls liked to listen to. I could overlook his dalliances. He served a purpose. But that's not what you want to know."

She's leading me. I'm trying not to let her do it, but clearly she knows why I'm really here.

"What you're really wondering is how did we do it? How did a bunch of technoilliterate farmers pull this off?" she asks.

"Belichick was a programmer," I reply.

"Belichick wrote manuals for knitting software. But, like Ezra, he was a useful idiot. People listened to him. We needed help. We needed someone who could show us how to start the fire. Fortunately, he found us."

Damn it. My skin burns. It's what I knew, but what I didn't really want to hear. Their helper, the man who made it possible, it's him. Heywood.

I do my best not to react. She wants to somehow use this as leverage.

"You know his price," asks Belinda, turning away. "You know what he wanted."

I hesitate before replying. "For you to kill me."

She nods. "Strange, though. I'm not sure if he actually wanted us to succeed." She stares off into the distance again. "Men . . . they're always fucking things up when they think with their—" Her hand slightly moves in her pocket, raising her jacket.

I lunge for her, but her gun goes off before I can get close. I tackle her to the ground, pinning her left hand with my knee and drawing my own weapon.

But it's too late. Her bullet already found its target.

A warm mist coats my face. My side aches and I think I've been shot, but realize it's my still-sore stab wound.

I look down. Blood gushes out of the bottom of Belinda's jaw. Her bulging eyes stare up at me. I can feel the beat of her heart as she bleeds out.

She thought she could get away with it, then she realized she didn't *want* to.

If you think the world is already lost, then there's no point to trying to save it.

EPILOGUE

THE MAN CALLED Michael Heywood by the court, and the War-lock by the world at large, woke up in his cell after 3:00 am and noticed something about it was different. It took a moment for his eyes to adjust. When they focused, he spotted the small white square resting on the metal sink.

He hadn't heard anyone enter his cell. He was a light sleeper. Yet he was certain it hadn't been there when he went to bed.

He raised himself off the cot, his fingers clinching the tooth-brush shiv he'd coated with a nerve paralyzer made from cleaning agents he'd managed to steal, and walked over to the sink.

It was a letter. He sat back down on his bed and read it in the dim light streaming through the small window on the cell door.

> *I looked at their faces. Every. Single. One.*
> *The old ones. The young ones.*
> *The ones too trusting to realize how they were manip-ulated.*

Some of them probably deserved to die. Not all.

Not most.

Not the little ones.

You twisted their beliefs to serve your own purposes.

Do they know what you are?

It doesn't matter. I do.

It's the faces of the little ones who died crying in the dark I want you to see as you try to tell yourself it was part of some grand plan.

I want those to be the last faces you'll ever see. Because you won't see my face.

You'll never see me coming.

Heywood held the note close to his nose, hoping there would be some scent of her. But there was none. He read the note again, imagining her saying the words aloud. After the third time, he put his weapon back in its hiding place and took out his prized possession, the one he liked to touch as he lay awake in the middle of the night.

Folded into the pages of his Bible, next to Exodus 22:18, was the silky strand of black hair.

He rolled it between his fingers and thought of her.

She'd come to him. He didn't know how. But she'd reached out to him.

He took her threat very seriously.

And it made him smile.

ACKNOWLEDGMENTS

THANKS TO MY parents, Jim and Pat. Thank you to my sounding boards, Justin Robert Young, Kenneth Montgomery, and Peter J. Wacks. Thank you to Joan Lawton and Erika Larsen for your kindness. Finally, special thanks to Hannah Wood and Erica Spellman Silverman for being Jessica's biggest champions.

ABOUT THE AUTHOR

Andrew Mayne started his first illusion tour while he was a teenager and was soon headlining in resorts and casinos around the world. He's worked behind the scenes creatively for David Copperfield, Penn & Teller, and David Blaine. With the support of talk show host and amateur magician Johnny Carson, Andrew started a program to use magic to teach critical thinking skills in public schools for the James Randi Educational Foundation. Andrew's "Wizard School" segments, teaching magic and science to children, aired nationwide on public television. He also starred in the reality show *Don't Trust Andrew Mayne*.